NEW STORIES
FROM THE SOUTH

The Year's Best, 1988

edited by
Shannon Ravenel

NEW STORIES
FROM THE SOUTH

The Year's Best, 1988

Algonquin Books of Chapel Hill
1988

published by
Algonquin Books of Chapel Hill
Post Office Box 2225, Chapel Hill, North Carolina 27515-2225
in association with Taylor Publishing Company
1550 West Mockingbird Lane, Dallas, Texas 75235

ISBN 0-912697-90-3
ISBN 0-912697-93-8 (pbk.)
ISSN 0897-9073

CONTENTS

PREFACE

The title of this series, *New Stories from the South,* holds out three promises: that the stories be new, that they be stories, and that they be from the South. The first two promises are easy to keep. I select these stories from those appearing in magazines published in the year preceding—so they are certainly new. And I don't *knowingly* include excerpts from longer pieces. I'm interested in stories that are conceived and written as stories.

But the third promise—that they be stories from the South—is complicated. Some of the stories here come from magazines published in the geographical South or Southwest. Most of the authors were born, if not raised, in the South. And all of the stories seem to me to have a "Southern" affect. But when I am asked to explain exactly what I mean by that, I find myself equivocating and trying not to be nailed down to an exclusive definition.

Flannery O'Connor, who greatly valued her Southern roots and experience, once defined the South as "a part of a society that has some real extension outside of the mind." I like this definition because it resists being nailed down, too. Convolute in expressing the meaning of her South, O'Connor was plain in her definition of the world as something to be "cherished while we struggle to endure it."

We Southerners like to brag about our indulgence of personal waywardness. In the South I knew as a child, deliberations upon the eccentricities of neighbors, teachers, cousins, and schoolmates were both entertainment and philosophy. So much so that the South might also be defined as a setting in which society has the inclination to mythologize what might, somewhere else, be considered deviant or just tiresome. But making easy generalizations about the

South, pro or con, can backfire. It's not even safe to offer the suggestion that there is perhaps more time for communal deliberation in a warmer climate. Just try to point out that there are more days in the year when the weather permits society to step outside and perform before a front porch audience and some wag will raise his hand and ask why there isn't, then, a great tradition of Cuban literature—the kind of question that Flannery O'Connor herself might have fired off.

But even she would probably have agreed that the more you watch human nature in action, the more intriguing becomes the shifting territory between normal and abnormal behavior. It is dangerous, but tempting, to claim this territory as particularly fertile ground for Southern writers. Consider Miss O'Connor herself and how she harvested it.

I believe the sixteen stories collected here make a case for this claim. Every story is a strategy for endurance. Human society offers an infinite variety of such strategies, all there for the fiction writer to pick among. Story lovers never tire of reading them well observed, described, deliberated upon—and cherished.

Some of these new stories from the South simply commemorate the joyful triumph of will over convention:

—in Annette Sanford's "Limited Access," a first TV set is successfully accommodated by an self-sufficient old woman who didn't want it in the first place;

—in Sunny Roger's "The Crumb," what the reader has every reason to believe is a rich man's self-indulgence metamorphoses into self-discovery;

—a whole town learns to reinterpret a "failure's" "successes" in Ellen Akins's wise story of community, "George Bailey Fishing";

—Jill McCorkle's single bank teller in "First Union Blues" throws out conventional security along with conventional wisdom;

—in "Gas," Jim Hall turns this theme inside out with Tina Blue. She makes a living looking weird ("She put on a leopard leotard, then an aquamarine-and-fushia nun's robe on top . . . and a necklace she'd made from the shells of dime-store turtles"), but comes to realize she's learned to "zing but . . . not sing."

In other stories, kids' figuring out their elders' battle plans provide classic recognitions:

—in "Half Measures," Trudy Lewis' oblique story of grief, a child comes to understand the size of her mother's loss and of her courage;

—a visiting boy's enthusiastic acceptance of his hosts' approach to sex renders him a wiser (though no longer desirable) guest in John Rolfe Gardiner's "Game Farm";

—in "Voice," Eve Shelnutt's young narrator senses more than she understands how lopsided love can pull lives crooked;

—a young country girl grows to love an outcast woman in "Rose-Johnny," by Barbara Kingsolver; and persists in her love even when she understands what her relatives mean when they call the woman "a Lebanese";

—"Like the Old Wolf in All Those Wolf Stories," by Nanci Kincaid, describes the first dawnings of a white child's perception of a black's position;

—and "Metropolitan," by Charlotte Holmes, gives us a teenaged witness's canny documentation of sexual intrigue in the local drug store.

Other stories are close-up studies of the human capacity for adjustment:

—Pam Durban's "Belonging" recreates the details of endurance so vividly that the reader sweats in the heat wave, tastes dust in the drought;

—Larry Brown goes even further: his story, "Facing the Music," takes us inside the very skin of a marriage where we are shaken by the violence of the struggle to keep it going.

Two other stories deal with extremes of eccentricity:

—"The Watch," Rick Bass's extraordinary story of interdependence, brings into play the obsessive dimension of eccentricity;

—In "The Man Who Knew Belle Starr," by Richard Bausch, eccentricity takes the fatal step across into insanity.

—And finally, Mark Richard's wild and jubilant "Happiness of the Garden Variety" is an out-and-out hymn to the lucky few who live life exactly as it suits them.

Flannery O'Connor didn't make the mistake of nailing down definitions of the South or Southern writing. But once, in a burst of regional pride, she did say this: "The Southern writer can outwrite anybody in the country . . . ." Read these sixteen stories and see if you don't think they make a case for that as well.

Shannon Ravenel

PUBLISHER'S NOTE

The stories reprinted in *New Stories from the South, The Year's Best, 1988* were selected from American short stories published in magazines issued between January 1986 and January 1987. Shannon Ravenel annually consults a list of more than 150 nationally-distributed American periodicals and makes her choices for this anthology based on criteria that include original publication first-serially in magazine form and publication as short stories. Direct submissions are not considered.

NEW STORIES
FROM THE SOUTH
The Year's Best, 1988

Mark Richard

HAPPINESS OF THE GARDEN VARIETY

(from *Shenandoah*)

I felt really bad about what we ended up having to do to Vic's horse Buster today, not that looking back all this could have been helped, all this starting when Steve Willis and I were ripping the old roof off of where we live in the shanty by the canal on Vic's acres. Vic was up to Norfolk again checking on a washing machine for his many-childed wife, Steve Willis and I left to rip off the roof and hammer in the new shingles. We were doing this in change for rent. Every month we do something in change for rent from Vic. Last month previous we strung three miles of pound net with bottom weights and cork toppers. What we change for rent usually comes to a lot more than what I'm sure the rent is for our four-room front porch shanty on the canal out back of Vic's, but Steve Willis and I like Vic and Vic lets us use his boat and truck for side business we do on new-moon nights.

Let me tell you something about what makes what we ended up doing to Vic's horse Buster all the worse. This is not to say about Vic less than Buster, me, I personally, and I know Steve Willis did too, hated Buster, Steve Willis having had to watch from far away Buster kill two of Vic's dogs. There'd be a stomp and a kick of dust then a splash in the canal and it's crab festival on old Tramp or Big Spot. Then there was Buster's biting and kicking of us humans, Buster having bit me on the shoulder once when I was scraping barnacles off one of Vic's skiffs in change for rent, and then he didn't even make a move back when I came at him with a sharp-sided hoe. Steve Willis had Buster kick in the driving side of his car door after Buster had been into some weeds Vic had sprayed with the wrong powder. Buster kicked in the door so hard Steve Willis still has to crawl in from the other way. It was this eating that got Buster in the end though not reading the right label is something about Vic which made him have us around.

This is what I mean, this about Vic, and about what we did to his horse to make things all the worse: Vic could not read nor write, and this about Vic affected the way we all were with him, what I mean all, means Vic's wife and his children and Buster and his dogs and all the acres we all lived on down by the canal, and everything on all the acres, and everything on all the acres painted aquamarine blue, because one thing about Vic, and I say this to show how Steve Willis and I made this all the worse, was that Vic not reading nor writing seemed to make him not to think about things like they had names that he had to remember by way of thinking that needed spelling, but instead Vic seemed to think about things in groups, like here is a group of things that are my humans, here is a group of things that are my animals, here is a group of things I got for free, here is a group of things I got off good deal making, and here is a group of things I should keep a long time because I got them from some people who had kept them a long time, and maybe because of a couple of these reasons put together, Vic had another group of things painted aquamarine blue because he had gotten a good deal on two fifty-five-gallon barrels of aquamarine paint, and everything, even Vic's humans and animals who could not help but rub against it somewhere because it was everywhere wet, everything was touched the color of aquamarine, though all of us calling it *ackerine*, because even spelling it out and sounding it out to Vic it still came out of his mouth that way, ackerine, keeping in mind here is a man who can't read nor write, and Steve Willis and I always saying ackerine like Vic said it, for fun, because it also always seemed like somehow we were always holding a brush of it somewhere putting it on something in change for rent.

So what made what we did to Buster worse were some ways in Vic's thinking which were brought on by him not reading nor writing. Just because somebody had kept Buster a long time to Vic made it seem Buster was very valuable, and even though the horse did come with some history tied to it, the real reason the people had Buster for so long was because they were old and could not seem to kill the horse by just shooting it with bird shot over and over even though they tried again and again, them just making Buster meaner and easier for Vic to buy when the two old people saw him in church and asked did he want a good deal on a historical horse. The history Buster had was he was the last of the horses they used at Wicomico Light Station to run rescue boats into the surf. To Steve Willis and I when we heard it said So what? but to Vic this was some history he could understand and appreciate, being an old sailor himself and it being some facts that did not have to be gotten from a history book that he could not read from in the first place.

What I came to find out later on was the heart tug Vic felt about this old horse that had to do with when Vic grew up, Vic's father having boarded a team of surf horses in a part of the house Vic slept in when he was a boy because all the children from Vic's parents spilled out of the two-room clapboard laid low in the dunes, not a far situation from Vic's own children who as long as Steve Willis and I have been living here I don't think I have seen all of because they keep spilling out of the house barefoot all year around and maybe it's because there are so many of them that Vic can't seem to remember all their names rather than the fact he can't place in his mind what they are called because Vic cannot read nor write.

Anyway, the point I'm leading to about the heart tug is that where Vic spent his life as a child was sleeping with two other brothers in a hayloft mostly empty at that, not even because there was no hay to be had on an island of sand but because the team always grazed on the wild sea oats in the dunes, and this is what makes what we did worse, this tug on Vic's heart to his younger days that Buster had, me hearing Vic tell it to Buster one day when Vic didn't know I did, the feeling Vic remembered best of laying snug warm with his brothers, all of them laid all over each other to keep warm during winter northeasters that shook the two-room clapboard and the tacked-on horse stalls where they slept, remembering them in the early mornings keeping warm while down below the horses would be stirring to go out, making droppings and the smell coming up to the warm, all over each other boys, the warm smell of wild sea oats passed through the two solid horses breathing sea fog breath.

So that was the heart tug Buster had and I don't mean to make Vic out strange owing to him liking the smell of an old horse passing gas, I think if you think about it there's really nothing there that doesn't fit with a man not thinking thoughts he has to read nor write, but fits well with a man who thinks of things as being good when they are human or animal especially if they came about by getting them free or from off a good deal.

I guess that is the main reason about Vic besides using his boat and truck on new-moon nights that Steve Willis and I stuck around, us in a couple of groups in Vic's mind mainly getting a good deal off of, us stringing nets, ripping roofs and painting everything not breathing what we called ackerine, and that is also the main reason what we ended up doing ended up all the worse.

So like I said, this all started when Steve Willis and I were ripping the old roof off our four-room front porch shanty by the canal in change for rent. Vic had gone to Norfolk because he had heard of a good deal some people from church told him about to do with some washing machines, and Vic, having stood in water barefoot while plugging his old washer in and getting thrown against a wall by the shock, naturally to his mind thought it was broken and needed replacing. Vic had left in the morning coming in to get Steve Willis and I up around dawn to finish the roof and said only one other simple thing, the real easy thing, to please keep Buster out of the garden no matter what we did. Then Vic was off through the gate in his good deal truck he had painted ackerine blue one night after supper the week before.

It was July hot, and before we started Steve Willis and I just walked around our shanty roof, just looking, because the island we live on is flat with just scrub pine and wandering dunes and from a single story up you can see Wicomico Light, the inlet bridge and the big dunes where the ocean breaks beyond. It was a good morning knowing Vic's wife would come soon out bringing us some sticks of fried fish wrapped in brown paper, her knowing for breakfast we usually had a cigarette and a Dr. Pepper. For a long time Steve Willis and I had not made any new-moon runs to Stumpy Point to make us watch the one lane down to Vic's acres for cars we wouldn't like the looks of and I could look at Steve Willis and Steve Willis could look at me and we could feel good to be one of Vic's humans in a house on all of Vic's acres.

About midway through the morning after their chores about a half a dozen of Vic's kids came spilling barefoot out of Vic's ackerine blue house to ride the ackerine bicycles and tricycles and to play on the good deal ackerine swing set and jungle gym. The older Vic's kids got to play fishing boat and battleship down on the canal dock as long as one of them stayed lookout to keep a count of heads and watch for snakes.

From over my shoulder I was watching what Buster was up to. He stood looking up at me in the middle of the midday morning hot yard not seeking shade like even a common ass would but just standing in the yard near where the incline made of good deal railway ties came out of the canal and to the boat shed. Buster stood not even slapping his tail at the blackflies that were starting to work on Steve Willis and I up on the roof ripping shingles, but standing so still as if knowing not to attract one bit of attention to himself on his way to he and I knew where. I would rip a row of shingles and then look over my shoulder and Buster would be standing perfectly still not even slapping his tail at the black flies or even showing signs of breath in and out of his big almost to the ground slouching belly. Just standing as if he was a big kid's toy some big kid was moving around in the yard when I wasn't looking, all the time moving closer by two or one feet to the garden.

So I would rip a row and look, rip a row and look, never seeing him move even by inches, and I saw Steve Willis was not even bothered by looking to keep an eye on Buster out of the garden even though Vic had told us both to do it, and the reason was a simple one for Steve Willis not to care and boiled down, this is it: the evening Vic went over to make the good deal off the old people who had Buster for so long he rode Buster home and when he showed up at the gate to Vic's acres needing one of us, me or Steve Willis to come down off the porch of our shanty to open the gate, it was me who came down to let Vic and Buster in the yard. That is the reason for Steve Willis not caring about Buster, not one thing more. Steve Willis stayed on the porch with his feet up on the railing watching Vic ride Buster by and me close the gate, and ever since, anything Vic tells us to do or about or with Buster, it is me who does it or me who listens even though Vic is telling us both, it is me and not Steve Willis, all from me getting down to open the gate that one time. That is why today Steve Willis was just ripping rows and not looking at Buster sneak, and I tell you, I like this forward thinking in Steve Willis when we make our new-moon runs but around Vic's back acres it can become tiresome and make you job-shy.

Just about lunch time, just about the time for the little Vic's children to come into their house to get cold pieces of fried fish and Kool-Aid for lunch, the big Vic's children down by the dock all shouted Snake and ran about fetching nets, poles and paddles. This was a good time for Steve Willis and I to break so Steve Willis and I broke for a cigarette to watch what would all Vic's kids be telling around the table all supper long. Vic's big kids ran up and back the dock trying to catch the snake with their poles and paddles, and the poor snake swam from side to side in the boat slip with his escape cut off by one of Vic's big kids poling around in a washtub, trailing a minnow seine. One of Vic's big girl kids caught the tired-out snake on the surface and dipped him out with a canoe paddle and one of Vic's big boys snapped it like a bullwhip, popping its neck so it went limp. Vic's dogs that Buster hadn't yet kicked into the canal barked and jumped up on the boys playing keepaway with the snake until the boys took it up to the outside sink where we clean fish to skin it out and dry what the dogs didn't eat in the sun.

As they all paraded up to the house I came to notice the yard seemed even emptier than it should have been with Vic's kids and dogs up at the big house, then I realized what piece was missing when between the wooden staked out rows of peabeans I saw a patch of sparrow-shot ragged horsehair and a big horse behind showing out by the tomatoes. I shouted a couple of times and spun a shingle towards where Buster was at work munching cabbage and cucumbers but the shingle just skipped off his big horse behind and went into the canal.

By the time I got down from the roof leaving Steve Willis up there ripping shingles, Steve Willis not being the one to open the gate that first time Buster came to Vic's acres, Buster had eaten half the cabbage heads we had. I knew better than to come up from behind a horse who can kick a full grown collie thirty yards so I picked up the canoe paddle the big Vic's girl had used to fling the snake on the dock with and went through the corn to cut Buster off at the cabbage.

But head to head, me shouting and making up and down wild slicing actions with the canoe paddle Buster had no focus on me.

Instead he was stopped in mid-chew. Then the sides of his almost-to-the-ground slouched belly heaved out then in and then more out so much that patches of horsehair popped and dropped off and I took a half a step backward fearing for an explosion. I called for Steve Willis to come down, to hurry up, but all Steve Willis said was what did I want, and I said I think Buster is sick from whatever Vic had sprayed on the cabbage probably not getting anybody to read the label to begin with, and then Buster side-stepped like he was drunk through two rows of stake-strung peabeans and then he pitched forward to where I was backing up with the canoe paddle of little good, I was thinking, against an exploding horse, and then Buster, I swear before God, Buster burped and farted at the exact same time before his knees shook out from under him and he went down among the tallest tomatoes in Vic's garden wiping out the un-ate cabbage and some cucumber pickles too.

By this time Steve Willis had come down off the roof to look at the tragedy we were having in Vic's garden. It was hard to count the amount of summer supper vegetables Buster had ruint and smushed. Steve Willis called Buster a son of a bitch for wiping out the tomatoes, Steve Willis' favorite sandwich being tomato with heavy pepper and extra mayonnaise.

Steve Willis asked me did I hit him in the head or what with the canoe paddle but I promised I hadn't given him a lick at all with it, though we were both looking at how hard I was holding on to the handle. Steve Willis pushed in on Buster's big blowing-up belly with his toe and air started to hiss out of Buster's mouth like a nail-struck tire, and the fear of explosion having not completely passed, we both stepped back. You could tell the little hiss was coming out near where Buster's big black and pink tongue stuck pretty far out of his mouth laying in the dirt between where the tomatoes were smushed and the cabbage used to be.

Steve Willis said This is not good.

Usually when Steve Willis and I have a problem in our on the side new-moon business, we say we have to do some Big Thinking, and we are always seeming to be doing Big Thinking in all our business, but since this was a Buster problem and since Steve Willis didn't come down off the porch that first time to open the gate, it was coming clear to me I would have to be the Big Thinker on this one. I stepped away to think really big about the tragedy, figuring from where the garden is situated around the boat shed by our shanty on the canal you can't see it from the big house. I figured I had a fair while to figure where to go with Buster after I got him out of the garden, hoping to find a hole nearby big enough for such a big animal and do it all while Vic's children went to afternoon summer Bible study.

In the first part of thinking big I went up to the garage to get a good deal riding lawn mower to yank Buster out until I remembered it had a broken clutch, and when I came back Steve Willis was holding back a laugh to himself, and I will say about Steve Willis, he is not one to laugh right in your face. He was holding back a laugh holding the rope I'd given him to put around Buster to yank him out. Steve Willis asked me what kind of knot would I suggest he tie a dead horse to a broken riding lawn mower with.

I could see how far I could get Steve Willis to help with the Buster tragedy so I took the line out of his hand and put a timber hitch around one of Buster's hind legs saying out loud A timber hitch seems to work pretty well thanks a whole hell of a lot. I paid the line out from the garden and started to get that sinking feeling of a jam panic, a jam closing in needing Very Big Thinking, with not the July hot sun in the yard baking waves of heat making me feel any better at all. You get that sinking jam panic feeling, and I got it so bad that while I was paying out the line across the yard, and even though I knew I could not ever possibly do it, I stopped and held hard to the line and gave it a good solid pull the hardest I could to yank Buster out, straining, pulling, even when I saw when it was hopeless, and even with the jam panic worse, I had to let go of the line, and all the difference I had made was that now there was air hissing out from where blackflies were moving around and settling back underneath the dirty place by Buster's big stringy tail.

This was even better than before to Steve Willis who stepped behind what tall tomatoes were left so he wouldn't have to laugh at me to my face. I picked up a shingle I'd thrown at Buster from the roof and spun it towards Steve Willis but it sliced to the right and shattered our side kitchen window and I could tell Steve Willis had to go behind the boat shed to laugh not in my face this time after you couldn't hear glass falling in the shanty anymore.

I gathered up the line bunched at my feet and trailed it over to the boat shed down to the dock. Vic's big Harker Island rig, our new-moon boat with the Chrysler inboard was gassed up with the key rusted in the ignition. I cleated the line that ran across the yard from Buster's hind leg onto the stanchion on the stern and shouted over to Steve Willis in the garden to at least help me throw the lines.

I felt for an instant better starting up the big Chrysler engine so that the floorboards buzzed my feet, feeling the feeling I get that starts to set in running the Harker Island rig over to the hidden dock on the south bay shore on new-moon nights, the feeling of the chance of sudden money and the possibility of anything, even danger and death, and feeling now in a July hot sun the feeling of Big Thinking a way out of a bad tragedy. With the engine running it was now possible in my mind that we wouldn't lose our place of life over something like letting a big horse die.

I was feeling better as Steve Willis threw off the stern line and I choked the wraps on the stanchion leading to where I could just see two big-legged hooves hung up in the tomatoes where I could snatch Buster out and decide what to do then, but the sound of the big engine turning over brought out the dogs from underneath the big house, them being used to going out with Vic in the mornings to check five miles of pound nets, and then some of the older kids not yet set off for Bible study, started to spill out of the house to see what Steve Willis and I were up to this time with their daddy's boat, and if I looked harder at the house, which I did, I could see the little Vic's children in the windows with diapers and the old Vic's T-shirts on wanting to follow the big kids out, but not coming, them having to sleep in away from the July hot sun.

Vic's dogs got down to us first, and even old Lizzie's tan and gray snout, a snout she let babies pull without snapping, and a snout which would, when you bent over fooling with getting the lawn hose turned on, come up and give you a friendly goose in your rear end, even old Lizzie's tan and gray snout snarled back to show sharp ripping wolflike teeth when she saw that old bastard of a horse Buster was down, and then she and all of Vic's other dogs were on the carcass and there was no keeping them away.

Now I had the problem of everybody in Vic's acres coming down to see what I had let happen to Buster, topped off by the dogs having their day going after Buster's body biting his hind legs and ripping away at the ears and privates. The sight of the dogs on Buster was no less than the sound they made, blood wild, and here came the rest of the kids to see all this, this even being better than chasing the watersnake around and out of the canal for a supper table story.

I had to Big Think quick so I pulled Steve Willis by his belt into the boat, starting over at that point about me and him and anything to do with Buster, forgetting that first time him not getting down to open the gate. I pushed forward on the throttle but did it cutting the bow off where I knew the sand bar was, still being in the right mind to know not to double up a dead horse tragedy with bad boatmanship. When I rounded the dock and the line leading to where the pack of wild-acting animals were in the tomatoes with the horse carcass snugged tight, our bow rose and our stern squared, and I really gave the big old lovey Chrysler the gas and, looking over my shoulder, I saw Buster slide from the garden with still the dogs around, this time giving chase to the dragging legs, because in their simple minds they were probably thinking the only way to stop something with legs is to bite its feet whether they are standing on them or not.

I knew that I was not just pulling Buster out of the garden now but that we had him sort of in tow, so that as we turned onto the canal proper and Buster skidded across the bulkhead and onto the dock that I knew wouldn't take his weight, I really had to pour the engine on, and I was right, Buster's big body humped the bulkhead over and came down splintering the dock we had just been tied to, but for an instant even over the dogs barking and the children yelling and the big Chrysler giving me any of anything making me feel better about all of this, just for an instant I heard Buster's hooves hit and scrape the good deal planking of the dock before bringing it down, and in that second of hearing horse's hooves on plank I had to turn back quick and look because it passed over me that maybe I would see Buster galloping behind us giving chase of me and Steve Willis out of Vic's garden instead of us dragging his big, dead body to sea in tow.

We still had plenty of canal to cover before we broke out into open ocean. The dogs raced along beside as far as they could but it was a game to them now, their wolf-like leaps mellowed out into tongue-flapping lopes. A couple of neighbors on down the canal came out to watch and the wake and spray from Buster cutting along ass backwards threw water into their yards. One of Vic's cousins Malcolm was working in a boat and seeing us coming he held up a pair of waterskis pointing to Buster laughing as we passed, but I could see open ocean so I throttled down and leaned hard forward to balance against the rising bow. I was glad I had enough forward thinking of my own to pull Steve Willis into the boat starting us over about Buster because I could look at him in the stern watching the big horse carcass we had in tow by a stiffed up leg like it was a weird submarine we were pulling by its periscope, and looking at Steve Willis I could see it was sinking in that when Vic came home from Norfolk and threw me out of the back acres by the canal it would be Steve Willis himself being thrown out too.

I burned up about three hours of fuel looking for the right place in the ocean to cut Buster loose. One problem we had was one time we stopped to idle the engine and pull up a floorboard so I could check the oil and while we set to drifting Steve Willis noticed that Buster floated. You could tell how the body was like a barrel just below the surface that it was the air or the gas or whatever was in Buster's big belly keeping him afloat. When I got up from checking the oil I threw to where Steve Willis was standing in the stern a marlin spike and he looked down at the marlin spike and then he looked up to me like he was saying Oh no I won't punch a hole, and I looked back at him wiping the oil off my hands, looking back like Oh yes you will too punch a hole, and when it came time for me to cut Buster loose out near the number nine sea buoy and it came time for Steve Willis to punch a hole, I did and he did and it was done.

So here we are really feeling bad about what we finally ended up doing to Vic's horse Buster, us drinking about it in the First Flight Lounge after we called Vic's wife at home and she said Un huh and Nunt uh to the sideways questions we asked her about Vic being home yet, trying to feel out how bad was the tragedy, and her hanging up not saying goodbye, and us wondering did she always do that and then us realizing we'd never talked to her on the telephone before.

After we tied up Vic's rig in the ditch behind the First Flight Lounge we started to wonder if shouldn't we have let Vic had his say about what to do with his finally dead horse, so therein started us having the lack of forward thinking and of Big Thinking, and instead we were left to second guessing and after we had left the rig with its better feeling hum and came in to drink, with the drink buzzes coming on ourselves, we started to feel naked in our thinking especially when a neighbor of Vic's came in and shook his head when he saw us and then walked back out.

So what Steve Willis and I have done is to get down off the wall the tide chart and figure out where the most likely place for Buster to wash in is. We'll head out over there when the tide turns and wait for Buster to come in on the surf and then drag him up to take him home in a truck we'll somehow Big Think our way to fetch by morning. The tide tonight turns at about two-thirty, just about when the lounge closes, too, so that is when we think we will make our move to the beach by the Holiday Inn, which is where we expect Buster back.

So Steve Willis and I sit in the First Flight Lounge not having the energy to begin to think about where we are to live after having to get ready to be kicked out of Vic's acres, much less having the energy to Big Think about pulling a sea-bloated horse out of the surf at two-thirty in the morning. Here we are sitting not having the energy to Big Think about all of this when Vic walks in barefooted and says Gintermen, gintermen, another one of the ways he says things because he can't read nor write and doesn't know how things are spelled to speak them correct.

There is a nervous way people who don't drink, say a preacher, act in bars but that is not Vic. Vic sits at our table open armed and stares at all the faces in the place, square in the eye, including our own we turn down. He sits at the table that is for drinking like it could be a table for anything else. Vic says he saw his rig in the ditch behind the lounge on his way home from Norfolk, would we want a ride home and come get it in the morning.

Steve Willis and I settle up and stand to go out with Vic who says he's excited about the good deal he's come back with. Looking at Steve Willis I still see it's to me to start telling Vic about us having to wait for his favorite animal in his animal group to wash up down the beach, all at our hands.

Out in the back of Vic's truck Vic runs his hands over six coin washing machines, something he does to all his new good deal things to make them really his. Vic says he got them from a business that was closing down, won't his wife be happy. Vic says our next change for rent will be to rewire the machines so they can run without putting in quarters, what did we think. I start to tell Vic about Buster and the tragedy in the garden. I can't see Vic in the dark when they turn off the front lights to the First Flight Lounge but I can hear him say Un huh, un huh as I talk.

When I finish the part with Steve Willis and I waiting for the tide to turn Vic says Come on boys, we ought to get on home oughten we. All three of us sit up front of the truck riding across the causeway bridges home. All Vic says for a while is Well, my horse, my old horse, not finishing the rest, if there is anything to finish, and I get the feeling Vic is rearranging groups in his mind like his animal group things and his human group things and his good deal off people things, and maybe making a new group of really awful people things with just me and Steve Willis in it. But then Vic starts talking about how in change for rent Steve Willis and I are also going to build a laundry platform with a cement foundation and a pine rafter shedding, and Vic starts to talk like even after taking a rearrangement of all his things in all his groups everything still comes up okay. Vic says oughten we lay the foundation around near the downside of the shanty where Steve Willis and I live so the soap water can drain into the canal, and after we figure how to put the sidings and braces up oughten we put a couple of coats of paint on it to keep the weather out, maybe in change for some rent, and what color would us boys say would look good, and Steve Willis and I both sit up and yell Ackerine! at the same time, us all laughing, and me feeling crossing the last causeway bridge home I'm happy heading there as a human in Vic's acres again.

John Rolfe Gardiner

GAME FARM

(from *The New Yorker*)

When Michael's mother said her three nieces could have been hotel girls, she didn't mean anything cheap. Quite the opposite. In Roanoke there was a set of families who shunned the outlying country clubs and made do with the city's grand old hotel. Their coming-out parties were held there. Their early dating and finest evenings were in its elegant dining room, among the marble columns of its panelled reception hall, and in its underground cocktail bar.

Michael's mother and his Aunt Ailene had been presented at the hotel in the same season. When their weddings came—Ailene's to Uncle Eddie nine years before Michael's mother's—the receptions had been held in the same familiar room. But long before his mother married she had lost her brother Eddie to a small farm in a forsaken northern corner of the state. And one reason he'd given for removing himself and Ailene to that wilderness was precisely to escape the society that still circled the old hotel—a society in which his sister had been an eligible beauty for too long.

A renunciation. His mother took it hard that Eddie should attack her just for taking her time, waiting for the right man, and using the hotel's elegant cover—its salon, bar, and ballroom. Still, they kept in touch. As Michael came to understand it, his mother could forgive Eddie's boorish reclusion if he could forgive her long dalliance. When she married a cotton salesman from South Carolina, the dalliance became moot, but Eddie continued selfishly secluding his wife and daughters, who were losing tone on the banks of a northern river.

Michael's mother had visited often, perhaps with a rescue in mind. She had seen for herself. Flies and mosquitoes with free flight over an unscreened porch. Dark water and detritus in the ice trays. Ailene fighting for the girls' grammar against the influence of a hired man and his son. Unsuitable clothes. Long hippie skirts on the children when they were playing in the fields, and jeans when they should have been in something nice for the evening.

Her brother had something to prove. He shaved his head, and wore black pajamas in the fields. According to her, he came ignorant to corn and machinery, thinking high intelligence could get him through. Actually, he lived at the mercy of swinging-door help, though some coincidence of weather and the grain markets had brought him an early profit.

Uncle Eddie, according to Michael's mother, had been an easy, irreverent scholar. The Latin prize in his high school. At the university, classical studies, in which, she said, he was doing beautifully when he dumped them for psychology. As if he could have sustained interest long enough to become a head doctor. Eddie, she maintained, could never settle. A wonder he'd gotten Ailene, a hotel girl, to marry him and accept the up-country horrors.

With her censure Michael's mother was creating the legend of a family pioneer. A forecast of a bad end for brains in a barnyard was just her way of saying, "My brother could have been anything. Never mind that he's chosen to go nowhere and be nothing." If she hadn't respected him, why so many visits to the farm before she was married? And afterward, why had she so often left Michael, her only child, to the care of Eddie and his family?

Years later, Michael could still remember hearing the exciting news: "Can you believe it? Eddie's turned the place on the Potomac into a game farm." Even more exciting, Michael's mother and father, needing private time again for the long quarrel their marriage had become, were sending him up for the summer. Eight years old, he was being passed along to Eddie and Aunt Ailene. And to his three older cousins, Georgia, Annalee, and Grace. Wild girls of the north, in his mother's estimation—the ones he couldn't wait to see.

Michael knew he shouldn't have shown such delight to his parents. But everything was turning out perfectly. At Easter he had seen the redbuds and dogwoods making little chapels of color in the dark woods. And his teacher had squeezed his arm gently and promised to promote him to the third grade.

Then the odd and wonderful report that his uncle's farm—the house, the woods behind, the sloping meadow down to the wide bottomland—had been turned over to the pleasure of a game. He wondered if his cousins would teach him Monopoly. Awkward to learn on arrival that there were no plans for checkers in the parlor or badminton in the fields; that his uncle was raising ducks for hunters.

That summer, Michael had been put on the bus in Roanoke and sent up the valley in a jacket and tie to Winchester. The whole Mason family came to collect him at the depot. He sat in the very back of their station wagon, and the girls kept turning in their seat to fuss over him and protest against the inches he'd grown during the winter.

The sisters had always been eager for his visits. He'd been told that when he was a toddler, the big one, Georgia, had put him in a carriage and pushed him up and down the long cinder drive. For a season he was her doll. She showed him off to anyone who would listen to outrageous matronly chatter: "A hard labor with this one. I don't really know if I want another." She was twelve then and quite theatrical, with corkscrew curls, pretty red springs that seemed to connect her bouncy head to her shoulders.

Georgia had changed. She looked at Michael as if a judgment had been made about him, not entirely favorable, and her full attention was going to be impossible. Michael noticed that her nose had gotten larger, and she was saying "unbearable" about each thing that displeased her.

The second sister, Annalee, was tugging on his silly tie, holding his gaze while she made fun of his grown-man outfit. Annalee was plump, alert for fun, with green eyes that she already knew how to promote with a green scarf. "If you get scared in the attic," Annalee told him, "you can sleep in my room." She talked about a blacksnake skin in the attic room until Aunt Ailene told her to be quiet.

The youngest, Grace, silent up to then, asked him suddenly in a remarkable, deep voice, "Do you know how old I am?" He was startled, as if quizzed by a bullfrog with spider legs. He didn't care to guess, unaware that the challenge in her little whiskey throat was only the armor of the smallest, and that the proud answer "Ten years old" was scorned by sisters already thirteen and eighteen. Grace reached back to tousle his hair as Annalee had done a moment before.

"Leave Michael alone," Aunt Ailene told them, and she said to Uncle Eddie, "How could his mother send him all that way by himself?"

He remembered the shadow falling over him at those words, and he remembered crying inconsolably in the back of the Masons' car. And how, when they got to the farm, Annalee had taken him for a tour to cheer him. "We haven't stopped growing corn," she said. "We've just added ducks."

The duck hatchery was the old barn, and a smooth concrete floor had been poured and rough boards nailed up for interior walls. On one side, where the floor was covered with sawdust, hundreds of baby ducks crowded under steel hovers, keeping warm. Across the room a great wooden cabinet hummed like a refrigerator. "It's not cold in there," Annalee told him. Inside, a large drum filled with eggs in wire baskets turned almost as slowly as the hand of a clock.

"I'm forbidden to do this," Annalee said, opening a panel and reaching in for an egg. She moved to a row of switches and suddenly the only light in the barn was coming from a little hole next to her. She held the egg up to the beam, showing him a small dark place inside. "That's blood," Annalee said, "little rivers of blood."

"Annalee! Are you in there?"

The lights came on and her father was standing across the floor. Annalee was sent to the house and Michael's tour of the hatchery was completed by Uncle Eddie, who took him into the penned areas with wire partitions, where hundreds of mallards were separated according to age. The oldest, his uncle explained, were down on the river waiting for the dinner bell. This was going to be Michael's daily chore, ringing the big iron bell each evening, watching the ducks fly home over the trees to the protein pellets waiting for them in their wire shelters.

When the hunters came that summer, Michael was forbidden to go outside. From his attic window he would hear his uncle's voice calling from the release ramp beside the pens and, moments later, the answering reports of shotguns from the meadow below the woods.

Alone, there was time to consider the mysteries of the farm: why Uncle Eddie's black pajamas went into a separate hamper and why he did his own laundry; why, each morning, Aunt Ailene made her girls drink a measure cup of grapefruit juice; why the surviving ducks flew home in the evenings only to be shot at another day.

Big cousin Georgia was locking her door for hours at a time. When she considered Michael, she was apt to speak about him, not to him. About the "unbearable situation" in Michael's home in Roanoke. "Never mind her," Aunt Ailene said. "She's going down to the university in September. She has reading to do. She's worried about her skin."

Annalee became his summer friend, treating his homesickness with hand-in-hand trips to a creek in the woods. Together they took off their clothes and waded into the water. Before he went home to Roanoke, Annalee gave him stationery with envelopes addressed to her.

His mother came for him at the end of August and was freshly appalled by conditions and her cold greeting by the girls. "What did you do all summer?" she asked him.

"I went swimming."

Alarmed, she recalled that she'd never packed his bathing suit.

At home, Michael thought of Annalee standing next to him in the creek, and could not write, too ashamed of his handwriting and the meagerness of the news he was able to spell. He supposed he'd see her the next year. But his mother wouldn't talk about another trip. She didn't like what was happening to his cousins. Something had come over them—of all things, an up-country snobbery. "The Masons have had enough of you for a while," she said.

The next spring, when Aunt Ailene wrote to ask which week he'd be coming, his mother was adamant. She took him visiting with her to friends in Lynchburg and Staunton. He remembered his humiliation in both cities being made to stand and recite three verses from "Hiawatha." Very much on display, the only prize of her marriage.

Michael's mother kept the memory of his cousins alive with lament and denunciation. "Coming to no good," she assured him. He wished he could be with them on their way to this bad end. There were brief visits to the Potomac farm, each one unsatisfactory. Years passing, but never without reference to his cousins. "That was the year Georgia matured so suddenly." Or "That was the year Annalee wasn't pretty."

Michael was fourteen before the Masons were allowed to have him for another season. He was still anxious to go, though there was summer sport ahead of him in his own city. And a door to watch on his block where a young lady went in and out.

Aunt Ailene had almost begged for him. They needed a steady young man was the way she put it. Someone to give Eddie and the girls a hand, since the last help had run off. And something to reestablish her connection with Roanoke.

On no condition, Michael's mother said, could he be allowed to handle a gun. With that solemn contract he was allowed up the valley again on the Greyhound. He travelled with the old memory of Annalee beside him in the water, wondering if there would be more secret swimming.

His aunt and Grace delighted in the enormous changes in his appearance. So tall! And the wonderful, naughty hair, as long as their own. His uncle seemed pleased to see him. Not Annalee. She was polite, distant, betraying him as Georgia had before her, preoccupied with things that couldn't be shared by a young boy cousin. He arrived in short sleeves, biceps for Annalee, but it was lithe Grace who ran her hands down his arms and gave him the big hug. Passed down again by the sisters, like old clothes.

"Georgia isn't even here," Grace said, when they were all in the car driving home. She had the same deep voice that cracked when she hurried it.

"Georgia is taking work in Charlottesville for the summer," Aunt Ailene said quickly.

"A little Roanoke camouflage," Uncle Eddie said.

"Be quiet," Aunt Ailene told him. "What do you know about Roanoke society? You never entered it."

Uncle Eddie turned around at the wheel and announced to everyone, "You don't enter society. You're born into it."

Grace leaned over to whisper in Michael's ear, "Georgia's living with her boyfriend from college, and she hasn't even had her party yet."

*   *   *

Sixteen, Grace was a power on the farm, giving crisp orders, even to Annalee. The hatchery was in full production. Ducks were being sold to other farms and wholesalers. Grace could run the whole thing herself, she told Michael, pleased to think she was in charge of eight thousand eggs. Michael watched attentively as she hurried from task to task, sweating through her T-shirts, cursing incompetence.

"We have to teach them to fly," she said, like a goddess. He didn't believe it was possible. Then he and Grace spent hours forcing one young mallard after another up a ramp from which he could either plop to earth or spread his wings and glide. In time each bird raced its wings, gained altitude through an opening in the trees, and glided down over meadow and cornfields to the river.

That summer, while the gunmen waited, ready in their meadow blinds, Michael worked the release gate with Grace, who called encouragement to the ducks as they took off. "Fly high, beauties!" Grace said the drakes' white neck rings were their charms against buckshot.

Obedient, Michael allowed her to take his arm and hurry him along from one job to the next. And from time to time Uncle Eddie would show up, taking them by surprise. To see how they were treating the eggs. Or how they were treating each other.

Michael had been staying in the attic again. Old enough now to think of the house as a network of exciting bedrooms, he was directly above Georgia's empty chamber, which she did not want used or explored in her absence. Next to that was the master bedroom, from which Michael could hear the muffled voices of his aunt and uncle in the dark. At the end of the hall, from a room shut tight, Annalee's tape machine played provocative music not quite low enough to be secret.

Grace was downstairs in a tiny room off the kitchen—quarters that had been used by the maid of a previous household. After the family turned their lights out there was no telling what Grace might be doing. Through the attic window Michael sometimes saw her in the moonlight, moving around the duck pens, checking her flock, or walking toward the river, stargazing.

Aunt Ailene kept the door to her room open at night. If Michael came downstairs to use the bathroom, she would call, "Is that you,

Michael?" or "Is that you, Annalee?" Sometimes she called all their names, "Annalee? Michael? Grace?"

In the house one afternoon, seeking relief from Grace's energy and orders, Michael stole a beer from the refrigerator, and was gulping it quickly in the side room Uncle Eddie used for his library. A small gilt-edged volume on the shelf caught his eye. Catullus? It was inscribed to Edward Mason II, first in Latin. Under that, in ink now pale blue, a line his uncle must have written to himself, "At last the poetry gets dirty."

Skipping through the pages, as if he could translate and find out if it was true, he heard his uncle's voice behind him: "If you're going to drink beer, pour it in a mug." But Eddie was more concerned with the effect of the book, which he took from Michael's hand. Replacing it on the shelf, he said, "Not worth a glance. Grace is looking for you."

Uncle Eddie moved to a window from which he could see Grace in the duck pens. His forehead against a pane, he began to speak in a peculiar voice. "If you're a stranger, anything is possible, even romance, but hospitality is difficult." Almost mumbling, he added, "If you're family, you're welcome in the bosom forever."

Meditation or lecture. Michael couldn't say which.

"Where are you, Eddie?" Aunt Ailene was coming through the door. "What are you telling Michael? What is his mother going to think?"

Michael left them arguing about whether he should be allowed to drink beer, and what his mother would think about that. And for the rest of the afternoon he moved eggs for Grace, even obeyed when she told him to explain what was going on in Roanoke.

He exaggerated. Still, there had been shouting as far back as he could remember. His father had inherited part of a small railroad with mortgaged equipment, and this complicated a pending divorce. Lawyers were taking years deciding how to divide things, how to divide him.

His parents still occupied the same house, living in separate rooms, each maintaining a squatter's right, lest a move jeopardize legal standing. Considered a split pair by the Roanoke crowd who danced and played cards together, they were each "seeing new friends," as their circle put it. Even careful to balance infidelities.

"Your mother was a long time getting married, wasn't she?" Grace asked him. "I suppose if you waited that long you could expect to catch a layabout."

"He's a cotton rep," Michael corrected her.

"What's that?"

He could only tell her what he'd heard at home: "A man who spends too much time in other cities asking pansies to put more natural fibres in the clothes they design."

It seemed there was something wrong with what he'd told Grace earlier. "People can get divorced," she said, "and decide the other things later." Big news, late arriving. Why hadn't he known that? "Anyway, your mother was one of those hotel people, wasn't she?"

"So was yours," Michael said.

"Yes, but she didn't use upstairs rooms."

Struck dumb, for the first time he considered the guest rooms of the old hotel as something more than the sad quarters of travellers. He watched a fertilized egg fall to the floor. His fault. Grace's head turned back to business.

After a while, she said, "You know, you're getting to be almost as old as I am." A two-year gift he was pleased to accept as he watched her lashes flutter at the tips of her long, pale bangs.

Among the visiting hunters there was much talk about makes and values of shotguns, chokes, bores, shot patterns. Though Uncle Eddie had his own shotgun, it hung over the mantel in his study like a museum piece. He shied away from the he-man chitchat. On the side of the ducks, he was more interested in the hatching and nurturing.

Most of the hunters did not care to pluck and eat. They left the dead with Aunt Ailene with best wishes—gifts of the mighty. She accepted politely, as if there were room for another shot-ridden carcass in her freezer.

One weekend a party of huge, happy men arrived—members of a professional football team down from New Jersey with shotguns on loan. They were pointing them at each other, taking mock aim, saying things like "Bet you're glad this isn't loaded."

They set off for the blinds, and before they reached the meadow one of the guns discharged. A hail of shot fell on the hatchery's metal roof. Uncle Eddie ran down the hill after the men, tore up their check, and told them to get off the property. They came up the path shamefaced and silent. But back in their van they spun their wheels all the way down the driveway.

As Michael watched, his uncle's anger passed quickly into rumination. "At first, the egg has no air cell," he said softly. "But the shell is porous, moisture escapes. What do we make of that?" Dreaming of an answer? Looking around and seeing that his nephew had been listening, he turned embarrassment into an order. "Make sure the breeder flock's getting enough calcium. We don't want any more leakers."

"Georgia is too quiet," Aunt Ailene announced when the summer was half over. Annalee was sent down to visit and report back on her sister's "involvement." But Annalee was introduced to someone else in Charlottesville and began to negotiate with her parents for time of her own there.

Aunt Ailene's "Absolutely not" was undercut by Uncle Eddie's indecision, and the visit dragged on. After a week of long-distance debate the girls stopped answering their phone.

"The two of them are useless anyway," Grace said. "So what's changed? Michael and I do all the work."

"So why is Michael still in the attic?" Uncle Eddie asked, and Aunt Ailene moved his things down to Annalee's room, where he could feel "more like real family."

What he felt was one floor closer to Grace, who would lean against him on the way from house to barn and ask, "Where would I be without you?"

With Annalee gone, it was that much easier to work hard for Grace. Standing beside her at the incubator, shifting eggs to the hatching trays, he imitated the robot action of her long, thin arms, still trying to please her with labor.

One evening on the way up to the house she asked him, "What would we do if my parents weren't here?"

"I suppose we'd work just as hard," he said, hoping he'd guessed right.

That same evening his mother called from Roanoke because he hadn't written a single line. He kept telling her, "No, everything's fine," until Aunt Ailene took the phone away from him. And he heard her say, "They're darling together. He's devoted to her."

Grace disappeared, and Michael went up to bed, slowly counting the steps in the staircase, the way he did at home, reluctant to leave anyone awake behind him. Later, he was doing his other number trick, counting the deep breaths it takes to reach sleep, when his door opened and Grace came to his bed. "This can only happen once," she said.

In the morning, right in front of her mother, Grace asked Michael if he'd slept well, and if he was ready to make ducks walk the plank. Aunt Ailene was measuring out grapefruit juice, getting them off to another healthy day.

Grace was not sooner out the front door with him than she asked, "Was it nice for you?," moving too quickly for him, from deceit to pleasure. He couldn't tell her there had been nothing in his life to compare it to.

Something had gone wrong the night before. As soon as Grace had left his room she had not seemed beautiful anymore but an ungainly farm girl who might need secrets and apologies. Lying in bed, he had begun to compare her face unfavorably with Georgia's and Annalee's. Grateful for her pledge "Only once," he fell asleep. Now her knobby knees were sticking through holes in her jeans. With sunburned arms and neck she looked her usual part again—hired help living in maid's quarters—the way he was used to her.

"Don't worry," Grace said. They were hardly out of sight of the house when she took his hand, raised it to her small breast, and told him, "I'm going to take care of you."

While they taught ducks to fly, Grace tried to convince him he was safe with her. "If cousins can't help each other into the world," she said, "who can?" They were pushing the mallards onto the ramp. Each time they put a duck on the bottom, another at the top was forced, against its will, into the air. With this for sport, they bet on the birds; which would fly to the river, and which would have to try again.

At supper that night, Uncle Eddie asked Michael if he knew why the lights in the barn were kept on all night, every night. Michael didn't know. "Because if ducks are startled in the dark, they stampede. Grace knows that. I'm surprised she hasn't told you."

Before the meal was over, his uncle had another pointed question, more husbandry. "How do you tell their sex before they grow up?"

"Stop it, Eddie," Aunt Ailene said.

"By their voices," Uncle Eddie told him leaning forward with the news. "The hens honk and the drakes belch."

Grace had left the table.

Later, awake in his bed, Michael was surprised at how quickly his plans changed. He rose, put on pants, and went barefoot from his room. In the hall he felt like a child playing Red Light, Green Light, the floor squeaking "Stop" at each small advance. It took him several minutes to reach the stairs. On the ground floor he went straight through the kitchen corridor to Grace.

"Why only once?" he asked.

A moment later, a light shone under the door and Aunt Ailene called, "What's going on in there?"

Next morning, first thing, Aunt Ailene phoned Michael's mother, who was starting north immediately. Grace could guess what his mother had said: "When I think they could have been hotel girls." Meaning Georgia, Annalee, and Grace. There was no counting the number of times his mother had said it, this refrain that gently mocked her own life.

"Never mind, young lady." Aunt Ailene was stripping all the beds, doing the white laundry with angry amounts of Clorox.

By the time his mother came, Georgia and Annalee were on their way, too, answering their mother's call for help. They arrived, surprising Michael with raised, adult eyebrows. He understood his aunt was making the house respectable again, filling the rooms with legitimate company.

The older sisters, with even tans and nicely made-up faces, had become a team with their own agenda. It was clear they thought Grace would have to wait a long time for honest love.

As Michael packed, he could hear his mother downstairs asking someone, "What can you expect in a house that doesn't even have television?"

She was moving through the ground-floor rooms, taking inventory of the house's deficiencies. And the next minute she was upstairs, standing arms akimbo in his doorway, telling Michael, "It's going to take a long time to live this down."

Trudy Lewis

HALF MEASURES

(from *Carolina Quarterly*)

My only problem with Tracy was that he never died. When the white man shot down the vine that held him suspended over a pit of crocodiles, or Cat Woman scratched his face with a poison finger-nail, he found a good spot in my yard, fainted down, spreading the fingers of one hand over the flared bones of his ribcage, and whispered to me that he was half dead.

Half dead. I always wondered how that happened, whether you got killed in only part of your body, so the living parts had to jiggle you awake again, or if it was like riding your bike down the alley behind our houses—when you got to the Ramseys' crinkly silver toolshed, you were halfway to the street. Then Tracy would say, "Let's raid their supply house, Trigger," or "Did you remember to bring the special munitions?" This was supposed to make me forget that his mother wouldn't let him go past the Ramseys'. But when we'd finished our mission and he was flicking up his kickstand and twisting his bike around, I'd say, "No, they've got that way covered. We have to get out of here." So he rode down to the street with me anyway. That used to make me laugh about the people who said boys were smarter than girls.

But the whole thing was enough to get me suspicious of the half dead business that Tracy threw into every game as regularly as a commercial I hated. His favorite place to do this was on a grill in the very back of my backyard. I remember my own yard, even, by the pirate's map he made of it. Oh, he didn't draw it on paper; it was far too secret for that. The map came out as a code on my back or arm: a knuckle scrape for the back porch, a roll of his wrist for the long hill after that, walking fingers for the stepping stones. Then came a pinch in the place where you buried the treasure. Or ambushed the enemy. Or where you were planning to convince someone you were about to die.

The most secret place of all was at the end of the yard, closed off by four walls of shaggy bushes with green berries that never ripened and smelled like my mother's cleaning powder when I split one open with a fingernail. Inside the hedge was a playground where no one else ever came. Eleven stalks of yellow-green corn rode up and over like the tails of circus animals. In coffee cans at the corners of the hedge, striped and speckled plants unrolled their tongues in the morning, curled them back up at night. And if you looked for fans of light green feathers in the grass, you could pull out a tiny carrot. Then there was the grill. It wasn't a regular backyard grill, more like the ones you saw in the park—just a metal screen set up on bricks over a pit of ashes.

The mystery was, though, my family never made any of those ashes. we never planted the carrots either, or the corn. Some unknown family before us had done all that. So when I opened a sheaf and wrapped a silk around my finger, or bit into a single kernel so its milky fruit spit into the roof of my mouth, I was eating after strangers, taking rides with strangers, talking to strangers whose histories were only accidental with my own.

"Why don't your folks fix up that patio for you?" Tracy's mother used to ask me when I went over for juice and cookies after school. She pushed the tip of her cigarette down into the ashtray and looked at the grayish freckles like little bits of ash on her skinny arm.

Mrs. Barton was much older than my mother, and wore stretch pants and sleeveless blouses around the house all day while she pulled weeds and washed dishes and then swept up under our feet during afternoon cartoons. But no matter what she did, she kept touching her hand to the small of her back with her elbow swinging out behind her, so I could never decide if she was really tired or just staying ready to turn around whenever she had to. Anyway, she asked a lot of questions for an adult.

"They don't like fixing up," I told her. "That's why we moved here, 'cuz people aren't so picky about their grass."

She stopped the cigarette at the edge of her mouth and pointed it to where I could see the tight cells of fire breathing inside. "Well, it could be nice and pretty out there," she said.

She looked over at Tracy scraping his cookie crumbs into an empty ice tray on the other side of the table.

"Mom, do you think if we got birds to come around here we could train them to do, you know, like military assignments?"

"I wouldn't be surprised, honey."

"Yeah," he said. "Come on, Trigger."

"The little girl's name is Laurie, hon."

"Oh, well Trigger's her code name."

Then we were outside again, but I was still thinking about Mrs. Barton and her sticky comments like mulberry leaves with insect eggs sewn inside them. I didn't care if Tracy called me Trigger or Laurie or anything really. I just didn't want her to bother him about it. She made me feel like my name was something disagreeable we had to put up with anyway, something on a level with rubber boots and brussels sprouts. I never wanted Tracy to think about me with that sort of thing in mind.

Then, about my parents. But Mrs. Barton didn't understand half the things she pretended to. Just because she had four kids, all bumping in and out the screen door like a television family, she thought she knew everything that happened—everything that could happen—to people in the whole world. She especially knew about little kids like Tracy and me. She thought we were so easy to take care of that she didn't even charge my mother for keeping an eye on me after school. "Since there's only one," she said.

Maybe she did know about what happened in her yard, but she didn't know about mine. I bet she couldn't begin to picture Tracy lying back on the grill like that with his eyes closed. Sometimes, the grill stood for an actual bonfire where Tracy was being burned alive. His face was pink enough for it. And his yellow hair was shaved so short it was just a glistening under the sun, one side then the other, depending on how I stood looking.

What I did then was try and ignore him for as long as I could. I'd pick out one thing and think all around it. Tracy's hair, for example. When I was six years old and living next to Tracy Barton, I was still settling the difference between boys and girls. The only obvious thing was hair. If Tracy's mother let his hair grow, would he be a girl like me than? What if I cut my hair off, so short I couldn't wear my clown barette over my ear anymore? What then? The silky patch under my ponytail shivered when I thought about it. I didn't want to be a boy. But it was important to act like one anyway. That was something I knew from Tracy's big sister Liz calling me a sissy when I wouldn't climb the television tower in the vacant lot. Or my own mother, who told me to stop primping when I looked in the mirror and complained about the way she tied my ribbons and sashes. At the same time, there wasn't anything more shameful than being mistaken for a boy, like one little girl who got sent to the wrong bathroom in the big Rexall where we shopped. This was a problem I worried over and over again, but I couldn't ask anyone about it. First off, I didn't know how to say it. Then it seemed too embarrassing to wonder at all, when everyone else had it figured out.

Once I asked Tracy if he had to wash his hair and he said no, he just rubbed a little soap on it when he took a bath. But I wasn't surprised because I'd expected as much. In our bathroom at home, we had two kinds of shampoo and a cream rinse. Only all of them had pictures of ladies flouncing their hair back, so it didn't look like there was anything for my father to use. In the morning when he was getting ready for work, though, I heard him jingling glass together and pumping plastic bottles. Maybe he couldn't find what he wanted, I thought. If I went into the bathroom after him, everything smelled funny—pressed-together and peppery. I picked up a towel half hanging off the toilet tank and it was peppery, too, spiked over with stiff black hairs. I held it up to my face. It had the same smell as the chapped, clingy skin of a kid I used to nap next to during kindergarten.

Then I'd go back to bed and listen to my mother scraping toast and talking to the radio in the kitchen.

"Try some enchanted morning yourself," she'd say. My father ate his toast burnt and could never remember to turn the setting back to normal. The scruffy noise of her knife raced the song on the radio until she came out way ahead and the knife fell ringing sharply in the sink.

"Sorry, Darla," my father said every morning when he came into the kitchen. "Maybe we could skip breakfast anyway. Take the kid out to Marvin's."

"Too late. Laurie's got to catch the carpool. I've got to iron my skirt. Besides, don't you know those gold star housedress mothers are just sniffing around and drooling for another example of how I spoil my child?"

"She's OK. She's fine. Give the kid a little slack. Give the neighbors a little slack. Now me, you can go ahead and beat up on me."

There was a little rocking of the silverware drawer and then she said, "You're not worth it." She walked out the kitchen, through the living room, past my door. When I got up she was ironing at the table in her high heels and complicated grown-up underwear with white tabs and lace windows everywhere. She pushed down on the iron with both hands so her smooth breasts small as a babysitter's pressed together, nearly touching. And my father would be gone.

Actually, that was the part I tried not to think about while I was in the backyard waiting for Tracy to get bored of being almost dead. But somehow, no matter where I started and how slow I went, I always ended up in my house in the morning with my parents going on in a way I didn't want to call fighting. It was like saying the alphabet to figure out whose name came first when we lined up to play kickball at recess. Even if you had everyone in order by T or so, you still had to keep talking all the way to Z. Otherwise, your tongue felt fat and itchy in your mouth and your mind kept stuttering over the letters you didn't say.

But once I got to my family, I'd have to stop. I'd have to give in before Tracy did and feed him some medicine I made up from plants in the yard or take his pulse and say how good it sounded. When I went to touch him, I felt his hot shadow before I got to the skin, where the heat clotted all around him. That wouldn't happen if he was dead, I thought.

We'd only lived next to Tracy a few months—it was still the beginning of first grade—when things started to go funny, so I couldn't count on anyone anymore. I remember, I was sitting at the kitchen table packing black four-o'clock seeds into a pillbox for ammunition. If you ever notice, they look just like little hand grenades. My mother was on the phone to my grandmother. I could tell because her voice got straighter, like she was trying to run it through a needle, and she kept rubbing at a spot on her chest.

"No. At least until next year. We've got the car and the refrigerator to pay off yet. Besides, I guess they'd have me canning and pickling all the contracts at work if they thought I was going to leave."

The rubbing got faster. It reminded me of Tracy testing out a gun-shot wound.

"She's not lonely, Mom. She's best friends with the little girl across the street. Inez. I know because she gave her that box of seashell soap she's been hoarding under her bed for six months now. Never even tried one before she gave it away."

I shot a seed from my placemat to my father's. It was true I played with Inez sometimes, but she wasn't my best friend. Tracy was my best friend. When Inez came over, she only wanted to play store. That meant she took inventory of my room while I wrote all the stuff down on a green notepad from her dad's office. Well, I couldn't write, really, but I could make all the letters. And I drew a lot of pictures to help me remember what the writing was about. It got to where I felt like the notepad was mine, since Inez never used it between times. Then one day I inventoried Inez, her ruffly jumper and hooked-together braids. I liked the picture so much I wanted Tracy to see it, so I asked if I could keep the notepad overnight.

"Want to trade?" Inez said.

She'd been looking around my room for a long time; she took the seashells and I kept the notepad for secret communications and just drawing to myself, sometimes.

"Mother," I said when she got off the phone and opened the re-frigerator. "Mother, Inez Ramsey is not my best friend."

"She's not, love?"

I could just see her sandal beneath the refrigerator door. Her heel was lifted up, not even touching the shoe, and the whole thing looked so pretty it made my teeth grit together like when I ate a mul-berry without washing it.

"Gosh, I don't even see Inez except on Saturday when you're home. Then she wants to talk to you all the time. It's just boring. Want to know who my best friend really is?"

"Not your mother, I guess."

"No. It's Tracy Barton and I'm going to call Grandma back and tell her."

"Like when you told on me for not making you enough cookies?"

"I'm not telling. I just want everyone to know. I just want to say the truth, like you say."

"Jeez, I told your father you were getting too much Sunday school. I don't think this is something your grandmother needs corrected right away. You can tell her next time you see her, all right?"

"No. I want to tell her now. And you can't say anything either. I wouldn't even have to do it if you even knew who my best friend is," I said. But I didn't call. Instead, I took my ammunition into the backyard and shook it out into the bushes. I wouldn't let myself shoot grenades, not after that. Then when I cried, it was about the four-o'clock seeds I'd have to gather all over again.

In Tracy's yard that same afternoon they were playing ponies. Liz stood up between every race with her knees green from the cut grass and told her father he'd better place his bets. He'd better pick his winner. Mr. Barton, who was arranging his gardening tools on the patio, said he bet against their mother, whatever she said. And Mrs. Barton bet wildly.

"Come on Tracy," I told him, when they finally let him win a race. "We've got to have a secret meeting."

His eyes were still bucking around to everyone in his family, making sure they knew he won. "Yeah, I've got to tell you some stuff, too," he said, but he looked more excited about the ponies.

Then Mrs. Barton was standing there with us. She crouched down toward us and the plaid of her long shorts made a funny jump at the hips, so it wasn't in straight lines anymore.

"Laurie, don't you want to race the winner? I'm just about to bring out the lemonade."

"I don't like horses," I said. "Besides, Tracy has to come over to my house. I'm not supposed to play here."

"Well why not? It seems like you were pretty safe in our yard all week."

"That's why. I'm not supposed to bother you on weekends."

"Oh, that's just silly, honey. If this is where the kids are playing today, this is just where they're playing. I'm sure your mom doesn't want to keep you out of any fun."

It was true about Mrs. Barton. She was sure. I remembered my mother saying "housedress mothers" and her voice going jiggly like a see-saw. But the Bartons had different voices completely, where they didn't have to listen to the ends and echoes of words to tell them what to do. I wondered how Mrs. Barton would take my mother's mean talk and fast arguments, her tall, awful prettiness that was also ugly in the way my grandmother meant when she said it was ugly for little girls to lie. I was ashamed, and wanted to protect my mother from being looked at like a wicked stranger. I was proud, too, and sucked at the inside of my lip when I thought about Mrs. Barton and my mother in a fight, our neighbor's eye wrinkles uncurling at the sight of my mother all stiff and beautiful and strange. But one thing I never wanted to happen: I never wanted my mother and Tracy's to be friends.

Mrs. Barton, though, thought I was sitting up and begging for her to rescue me. She thought she was some kind of good fairy who could show up and change the ending without breaking any of the rules.

"I'll go over and talk to her," she said. Her face got thinner, so I could see the sharp mask underneath. Then I knew this was what she was waiting for all along, and it was my fault, I'd finally given her a chance to do it.

So I wasn't very happy when she went in our back door and I sat outside on the steps picking up paint curls and flattening them up to my nose for the bare, chalky smell of them. And even though Tracy sat there with me, we didn't say anything special; nothing seemed secret enough to count.

When Mrs. Barton came back out the door, my mother's face looked out from behind her. It was the telephone face, a hard, gathered smile. I'd done it twice today now, tried to tell on her. But every time, I got confused and couldn't really measure what I had to tell.

From then on, my mother didn't honk for me when she came home from work. I was never untwisted from my games anymore by the in-and-out, up-and-over drone of the car horn. Instead, she dropped into Mrs. Barton's kitchen and waited for me to find her. When I did, she was sitting there rubbing the rim of her coffee cup with one finger. Her high-heeled shoes hung by their straps from the knobs on back of her chair; her feet rested on the wide base of the table like roots running from a tree.

She didn't see me. Mrs. Barton was talking to her, or she was talking to Mrs. Barton. The spark of their conversation passed between them as fast as the gleam on Mrs. Barton's cigarette.

"What's the deal?" I said to Tracy. "I thought they didn't like each other."

"Shh, she's getting information." His thick fingers ran over my lips, then crossed in an X over his.

I shifted my chewing gum. "Which one?"

He twitched his eyes in that half wink, half squint I'd been practicing for weeks. "I don't trust both of them, Trigger. Anyway, we
have to do another mission. Let's get on it."

I looked back to the table first. My mother was spreading her hand
out like a starfish, tracing each finger. Mrs. Barton smashed her cigarette and adjusted a ring. Something scary was happening, I knew
it. And it would keep on going, edging forward, back and forth, until I made it stop.

One day they went back into the den where Mrs. Barton was folding clothes.

"Go scalp your Indians, love," my mother said when I walked in
behind them and pretended to look at the pictures all around the
room. I especially liked the newspaper clippings glued onto thick
slices of yellow wood. Mr. Barton spraying the church sidewalk.
Mrs. Barton holding up a spatula at a pancake breakfast. Tracy's
brother turning into an Eagle Scout. I looked at the writing underneath and thought I saw the story for every one, how Tracy's family
was important in an ordinary way and mine was secretly dramatic.

All our pictures were like part of an adventure—my father jumping off a cliff at the camp where he got sent home for tying his
brother to a running pump, or my mother riding bareback with her
cousin. There were a few of my parents together on top of an old car
with the bumps in the wrong places and in front of a fancy ferris
wheel. Then came some shots of a bald-headed baby they said was
me. Nothing else then, not for a long time, until it got to me on my
first day of kindergarten—a flimsy girl with a tassel of hair the color
of tree sap. Pink eyes, blue sandals. I wasn't pretty like my mother.
But I wasn't ugly either. My white, unfreckled face was just a blank
to me, so that I longed for glasses, braces, or makeup. Or something, anyway, to show I was just as exciting as the rest of my family.

"We're not convinced we want to stay anywhere just yet," my
mother was saying to Mrs. Barton. But her eyes were fidgeting
around so much I knew she still saw me there listening.

People said I was like my mother. For as long as I could remember,
though, I'd felt like someone different, separate, not myself. Getting
up from my nap sometimes, I couldn't find my hand. It was still
asleep and when I shook it out the pain spangled down from my
wrist like the fuzzy dots on the TV screen when Mrs. Barton turned
on the vacuum cleaner. Once, it was even part of my dream. I was
lying on the sofa and felt something uneven against my side, coming

up from under the cushion. I pulled it out with my eyes close and didn't look until I thought over everything it could be—rat, fish, rattlesnake. It was a dead hand. Like the one they had in the spook house at the school carnival—all green and rubbery. Then I woke up and figured out what was going on. The dead hand was my hand that had fallen asleep all over again. In a way, it was worse than the dream. I found my mother in the bathroom plucking her eyebrows and hugged her from behind so that she pulled harder than she wanted and cursed the seven deadly bells of hell. Then she said she was sorry. I stayed there, sitting on the edge of the toilet, until she finished up with cold cream and water. But I never told her what I dreamed.

"Laurie," my mother said. "This is going to be an adult conversation as soon as you leave the room."

"I think they're getting out the kickball." Mrs. Barton flapped out a sheet as far as it would go. I could feel its windy shadow snap at my face. She didn't fool me, not ever. She couldn't do anything to my mother until I was gone.

But my mother straightened her face up so it looked as plain as mine, which meant I had to go anyway.

"She's a good little girl," I heard Mrs. Barton say when I was going down the hall. "But she sure can be contrary."

"She's going to be a lawyer, I know she is. With that Puritan pucker of hers and those dryclean only eyes." That was my mother, talking about me the way she talked about our neighbors in the kitchen every morning.

"How do you get on with those lawyers out there where you work?"

"We get on like sharks and armies," she said. Her voice got wider. "Maybe I should have been a lawyer, too."

Yeah, I thought, slamming the door in the way I could get away with at the Bartons'. Then you could be even meaner.

Outside, Tracy was twirling the big, clay-colored kickball in his hands.

"Hey Trigger, two-man stud."

"You don't even know what that means. Besides, I'm not a man. And besides, you're not either."

The pink in his face slid around, all slinky, trying to decide where to go. "Hey, don't you want to play ball?"

"OK, but let me kick first."

I ran over to the mulberry tree that was always first base. Kick one, I kicked a foul ball. Kick two, I felt my toes stinging happily through my tennis shoe and the ball went high and wide, slowly sighing the echo of the kick while Tracy staggered back like a gangster who'd been shot with a powerful pistol and then finally caught the ball. Which meant he won or I was out or whatever. But I didn't care, not really, it felt so good to kick the ball and have it swoop up in a perfect red rainbow from me to him.

"Tracy," I said when I tagged him on my way to the outfield. "Who's the boss of us?"

"God," he said. "Or the President. No one can boss me except God and the President."

"Me neither," I wanted to say, but I didn't. I just patted the ball and rolled it over the thick, minty grass.

When Tracy kicked it back, it came fast and smooth, barely lifted from the ground, and went all the way past the corner of the house. I ran after it with my lungs jogging in my chest. Then when I got there and saw the ball jammed up against a lawn chair, I did something no one knew about. I kicked it further. I kicked it all the way to the window by the den. Squatting down to get it, I heard my knees unbuckle—loud, too loud—and bounced three times to keep my balance. My hand wobbled on the ball.

"Same thing happened to my sister," Mrs. Barton was saying. "They didn't have him six months when it came on. And they didn't even know he was sick."

That noise, the iron scraping against some rough fabric and being set up on its end again. I remembered it from my sleep. The patchy scrape and the quick, internal click.

"But they've got three now, healthy as farm animals. Too healthy, if you really want to know. Make mine look like strays. You know, Darla, when I first saw you I figured it was something. I couldn't say exactly what, but I could tell you were thinking too much. Like about Laurie. You shouldn't let the child worry you that way."

"Oh, she couldn't have known what was happening. At least, I don't think so. But then sometimes I'm not so sure. Kids that age are wicked little trolls, aren't they? They're only partly human. They can always pretend they don't know what's going on, then slam it home on you later. Laurie was like that. When I came in, she was sliding toys through the crib bars—one after another, like quarters in a slot machine. I didn't wake the baby up, she said when she saw me. She wasn't supposed to play in there. She was too wild, tried to frazzle him up all the time. Anyway, I looked at him and thought everything was OK. His face had a little pink map of wrinkles in the sheet and he was holding onto this plastic teething ring his grandmother gave him, the kind with plastic animals floating in colored water inside. Laurie put that in, I remember thinking. That was on the basinet before lunch. Then I'm all of a sudden feeling my heart beat, hard, in my fingers like I have ten hearts, and there's nothing coming back. No beat. I'm holding onto his ankle and there's nothing, just this cool blank feel like the stem of a plant."

Then I think I heard her cry.

When the jagged humming stopped it made me dizzy and I grabbed the toes of my tennis shoes, found a cricket on one of them, pulled back to smell the cricket juice on my fingers. I had a little brother. I used to have a brother.

Mrs. Barton started ironing again. I guessed she was happy now. But I thought the whole thing was a lie, or at least that it wouldn't be true if she didn't make my mother say it. She made it all up and then she made her say it. She made her say it about me, so I couldn't even act normal anymore.

I wiped my hands on the side of the house. Liz and Tracy came around the corner kicking a pine cone, pushing each other out of the way with their shoulders. Tracy gave Liz an extra hard push and she flung away like a dancer with her arms curved out in front.

"What happened to you?" Tracy said, stopping. It looked like he was giving up on the pine cone. "Lizzie wants to play with us now. Only you're pigging the ball."

"I'm tired of playing," I said. "Besides, it's just a dumb boys' game anyway."

"Then give me the ball, kid," Liz said. She nudged it toward her with her foot, then tossed it in the air, spinning around to catch it. Her hair spun out in a clean yellow fizz around her.

"Well, what's Trigger going to play?" Tracy said.

"I'm going home to play in my yard. I'm going to play Batman. Want to come?"

His face crinkled in the sun. He rubbed at the front of his shirt. Of course he wanted to play. He couldn't wait to go dead on me.

"Let's do the one where they catch the Joker in the wax museum," he said.

We went down to the alley and back up into my yard. He said the corn could stand for the statues and the grill could be the fountain where the Joker threw piranhas instead of pennies. He had to act like Batman and be fighting all the time, so I did Robin and Joker both, back and forth, until I had him in with the piranhas and had to change back into a good guy to pull him out again.

I slid my hands under his shoulders and pretended to pick him up. My face was warm against his chest and from there he smelt like grass and four-o'clocks and the lighter fluid from his mother's cigarette lighter that he wasn't supposed to play with anyway.

"They got me in the guts," he said when I set him back down. "Play like I'm half dead now."

I held up his hand to take his pulse. It came sprinting through in the beats between mine. Then I saw something I'd never seen before: the crisscross lines on his hand, all over his skin, the way a kindergartner draws a star. My breath started going backwards. I felt like I was sucking in the whole dizzy spiral of my family. But this time I didn't wait. I didn't even try. I kissed Tracy's hand, hard. I felt the sharp bones of his fingers. And when we both flexed away I wanted to ask—I was afraid to to ask—did he really think I meant it.

Richard Bausch

THE MAN WHO KNEW BELLE STARR

(from *The Atlantic*)

On his way west McRae picked up a hitcher, a young woman carrying a paper bag and a leather purse, wearing jeans and a shawl—
which she didn't take off, though it was more than ninety degrees
out and McRae had no air-conditioning. He was driving an old
Dodge Charger with a bad exhaust system and one long crack in the
wraparound windshield. He pulled over for her, and she got right
in, put the leather purse on the seat between them, and settled herself with the paper bag on her lap between her hands. He had just
crossed into Texas from Oklahoma. This was the third day of the
trip.
"Where you headed?" he asked.
She said, "What about you?"
"Nevada, maybe."
"Why maybe?"
And that fast he was answering *her* questions. "I just got out of
the Air Force," he told her, though this wasn't exactly true. The Air
Force had given him a dishonorable discharge, after four years at
Leavenworth, for assaulting a staff sergeant. He was a bad character.
He had a bad temper that had got him into a load of trouble already,
and he just wanted to get out west, out to the wide open spaces. Just
to see it, really. He had the feeling that people didn't require as much
from a person way out where there was that kind of room. He didn't

have any family now. He had five thousand dollars from his father's insurance policy, and he was going to make the money last a while. He said, "I'm sort of undecided about a lot of things."

"Not me," she said.

"You figured out where you're going?"

"You could say that."

"So where might that be?"

She made a fist and then extended her thumb, and turned it over. "Under," she said. "Down."

"Excuse me?"

"Does the radio work?" she asked, reaching for it.

"It's on the blink," he said.

She turned the knob anyway. Then she sat back and folded her arms over the paper bag.

He took a glance at her. She was skinny and long-necked, and her hair was the color of water in a metal pail. She looked just old enough for high school.

"What's in the bag?" he said.

She sat up a little. "Nothing. Another blouse."

"Well, so what did you mean back there?"

"Back where?"

"Look," he said, "we don't have to do any talking if you don't want to."

"Then what will we do?"

"Anything you want," he said.

"What if I just want to sit here and let you drive me all the way to Nevada?"

"That's fine," he said. "That's just fine."

"Well, I won't do that. We can talk."

"Are you going to Nevada?" he asked.

She gave a little shrug of her shoulders. "Why not?"

"All right," he said, and for some reason he offered his hand. She looked at it and then smiled at him, and he put his hand back on the wheel.

It got a little awkward almost right away. The heat was awful, and she sat there sweating, not saying much. He never thought he was very smooth or anything, and he had been in prison; it had been a long time since he had found himself in the company of a woman.

Finally she fell asleep, and for a few miles he could look at her without worrying about anything but staying on the road. He decided that she was kind of good-looking around the eyes and mouth. If she ever filled out, she might be something. He caught himself wondering what might happen, thinking of sex. A girl who traveled alone like this was probably pretty loose. Without quite realizing it, he began to daydream about her, and when he got aroused by the daydream he tried to concentrate on figuring his chances, playing his cards right, not messing up any opportunities—but being gentlemanly, too. He was not the sort of man who forced himself on young women. She slept very quietly, not breathing loudly or sighing or moving much; and then she simply sat up and folded her arms above the bag again and stared out at the road.

"God," she said. "I went out."

"You hungry?" he asked.

"No."

"What's your name? I never got your name."

"Belle Starr," she said, and, winking at him, she made a clicking sound out of the side of her mouth.

"Belle Starr," he said.

"Don't you know who Belle Starr was?"

All he knew was that it was a familiar-sounding name. "Belle Starr."

She put her index finger to the side of his head and said, "Bang."

"Belle Starr," he said.

"Come on," she said. "Annie Oakley. Wild Bill Hickok."

"Oh," McRae said. "Okay."

"That's me," she said, sliding down in the seat. "Belle Starr."

"That's not your real name."

"It's the only one I go by these days."

They rode on in silence for a time.

"What's *your* name" she asked.

He told her.

"Irish?"

"I never thought about it."

"Where you from, McRae?"

"Washington, D.C."

"Long way from home."

"I haven't been there in years."

"Where *have* you been?"

"Prison," he said. He hadn't known he would say it, and now that he had, he kept his eyes on the road. He might as well have been posing for her; he had an image of himself as he must look from the side, and he shifted his weight a little, sucked in his belly. When he stole a glance at her, he saw that she was simply gazing out at the Panhandle, one hand up like a visor to shade her eyes.

"What about you?" he asked, and felt like somebody in a movie—two people with a past come together on the open road. He wondered how he could get the talk around to the subject of love.

"What *about* me?"

"Where you from?"

"I don't want to bore you with all the facts," she said.

"I don't mind," Mcrae said. "I got nothing else to do."

"I'm from way up north."

"Okay," he said, "you want me to guess?"

"Maine," she said. "Land of moose and lobster."

He said, "Maine. Well, now."

"See?" she said. "The facts are just a lot of things that don't change."

"Unless you change them," McRae said.

She reached down and, with elaborate care, as if it were fragile, put the paper bag on the floor. Then she leaned back and put her feet up on the dash. She was wearing low-cut tennis shoes.

"You going to sleep?" he asked.

"Just relaxing," she said. But a moment later, when he asked if she wanted to stop and eat, she didn't answer. He looked over and saw that she was sound asleep.

His father had died while he was at Leavenworth. The last time McRae saw him, he was lying on a gurney in one of the bays of D.C. General's emergency ward, a plastic tube in his mouth, an IV set into an ugly yellow-blue bruise on his wrist. McRae had come home on leave from the Air Force—which he had joined on the suggestion of a juvenile judge—to find his father on the floor in the living room, in a pile of old newspapers and bottles, wearing his good suit, with no socks or shoes and no shirt. He looked like he was dead. But the ambulance drivers found a pulse and rushed him off to the hospital. McRae cleaned the house up a little and then followed in the

Charger. The old man had been going steadily downhill from the time McRae was a boy, so this latest trouble wasn't new. In the hospital they got the tube in his mouth and hooked him to the IV, and then left him there on the gurney. McRae stood at his side, still in uniform, and when the old man opened his eyes and looked at him, it was clear that he didn't know who it was. The old man blinked, stared, and then sat up, took the tube out of his mouth, and spit something terrible-looking into a small metal dish that was suspended from the complicated apparatus of the room, which made a continual water-dropping sound, like a leaking sink. He looked at McRae again, and then he looked at the tube. "Jesus Christ," he said.

"Hey," McRae said.

"What."

"It's me."

The old man put the tube back in his mouth and looked away.

"Pops," McRae said. He didn't feel anything.

The tube came out. "Don't look at me, boy. You got yourself into it. Getting into trouble, stealing and running around. You got yourself into it."

"I don't mind it, Pops. It's three meals a day and a place to sleep."

"Yeah," the old man said, and then seemed to gargle something. He spit into the little metal dish again.

"I got thirty days of leave, Pops."

"Eh?'

"I don't have to go back for a month."

"Where you going?"

"Around," McRae said.

The truth was that he hated the Air Force, and he was thinking of taking the Charger and driving to Canada or someplace like that, and hiding out for the rest of his life. The Air Force felt like punishment—it *was* punishment—and he had already been in trouble for his quick temper and his attitude. That afternoon he left his father to whatever would happen, got in the Charger, and started north. But he didn't make it. He lost heart a few miles south of New York City, and he turned around and came back. The old man had been moved to a room in the alcoholic ward, but McRae didn't go to see him. He stayed in the house, watching television and drinking beer, and when old high school buddies came by he went around with them a little. Mostly he stayed home, though, and at the end of his leave he locked the place and drove back to Chanute, in Illinois, where he was stationed. He hadn't been there two months before he got into the scrape that landed him in prison. A staff sergeant caught him drinking beer in the dayroom of one of the training barracks and asked for his name. McRae walked over to him, said, "My name is trouble," and, at the word *trouble*, struck the other man in the face. He'd had a lot of beer, and he had been sitting there in the dark, going over everything in his mind, and the staff sergeant, a baby-faced man with spare tire of flesh around his waist and an attitude about the stripes on his sleeves, had just walked into it. McRae didn't even know him. Yet he stood over the sergeant where he had fallen and started kicking him. The poor man wound up in the hospital with a broken jaw (the first punch had done it), a few cracked ribs, and multiple lacerations and bruises. The court-martial was swift. The sentence was four years at hard labor, along with a dishonorable discharge. He'd had less than a month on the sentence when he got the news about his father. He felt no surprise, nor, really, any grief, yet there was a little thrill of something like fear; he was in his cell, and for an instant some part of him actually wanted to remain there, inside walls, where things were certain and no decisions had to be made. A week later he learned of the money from the insurance, which would have been more than the five thousand except that his father had been a few months behind on the rent and on other payments. McRae settled what he had to of those things, and kept the rest. He had started to feel like a happy man, out of Leavenworth and the Air Force. And now he was on his way to Nevada, or someplace like that—and he had picked up a girl.

He drove on until dusk, stopping only for gas, and the girl slept right through. Just past the line into New Mexico he pulled off the interstate and went north for a mile or so, looking for some place other than a chain restaurant to eat. She sat up straight and pushed the hair back from her face. "Where are we?"

"New Mexico," he said. "I'm looking for a place to eat."

"I'm not hungry."

"Well," he said, "you might be able to go all day without eating, but I got a three-meal-a-day habit to support."

She brought the paper bag up from the floor and held it in her lap.

"You got food in there?"

"No."

"You're very pretty—childlike, sort of, when you sleep."

"I didn't snore?"

"You were quiet as a mouse."

"And you think I'm pretty."

"I guess you know a thing like that. I hope I didn't offend you."

"I don't like dirty remarks," she said. "But I guess you don't mean to be dirty."

"Dirty."

"Sometimes people can say a thing like that and mean it very dirty, but I could tell you didn't."

He pulled in at a roadside diner and turned the ignition off. "Well?" he said.

She sat there with the bag on her lap. "I don't think I'll go in with you."

"You can have a cold drink or something," he said.

"You go in. I'll wait out here."

"Come on in there with me and have a cold drink," McRae said. "I'll buy it for you. I'll buy you dinner, if you want."

"I don't want to," she said.

He got out and started for the entrance, and before he reached it, he heard her door open and close, and turned to watch her come toward him, thin and waiflike in the shawl, which hid her arms and hands.

The diner was empty. A long, low counter ran along one side, with soda fountains and glass cases in which pies and cakes were set. There were booths along one wall. Everything seemed in order, except that no one was around. McRae and the girl stood in the doorway for a moment and waited, and finally she stepped in and took a seat in the first booth, "I guess we're supposed to seat ourselves," she said.

"This is weird," McRae said.

"Hey," she said, rising. "A jukebox." She strode over to it and leaned on it, crossing one leg behind the other at the ankle, her hair falling down to hide her face.

"Hello?" McRae said. "Anybody here?"

"Got any change?" the girl asked.

He gave her a quarter and then sat at the counter. A door at the far end of the diner swung in and a big, red-faced man entered, wearing a white cook's apron over a sweat-stained baby-blue shirt, the sleeves of which he had rolled up past the meaty curve of his elbows. "Yeah?" he said.

"You open?" McRae asked.

"That jukebox don't work, honey," the man said.

"You open?" McRae said, as the girl came and sat down beside him.

"I guess maybe I am."

"Place is kind of empty."

"What do you want to eat?"

"You got a menu?"

"You want a menu?"

"Sure," McRae said. "Why not."

"Truth is," the big man said, "I'm selling this place. I don't have menus anymore. I make hamburgers and breakfast stuff. Some french fries and cold drinks. A hot dog, maybe. I'm not keeping track."

"Let's go somewhere else," the girl said.

"Yeah," the big man said, "why don't you do that."

"Look," McRae said, "what's the story here?"

The other man shrugged. "You came in at the end of the run, you know what I mean? I'm going out of business. Sit down and I'll make you a hamburger, on the house."

McRae looked at the girl.

"Okay," she said, in a tone that made it clear that she would've been happier to leave.

The big man put his hands on the bar and leaned toward her. "Miss, if I were you, I wouldn't look a gift horse in the mouth."

"I don't like hamburger," she said.

"You want a hot dog?" the man said. "I got a hot dog for you. Guaranteed to please."

"I'll have some french fries," she said.

The big man turned to the grill and opened the metal drawer under it. He was very wide at the hips, and his legs were like tree trunks. "I get out of the Army after twenty years," he said, "and I got a little money put aside. The wife and I decide we want to get into the restaurant business. The government's going to be paying me a nice pension, and we got the savings, so we sink it all in this goddamn diner. Six and a half miles from the interstate. You get the picture? The guy's selling us this diner at a great price, you know? A terrific price. For a song, I'm in the restaurant business. The wife will cook the food and I'll wait tables, you know, until we start to make a little extra, and then we'll hire somebody—a high school kid, or somebody like that. We might even open another restaurant, if the going gets good enough. But, of course, this is New Mexico. This is six and a half miles from the interstate. You know what's up the road? Nothing." He had put the hamburger on, and a basket of frozen french fries. "Now the wife decides she's had enough of life on the border, and off she goes to Seattle to sit in the rain with her mother, and here I am trying to sell a place nobody else is dumb enough to buy. You know what I mean?"

"That's rough," McRae said.

"You're the second customer I've had all *week*, bub."

The girl said, " I guess that cash register's empty, then, huh."

"It ain't full, honey."

She got up and wandered across the room. For a while she stood gazing out the windows over the booths, her hands invisible under the woolen shawl. When she came back to sit next to McRae again, the hamburger and french fries were ready.

"On the house," the big man said.

And the girl brought a gun out from under the shawl—a pistol that looked like a toy. "Suppose you open up that register, Mr. Poor Mouth," she said.

The big man looked at her, then at McRae, who had taken a large bite of his hamburger and had it bulging in his cheeks.

"This thing is loaded, and I'll use it."

"Well, for Christ's sake," the big man said.

McRae started to get off the stool. "Hold on a minute," he said to them both, his words garbled by the mouthful of food, and then everything started happening at once. The girl aimed the pistol. There was a popping sound—a single small pop, not much louder than the sound of a cap gun—and the big man took a step back, into the dishes and pans. He stared at the girl, wide-eyed, for what seemed like a long time, and then went down, pulling dishes with him in a tremendous shattering.

"Jesus Christ," McRae said, swallowing, standing back far from her, raising hands.

She put the pistol back in her jeans, under the shawl, and then went around the counter and opened the cash register. "Damn," she said.

And now she looked at him; it was as if she had forgotten he was there. "What're you standing there with your hands up like that?"

"God," he said, "oh, God."

"Stop it," she said. "Put your hands down."

He did so.

"Cash register's empty." She sat down on one of the stools and gazed over at the body of the man where it had fallen. "Damn."

"Look," McRae said, "take my car. You can have my car."

She seemed puzzled. "I don't want your car. What do I want your car for?"

"You—" he said. He couldn't talk, couldn't focus clearly, or think. He looked at the man, who lay very still, and then he began to cry.

"Will you stop it?" she said, coming off the stool, reaching under the shawl and bringing out the pistol again.

"Jesus," he said. "Good Jesus."

She pointed the pistol at his forehead. "Bang," she said. "What's my name?"

"Your—name?"

"My name."

"Belle—" he managed.

"Come on," she said. "The whole thing. You remember."

"Belle—Belle Starr."

"Right." She let the gun hand drop to her side, into one of the folds of the shawl. "I like that so much better than Annie Oakley."

"Please," McRae said.

She took a few steps away from him and then whirled and aimed the gun. "I think we better get out of here. What do you think?"

"Take the car," he said, almost with exasperation; he was frightened to hear it in his voice.

"I can't drive," she said simply. "Never learned."

"Jesus," he said. It went out of him like a sigh.

"Lordy," she said, gesturing with the pistol for him to move to the door, "it's hard to believe you were ever in *prison*."

The interstate went on into the dark, beyond the glow of the headlights. He lost track of miles, road signs, other traffic, time; trucks came by and surprised him, and other cars seemed to materialize as they started the lane change that would bring them over in front of him. He saw their taillights grow small in the distance, and all the while the girl sat watching him, her hands somewhere under the shawl. For a long time he heard only the sound of the rushing night air at the windows, and then she moved a little, shifted her weight, bringing one leg up on the seat.

"What were you in prison for, anyway?"

Her voice startled him, and for a moment he couldn't think of an answer.

"I—beat up a guy."

"That's all?"

"Yes, that's all." He couldn't keep the irritation out of his voice.

"Tell me about it."

"It was just—I just beat up a guy. It wasn't anything."

"I didn't shoot that man for money, you know."

McRae said nothing.

"I shot him because he made a nasty remark to me about the hot dog."

"I didn't hear any nasty remark."

"If he hadn't said it, he'd still be alive."

McRae held tight to the wheel.

"Don't you wish it was the Wild West?" she said.

"Wild West," he said. "Yeah." He could barely speak for the dryness in his mouth and the deep ache of his own breathing.

"You know," she said, "I'm not really from Maine."

He nodded.

"I'm from Florida."

"Florida," he managed.

"Yes, only I don't have a southern accent, so people think I'm not from there. Do you hear any trace of a southern accent at all when I talk?"

"No," he said.

"Now you—you've got an accent. A definite southern accent."

He was silent.

"Talk to me," she said.

"What do you want me to say?" he said. "Jesus."

"You could ask me things."

"Ask you things—"

"Ask me what my name is."

Without hesitating, McRae said, "What's your name?"

"You know."

"No, really," he said, trying to play along.

"It's Belle Starr."

"Belle Starr," he said.

"Nobody *but*," she said.

"Good," he said.

"And I don't care about money, either," she said. "That's not what I'm after."

"No," McRae said.

"What I'm after is adventure."

"Right," McRae said.

"Fast living."

"Fast living, right."

"A good time."

"Good," he said.

"I'm going to live a ton before I die."

"A ton, yes."

"What about you?"

"Yes," he said. "Me too."

"Want to join up with me?"

"Join up," he said. "Right." He was watching the road.

She leaned toward him a little. "Do you think I'm lying about my name?"

"No."

"Good," she said.

He had begun to feel as though he might start throwing up what he'd had of the hamburger. His stomach was cramping on him, and he was dizzy. He might even be having a heart attack.

"Your eyes are as big as saucers," she said.

He tried to narrow them a little. His whole body was shaking now.

"You know how old I am, McRae? I'm nineteen."

He nodded, glanced at her and then at the road again.

"How old are you?"

"Twenty-three."

"Do you believe people go to heaven when they die?"

"Oh, God," he said.

"Look, I'm not going to shoot you while you're driving the car. We'd crash if I did that."

"Oh," He said. "Oh, Jesus, please—look, I never saw anybody shot before—"

"Will you *stop* it?"

He put one hand to his mouth. He was soaked: he felt the sweat on his upper lip, and then he felt the dampness all through his clothes.

She said, "I don't kill everybody I meet, you know."

"No," he said. "Of course not." The absurdity of this exchange almost brought a laugh up out of him. How astonishing, that a laugh could be anywhere in him at such a time, but here it was, rising up in his throat like some loosened part of his anatomy. He held on with his whole mind, and a moment passed before he realized that *she* was laughing.

"Actually," she said, "I haven't killed all that many people."

"How—" he began. Then he had to stop to breathe. "How many?"

"Take a guess."

"I don't have any idea," he said.

"Well," she said, "you'll just have to guess. And you'll notice that I haven't spent any time in prison."

He was quiet.

"*Guess*," she said.

McRae said, "Ten?"

"No."

He waited.

"Come on, keep guessing."

"More than ten," he said.

"Maybe."

"More than ten," he said.

"Well, all right. Less than ten."

"Less than ten," he said.

"Guess," she said.

"Nine."

"No."

"Eight."

"No, not eight."

"Six?"

"Not six."

"Five?"

"Five and a half people," she said. "You almost hit it right on the button."

"Five and a half people," McRae said.

"Right. A kid who was hitchhiking, like me; a guy at a gas station; a dog that must've got lost—I count him as the half; another guy at a gas station; a guy that took me to a motel and made an obscene gesture to me; and the guy at the diner. That makes five and a half."

"Five and a half," McRae said.

"You keep repeating everything I say. I wish you'd quit that."

He wiped his hand across his mouth and then feigned a cough to keep from having to speak.

"Five and a half people," she said, turning a little in the seat, putting her knees up on the dash. "Have you ever met anybody like me? Tell the truth."

"No," McRae said, "nobody."

"Just think about it, McRae. You can say you rode with Belle Starr. You can tell your grandchildren."

He was afraid to say anything to this, for fear of changing the delicate balance of the thought. Yet he knew the worst mistake would be to say nothing at all. He was beginning to sense something of the cunning that he would need to survive, even as he knew that the slightest miscalculation might mean the end of him. He said, with fake wonder, "I knew Belle Starr."

She said, "Think of it."

"Something," he said.

And she sat farther down in the seat. "Amazing."

He kept to fifty-five miles an hour and everyone else was speeding. The girl sat straight up now, nearly facing him on the seat. For long periods she had been quiet, simply watching him drive. Soon they were going to need gas; they had less than half a tank.

"Look at those people speeding," she said. "We're the only ones obeying the speed limit. Look at them."

"Do you want me to speed up?"

"I think they ought to get tickets for speeding, that's what I think. Sometimes I wish I were a policeman."

"Look," McRae said, "we're going to need gas pretty soon."

"No, let's just run it until it quits. We can always hitch a ride with somebody."

"This car's got a great engine," McRae said. "We might have to outrun the police, and I wouldn't want to do that in any other car."

"This old thing? It's got a crack in the windshield. The radio doesn't work."

"Right. But it's a fast car. It'll outrun a police car."

She put one arm over the seat back and looked out the rear window. "You really think the police are chasing us?"

"They might be," he said.

She stared at him a moment. "No. There's no reason. Nobody saw us."

"But if somebody did—this car, I mean, it'll go like crazy."

"I'm afraid of speeding, though," she said. "Besides, you know what I found out? If you run slow enough, the cops go right past you. Right on past you, looking for somebody who's in a hurry. No, I think it's best if we just let it run until it quits and then get out and hitch."

McRae thought he knew what might happen when the gas ran out: she would make him push the car to the side of the road, and then she would walk him back into the cactus and brush there, and when they were far enough from the road, she would shoot him. He knew this as if she had spelled it all out, and he began again to try for the cunning he would need. "Belle," he said. "Why don't we lay low for a few days in Albuquerque?"

"Is that an obscene gesture?" she asked.

"No!" he said, almost shouted. "No! That's—it's outlaw talk. You know. Hide out from the cops—lay low. It's—it's prison talk."

"Well, I've never been in prison."

"That's all I meant."

"You want to hide out."

"Right," he said.

"You and me?"

"You—you asked if I wanted to join up with you."

"Did I?" She seemed puzzled by this.

"Yes," he said, feeling himself press it a little. "Don't you remember?"

"I guess I do."

"You did," he said.

"I don't know."

"Belle Starr had a gang," he said.

"She did?"

"I could be the first member of your gang."

She sat there thinking this over. McRae's blood moved at the thought that she was deciding whether or not he would live. "Well," she said, "maybe."

"You've got to have a gang, Belle."

"We'll see," she said.

A moment later she said, "How much money do you have?"

"I have enough to start a gang."

"It takes money to start a gang?"

"Well—" He was at a loss.

"How much do you have?"

He said, "A few hundred."

"Really?" she said. "That much?"

"Just enough to—just enough to get to Nevada."

"Can I have it?"

He said, "Sure." He was holding the wheel and looking out into the night.

"And we'll be a gang?"

"Right," he said.

"I like the idea. Belle Starr and her gang."

McRae started talking about what the gang could do, making it up as he went along, trying to sound like all the gangster movies he'd seen. He heard himself talking about things like robbery and getaway cars and not getting nabbed and staying out of prison, and then, as she sat there staring at him, he started talking about being at Leavenworth, what it was like. He went on about it, the hours of forced work and the time alone, the harsh day-to-day routines, the bad food. Before he was through, feeling the necessity of deepening her sense of him as her new accomplice—and strangely as though in some way he had indeed become exactly that—he was telling her everything, all the bad times he'd had: his father's alcoholism, and growing up wanting to hit something for the anger that was in him; the years of getting into trouble; the fighting and kicking and what it had got him. He embellished it all, made it sound worse than it really was, because she seemed to be going for it and because, telling it to her, he felt oddly sorry for himself; a version of this story of pain and neglect and lonely rage was true. He had been through a lot. And as he finished describing for her the scene at the hospital the last time he saw his father, he was almost certain he had struck a chord in her. He thought he saw it in the rapt expression on her face.

"Anyway," he said, and smiled at her.

"McRae?" she said.

"Yeah?"

"Can you pull over?"

"Well," he said, his voice shaking, "why don't we wait until it runs out of gas?"

She was silent.

"We'll be that much farther down the road," he said.

"I don't really want a gang," she said. "I don't like dealing with other people that much. I mean, I don't think I'm a leader."

"Oh, yes," McRae said. "No—you're a leader. You're definitely a leader. I was in the Air Force and I know leaders, and you are definitely what I'd call a leader."

"Really?"

"Absolutely. You are leadership material all the way."

"I wouldn't have thought so."

"Definitely," he said. "Definitely a leader."

"But I don't really like people around, you know."

"That's a leadership quality. Not wanting people around. It is definitely a leadership quality."

"Boy," she said, "the things you learn."

He waited. If he could only think himself through to the way out. If he could get her to trust him, get the car stopped—be there when she turned her back.

"You want to be in my gang, huh?"

"I sure do," he said.

"Well, I guess I'll have to think about it."

"I'm surprised nobody's mentioned it to you before."

"You're just saying that."

"No, really."

"Were you ever married?" she asked.

"Married?" he said, and then stammered over the answer. "Ah—uh, no."

"You ever been in a gang before?"

"A couple times, but—they never had good leadership."

"You're giving me a line, huh."

"No," he said, "it's true. No good leadership. It was always a problem."

"I'm tired," she said, shifting toward him a little. "I'm tired of talking."

The steering wheel was hurting the insides of his hands. He held tight, looking at the coming-on of the white stripes in the road. There were no other cars now, and not a glimmer of light anywhere beyond the headlights.

"Don't you ever get tired of talking?"

"I never was much of a talker," he said.

"I guess I don't mind talking as much as I mind listening," she said.

He made a sound in his throat which he hoped she took for agreement.

"That's just when I'm tired, though."

"Why don't you take a nap?" he said.

She leaned back against the door and regarded him. "There's plenty of time for that later."

"So," he wanted to say, "you're not going to kill me—we're a gang?"

They had gone for a long time without speaking, an excruciating hour of minutes, during which the gas gauge had sunk to just above empty, and finally she had begun talking about herself, mostly in the third person. It was hard to make sense of most of it, yet he listened as if to instructions concerning how to extricate himself. She talked about growing up in Florida, in the country, and owning a horse; she remembered when she was taught to swim by somebody she called Bill, as if McRae would know who that was; and then she told him how when her father ran away with her mother's sister, her mother started having men friends over all the time. "There was a lot of obscene things going on," she said, and her voice tightened a little.

"Some people don't care what happens to their kids," McRae said.

"Isn't it the truth?" she said. Then she took the pistol out of the shawl. "Take this exit."

He pulled onto the ramp and up an incline to a two-lane road that went off through the desert, toward a glow that burned on the horizon. For perhaps five miles the road was straight as a plumb line, and then it curved into long, low undulations of sand and mesquite and cactus.

"My mother's men friends used to do whatever they wanted to me," she said. "It went on all the time. All sorts of obscene goings-on."

McRae said, "I'm sorry that happened to you, Belle." And for an instant he was surprised by the sincerity of his feeling: it was as if he couldn't feel sorry enough. Yet it was genuine: it had to do with his own unhappy story. The whole world seemed very, very sad to him. "I'm really very sorry," he said.

She was quiet a moment, as if thinking about this. Then she said, "Let's pull over now. I'm tired of riding."

"It's almost out of gas," he said.

"I know, but pull it over anyway."

"You sure you want to do that?"

"See?" she said. "That's what I mean—I wouldn't like being told what I should do all the time, or asked if I was sure of what I wanted or not."

He pulled the car over and slowed to a stop. "You're right," he said. "See? Leadership. I'm just not used to somebody with leadership qualities."

She held the gun a little toward him. He was looking at the small, dark, perfect circle at the end of the barrel. "I guess we should get out," she said.

"I guess so," he said.

"Do you have any relatives left anywhere?"

"No."

"Your folks are both dead?"

"Right, yes."

"Which one died first?"

"I told you," he said. "Didn't I? My mother, my mother died first."

"Do you feel like an orphan?"

He sighed. "Sometimes." The whole thing was slipping away from him.

"I guess I do too." She reached back and opened her door. "Let's get out now."

And when he reached for the door handle, she aimed the gun at his head. "Get out slow."

"Aw, Jesus," he said. "Look, you're not going to do this, are you? I mean, I thought we were friends and all."

"Just get out real slow, like I said to."

"Okay," he said. "I'm getting out." He opened his door, and the ceiling light surprised and frightened him. Some wordless part of him understood that this was it, and all his talk had come to nothing: all the questions she had asked him, and everything he had told her—it was all completely useless. This was going to happen to him, and it wouldn't mean anything; it would just be what happened.

"Real slow," she said. "Come on."

"Why are you doing this?" he asked. "You've got to tell me that before you do it."

"Will you please get out of the car now?"

He just stared at her.

"All right, I'll shoot you where you sit."

"Okay," he said. "Don't shoot."

She said in an irritable voice, as though she were talking to a recalcitrant child, "You're just putting it off."

He was backing himself out, keeping his eyes on the little barrel of the gun, and he could hear something coming, seemed to notice it the same instant that she said, "Wait." He stood half in and half out of the car, doing as she said, and a truck came over the hill ahead of them, a tractor trailer, all white light and roaring.

"Stay still," she said, crouching, aiming the gun at him.

The truck came fast, was only fifty yards away, and without having to decide about it, without even knowing that he would do it, McRae bolted into the road. He was running; he heard the exhausted sound of his own breath, the truck horn blaring, coming on, louder, the thing bearing down on him, something buzzing past his head. Time slowed. His legs faltered under him, were heavy, all the nerves gone out of them. In the light of the oncoming truck he

saw his own white hands outstretched as if to grasp something in
the air before him, and then the truck was past him, the blast of air
from it propelling him over the side of the road and down the embankment, in high, dry grass, which pricked his skin and crackled
like hay.

He was alive. He lay very still. Above him was the long shape of
the road, curving off in the distance, the light of the truck going on.
The noise faded and was nothing. A little wind stirred. He heard the
car door close. Carefully he got to all fours and crawled a few yards
away from where he had fallen. He couldn't be sure of which direction—he only knew he couldn't stay where he was. Then he heard
what he thought were her footsteps in the road, and he froze. He lay
on his side, facing the embankment. When she appeared there he
almost cried out.

"McRae?" she said. "Did I get you?" She was looking right at
where he was in the dark, and he stopped breathing. "McRae?"

He watched her move along the edge of the embankment.

"McRae?" She put one hand over her eyes and stared at a place a
few feet over from him, and then she turned and went back out of
sight. He heard the car door again, and again he began to crawl farther away. The ground was cold and rough, sandy.

He heard her put the key in the trunk. He stood up, tried to run,
but something went wrong in his leg, something sent him sprawl-
ing, and a sound came out of him that seemed to echo, to stay on
the air, as if to call her to him. He tried to be perfectly still, tried not
to breathe, hearing now the small pop of the gun. He counted the
reports: one, two, three. She was standing there at the edge of the
road, firing into the dark, toward where she must have thought she
heard the sound. Then she was rattling the paper bag. She was re-
loading—he could hear the click of the gun. He tried to get up and
couldn't. He had sprained his ankle, had done something very bad
to it. Now he was crawling wildly, blindly, through the tall grass,
hearing again the small report of the pistol. At last he rolled into a
shallow gully. He lay there with his face down, breathing the dust,
his own voice leaving him in a whimpering, animal-like sound that
he couldn't stop, even as he held both shaking hands over his mouth.

"McRae?" She sounded so close. "Hey'" she said. "McRae?"

He didn't move. He lay there perfectly still, trying to stop himself
from crying. He was sorry for everything he had ever done. He

didn't care about the money, or the car, or going out west, or anything. When he lifted his head to peer over the lip of the gully and saw that she had started down the embankment with his flashlight, moving like someone with time and the patience to use it, he lost sense of himself as McRae; he was just something crippled and breathing in the dark, lying flat in a little winding gully of weeds and sand. McRae was gone, was someone far, far away, from ages ago— a man fresh out of prison, with the whole country to wander in and insurance money in his pocket, who had headed west with the idea that maybe his luck, at long last, had changed.

Jill McCorkle

FIRST UNION BLUES

(from *Southern Magazine*)

I'm sitting here at work knowing full well that the Mr. Coffee that my cousin Eleanore gave me for Christmas is going full blast and there's not a thing I can do about it. I knew as soon as I pulled into the parking lot that I forgot to turn it off. I knew when I looked up at our sign here in front of the bank that gives the time and temp; it said 80 F and I thought, hot, Jesus it is hot, blazing hot, and since I have a fear of fire and have my entire life since I saw the movie *Jane Eyre*, I happened to think of the Mr. Coffee and how I had thought I might want to drink that little bit there in the bottom after I put on my makeup and somehow in the midst of mascara and cover up, my mind wandered right on into wanting to wax my legs and see how it did. "It hurts like hell," Eleanore has said and that's what I was thinking right up until I parked and saw the time and temp sign. I don't tell anybody this but I've yet to learn the C temp and how to figure it out and so I always have to wait around for the F one. What bothers me is that some days waiting to get the time to flash up is like waiting for Christmas and other days before you can make it out (all the dots don't always work) then it's changed on you. That's how it was this morning. I don't know who here is in charge of that sign; I'm not. I'm a teller, which they tell me is "a foot in the door," "a base to grow upon," and so on. A check to pay off Visa is more like it.

There's nothing I can do about the Mr. Coffee right this second. I barely get a coffee break and I know they aren't going to let me drive clear across town to check on something that I might or might not have done. It's happened before that I have thought the oven was on and such, only to find that I had turned it off without even knowing. "I live by my instincts," I've told Eleanore and that's true. And so I could've cut it off, instinctively. All of us have done things instinctively only to find out we didn't remember doing it. Some people spend years that way.

Eighty-two degrees Farenheit. I can read it loud and clear, not a dot out of place and I know that any minute now that condo that I rent is going to bust into flames. It starts there at the Mr. Coffee, wedged right between the microwave and the wok. A little piece of paper towel ignites, catches hold of my new Dinah Shore kitchen rags, which are just for show and stay dry as a bone since my condo has a dishwasher and I let them air dry. It spreads from there past the condo's mini-blinds to my little oil lamp that says "Light My Fire" that I won at a fair once for hitting a woman's big round butt with a bean bag. I never would've picked that lamp but free is free and so I took it and went ahead with Larrette over to the funny mirrors which is all she wanted to do. "Fat," she would say and hide between my legs. She is only two and doesn't have many more words than what she saw in the mirrors—big, little, funny, and, of course, kitty and puppy. There weren't any animals at the fair but those are her favorite words. If she likes something she'll call it kitty. If I could rig up some mirrors at home like that, she'd stay busy for hours but I'm not real sure how it's all done which I guess is why you only see them at a fair or some place special. I bought a little compact at Woolworth's that was on the sale table and that mirror was so bad and wavy, I just knew Larrette would love it. She threw it to the floor and it cracked and sparkled all over the condo kitchen. "Seven years, puppy," I said to her but I'm not worried. I figure I've had my seven already.

Larrette is my daughter by Larry Cross of Shallotte, North Carolina, and he is—cross I mean. So we never see him at all, mainly because he lives in California doing odd jobs. "The sea is in my blood," he used to say just because he grew up in Shallotte, which is nothing but a spit from the ocean. And I told him that, yeah, if stretching out in the sun with little to no clothes on, sipping a Bud, and riding the waves is what it takes to have the sea in your blood, well then, yeah boy, I've got it in mine, too. "Only that kind of blood

calls for money," I told him. "The average American cannot sun-
bathe straight from May to September." I meant due to finances, of
course, but I couldn't even if I was Jackie O. because I'm fair-
skinned; a strawberry blonde almost always is and my dermatologist
tells me that skin cancer is bad in this area. That's probably one reason right there why I instinctively took up with Larry Cross. He had
the tan that I had never had; he could have passed for Spanish if he
could have kept his mouth shut which he couldn't. Open his mouth
and Shallotte was written all over him.

I tell people that Larry Cross does odd jobs in California when
the truth is that I have no earthly idea what he does and I didn't
when I was staying there with him in Fuquay-Varina. I think he
must've dealt in drugs or something underhanded from the looks of
the people that would appear at my door at all hours of the night
and day when decent people are either at work or at home watching
TV.

I never married Larry Cross because I wasn't about to saddle myself with trash. I say that now, but I guess there were some times
when I thought we would get married; I guess I was thinking that
when I was carrying Larrette and he was so proud of himself for getting me that way. But my instincts told me it wouldn't work just as
soon as Larrette had popped out and Larry went and bought himself a surfboard with no surf whatsoever there in Fuquay-Varina.
There were bills to pay which I had always paid and he was over there
drinking a beer and listening to the Beach Boys singing, "Catch a
wave and you're sitting on top of the world."

"What're you going to do come low tide?" I asked him. What we
had wasn't a home so one day I just up and left, me and Larrette. We
moved to Raleigh and stayed with Eleanore until I got my job here.
Then before I knew it, I was going to the state fair and living in a
condo with a wreath on every wall and a big hooked rug that I
bought at the outlet mall over near the airport. That place has got
everything you might want and then some. Everything.

If that oil lamp catches fire it's all over. Everything I own will bust
right into flames and I'll have to start all over putting my life into
perspective. And I like that word—perspective—it can make something sound a lot more important than it is. Not that I don't value
my life, because I do, but sometimes I wish that I could spread it all
out on a piece of paper and take some white-out to it. Larry Cross

would be the first to go. I tell people (if they happen to ask) that he does odd jobs down in California. I don't tell that I think he's a drug pusher because that would stick and get turned right back around and follow me wherever I may go in this life like gum on a shoe. They'd say, "That's Maureen Roach who works as a teller and used to live with a pusher down in Fuquay-Varina," and I can't have that. Now people just say things like, "That's Maureen Roach who works down there at the First Union Bank; she's the teller with the strawberry blonde hair that looks a little tiny bit like Krystle Carrington off of 'Dynasty.' She has a cute little girl by the name of Larrette. No, she's a single parent."

If my Daddy wasn't already dead, I'd want to kill him for not changing our name legal to something other than Roach. "Roach Eyes!" That's what children said to me at school and I know they'll do it to Larrette if I don't get married and have whoever adopt her first. Some things never change—children teasing other children and people taking a little information and turning it all around and sticking it to you like a wad of Juicy Fruit. We can't chew gum while on the window or smoke cigarettes. "It looks bad," my boss, Mr. Crown, says, and I could bust his crown. I work right here and yet when I decided to get me a Visa card, I had one hell of a time. To get a card you have to show that you charge up a blue streak, that you owe money here and there. "I have always paid what I owe," I told him only to be told that I have no credit. I went and got me a microwave and a washer and dryer on time so I could owe some money and get a card so I'd be able to write a check in the grocery store. I probably couldn't have done that if Earl Taylor hadn't been working there in Sears and hadn't been taken with me. He asked me to go for dinner and I asked him to let me charge and pay on time and we shook on it, ate Chinese food and the next day my things were delivered. Larrette had a fit over those big pasteboard boxes. I've been going out with Earl ever since.

I figure Larry Cross has himself one of those sticks that'll beep if he's walking there on the strand and happens upon some change. That's what he does all day long, that and take pills and sell pills and do sex stuff. I'd be stupid to tell all of that and I am not stupid. "Why did you take a check that wasn't endorsed?" Mr. Crown asked me first thing this morning, those other girls studying papers like they were in school, scared to death I know that they had done it and not me. "You're not stupid, Maureen," he said and I said, "No sir, I am not." I can admit to a mistake; it's easy if you've got the right perspective on it all, such as, Mr. Crown sits in a leather chair all day long and never once has to touch a nasty old piece of money that has been God only knows where and might have some AIDS on it. If Mr. Crown sat here at the window and saw what's going in and out of this place, who's bouncing and who's scrimping, then he'd be likely to mess up occasionally, too. "You've got to concentrate, Maureen."

And I'm certainly not stupid. Stupid would be if I told all I know about Larry Cross. Sex stuff, that's the only reason I got hooked up with Larry Cross to begin with and that ties right in with that Spanish tan and hairy chest because he was right good-looking in a ape-like way. He looked like those little he-men dolls, except his hair was black and he had a real full beard like that man on "Little House on the Prairie," not Little Joe Cartwright but that other man that lived all alone most of the shows and dated that schoolteacher a time or two. Larry Cross was all right but I'm not stupid. I mean why would I marry trash? Especially trash with a last name that isn't too much better than my own. Taylor—that's Earl's last name and one I'm thinking I could probably live with.

Sometimes my mouth gets all worked up with saliva handling this money. I am not good with money. That's my biggest fault. It's a fault I've always had; if it's in my wallet then I just naturally think it's for spending and that outlet mall can get me in a whip-snap. Larry Cross had the fault of spending worse than me. If I was still with him he'd probably be sitting in the living room of that condo with those long legs stretched out on the coffee table and he'd be wearing nothing but some bathing trunks, letting the kitchen burn down, while he drew up a plan of how I could slip a little money every now and then. Embezzle is the word and I'd put my body on the street before I ever did that. I've got Larrette to think of but would he have ever thought of Larrette as something other than a Frisbee fetcher? No, no way. "I am not a dog," I told him when he'd say, "Honey, can you reach that Frisbee?" and that Frisbee about a hundred feet from where I was sitting. "If I had a rubber arm," I said.

I'd like for somebody to run my business. It isn't that I'm not into liberation. God knows, you can just look at me and know that I am;

you can know by my credit cards in my wallet, Visa, Ivey's, and Texaco. But still, it would be so nice to have somebody run my business, somebody who would say, "Now, honey, look here. You just thought you threw out your W-2 and here it is right under this stack of Christmas cards that you forgot to open." Take Earl Taylor, for example.

"I'd rather not," Eleanore always says when I say that. Eleanore is a teacher's aide in the elementary school and that has slowed her thoughts down some, though she's real good with Larrette. She was the first one to get Larrette to say kitty and to learn to meow.

Eleanore goes with a man who already has a wife so she can't really talk much. She only gets to see him every now and then at the Ramada Inn in Apex. She thinks he's going to leave that wife that drives a mini-van and heads up Easter Seals every year, and those two babies and that house that looks like a little fairy cottage out in a nice part of town for her. She likes for me to get in my car and drive her by that house late at night and she'll say things like, "Yep, TV's on. I knew he'd be watching TV. I know that man like the back of my hand. He's sitting up late watching the TV so he doesn't have to get in the bed with *her*." Eleanore doesn't know any better. She's two years older than me, thirty-one, but she doesn't know a bit better. She hasn't had life's lessons taught to her like I did staying in Fuquay with Larry Cross. I shouldn't encourage that. I shouldn't even drive her past that house for her to fill her head with stories, but sometimes it's fun. Sometimes we say we're going to disguise ourselves in case a cop should pull us over right there in front of that house, so I put on some sunglasses and tie a scarf to my head and I must admit that I like to do that because it makes me feel like I look a little like Susan Hayward and so I say things like "I Want to Live!" or "I'll Climb the Highest Mountain!" or let's ride on "Back Street!" and Eleanore will take it in her head that if she wears a gingham shirt and sunglasses that she looks like Doris Day and she will say, "Lover Come Back!" and "Where were you when the lights went out?" We have some fun times, me and Eleanore, and we always have, but then I have to get serious.

"Eleanore, you might as well look elsewhere," I say and she rolls those big blue eyes that are common among us Roaches (her mama was a Roach) like I might be a little breeze whistling past her ear. You can't tell her.

"I don't know what you see in Earl Taylor," she says. "Earl Taylor is a little nerd." I can see where she gets that. I can. To somebody who doesn't know Earl Taylor like I know him, he might look that way because of the way his hair is so thin and weak-looking and those glasses he has to wear. But Earl is smart and that's how he looks. He looks like somebody that can handle figures and money. Now, he doesn't make a bed slope way off to one side or creak and groan like Larry Cross did and he doesn't make *me* creak and groan like Larry Cross did. As a matter of fact, Earl can get in and out of a bed and you don't even know he's been there. Now, I don't want anybody getting me wrong because there is no such goings on in that condo with Larrette right there in the same dwelling. The only time that Earl and me have actually spent the night until dawn in a bed together was the weekend that Eleanore kept Larrette and we went down to Ocean Drive, which might as well be Myrtle Beach the way it's grown. "Myrtle Beach, Ocean Drive, they run right together," Earl said and he was right. I couldn't have drawn a line between the two if I had had to. Other than that, we just pop over to Earl's place every now and then. He has a bed that's just on a frame with a green glass-shaded floor lamp right there beside it so he can read in bed. Earl likes those green glass lamp shades because it's related to his profession, but that green glass is the only adornment of any kind that he owns. Plain. It's all real plain but it's clean.

Earl is smarter than Larry Cross was even before he killed off so many brain cells. I looked it all up in the library while I was in Fuquay. I looked up drugs and one thing led to another till pretty soon I was reading on brain cells and come to find out that once they're dead, they're dead. As dead as that rubber tree that Eleanore has in her living room thinking it's gonna bush back and be something. Larry Cross will never be something.

Earl Taylor is already something; he's in charge of the finances in Sears. He banks here with us and so I've seen his savings account and it is a fat one. That doesn't surprise me a bit because it's obvious that he doesn't throw money away; it's obvious by the way that his place is so plain and the way that he wears clothes that mix and mingle to the degree that it seems like he has on the same outfit every single day. When I think of Earl, I think khaki and oxford cloth. When I think of Larry Cross, I think Levi's and loud Hawaiian shirts, and loud-colored swim trunks and gym shorts. Flashy—

Larry Cross is flashy with the money he doesn't have and that little Spitfire convertible in bright orange that I was forever needing to jump with my VW Bug. Earl Taylor drives a Mazda, a nice, neat, plain, navy Mazda that he vacuums on a regular basis. Sometimes we'll be on our way out to eat and Earl will whip right in the Drive-Thru Klean-a-Kar and pop a quarter into that vacuum and run over things. He took the shoes right off of my feet and cleaned up the bottom of them for me. Night and day. That's what Larry Cross and Earl Taylor are.

"You are making a big mistake if you get hooked up with him," Eleanore tells me. Eleanore comes over every Tuesday night and fills my washer full of slinky nightwear she only wears in Apex. "What you like about Earl is how he isn't like Larry. Now tell the truth." Eleanore always says that, "Now tell the truth," but she only wants your truth; she turns a deaf ear if you discuss her truth.

"That's not the only reason," I tell her. "Earl is a good businessman."

"And Larry Cross was not," she'll snap though I know he must've done all right to have had that stream of weirdos coming by all the time. Of course, I never say that.

"Earl is neat as a pin."

"And Larry Cross was a slob," she says and doesn't even pause to breathe. "And I'll give you the last one: Larry Cross, as worthless as he is, is good-looking and Earl Taylor is not."

"Beauty is in the eye of the beholder," I tell her though I know better. "Beauty is only skin deep and Earl goes through and through."

"How? Name one way." Eleanore is so persistent with perspectives other than her own.

"He fixed it so I could get myself established with credit."

"That's his job. Name another."

"He's sweet to Larrette," I say and Eleanore can't deny that one because she's never seen Earl around Larrette that much.

"What does he think about the way you spend money? What does he think about the way you order just about everything that Yield House has to offer?"

"Earl doesn't care." I tell her and that's true. Half the time Earl doesn't even notice, which is, I guess, another difference between him and Larry Cross. If Larry Cross was to slap those long legs up on a brand new butler's table, he'd at least notice. He'd say, "Where'd you get this?" and I'd say what I always said, "At the getting place." Larry Cross didn't know a thing about the business because I made the money and I paid the bills and I just about lost my mind doing it.

There's a woman leaning out of her car window right now with a check and deposit slip in her hand and a diamond that would make anybody proud sparkling on her finger. "Hi, Gail, how are you today?" I say before I even open that drawer and pull it back in. I know her without even looking at the name on her deposit slip because she comes in every Monday morning with her husband's check that he got on Friday. William Anderson MD, and her name is right there under his, Gail Mason-Anderson. That check is something, too; I bet the United States of this country makes more off of one of William Anderson's checks than I make in four months gross. They live on Winona in a two-story house that's got a pool in the back. I know because I looked for that house when I rode Eleanore by to see whether or not her boyfriend was really out of town on the weekend when they were supposed to meet in Apex. He wasn't. He was right there in his backyard wearing an apron and carrying barbecue tongs with cars lined up on either side of the street. "He's out of town all right," I told Eleanore.

"It's *her*," she said. "*She* makes him do all these social things with people he can't stand. He does it to keep her off his back just a little bit."

"He lied," I told her.

"He didn't want me to be hurt by it." She had taken off her Doris Day glasses and wiped her eyes. "He's protective of my feelings."

I sang "Que Sera Sera" but it didn't perk her up. It made her mad, to be perfectly honest, and so she lit into Earl Taylor like a fly on you know what, because that's what she always does when her own life is going bad and she has no choice but to admit it.

"I hope you had a nice weekend, Gail," I say when I slip back that deposit slip minus the fifty dollars that I put in one of our little envelopes. Now she's going over to Kroger's and put that fifty to use, does it every Monday. I know Gail Mason-Anderson like the back of my hand.

"I did," Gail says but she doesn't look at me because she's checking to make sure that I gave her the fifty she requested. Two twenties and a ten, can't get any closer to fifty than that, though I'm not offended when people do that. I'm glad people sit right there and check it because if she got to Kroger's and then came back it would be her word against mine and Mr. Crown would take hers and chew me out whether I was in the right or wrong. "Think of the ways people could trick us out of money," I told him one day and it's the truth. There are numerous ways that you might trick a teller out of money and it is my job to keep that from happening. Not that I think Gail Mason-Anderson would do any such thing. She doesn't have to. I bet she and William Anderson have a man who looks a lot like Earl Taylor to just figure it all up for them.

I like to think of having a hyphenated name myself. Maureen Roach hyphen something. Maureen Roach-Taylor with right above it Earl Sinco Taylor. "Your name sounds like a plumbing product," I told him only to find that I had hurt his feelings. Sinco is a name from somewhere on his mama's family, and since his mama is dead, it made him real defensive that I should laugh at that name.

"Thank you," Gail says. I read her lips because I've already cut off my speaker. She drives a diesel-powered Audi and it wrecks my ears to hear it going on and on and ricocheting off the little drive-through area. I just nod and watch Gail Mason-Anderson go straight to Kroger's.

Eighty-five degrees F and 11:37. I decide I'll go and take my lunch hour a little early. I do that every now and again when it's important like today where I am not going to go sit in Eckerd's and order a grilled cheese but am going home and make sure there's no fire started. It will take the whole hour but it's the only way that I can stay in my seat the rest of the afternoon not to mention that I have got a little nic craving that I can't hold off anymore. I don't even bring my cigarettes into this building because it would be such a temptation, not to mention that Trish who sits at the other little opening wears one of those badges that has a picture of a cigarette with a slash through it. A picture paints a thousand words and I don't need to be hit over the head. Trish has a husband and that's how she can afford to be so outspoken. She hates cigarettes and loves manatees, the Cape Hatteras lighthouse, Statue of Liberty, 96LITE, and Jesus. You can read it all right there on the bumper of her car. I personally would not open my life like a book to the world. I have a bumper sticker that says, "Get Off My Rear!" and that's all. Trish brakes for animals but won't even answer a person when they say they're going to lunch. She just looks at the clock machine and rolls her eyes like I'm going to abuse the system and stay out until one instead of returning at 12:53 which will be exactly an hour from when my car exits the lot give or take a few minutes. Trish supports the system, the public schools, the Little Theatre, the President, and whales. All I know about Trish I've learned right off of that car. Her savings account shared with Edwin Hunter cannot touch the savings account of Gail Mason-Anderson and William or that of Earl Sinco Taylor.

Now I feel like I can't get this Bug to go fast enough. It's like all of a sudden I'm in a panic to see my condo still standing with my potted geranium on the door stoop and my straw hat with lacy ribbons on my door. Welcome and welcome relief it is when I turn this corner a little and see it. What I don't welcome is Eleanore standing out on the sidewalk with what looks like ketchup or poster paints there on the front of her blouse that I gave her for her birthday two years ago. That blouse not only is out of style but if it was in style it is far too frilly for a Monday morning in the elementary school. "It's a church blouse," I told her and she gave me the Roach eye.

Eleanore has always taken things personally. The time I told her that there is a difference in the country look that is authentic and the country look that is a hodge-podge of too much of a good thing, she took it personally and I certainly didn't mean it for her personally even though she does not need one more rooster looking like it's about to crow tacked up on her kitchen wall. I think it's symbolic that she's so into roosters, all that strutting and taking hold of every hen and that's not even touching the biblical symbol, three crows and you're out.

"Where have you been?" she asks just as soon as I step out of the Bug and this heat hits my head like a ton of bricks. "I've been waiting forever."

"I didn't know you were coming," I tell her. I do more than tell her. I state it like the fact that it is. This isn't the first time Eleanore has pulled such a visit only to turn it around and make it my fault that she's been waiting. And where else would I have been but at the bank, here in this green linen suit with matching espadrilles, and little canvas clutch. Every fiber of my Monday-through-Friday wardrobe says "teller."

I get up close and I can see that Eleanore has been crying and it takes me a second to remember why I trucked clean across town home—the Mr. Coffee. "Come on in," I tell her. "I'm afraid I left the Mr. Coffee on." Eleanore follows me in and just about falls down on a Fisher-Price bathtub frog which Larrette meows to. We both have tried to teach her to say "frog" but she is as stubborn in that way as Larry Cross. "Gotta love that Squeaky," he used to say to me and throw those gorilla arms around my hips. He called me Squeaky because he thought I looked like that woman that tried to shoot Gerald Ford that time and I don't. "I love my Squeaky," he would say because he didn't have much sense, but God, just the thought of that bed breaking down and not even fazing that man makes my heart skip a beat or two.

It's on. Plugged in and on, that pot bottom dried into nothing but crisp brown sludge. "I did it," I say to Eleanore, who is at that kitchen table with a Kleenex up to her face. "Thank God there wasn't a fire."

"He's gone back to his wife," Eleanore sobs. "Don't you say 'I told you so' one time since I'm going ahead and saying it for you."

I'm a little confused since to my knowledge he never left his wife to begin with. "I didn't know he had left her."

"He left her a year ago. He left her that first night we stayed in Apex and he told me that he loved me like he had never loved anybody." Eleanore primps up and sobs again, wiping her mascara on my linen pineapple print napkins. "I mean he still lived there, with *her*, but it was me he loved." I listen to Eleanore telling the details of it all while the Mr. Coffee pot cools enough that I can rinse out that crud, but while Eleanore is going on, my mind is thinking over that word *love*, and how it is used and misused and abused. Earl Taylor has said that word one time when it referred to me. Once, and I'm thinking that that isn't good enough. I'm thinking of "Love my Squeaky" and Larry Cross might have meant it as much as if he'd said, "Love my Carpet," but still he said it.

"He said if he could live his life over that he would be with me," Eleanore says and looks up from my napkin, black smudges all over it. "He said it on the phone and then there came a sweetheart rose

to the school office. No card. It's right out there in my car if you
want to see it."

"I don't need to see it," I tell her. "But what would you have done
if I hadn't come to lunch?"

"You usually do come to lunch," Eleanore says. "You're usually
here by eleven-thirty."

"Well," I say because I've never thought that anybody would busy
themself to pick up on my daily patterns.

"Mr. Coffee, iron, oven, it's always something." Eleanore goes
over and gets Larrette's little frog and hugs it. It squeaks. I hear a
squeak squeaky loud and clear, Larry Cross and bedsprings that Earl
Taylor couldn't squeak if he did a somersault with bricks tied
around his neck. "I know you like a book, Maureen."

"I reckon you do," I say and rinse that napkin out in cold water
and a little Stanley spot remover. "Must be the Roach in us."

"I know Tuesday is my wash night but I was wondering if I could
come over tonight instead," Eleanore says and there's no way I can
tell her no. It's my night to cook a little something for me and Earl
and for us to sit and watch "Cagney and Lacey" and I don't even
care. I don't even care that I'm going to break that pattern starting
tonight and if Gail Mason-Anderson had some sense she'd break her
habit and occasionally go to Harris Teeter where they've got fresh
seafood coming in by the barrel.

"I think that's a good idea," I tell her and go over to touch that
pot to see if it's cooled down enough that it won't crack.

"What about Earl Taylor?"

"Well, Earl Taylor can do something else. Earl Taylor can vacuum
his Mazda, for example." I run warm water first and take my Tuffy
pad to the bottom of that pot. "Let's go to Harris Teeter and buy
some scallops," I say when I'm so happy that pot doesn't crack and
splinter in my hands. "Let's get some wine and some cheese, not
dairy counter but deli cheese. And let's go in Ivey's and buy you
some cologne and a blouse that's in style." Eleanore has taken that
personally I can tell, but she is too upset to argue.

"I can't buy a new blouse," she says, her eyes watering again. "I
don't get paid until the end of the month."

"We'll just put it right on my card," I tell her. "If it weren't for you,
Larrette probably wouldn't be speaking at all. I'm expecting any day
now that she's going to get up and say frog and Kermit and every-

thing that goes with it." That pot comes clean as a whistle and while it's air drying, I go and call Trish to say I won't be back.

"I've taken ill," I tell her. "I could barely get myself to the bathroom."

"Didn't you take ill last week?" Trish asks and I figure she doesn't even deserve an answer. "Are you expecting?" Trish asks and I can't help but laugh a little in between making my voice sound sick, low and slow and sick; I've always been able to make my voice that way instinctively. I'd do my voice that way and Larry Cross would make all kinds of promises that he never kept. I did it to Earl once and he didn't even notice. I'd rather be told a lie than nothing at all, and Trish should feel that way, too.

"I may be," I tell her. "You might have hit the nail on the head, Trish."

"Don't you date Earl Taylor down at Sears?"

"Yes, yes I do." I tell Trish that I think I'll go to the doctor and that I'll see her in the morning. But first I tell her that my cousin, Eleanore Tripper, works in the public schools and once saw a manatee down in Florida. This is the most me and Trish have ever conversed. Now I call Earl to say I'm tied up for the evening.

"But it's Monday," he says. " 'Cagney and Lacey' comes on." He states all that as a fact and I realize that all Earl has ever done to me is state facts. I hate facts. I think facts are boring. A fact is just a base, a foot in the door, to perspectives and instincts. Earl Taylor has got a lot to learn. "What am I going to do?" he asks and I can tell he is in a hurry because he is not one to squander work time.

"You could vacuum your car."

"I did that yesterday."

"You could go shopping."

"I don't need anything," he says, which is a lie though he thinks it's the truth. He needs some pictures on his wall and to rip up that shag carpet, finish those floors and buy himself some pretty braided rugs. He could use a grape vine wreath, a shower curtain other than a white cheapo liner, and some pretty towels that match. He needs a headboard and an Alexander Julian shirt and some contact lenses and some hair conditioner that'll give body. He needs a body, a membership at a spa, barbells.

"Oh now, Earl," I say. "I bet if you went to the mall you could find some things you need."

"I don't believe in just going out and spending money," he says and sounds a little exasperated and I know just how he's looking with that exasperation: red-eared, bleary-eyed, and dull in an official way. "And I really can't talk. I'm working. You should be working."

I start to tell him that he could gain some weight but I don't. I just hang up, put on my sunglasses and go get my scarf to tie on my head. "Let's wear our outfits to the Harris Teeter," I say. "No telling who might see me and run by First Union to tell it." For the first time Eleanore smiles; it's a weak smile and I know the whole night is going to be potato chips and Coke and her tears working like a faucet. She puts on her glasses and says she'll pretend she's wearing a gingham shirt and off we go once I check to make sure the hot rollers or Larrette's vaporizer isn't still going.

We pass the North Carolina Bank and Trust and their sign says 88 F and I can believe it. It's hot and clear and feels so good I could stretch out like a dog with little to no clothes on and I imagine Larry Cross out walking some strand with his beeper stick and thinking of me, thinking that he was a fool not to know what he had when he had it. I know that's probably a lie but right now I like to believe it. Right now I can believe in that lie and keep it all in perspective.

"Lover Come Back," Eleanore says, and though the tears come to her eyes, she sings a little of "Que Sera Sera." *Will I be pretty? Will I be rich?*

"I Want to Live," I tell her and I toot that VW horn to do a "Que Sera Sera," and that's no lie. We pass by First Union and I hold my head high since I've got on my costume and I don't even look to see what time of day it may be and I don't even care that that fair-skinned arm of mine hanging out the window could get burned to a Jane Eyre crisp on a day like today. And I wouldn't trade places with Trish sitting there under the green lights, or Gail Mason-Anderson with her cabinets overflowed with Kroger bags or her purse filled up with deposit slips with my initials, or my cousin Eleanore who is staring out the window through a steady stream of tears while she tries to get a better perspective on things.

Eve Shelnutt

VOICE

* (from *The Chariton Review*)

It was the season when odors rose like invisible flame against the landscape of suffocating heat. Beneath the burnt grass and withered kudzu, rodents, skunks, knots of insects were dying, for we saw daily buzzards circling the folds of the hills.

The hills lay belly-up and reddish against the skyline, the kudzu, with nothing to hold it, having slipped like a robe downward. As if to anchor these sleeping Buddhas, an occasional tree rose from their navels. Without the trees, they might have rolled down into the valley, leaving the horizon deserted and more still.

We waited and, although we were accustomed to waiting, this time it seemed to be for something ineffable, as for a revelation heat promises when it becomes intense enough to purify.

Other times we had waited in towns, tethered, it seemed, at a carnival we might join.

I was ten that summer. I think, now, that nerve-endings can become fecund, sprout in a perfect coupling of time, place, our suspended bodies.

We needed ragged time, and freedom.

Claire was twelve, her one chant: "You don't know the *half* of it," meaning the lives of our parents in whom, so casually lodged, our freedom gestated.

There was, then, time which came in waves—the barking of dogs owned by a neighbor so far away we had not met, as if his roaming hounds were his surrogate into our world. And at noon came the mail truck on the valley road, its sound coming in crests as it wove through the stands of trees where farmers kept stills—on clear nights we had seen wisps of smoke punctuating the moonlit silence. We got no mail, drank no moonshine.

At three in the afternoon, the royal blue bus of the Church of the Holiest Redeemer ("How many Redeemers *were* there?" our mother had asked) rumbled over the hills near our house, empty of children already delivered home from Bible school in Greer.

Then, at twilight, rose the cacaphony of crickets, and frogs venturing from their panoply of thatch. I couldn't eat their legs when our mother cut them loose for our supper, throwing their scaly bodies in a cardboard box by the two-eyed stove. Perhaps I thought their voices were unsullied, would rise from the box to admonish me for hunger.

My bare feet padding in the red dust of the road to the deserted house across from ours was another sound, mid-mornings when I went to sit on the porch, a look-out, the old farmhouse sitting on the rise from which anything approaching was visible.

And where was Claire when the morning sun hit the tin roof of our one-room house, a flare in the opaque heat? She slept on, I thought, for her appearance that summer was of someone drugged with sleep, her gold hair matted, dark and wet at the ends as if she chewed it in a dream of fury. Or, I sometimes thought, she never slept, learning by every sound what our parents had planned. Our mother whimpering in what she imagined as her privacy? Or getting up in the middle of the night to make lists of where one might go? Did Claire see our mother remove her housedress? Was her body still beautiful?

Like our dog, Claire rarely made a sound. But, unlike the dog, whose fur matted with burrs our father would hate when he saw her again, Claire did not roam. She was a shadow of our mother, popping up behind her like the India-rubber ball I had read about. What *was* her use to our mother?

He would arrive sometime during the summer—Father, who had set us here and would retrieve us in his own time: California time, of being at the right spot at the right time, as he had taught us was the way the rich world ran. I had no idea but from movies what he meant: the black DeSoto of the heroine rounding the mountain curve unaware that ahead of her the truck with no brakes careened toward her; the phone which rang one second after the man in the double-breasted suit pulled the trigger.

I watched the road. I would call it waiting for the denouement but I know, now, it is yet to come.

Our house had been built by our paternal grandfather as the place where our grandmother and the eight children would wait while he built the rock house in the valley. In the little house there was no flooring, and so at night we laid our pallets on clay which seemed by contrast cool as spring water. Sometimes I lifted the quilt to lay one leg against the clay itself. But Claire was right—what did I know, especially of luxury.

We lived, said Claire, on Father's residuals, and it would be years before I knew they were a form of tender.

Father, the last of the children, had been born in the rock house, its christening. And it, in turn, had bestowed on him his looks, which our mother said led him straight to Hollywood. Meaning what, when all of us were beautiful? This I asked Claire, who rolled her eyes in her head, shaking it in despair of ignorance such as mine.

Was our mother proud of him?

We were not to start the stove with pages from his copies of *Variety* stacked by the boxes of books in a corner. "Don't touch them," he'd said, raising one finger, looking each of us in the eyes. "Don't touch them," our mother echoed as his maroon Nash Ambassador pulled from the roadside.

His teeth were perfectly straight and white. In sleep he ground them together all night in a rhythm, and we never forgot the sound.

The birds, too, made a covenant of sound. If, flaring up from the trees, they swooped down to sheet the yard in black and tawny wings, rain would come.

In that miasma, I stand Claire on the hard ground by our mother's garden where, in fact, she must often have stood as our mother, on her knees, rooted out weeds and insects from the tomato plants, lifting even the furry leaves of squash to search underneath. I must have watched Claire from the farmhouse porch, one finger in my book (for we believed in books) and, in the absence of color, rested my eyes over and over on her white dress, that wisp at the garden's edge. She looked over the hillside in pure motionlessness.

"I knew a woman lovely in her bones," I would read much later in a book by Roethke; and I know the poem goes on. It should end there.

*   *   *

Then neighbors came. We had gathered in the night at our front window to watch the man unload a pickup as our dog, refusing still to bark, raced back and forth on the dirt road. It was, I think, the only time he ever used the front door, propping it open with a stump from the yard. Someone ("It's a woman," our mother said) turned on all the lights and, although it was only nine o'clock, we didn't light our Coleman lanterns in answer. We lay back down, listening to the sounds coming in from the window above our pallets. Before I slept again I heard our mother say, "Well," by which I knew anything could happen, a word so airborn.

They were not like us, which I knew first upon discovering his stains of tobacco juice on the road and then, later, when the woman did my hair. She had come over to ask our mother if she might put their name on our mailbox. "Certainly," our mother said, and, walking back up the path to the farmhouse, the woman repeated, "Certainly, certainly."

At the steps of the farmhouse, where I had not gone since the couple moved in, she turned on me: "Look at you." She lifted my braids in both hands, on which the nails were the brightest pink, and sighed, dropping them. "*Lord*. Well come on in." And so I followed her, or followed the smell of Juicy Fruit gum and perfume and the click of her high-heeled sandals on the faded linoleum. Her yellow hair swayed across her back.

Toward twilight, coming out of the house just as the last sun hit the rise above our house, I almost stumbled, my eyes readjusting to the light, my head still hot from her hair dryer. In my ears was her voice and in my mind's eye were the names of lotions and sprays on the vanity with its red crepe-paper skirt.

I walked down the steps as if a crown rested on my head. The husband drove past as I stood on the roadside. His face looked dark and sullen in the shade of the truck's hood, and I heard him slam the truck door as I opened the door to our house.

Inside, Claire, sitting on our mother's quilts with her back against the wall, touched our mother with one toe and said, "Look," lifting her chin up to me.

"A bee hive," our mother said. "A bee hive." And, putting down her book and getting up to drag me outside to the rain barrel, she said, "Wouldn't you know, wouldn't you know." And, with water, she sealed into my head all I had heard and seen—the most ordinary things, I know now: the lure our mother feared.

It rained once, the cracks in the ground filling and overflowing into a thousand rivulets, ditches, and gullies full of sound the reddish water made as it raced down to the valley where the rock house sat crumbling. For a week Claire and I did not have to bring water from the spring, but I went to look at it overflowing to the creek nearby, our gourd dipper stuck on a tree limb out of reach. When the rain stopped, worms lay atop the ground, dazed or dead, and the birds loosened themselves from the trees to feast. Watching the birds, I realized that I had not noticed them just before the rain, either distracted by the novelty of neighbors or it wasn't true—birds as heraldic.

She, Mrs. R.C. Campbell, had nailed a sign on the tree by the porch: Salon of Beauty, and another almost like it by the cut-off to the road the postman used.

"Ha!" our mother said, seeing the sign. But perhaps Mrs. Campbell thought the postman would tell people on his route and, now that it had rained, they would—the women and girls like me—feel like fixing themselves up.

Our mother had, the first evening of the three-day rain, opening for the first time the trunks which sat along the walls. I had been playing in the creek until dark. As I came into the house, my dress and hair dripped around my feet. Our dog stood shaking behind me at the open door. And there she was, pulling on hose. When she stood to ask Claire if the seams were straight, our dog barked once, as if a stranger were in the house. She held the emerald Father had given her, letting it sway on the chain, her dress its color, and she sat on the pallet by Claire so that Claire could hook it.

"How do I look, you two?" our mother asked.

I closed the door, and for minutes there was only the sound of the drops falling from the sashes of my dress, and of our mother waiting.

"You look fine, Momma," said Claire. And, hearing Claire's voice then, I thought that Claire was somehow older than our mother; she waited for nothing.

I can no longer remember whether or not our mother took off her dress then, or if it was Claire who unclasped the necklace, or when, that night, our mother slept.

Sometimes we waken with passion for someone we've loved, say under our breaths, "Please come flying," meaning *now, now, now*, to catch a truth which would transform. But the time passes, having nothing to do with how another person moves.

Then, when the sky was washed and kudzu robed the hills again, Father drove up, all of California and states between on his windshield—gray feathery splats—and across the front, a grille of feathers. He wore his pin-stripe suit, the gray hat, and a grin. "Hello, sweets," he said as I climbed from the tree, "been holding down the fort?" He brought with him steaks from the A & P on the outskirts of Greer and, spread out on the back seat, all he had taken to pawn for gas on the trip out—the cuff links with ruby eyes, our mother's violin, the Chinese vase, and the autoharp.

That night he said of Claire, "*Make* her eat," to our mother, but I knew: if Claire ate what we ate, protruding from the inside we would see the perfect shape of steak.

From our place that night on the Nash Ambassador's fold-down bed, Claire said, "When he makes love to her and nothing happens, he takes her over against a wall and bangs her against it until something does. I bet you didn't know that."

And did Claire wait to see the walls of our house shake?

Of course he met the neighbors—Raymond, who worked at the West End Mill in Greer when he wasn't helping tend his father's cows on the other side of Greer. And Joyce, who said she didn't know a thing about it when our father, having gone to inspect the rock house, noticed a chifforobe missing from the room he had been born in.

"They're just poor white trash," he said, "but they've got a phone."

Did Joyce say to Raymond when he came in from work that night, "He wears this double-breasted suit and a blue shirt with a white collar and cuffs and cuff links in the shape of snakes with little red eyes, you know? And a tie, all the time, in this weather. He don't even sweat."

I think not.

And I would liked to have told her, It's all the clothes he's got. But our mother would not let me cross into their yard.

* * *

If I imagine the land we occupied then, from high up, as a buzzard or a hawk sees, I envision her backyard where the clothes line swayed in the morning breeze. The well would be there, its cover weathered and gray, and two oak trees overshadowing the house. Her shop must have been in the back room where she had taken me; its door opened onto the back porch.

I think, first, she walked to the front windows to look out at our car parked on the rise and, seeing our heads, she may have waited for the car doors to slam, morning heat filling the space in which Claire and I had slept. Then, barefoot, she would have walked over the cool linoleum to her shop and, opening the bottle of Evening in Paris, spread it on the backs of her legs. She would take the net off her hair, slip on her shorts and the pink halter, strap on the sandals, and look at herself in the vanity mirror.

The door would not slam behind her, and, I think, she would tiptoe across the porch. She might trail one hand along the clothesline, spit on the black mark the wire made on her palm. She would walk past the tree to the left and, over time, make a path through the weeds to the road. If it were especially hot, gnats might round her eyes, and so she would lift one hand and fan, her nails catching the light.

By then, we would be positioned: I in the tree, our father washing the car or raising the flag on the mailbox, our mother in the garden, stooping or pulling behind her the section of cardboard on which she knelt, Claire standing apart but near her. Across the valley, the bus would be heading toward Greer, empty but for the driver, whistling hymns.

Down the road she would come, swinging her arms, her hips swaying, her shoes making little eddies of dust, and her nails the only moving color below her waist. Her halter held her breasts tight, but above them the flesh quivered, like that of a new bird, still featherless.

Sometimes she stopped to talk to our father; other times, she lifted her chin and looked at a point beyond his head, as if searching the sky for a kite or a blimp.

"Out for a little airing?" our father might say.

"You're going to burn up in that suit-coat," she might answer.

Below the rise, our mother would turn her head once, sniffing the humid air, and Claire's pinafore would ruffle as she turned toward the hills.

Sometimes Mrs. Campbell wore all white, and the shorts looked homemade. I think across the hall from the room she called her shop there was a sewing machine left by whoever owned the house. Raymond might sleep to the sound of the treadle.

Of course, too, our father used the Campbell's telephone. He sat after breakfast at the card table and made notes on cards he carried in his breast pocket. Copies of *Variety* sat where the dishes had been. On the cards he wrote: *Jay Smith: pilot?* and *WLAC: Paul Allen, mgr.* Then, late in the morning, when the sun was as hot as it would be, he crossed the road. "Thanks, kindly," we could hear him call, later, as he came down the steps. But what she answered, we couldn't hear. Maybe, at first, she said softly, "Any time," and he winked at her, turning. Then she might have whispered it to herself, her right hand rubbing the frayed wood of the screen.

We waited daily to hear the rattle of Mr. Campbell's truck. I had seen men come from a cotton mill; tiny balls of cotton clung to their clothes, and I imagined Raymond leaning over her hand, where a splinter might have stuck, light suffused through the wisps of cotton as she said, "Shoot, shoot, shoot, it *hurts*."

By the creek where Claire and I had taken the dog to clean her fur of burrs and wash her because our father had said we had to, though it was useless, Claire stopped to drink spring water from the dipper. Over its rim she looked at me for a long time, I think, before I sensed her eyes on my back. She must have been deciding to tell me.

"If," she said, "he does it to her, I'll kill her."

"Kill who?" I asked.

"Mrs. R.C. Campbell! Who else?"

And so I waited; my body waited, seemingly still but learning of its own accord its fragile parts. When our mother asked where we two might next be in school, and our father said, "Not in Greer, by a long shot, with boys such as Raymond once was," I knew it was where I *should* be—with them whose boots laced tight and on their hands pads of calluses grew.

This Claire taught me.

*   *   *

Then Joyce did something she should not have done. She must have carried the picture of our mother in her eyes or looked over at her each day she rounded the bend by the garden. Studying. Or, when it was too hot to move, she lay on a chenille bedspread or on the linoleum itself and leafed through magazines, looking up now and then to envision that which she could never be.

For, one afternoon, when she had not that morning taken her walk or received our father with his handful of cards, she walked to our garden, looking like someone else.

Our father sat in a folding canvas chair under the chinaberry tree, our mother was pulling the last of the tomatoes, Claire walking beside her with the lard bucket. I had followed Mrs. Campbell from my tree and stood to one side, looking.

She had dyed her hair brown, like our mother's, and cut it, curled it into a page-boy such as our mother wore. Her nails were clean of polish, and she wore a printed dress; a slip showed from underneath when she clasped her hands before her as she breathed deeply, stilling herself.

"I wonder," she said, her voice soft, "if y'all'd care to come over for tea? Under the trees, maybe. I could spread a cloth."

Then our mother was smiling wryly, all that her face had gathered into it over the weeks breaking open. She almost giggled, one hand at her mouth.

"I think not," she said. "But thank you for the invitation."

Our father did not, then, wink at Mrs. Campbell. He was watching our mother, looking at her as he might have studied a film clip enlarged in a darkened studio.

And there was nothing Mrs. Campbell could do, then, but unfold her hands and back away. Claire watched her retreating form all the way, and we heard the door close softly.

I used to think that words and music (and money, Father said) were honey outpouring: *luxury*, Claire, I would have said, borne up from any field of silence, any time. The surprises of America, which land our father loved.

But no, not even, you see, if I can imagine Mrs. Campbell's voice rising as she shows our father his part of the telephone bill, the long part, saying, "Los Angeles? New York City? Miami, Florida? and all them places?"

For three days we didn't hear his truck. We heard the dog chasing rabbits through the undergrowth, the hollow of silence left by the bus when Bible school was over, and the sound of the mail truck, which came up our road now when the flag was up. At night: crickets, our mother humming, Claire eating dry cereal from the box.

Then, on the third day, when we were packing boxes for the move to Lexington, Kentucky, WYAX, said the letterhead, our mother lifted her head from a trunk, saying "She must have left."

We did not answer her.

It was dark outside now. The dog circled the house, then came panting to sit outside the door. We heard her turning around three times, then settling. Our mother tried on clothes from the trunk, turning to ask, "How's this, Jim?"

It was almost our bedtime. We would sleep in the absence of light from the farmhouse, and the Nash Ambassador would seem colder. Claire would lock the car doors.

Then Raymond, kicking out at the dog, I think, came bursting in. His face was tight, as if his teeth held the skin on, and his body looked larger than it was from where we sat on the quilts. He stopped at the doorway, looking down once at our father, and then to our mother, who half rose, her rose-colored dress shining in the light of the lanterns. I don't think that he spoke. It was the kind of quiet one hears in a church before the baptismal immersion, when, in sympathy, everyone holds his breath. He looked for a minute at our mother, as if the color of her dress filled his eyes.

Then he saw Claire, standing now with her back against the wall by the trunk, which made a shadow on her legs. She wore a cotton slip; light shone on it and on her skin, so white that it seemed the slip was part of her skin.

He looked at her for a long time, and it was as if only they were in the room. Then he shivered, his body, it seemed, saying: You didn't expect it.

His chest seemed to sink, air escaping from every pore. He grew smaller and his eyes changed—they darkened and, for a second, shut tightly. While his eyes were shut, he reached for the door knob and, without lifting his head again, he closed the door behind him. We heard him run.

I wish now, thinking of Claire, we had let her go with him. I imagine a day in the heat of August. His mouth would be dry, always now, and somehow cool. She would be standing quietly, as she does, by a chinaberry tree, where a slight wind might lift her blond hair.

"First things first," he would say, his only words, and pulling her against his chest, they would hear the beating of wings in the seal of one another's ribs. And the cry we would have to imagine would set us free.

Annette Sanford

LIMITED ACCESS

(from *The Ohio Review*)

Miss Ettie is not a house person. She works in her yard most days until it's dark enough to go to bed and she gets out again as soon as it's daylight. I'm putting on my coffee and I can see her over there creeping out of the back door in her outfit: rubber boots, knit pants tucked in the tops, a long-sleeved shirt, a wool cap pulled down over her ears even if it's summer.

If she stood up straight she would be maybe five feet tall. But she is bent from the waist, like a street going around a corner. Arthritis, she says.

She blacks out sometimes: digging in her flower beds, eating Christmas dinner with me. Once in the drugstore.

Miss Ettie says: It's constipation.

We don't know how old she is. Clara says nearly eighty. Another niece, Francey, says eighty-three. There is not much communication between the aunt and the nieces.

Miss Ettie says: They don't care about me. They send their children over here with cabbages and figs. I already have cabbages and figs.

Miss Ettie's yard she keeps shipshape. Around the back she has dewberry vines, persimmon and fig trees, tomatoes, her cabbages. Growing along the south side of the house she has roses, cantaloupe vines that grew from seeds she threw out the kitchen window, portulaca in all colors and periwinkles. In the front yard purple and white iris grow, and pink verbenas. In April the place looks like an Easter basket.

Under a tree she has potted ferns on a staircase arrangement of boards stacked on lard cans. No grass. If any comes up she chops it out with a hoe. How does she tend to it all? She crawls around on her knees.

The house on the inside is a different story.

When I go for a visit she lets me in at the back onto a cement porch where the washing machine leaks and she's hung a clothesline the right height to choke you.

Back off in her bedroom the windows are still boarded up from the last threat of hurricane. A cave is what it is, like a shah's boudoir with pillows piled everywhere and bedspreads draping the furniture and a lot of blankets bunched around on a lumpy bed.

The living room she uses mainly to wait for the mail in. The kitchen is a battleground. Open jars all over. Flour sprinkled around. Miss Ettie's radio broadcasts from the drainboard. It picks up two stations: one plays polkas all day, one gives the news, first in English, then in Czech.

Clara and Francey want to give her a TV.

Miss Ettie says: I've got my radio. What do I need a TV for?

Clara and Francey have talked to the welfare woman. They want her in a home. They want her well taken care of. They would see to it themselves, but she doesn't allow them to set foot on her place.

The reason is because forty years ago at the home place in the country Miss Ettie fell out with Clara and Francey's mother, her sister Abigail. The tale has two sides, one common element: Miss Ettie's father's false teeth, kept in the back bedroom after he died.

Abigail off in Hoxley with her husband the barber and her two precious daughters wanted the teeth done away with. Miss Ettie and her mother, in whose house the teeth resided, felt satisfied they were in the right place, on top of the chifforobe where the old man left them.

Clara says: To spend the night in that room would scare the liver out of you.

Miss Ettie says that Clara is scared of everything and so was her mother.

Whatever the case, the teeth disappeared. Abigail stole them, Miss Ettie says. On a visit one day she slipped them in her purse and dumped them in the frog pond. Miss Ettie's horse drank there and drank up the teeth. They were found clamped to his tonsils when the rendering plant rendered him.

Miss Ettie says: That is the truth.

Clara and Francey say it is nothing of the sort. According to them, the teeth were mislaid during a once-a-year clean-up supervised by Abigail from Hoxley. A big load of rubbish was dumped in the pond. A pig wallowing there hooked the teeth on his snout and wore them back to the house. Abigail, fanning on the porch, spotted the pig and fell off in the fern bed. Miss Ettie's mother rescued the teeth and flung them in a stewpan Clara had set aside for a sixth-grade scrap drive to knock the Japanese kamikazes out of the sky. Clara delivered the stewpan to the scrap heap herself. She heard the rattling inside but paid no attention.

Francey says the whole misunderstanding is pre-nuclear anyway. She and Clara could do a lot for Aunt Ettie if Aunt Ettie would let them.

Miss Ettie says to me: Do what? If I have to see a doctor, *you* can carry me there. Of course, I'll pay you whatever you charge.

She calls me up one day, but not to see the doctor. She wants to see the government dam built on the outskirts of town. The backed-up water covers the farm where the frog pond was.

We set out late, following the cattle egrets to where they nest in the drowned trees. On the way I ask: How big was the farm?

Miss Ettie says: Too small to make a living. Too big for mules. The land was good for watermelons and peanuts. Her father raised corn and killed himself trying.

Miss Ettie took care of her mother. Without welfare. She sold eggs. She sold cabbages and figs and fat dressed hens. She sold pies and jelly. She ironed and took in sewing. She looked after babies and watched over sick people. She picked cotton. She pieced quilts. She sold off a few acres at a time down to the yard fence. When her mother died, she sold that, too, and bought the house in town.

Nobody helped you? I ask.

I never needed help.

Miss Ettie takes a look at the government dam. She wants to drive right down to the water, but you can't do that.

There's a road, she says. Don't you see it?

I point out a sign. LIMITED ACCESS.

What's that mean?

It means we can't use the road because we're not authorized.

The idea appeals to her. The next morning she tromps out in her boots and sticks a sign in the verbenas: LIMITED ACCESS. THAT MEANS YOU.

Clara and Francey ring up right away. What's the cause of that sign?

The cause is the same reason she won't let the grass grow. One blade makes two and the first thing you know you have to buy a lawn mower.

But I don't tell them that. I say the sign is for dogs.

Clara says: We bought the TV.

Francey says: She'll love it once she gets used to it.

They appoint me to make her see she wants it. I go over after breakfast. She is out in the back forty, picking dewberries in a tin pail.

I say: The girls bought the TV.

Miss Ettie says: You know why, don't you? They've got an old aunt they don't do anything for.

Is there something you'd like done?

Not by them.

I say: What about the TV? Don't you think you might like it?

Miss Ettie says: Could I get the weather on it?

The weather and everything.

I get all that on my radio.

It's no use, I tell the girls. Maybe you can trade the thing in on something you'd like yourselves.

They don't listen. They go over there while she's chopping out clover on the other side of the house and put it in the living room. A man they brought along hooks it up. Miss Ettie is deaf so she doesn't hear the commotion. She doesn't know anything is going on until the antenna shoots up.

Clara hollers, standing close to her car: It's installed, Aunt Ettie. There's nothing you can do about it so you might as well enjoy it.

Francey says: I'll show you how to change channels, Aunt Ettie, if you'll let me in the house.

Miss Ettie says: If it's my TV I don't need you to show me how to work it.

I wait until the smoke clears and then I go over. The radio is blaring. I knock on the back door.

Miss Ettie says: I guess you know they did it anyway.

I say: Let's have a look at it.

She has a doily on top of it and in the middle of the doily is a china dancing doll whose skirt is a pincushion.

Have you turned it on? I say.

Miss Ettie says: I've been busy.

Francey calls up as soon as I get home: I bet she already loves it.

I say: It was really nice, Francey, of you girls to do that.

We want her to enjoy it. She can't read anymore. She has all that time on her hands. And in the winter when it rains, won't it be a blessing.

I do a few things in the kitchen. Then I eat my supper and go to bed. I wake up about midnight needing something for heartburn. Out of the kitchen window I see Miss Ettie's living room aglow. Fire! I think first. Then I think TV. I don't want to scare her, poking around, but I have to know which it is before I go back to bed. She could be blacked out on the floor. Her hip could be broken.

I knock where I always do and then I go around to the front where the noise is coming from.

She lets me in. She's all tuckered out.

I have company already, she says. She has a gray, fuzzy nightgown on and chartreuse slippers she bought at a garage sale: plastic eyes on the toes and red felt tongues.

She points to the TV screen, jumping with activity.

They're cooking, she says. In the middle of the night.

She switches channels and gets a stock car race. She turns the dial again. A man in a black coat stabs a woman wearing rompers.

If you're okay, I say, I'm going back home.

Miss Ettie says: When do these people sleep?

You can turn it off. I show her how.

They're still there, she says. Back of that window.

No, they're not.

They are. She proves it. She heads off toward the kitchen. I'll take a broom to that thing.

I should explain how it's possible for people to cook in New York and show up a long time later in somebody's living room. But I don't know myself. Anyway, facts don't concern her. She just wants to put a stop to it.

Don't bang it up, I say. We'll unplug it.

I don't want to look at it. I don't want it sitting there.

She'll be up all night, I see, wearing herself out. I go off to the bedroom. Without making a dent in the decor I bring back a Russian shawl, three or four pillows and a dime store vase with a fake lily in it.

Miss Ettie watches me set things around. Under. On top of.

Hocus pocus, I say.

She looks at her new lounge table beside the Nile River. Okay, she says. You can go home now.

You won't wreck it?

Not before tomorrow, she says. And only the insides. All cleaned out it ought to make a fine coop for a setting hen.

The girls are upset that Aunt Ettie doesn't like the TV.

Francey says: She could at least give it a fair trial.

Clara says: She's a hardheaded old fool. I wash my hands of her.

It's a good sign, I say, that it's still in one piece.

I go over in a day or two, just to make sure. The fake lily and the pillow are right where I left them, but one corner of the Russian shawl is hiked up to clear the screen.

Miss Ettie sees me looking at it. Sparks could fly out, she says. I have to keep a watch in case of fire.

For the next couple of weeks I put up pickles. I get on a bus and go visit my cousin. When I come home again Miss Ettie's yard looks worse than her kitchen. I stand on the curb and I can't hear the radio.

She's died, I think, and rush to the phone.

She's watching TV, Clara says.

Francey says: We really think she is!

I unpack my suitcase and go knock on the back door. Nobody comes, so I go around to the front.

Miss Ettie lets me in. She's wearing her gray nightgown. She's gray all over.

Are you sick? I say.

I'm sick of all the racket that comes out of this box. How long will it be before the bulbs burn out?

I say: What would be the harm in just turning it off?

Miss Ettie says: There's shows every hour. I wasn't raised to be wasteful.

She droops in the mail chair to watch a dogfood commercial.

I sympathize with the fix she's in. There's nothing worse in the world than prejudice gone soft. Unless it's a flower bed chock full of weeds.

I try to think what to do. Finally, I say: It's too bad, Miss Ettie, about your radio.

What about my radio?

There's all that music and nobody to hear it.

The next morning at six she's out hoeing the verbenas. The yard is full of polkas and Czech versions of the news. I go over at ten when she's resting on the steps drinking cistern water.

Here's some pickles, I tell her.

She squints off toward the fire house. I put it on low, she says, and shut the cat in there.

How are your knees? I say.

Stiff, she says. It's a sin how the grass grows.

Rick Bass

THE WATCH

(from *The Quarterly*)

When Hollingsworth's father, Buzbee, was seventy-seven years old, he was worth a thousand dollars, that summer and fall. His name was up in all the restaurants and convenience stores, all along the interstate, and the indistinctions on the dark photocopies taped to doors and walls made him look distinguished, like someone else. The Xerox sheets didn't even say *Reward*, *Lost*, or *Missing*. They just got right to the point: *Mr. Buzbee, $1,000.*

The country Buzbee had disappeared in was piney woods, in the center of the state, away from the towns, the Mississippi—away from everything. There were swamps and ridges, and it was the hottest part of the state, and hardly anyone lived there. If they did, it was on those ridges, not down in the bottoms, and there were sometimes fields that had been cleared by hand, though the soil was poor and red, and could really grow nothing but tall lime-colored grass that bent in the wind like waves in a storm, and was good for horses, and nothing else—no crops, no cattle, nothing worth a damn—and Hollingsworth did not doubt that Buzbee, who had just recently taken to pissing in his pants, was alive, perhaps even just lying down in the deep grass somewhere out there, to be spiteful, like a dog.

Hollingsworth knew the reward he was offering wasn't much. He had a lot more money than that, but he read the papers and he knew that people in Jackson, the big town seventy miles north, offered that much every week, when their dogs ran off, or their cats went away somewhere to have kittens. Hollingsworth had offered only a thousand dollars for his father because nine hundred dollars or some lesser figure would have seemed cheap—and some greater number would have made people think he was sad and missed the old man. It really cracked Hollingsworth up, reading about those lawyers in Jackson who would offer a thousand dollars for their tramp cats. He wondered how they came upon those figures—if they knew what a thing was really worth when they liked it.

It was lonely without Buzbee—it was bad, it was much too quiet, especially in the evenings—and it was the first time in his life that Hollingsworth had ever heard such a silence. Sometimes cyclists would ride past his dried-out barn and country store, and one of them would sometimes stop for a Coke, sweaty, breathing hard, and he was more like some sort of draft animal than a person, so intent was he upon his speed, and he never had time to chat with Hollingsworth, to spin tales. He said his name was Jesse; he would say hello, gulp his Coke, and then this Jesse would be off, hurrying to catch the others, who had not stopped.

Hollingsworth tried to guess the names of the other cyclists. He felt he had a secret over them: giving them names they didn't know they had. He felt as if he owned them: as if he had them on some invisible string and could pull them back in just by muttering their names. He called all the others by French names—François, Pierre, Jacques—as they all rode French bicycles with an unpronounceable name—and he thought they were pansies, delicate, for having been given such soft and fluttering names—but he liked Jesse, and even more, he liked Jesse's bike, which was a black Schwinn, a heavy old bike that Hollingsworth saw made Jesse struggle hard to stay up with the Frenchmen.

Hollingsworth watched them ride, like a pack of animals, up and down the weedy, abandoned roads in the heat, disappearing into the shimmer that came up out of the road and the fields: the cyclists disappeared into the mirages, tracking a straight line, and then, later in the day—sitting on his porch, waiting—Hollingsworth would see them again when they came riding back out of the mirages.

The very first time that Jesse had peeled off from the rest of the pack and stopped by Hollingsworth's ratty-ass grocery for a Coke— the sound the old bottle made, sliding down the chute, Hollingsworth still had the old formula Cokes, as no one—no one—ever came to his old leaning barn of a store, set back on the hill off the deserted road—that first time, Hollingsworth was so excited at having a visitor that he couldn't speak: he just kept swallowing, filling his stomach fuller and fuller with air—and the sound the Coke bottle made, sliding down, made Hollingsworth feel as if he had been struck in the head with it, as if he had been waiting at the bottom of the chute. No one had been out to his place since his father ran away: just the sheriff, once.

The road past Hollingsworth's store was the road of a ghost town. There had once been a good community, a big one—back at the turn of the century—down in the bottom, below his store—across the road, across the wide fields—rich growing grasses there, from the river's flooding—the Bayou Pierre, which emptied into the Mississippi, and down in the tall hardwoods, with trees so thick that three men, holding arms, could not circle them, there had been a colony, a fair-sized town actually, that shipped cotton down the bayou in the fall, when the waters started to rise again.

The town had been called Hollingsworth.

But in 1903 the last survivors had died of yellow fever, as had happened in almost every other town in the state—strangely enough, those lying closest to swamps and bayous, where yellow fever had always been a problem, were the last towns to go under, the most resistant—and then in the years that followed, the new towns that reestablished themselves in the state did not choose to locate near Hollingsworth again. Buzbee's father had been one of the few who left before the town died, though he had contracted it, the yellow fever, and both Buzbee's parents died shortly after Buzbee was born.

Malaria came again in the 1930s, and got Buzbee's wife—Hollingsworth's mother—when Hollingsworth was born, but Buzbee and his new son stayed, dug in and refused to leave the store. When Hollingsworth was fifteen, they both caught it again, but fought it down, together, as it was the kind that attacked only every other day—a different strain than before—and their days of fever alternated, so that they were able to take care of each other: cleaning up the spitting and the vomiting of black blood, covering each other with blankets when the chills started, and building fires in the fireplace, even in summer. And they tried all the roots in the area, all the plants, and somehow—for they did not keep track of what they ate, they only sampled everything, anything that grew—pine boughs, cattails, wild carrots—they escaped being buried. Cemeteries were scattered throughout the woods and fields; nearly every place that was high and windy had one.

So the fact that no one ever came to their store, that there never had been any business, was nothing for Buzbee and Hollingsworth; everything would always be a secondary calamity, after the two years of yellow fever, and burying everyone, everything. Waking up in the night, with a mosquito biting them, and wondering if it had the fever. There were cans of milk on the shelves in their store that were forty years old; bags of potato chips that were twenty years old, because neither of them liked potato chips.

Hollingsworth would sit on his heels on the steps and tremble whenever Jesse and the others rode past, and on the times when Jesse turned in and came up to the store, so great was Hollingsworth's hurry to light his cigarette and then talk, slowly, the way it was supposed to be done in the country, the way he had seen it in his imagination, when he thought about how he would like his life to really be—that he spilled two cigarettes, and had barely gotten the third lit and drawn one puff when Jesse finished his Coke and then stood back up, and put the wet empty bottle back in the wire rack, waved, and rode off, the great backs of his calves and hamstrings working up and down in swallowing shapes, like things trapped in a sack, like ominous things, too. So Hollingsworth had to wait again for Jesse to come back, and by the next time, he had decided for certain that Buzbee was just being spiteful.

Before Buzbee had run away, sometimes Hollingsworth and Buzbee had cooked their dinners in the evenings, and other times they had driven into a town and ordered something, and looked around at people, and talked to the waitresses—but now, in the evenings, Hollingsworth stayed around, so as not to miss Jesse should he come by, and he ate briefly, sparingly, from his stocks on the shelves: dusty cans of Vienna sausage, sardines, and rock crackers. Warm beer, brands that had gone out of business a decade earlier, two decades. Holding out against time was difficult, but was also nothing after holding out against death. In cheating death, Hollingsworth and Buzbee had continued to live, had survived, but also, curiously, they had lost an edge of some sort: nothing would ever be quite as intense, nothing would ever really matter, after the biggest struggle.

The old cans of food didn't have any taste, but Hollingsworth didn't mind. He didn't see that it mattered much. Jesse said the other bikers wouldn't stop because they thought the Cokes were bad for them: cut their wind, slowed them down.

Hollingsworth had to fight down the feelings of wildness sometimes, now that his father was gone. Hollingsworth had never married, never had a friend other than his father. He had everything brought to him by the grocery truck, on the rarest of orders, and by the mail. He subscribed to *The Wall Street Journal*. It was eight days late by the time he received it—but he read it—and before Buzbee had run away they used to tell each other stories. They would start at sundown and talk until ten o'clock: Buzbee relating the ancient things, and Hollingsworth telling about everything that was in the paper. Buzbee's stories were always better. They were things that had happened two, three miles away.

As heirs to the town, Hollingsworth and Buzbee had once owned, back in the thirties, over two thousand acres of land—cypress and water oak, down in the swamp, and great thick bull pines, on the ridges—but they'd sold almost all of it to the timber companies—a forty- or eighty-acre tract every few years—and now they had almost no land left, just the shack in which they lived.

But they had bushels and bushels of money, kept in peach bushel baskets in their closet, stacked high. They didn't miss the land they had sold, but wished they had more, so that the pulpwood cutters would return: they had enjoyed the sound of the chain saws.

Back when they'd been selling their land, and having it cut, they would sit on their porch in the evenings and listen to it, the far-off cutting, as if it were music, picturing the great trees falling, and feeling satisfied, somehow, each time they heard one hit.

The first thing Jesse did in the mornings when he woke up was to check the sky, and then, stepping out onto the back porch, naked, the wind. If there wasn't any, he would be relaxed and happy with his life. If it was windy—even the faintest stir against his shaved ankles, up and over his round legs—he would scowl, a grimace of concentration, and go in and fix his coffee. There couldn't be any letting up on windy days, and if there was a breeze in the morning, it would build to true and hard wind for sure by afternoon: the heat of the fields rising, cooling, falling back down: blocks of air as slippery as his biking suit, sliding all up and down the roads, twisting through trees, looking for places to blow, paths of least resistance.

There was so much Hollingsworth wanted to tell someone! Jesse, or even François, Jacques, Pierre! Buzbee was gone! He and Buzbee had told each other all the old stories, again and again. There wasn't anything new, not really, not of worth, and hadn't been for a long time. Hollingsworth had even had to resort to fabricating things, pretending he was reading them in the paper, to match Buzbee during the last few years of storytelling. And now, alone, his imagination was turning in on itself, and growing, like the most uncontrollable kind of cancer, with nowhere to go, and in the evenings he went out on the porch and looked across the empty highway, into the waving fields in the ebbing winds, and beyond, down to the blue line of trees along the bayou, where he knew Buzbee was hiding out, and Hollingsworth would ring the dinner bell, loudly and clearly, with a grim anger, and he would hope, scanning the fields, that Buzbee would stand up and wave, and come back in.

Jesse came by for another Coke in the second week of July. There was such heat. Hollingsworth had called in to Crystal Springs and had the asphalt truck come out and grade and level his gravel, pour hot slick new tar down over it, and smooth it out. It cooled, slowly, and was beautiful, almost iridescent, like a blacksnake in the bright green grass: it glowed its way across the yard as if it were made of glass, a path straight to the store, coming in off the road. It beckoned.

"So you got a new driveway," Jesse said, looking down at his feet.

The bottle was already in his hand; he was already taking the first sip.

Nothing lasted; nothing!

Hollingsworth clawed at his chest, his shirt pocket, for cigarettes. He pulled them out and got one and lit it, and then sat down and said, slowly, "Yes." He looked out at the fields and couldn't remember a single damn story.

He groped, and faltered.

"You may have noticed there's a sudden abundance of old coins, especially quarters, say, 1964, 1965, the ones that have still got some silver in them," Hollingsworth said casually, but it wasn't the story in his heart.

"This is nice," Jesse said. "This is like what I race on sometimes." The little tar strip leading in to the Coke machine and Hollingsworth's porch was as black as a snake that had just freshly shed its skin, and was as smooth and new. Hollingsworth had been sweeping it twice a day, to keep twigs off it, and waiting.

It was soft and comfortable to stand on; Jesse was testing it with his foot—pressing down on it, pleasurably, admiring the surface and firmness, yet also the give of it.

"The Russians hoarded them, is my theory, got millions of them from our mints in the sixties, during the cold war," Hollingsworth said quickly. Jesse was halfway through with his Coke. This wasn't the way it was with Buzbee at all. "They've since subjected them to radiation—planted them amongst our populace."

Jesse's calves looked like whales going away; his legs, like things from another world. They were grotesque when they moved and pumped.

"I saw a man who looked like you," Jesse told Hollingsworth in August.

Jesse's legs and deep chest were taking on a hardness and slickness that hadn't been there before. He was drinking only half his Coke, and then slowly pouring the rest of it on the ground, while Hollingsworth watched, crestfallen: the visit already over, cut in half by dieting, and the mania for speed and distance.

"Expect he was real old," Jesse said. "I think he was the man they're looking for." Jesse didn't know Hollingsworth's first or last name; he had never stopped to consider it.

Hollingsworth couldn't speak. The Coke had made a puddle and was fizzing, popping quietly in the dry grass. The sun was big and orange across the fields, going down behind the blue trees. It was beginning to cool. Doves were flying past, far over their heads, fat from the fields and late-summer grain. Hollingsworth wondered what Buzbee was eating, where he was living, why he had run away.

"He was fixing to cross the road," said Jesse.

He was standing up, balancing carefully, in the little cleat shoes that would skid out from underneath him from time to time when he tried to walk in them. He didn't use a stopwatch the way other cyclists did, but he knew he was getting faster, because just recently he had gotten the quiet, almost silent sensation—just a soft hushing—of falling, the one that athletes, and sometimes other people, get when they push deeper and deeper into their sport, until—like pushing through one final restraining layer of tissue, the last and thinnest, easiest one—they are falling, slowly, and there is nothing left in their life to stop them, no work is necessary, things are just happening, and they suddenly have all the time in the world to perfect their sport, because that's all there is, one day, finally.

"I tried to lay the bike down and get off and chase him," Jesse said. "But my legs cramped up."

He put the Coke bottle in the rack.

The sun was in Hollingsworth's eyes: it was as if he was being struck blind. He could smell only Jesse's heavy body odor, and could feel only the heat still radiating from his legs, like thick andirons taken from a fire: legs like a horse's, standing there, with veins wrapping them, spidery, beneath the thin browned skin.

"He was wearing dirty old overalls and no shirt," said Jesse. "And listen to this. He had a live carp tucked under one arm, and it didn't have a tail left on it. I had the thought that he had been eating on that fish's tail, chewing on it."

Jesse was giving a speech. Hollingsworth felt himself twisting down and inside with pleasure, like he was swooning. Jesse kept talking, nailing home the facts.

"He turned and ran like a deer, back down through the field, down toward the creek, and into those trees, still holding on to the fish." Jesse turned and pointed. "I was thinking that if we could catch him on your tractor, run him down and lasso him, I'd split the reward money with you." Jesse looked down at his legs, the round swell of them so ballooned and great that they hid completely his view of the tiny shoes below him. "I could never catch him by myself, on foot, I don't think," he said, almost apologetically. "For an old fucker, he's fast. There's no telling what he thinks he's running from."

"Hogson, the farmer over on Green Gable Road, has got himself some hounds," Hollingsworth heard himself saying, in a whisper.

"He bought them from the penitentiary, when they turned mean, for five hundred dollars. They can track anything. They'll run the old man to Florida if they catch his scent; they won't ever let up."

Hollingsworth was remembering the hounds, black and tan, the colors of late frozen night, and cold honey in the sun, in the morning, and he was picturing the dogs moving through the forest, with Jesse and himself behind them: camping out! The dogs straining on their heavy leashes! Buzbee, slightly ahead of them, on the run, leaping logs, crashing the undergrowth, splashing through the bends and loops in the bayou: savage swamp birds, rafts of them, darkening the air as they rose in their fright, leaping up in entire rookeries ... cries in the forest, it would be like the jungle.... It might take days! Stories around the campfire! He would tear off a greasy leg of chicken, from the grill, reach across to hand it to Jesse, and tell him about anything, everything.

"We should try the tractor first," Jesse said, thinking ahead. It was hard to think about a thing other than bicycling, and he was frowning and felt awkward, exposed, and, also, trapped: cut off from the escape route. "But if he gets down into the woods, we'll probably have to use the dogs."

Hollingsworth was rolling up his pants leg, cigarette still in hand, to show Jesse the scar from the hunting accident when he was twelve: his father had said he thought he was a deer, and had shot him. Buzbee had been twenty-six.

"I'm like you," Hollingsworth said faithfully. "I can't run worth a damn, either." But Jesse had already mounted his bike; he was moving away, down the thin black strip, like a pilot taking a plane down a runway, to lift off, or like a fish running to sea; he entered the dead highway, which had patches of weeds growing up even in its center, and he stood up in the clips and accelerated away, down through the trees, with the wind at his back, going home.

He was gone almost immediately.

Hollingsworth's store had turned dark; the sun was behind the trees. He did not want to go back inside. He sat down on the porch and watched the empty road. His mother had died giving birth to him. She, like his father, had been fourteen. He and his father had always been more like brothers to each other than anything else. Hollingsworth could remember playing a game with his father, perhaps when he was seven or eight, and his father then would have been twenty-one or so—Jessie's age, roughly—and his father would run out into the field and hide, on their old homestead—racing down the hill, arms windmilling, and disappearing suddenly, diving down into the tall grass, while Hollingsworth—Quieter, Quiet—tried to find him. They played that game again and again, more than any other game in the world, and at all times of the year, not just in the summer.

Buzbee had a favorite tree, and he sat up in the low branch of it often and looked back in the direction from which he had come. He saw the bikers every day. There weren't ever cars on the road. The cyclists sometimes picnicked at a little roadside table off of it, oranges and bottles of warm water and candy bars by the dozens—he had snuck out there in the evenings, before, right at dusk, and sorted through their garbage, nibbled some of the orange peelings—and he was nervous, in his tree, whenever they stopped for any reason.

Buzbee had not in the least considered going back to his maddened son. He shifted on the branch and watched the cyclists eat their oranges. His back was slick with sweat, and he was rank, like the worst of animals. He and all the women bathed in the evenings in the bayou, in the shallows, rolling around in the mud. The women wouldn't go out any deeper. Snakes swam in evil S-shapes, back and forth, as if patrolling. He was starting to learn the women well, and many of them were like his son in every regard, in that they always wanted to talk, it seemed—this compulsion to communicate, as if it could be used to keep something else away, something big and threatening. He thought about what the cold weather would be like, November and beyond, himself trapped, as it were, in the abandoned palmetto shack, with all of them around the fireplace, talking, for four months.

He slid down from the tree and started out into the field, toward the cyclists—the women watched him go—and in the heat, in the long walk across the field, he became dizzy, started to fall several times, and for the briefest fragments of time he kept forgetting where he was, imagined that one of the cyclists was his son, that he was coming back in from the game that they used to play, and he stopped, knelt down in the grass and pretended to hide. Eventually, though, the cyclists finished eating, got up and rode away, down the road again. Buzbee watched them go, then stood up and turned and raced back down into the woods, to the women. He had become very frightened, for no reason, out in the field like that.

Buzbee had found the old settlement after wandering around in the woods for a week. There were carp in the bayou, and gar, and catfish, and he wrestled the large ones out of the shallow oxbows that had been cut off from the rest of the water. He caught alligators, too, the small ones.

He kept a small fire going, continuously, to keep the mosquitoes away, and as he caught more and more of the big fish, he hung them from the branches in his clearing, looped vine through their huge jaws and hung them like villains, all around in his small clearing, like the most ancient of burial grounds. All these vertical fish, out of the water, mouths gaping in silent death, as if preparing to ascend— they were all pointing up.

The new pleasure of being alone sometimes stirred Buzbee so that he ran from errand to errand, as if on a shopping spree or a game show: he was getting ready for this new life, and with fall and winter coming on, he felt young.

After a couple of weeks, he had followed the bayou upstream, to-ward town, backtracking the water's sluggishness; sleeping under the large logs that had fallen across it like netting, and he swatted at the mosquitoes that swarmed him whenever he stopped moving, in the evenings, and he had kept going, even at night. The moon came down through the bare limbs of the swamp-rotted ghost trees, skel-eton-white, disease-killed, but as he got higher above the swamp and closer to the town, near daylight, the water moved faster, had some circulation, was still alive, and the mosquitoes were not a threat.

He lay under a boxcar on the railroad tracks and looked across the road at the tired women going in and out of the washateria, moving so slowly, as if old. They were in their twenties, their thirties, their forties; they carried their baskets of wet clothes in front of them with a bumping, side-to-side motion, as if they were going to quit living on the very next step; their forearms sweated, glistened, and the sandals on their wide feet made flopping sounds, and he wanted to tell them about his settlement. He wanted five or six, ten or twenty of them. He wanted them walking around barefooted on the dark earth beneath his trees, beneath his hanging catfish and alligators, by the water, in the swamp.

He stole four chickens and a rooster that night, hooded their eyes, and put them in a burlap sack, put three eggs in each of his shirt pockets, too, after sucking ten of them dry, greedily, gulping, in the almost wet brilliance of the moon, behind a chicken farm back west of town, along the bayou—and then he continued on down its banks, the burlap sack thrown over his back, the chickens and rooster warm against his damp body, and calm, waiting.

He stopped when he came out of the green and thick woods, over a little ridge, and looked down into the country where the bayous slowed to heavy swamp and where the white and dead trees were and the bad mosquitoes lived—and he sat down and leaned his old back against a tree, and watched the moon and its blue light shining on the swamp, with his chickens. He waited until the sun came up and it got hot, and the mosquitoes had gone away, before starting down toward the last part of his journey, back to his camp.

The rest of the day he gathered seeds and grain from the little raised hummocks and grassy spots in the woods, openings in the forest, to use for feed for the chickens, which moved in small crooked shapes of white, like little ghosts in the woods, all through his camp, but they did not leave it. The rooster flew up into a low tree and stared wildly, golden-eyed, down into the bayou. For weeks Buzbee had been hunting the quinine bushes said to have been planted there during the big epidemic, and on that day he found them, because the chickens went straight to them and began pecking at them as Buzbee had never seen chickens peck: they flew up into the leaves, smothered their bodies against the bushes as if mating with them, so wild were they to get to the berries.

Buzbee's father had planted the bushes, and had received the seeds from South America, on a freighter that he met in New Orleans the third year of the epidemic, and he had returned with them to the settlement, that third year, when everyone went down finally.

The plants had not done well; they kept rotting, and never, in Buzbee's father's time, bore fruit or made berries. Buzbee had listened to his father tell the story about how they rotted—but also how, briefly, they had lived, even flourished, for a week or two, and how the settlement had celebrated and danced, and cooked alligators and cattle, and prayed, and everyone in the settlement had planted quinine seeds, all over the woods, for miles, in every conceivable location . . . and Buzbee knew immediately, when the chickens began to cluck and feed, that it was the quinine berries, which they knew instinctively they must eat, and he went and gathered all the berries, and finally, he knew, he was safe.

The smoke from his fire, down in the low bottom, had spread through the swamp, and from above would have looked as if that portion of the bayou, going into the tangled dead trees, had simply disappeared: a large spill of white, a fuzzy, milky spot—and then, on the other side of the spill, coming out again, bayou once more.

Buzbee was relieved to have the berries, and he let the fire go down; he let it die. He sat against his favorite tree by the water and watched for small alligators. When he saw one, he would leap into the water, splash and swim across to meet it, and wrestle it out of the shallows and into the mud, where he would kill it savagely.

But the days were long, and he did not see that many alligators, and many of the ones he did see were a little too large, sometimes far too large. Still, he had almost enough for winter, as it stood: those hanging from the trees, along with the gaping catfish, spun slowly in the breeze of fall coming, and if he waited and watched, eventually he would see one. He sat against the tree and watched, and ate berries, chewed them slowly, pleasuring in their sour taste.

He imagined that they soured his blood: that they made him taste bad to the mosquitoes, and kept them away. Though he noticed they were still biting him, more even, now that the smoke was gone. But he got used to it.

A chicken had disappeared, probably to a snake, but also possibly to anything, anything.

The berries would keep him safe.

He watched the water. Sometimes there would be the tiniest string of bubbles rising, from where an alligator was stirring in the mud below.

Two of the women from the laundry came out of the woods, tentatively, having left their homes, following the bayou, to see if it was true what they had heard. It was dusk, and their clothes were torn and their faces wild. Buzbee looked up and could see the fear, and he wanted to comfort them. He did not ask what had happened at their homes, what fear could make the woods and the bayou journey seem less frightening. They stayed back in the trees, frozen, and would not come with him, even when he took each by the hand, until he saw what it was that was horrifying them: the grinning reptiles, the dried fish, spinning from the trees—and he explained to them that he had put them there to smoke, for food, for the winter.

"They smell good," said the shorter one, heavier than her friend, her skin a deep black, like some poisonous berry. Her face was shiny.

Her friend slapped at a mosquito.

"Here," said Buzbee, handing them some berries. "Eat these."

But they made faces and spat them out when they tasted the bitterness.

Buzbee frowned. "You'll get sick if you don't eat them," he said. "You won't make it otherwise."

They walked past him, over to the alligators, and reached out to the horned, hard skin, and touched them fearfully, ready to run, making sure the alligators were unable to leave the trees and were truly harmless.

"Don't you ever, you know, get lonely for girls?" Hollingsworth asked, like a child. It was only four days later, but Jesse was back for another half-Coke. The other bikers had ridden past almost an hour earlier, a fast *rip-rip-rip*, and then, much later, Jesse had come up the hill, pedaling hard, but moving slower.

He was trying, but he couldn't stay up with them. He had thrown his bike down angrily, and glowered at Hollingsworth, when he stalked up to the Coke machine, scowled at him as if it was Hollingsworth's fault.

"I got a whore," Jesse said, looking behind him and out across the road. The pasture was green and wet, and fog, like mist, hung over it, steaming from a rain earlier in the day. Jesse was lying; he didn't have anyone, hadn't had anyone in over a year—everybody knew he was slow in his group, and they shunned him for that—and Jesse felt as if he was getting farther and farther away from ever wanting anyone, or anything. He felt like everything was a blur: such was the speed at which he imagined he was trying to travel. Beyond the fog in the pasture were the trees, clear and dark and washed from the rain, and smelling good, even at this distance. Hollingsworth wished he had a whore. He wondered if Jesse would let him use his.

He wondered if maybe she would be available if Jesse was to get fast and go off to the Olympics, or something.

"What does she cost?" Hollingsworth asked timidly.

Jesse looked at him in disgust. "I didn't mean it *that* way," he said. He looked tired, as if he was holding back, just a few seconds, from having to go back out on the road. Hollingsworth leaned closer, eagerly, sensing weakness, tasting hesitation. His senses were sharp, from deprivation: he could tell, even before Jesse could, that Jesse was feeling thick, laggard, dulled. He knew Jesse was going to quit. He knew it the way a farmer might see that rain was coming.

"I mean," sighed Jesse, "that I got an old lady. A woman friend. A girl."

"What's her name?" Hollingsworth said quickly. He would make Jesse so tired that he would never ride again. They would sit around on the porch and talk forever, all of the days.

"Jemima."

Hollingsworth wanted her, just for her name.

"That's nice," he said, in a smaller voice.

It seemed to Hollingsworth that Jesse was getting his energy back. But he had felt the tiredness, and maybe, Hollingsworth hoped, it would come back.

"I found out the old man is your father," said Jesse. He was looking out at the road. He still wasn't making any move toward it. Hollingsworth realized, as if he had been tricked, that perhaps Jesse was just waiting for the roads to dry up a little, to finish steaming.

"Yes," said Hollingsworth, "he has run away."

They looked at the fields together.

"He is not right," Hollingsworth said.

"The black women in town, the ones that do everyone's wash at the laundromat, say he is living down in the old yellow-fever community," Jesse said. "They say he means to stay, and that some of them have thought about going down there with him: the ones with bad husbands and too much work. He's been sneaking around the laundry late in the evenings, and promising them he'll cook for them, if any of them want to move down there with him. He says there aren't any snakes. They're scared the fever will come back, but he promises there aren't any snakes, that he killed them all, and a lot of them are considering it." Jesse related all this in a monotone, still watching the road, as if waiting for energy. The sun was burning the steam off. Hollingsworth felt damp, weak, unsteady, as if his mind was sweating with condensation from the knowledge, the way glasses suddenly fog up when you are walking into a humid setting.

"Sounds like he's getting lonely," Jesse said.

The steam was almost gone.

"He'll freeze this winter," Hollingsworth said, hopefully.

Jesse shook his head. "Sounds like he's got a plan. I suspect he'll have those women cutting firewood for him, fanning him with leaves, fishing, running traps, bearing children. Washing clothes."

"We'll catch him," Hollingsworth said, making a fist and smacking it in his palm. "And anyway, those women won't go down into the woods. They're dark, and the yellow fever's still down there. I'll go into town, and tell them it is. I'll tell them Buzbee's spitting up black blood and shivering, and is crazy. Those women won't go down into the woods."

Jesse shook his head. He put the bottle into the rack. The road was dry; it looked clean, scrubbed, by the quick thunderstorm. "A lot of those women have got bruises on their arms, their faces, have got teeth missing, and their lives are too hard and without hope," Jesse said slowly, as if just for the first time seeing it. "Myself, I think they'll go down there in great numbers. I don't think yellow fever means anything compared to what they have, or will have." He turned to Hollingsworth and slipped a leg over his bike, got on, put his feet in the clips, steadied himself against the porch railing. "I bet by June next year you're going to have about twenty half brothers and half sisters."

When Jesse rode off, thickly, as if the simple heat of the air were a thing holding him back, there was no question, Hollingsworth realized, Jesse was exhausted, and fall was coming. Jesse was getting tired. He, Hollingsworth, and Buzbee, and the colored women at the washhouse, and other people would get tired, too. The temperatures would be getting cooler, milder, in a month or so, and the bikers would be riding harder than ever. There would be smoke from fires, hunters down on the river, and at night the stars would be brighter, and people's sleep would be heavier, and deeper. Hollingsworth wondered just how fast those bikers wanted to go. Surely, he thought, they were already going fast enough. He didn't understand them. Surely, he thought, they didn't know what they were doing.

The speeds that the end of June and the beginning of July brought, Jesse had never felt before, and he didn't trust them to last, didn't know if they could; and he tried to stay with the other riders, but didn't know if there was anything he could do to make the little speed he had last, in the curves, and that feeling, pounding up the hills, his heart working thick and smooth, like the wildest, easiest, most volatile thing ever invented. He tried to stay with them.

Hollingsworth, the old faggot, was running out into the road some days, trying to flag him down, for some piece of bullshit, but there wasn't time, and he rode past, not even looking at him, only staring straight ahead.

The doves started to fly. The year was moving along. A newspaper reporter wandered down, to do a short piece on the still-missing Buzbee. It was rumored he was living in an abandoned, rotting shack, deep into the darkest, lowest heart of the swamp. It was said that he had started taking old colored women, maids and such, women from the laundromat, away from town, that they were going back down into the woods with him and living there, and that he had them in a corral, like a herd of wild horses. The reporter's story slipped further from the truth. It was all very mysterious, all rumor, and the reward was increased to twelve hundred dollars by Hollingsworth, as the days grew shorter after the solstice, and lonelier.

Jesse stopped racing. He just didn't go out one day; and when the Frenchmen came by for him, he pretended not to be in.

He slept late and began to eat vast quantities of oatmeal. Sometimes, around noon, he would stop eating and get on his bike and ride slowly up the road to Hollingsworth's—sometimes the other bikers would pass him, moving as ever at great speed, all of them, and they would jeer at him, shout yah-yah, and then they were quickly gone; and he willed them to wreck, shut his eyes and tried to make it happen—picturing the whole pack of them getting tangled up, falling over one another, the way they tended to do, riding so close together—and the pain of those wrecks, the long slide, the drag and skid of flesh on gravel.

The next week he allowed himself a whole Coca-Cola, with Hollingsworth, on the steps of the store's porch. The old man swooned, and had to steady himself against the railing when he saw it was his true love. It was a dry summer. They talked more about Buzbee.

"He's probably averse to being captured," Hollingsworth said. "He probably won't go easy."

Jesse looked at his shoes, watched them, as if thinking about where they were made.

"If you were to help me catch him, I would give you my half of it," Hollingsworth said generously. Jesse watched his shoes.

Hollingsworth got up and went in the store quickly, and came back out with a hank of calf-roping lariat, heavy, gold as a fable, and corded.

"I been practicing," he said. There was a sawhorse standing across the drive, up on two legs, like a man, with a hat on it, and a coat, and Hollingsworth said nothing else, but twirled the lariat over his head and then flung it at the sawhorse, a mean heavy whistle over their heads, and the loop settled over the sawhorse, and Hollingsworth stepped back quickly and tugged, cinched the loop shut. The sawhorse fell over, and Hollingsworth began dragging it across the gravel, reeling it in as fast as he could.

"I could lasso you off that road, if I wanted," Hollingsworth said.

Jesse thought about how the money would be nice. He thought about how it was in a wreck, too, when he wasn't able to get his feet free of the clips and had to stay with the bike, and roll over with it, still wrapped up in it. It was just the way his sport was.

"I've got to be going," he told Hollingsworth. When he stood up, though, he had been still too long, and his blood stayed down in his legs, and he saw spots and almost fell.

"Easy now, hoss," Hollingsworth cautioned, watching him eagerly, eyes narrowed, hoping for an accident and no more riding.

The moonlight that came in through Hollingsworth's window, onto his bed, all night—it was silver. It made things look different: ghostly. He slept on his back, looking up at the ceiling until he fell asleep. He listened to crickets, to hoot owls, and to the silence, too.

We'll get him, he thought. We'll find his ass. But he couldn't sleep, and the sound of his heart, the movement of his blood pulsing, was the roar of an ocean, and it wasn't right. His father did not belong down in those woods. No one did. There was nothing down there that Hollingsworth could see but reptiles, and danger.

The moon was so bright that it washed out all stars. Hollingsworth listened to the old house. There was a blister on the inside of his finger from practicing with the lariat, and he fingered it and looked at the ceiling.

Jesse went back, again and again. He drank the Coke slowly. He wasn't sweating.

"Let's go hunt that old dog," Hollingsworth said—it was the first thing he said, after Jesse had gotten his bottle out of the machine and opened it—and like a molester, a crooner, Hollingsworth seemed to be drifting toward Jesse without moving his feet: just leaning forward, swaying closer and closer, as if moving in to smell blossoms. His eyes were a believer's blue, and for a moment, still thinking about how slowly he had ridden over and the Coke's coldness and wetness, Jesse had no idea what he was talking about and felt dizzy. He looked into Hollingsworth's eyes, such a pale wash of light, such a pale blue that he knew the eyes had never seen anything factual, nothing of substance—and he laughed, thinking of Hollingsworth trying to catch Buzbee, or anything, on his own. The idea of Hollingsworth being able to do anything other than just take what was thrown at him was ridiculous. He thought of Hollingsworth on a bike, pedaling, and laughed again.

"We can split the reward money," Hollingsworth said again. He was grinning, smiling wildly, trying as hard as he could to show all his teeth and yet keep them close together, uppers and lowers touching. He breathed through the cracks in them in a low, pulsing whistle: in and out. He had never in his life drunk anything but water, and his teeth were startlingly white; they were just whittled down, was all, and puny, from aging and time. He closed his eyes, squeezed them shut slowly, as if trying to remember something simple, like speech, or balance, or even breathing. He was like a turtle sunning on a log.

Jesse couldn't believe he was speaking.

"Give me all of it," he heard himself say.

"All of it," Hollingsworth agreed, his eyes still shut, and then he opened them and handed the money to Jesse slowly, ceremoniously, like a child paying for something at a store counter, for the first time.

Jesse unlaced his shoes, and folded the bills in half and slid them down into the soles, putting bills in both shoes. He unlaced the drawstring to his pants and slid some down into the black dampness of his racing silks: down in the crotch, and padding the buttocks, and in front, high on the flatness of his abdomen, like a girdle, directly below the cinching lace of the drawstring, which he then tied again, tighter than it had been before.

Then he got on the bike and rode home, slowly, not racing anymore, not at all; through the late-day heat that had built up, but with fall in the air, the leaves on the trees hanging differently. There was some stillness everywhere. He rode on.

When he got home he carried the bike inside, as was his custom, and then undressed, peeling his suit off, with the damp bills fluttering slowly to the old rug, like petals and blossoms from a dying flower, unfolding when they landed, and it surprised him at first to see them falling away from him like that, all around him, for he had forgotten that they were down there as he rode.

Buzbee was like a field general. The women were tasting freedom, and seemed to be like circus strongmen, muscled with great strength suddenly, from not being told what to do, from not being beaten or yelled at. They laughed and talked, and were kind to Buzbee. He sat up in the tree, in his old khaki pants, and watched, and whenever it looked like his feeble son and the ex-biker might be coming, he leaped down from the tree, and like monkeys they scattered into the woods: back to another, deeper, temporary camp they had built.

They splashed across the river like wild things, but they were laughing, there was no fear, not like there would have been in animals.

They knew they could get away. They knew that as long as they ran fast, they would make it.

Buzbee grinned too, panting, his eyes bright, and he watched the women's breasts float and bounce, riding high as they charged across—ankle-deep, knee-deep, waist-deep—hurrying to get away from his mad, lonely son, running fast and shrieking, because they were all afraid of the alligators.

Buzbee had a knife in one hand and a sharpened stick in the other, and he almost wished there would be an attack, so that he could be a hero.

The second camp was about two miles down into the swamp. No one had ever been that far into it, not ever. The mosquitoes were worse, too. There wasn't any dry land, not even a patch, but they sat on the branches, and dangled their feet, and waited. Sometimes they saw black bears splashing after fish, and turtles. There were more snakes, too, deeper back, but the women were still bruised, and some of them fingered their scars as they watched the snakes, and no one went back.

They made up songs, with which they pretended to make the snakes go away.

It wasn't too bad.

They sat through the night listening to the cries of birds, and when the woods began to grow light again, so faintly at first that they doubted it was happening, they would ease down into the water and start back toward their dry camp.

Hollingsworth would be gone, chased away by the mosquitoes, by the emptiness, and they would feel righteous, as if they'd won something: a victory.

None of them had a watch. They never knew what time it was, what day even.

"Gone," said Hollingsworth.

He was out of breath, out of shape. His shoelaces were untied, and there were burrs in his socks. The camp was empty. Just chickens. And the godawful reptiles, twisting from the trees.

"Shit almighty," said Jesse. His legs were cramping, and he was bent over, massaging them: he wasn't used to walking.

Hollingsworth poked around in the little grass-and-wood shacks. He was quivering, and kept saying, alternately, "Gone" and "Damn."

Jesse had to sit down, so bad was the pain in his legs. He put his feet together like a bear in the zoo and held them there, and rocked, trying to stretch them back out. He was frightened of the alligators, and he felt helpless, in his cramps, knowing that Buzbee could come up from behind with a club and rap him on the head, like one of the chickens, and that he, Jesse, wouldn't even be able to get up to stop him, or run.

Buzbee was in control.

"Shit. Damn. Gone," said Hollingsworth. He was running a hand through his thinning hair. He kicked a few halfhearted times at the shacks, but they were kicks of sorrow, not rage yet, and did no damage.

"We could eat the chickens," Jesse suggested, from his sitting position. "We could cook them on his fire and leave the bones all over camp." Jesse still had his appetite from his riding days, and was getting fat fast. He was eating all the time since he had stopped riding.

Hollingsworth turned to him, slightly insulted. "They belong to my father," he said.

Jesse continued to rock, but thought: My God, what a madman.

He rubbed his legs and rocked. The pain was getting worse.

There was a breeze stirring. They could hear the leather and rope creaking, as some of the smaller alligators moved. There was a big alligator hanging from a beech tree, about ten feet off the ground, and as they watched it, the leather cord snapped, from the friction, and the dead weight of the alligator crashed to the ground.

"The mosquitoes are getting bad," said Jesse, rising, hobbled, bent over. "We'd better be going."

But Hollingsworth was already scrambling up through the brush, up toward the brightness of sky above the field. He could see the sky, the space, through the trees, and knew the field was out there. He was frantic to get out of the woods; there was a burning in his chest, in his throat, and he couldn't breathe.

Jesse helped him across the field and got him home; he offered to ride into Crystal Springs, thirty miles, and make a call for an ambulance, but Hollingsworth waved him away.

"Just stay with me a little while." he said. "I'll be OK."

But the thought was terrifying to Jesse—of being in the same room with Hollingsworth, contained, and listening to him talk, forever, all day and through the night, doubtless.

"I have to go," he said, and hurried out the door.

He got on his bike and started slowly for home. His knees were bumping against his belly, such was the quickness of his becoming fat, but the relief of being away from Hollingsworth was so great that he didn't mind.

Part of him wanted to be as he had been, briefly: iron, and fast, racing with the fastest people in the world, it seemed—he couldn't remember anything about them, only the blaze and rip of their speed, the *whish-whish* cutting sound they made, as a pack, tucking and sailing down around corners—but also, he was so tired of that, and it felt good to be away from it, for just a little while.

He could always go back.

His legs were still strong. He could start again any time. The sport of it, the road, would have him back. The other bikers would have him back, they would be happy to see him.

He thought all these things as he trundled fatly up the minor hills, the gradual rises, coasting, relievedly, on the down sides.

Shortly before he got to the gravel turnoff, the little tree-lined road that led to his house, the other bikers passed him, coming out of the west, and they screamed and howled at him, passing, and jabbed their thumbs down at him, as if they were trying to unplug a drain or poke a hole in something; they shrieked, and then they were gone, so quickly.

He did not stop blushing for the rest of the day. He wanted to hide somewhere, he was so ashamed of what he had lost, but there was nowhere to hide, for in a way it was still in him: the memory of it.

He dreamed of going down into the woods, of joining Buzbee and starting over, wrestling alligators; but he only dreamed it—and in the morning, when he woke up, he was still heavy and slow, grounded.

He went into the kitchen, and looked in the refrigerator, and began taking things out. Maybe, he thought, Hollingsworth would up the reward money.

Buzbee enjoyed cooking for the women. It was going to be an early fall, and dry; they got to where they hardly noticed the mosquitoes that were always whining around them—a tiny buzzing—and they had stopped wearing clothes long ago. Buzbee pulled down hickory branches and climbed up in trees, often—and he sat hunkered above the women, looking down, just watching them move around in their lives, naked and happy, talking; more had come down the bayou since the first two, and they were shoring up the old shelter; pulling up palmetto plants from the hummocks and dragging logs across the clearing, fixing the largest of the abandoned cabins into a place that was livable, for all of them.

He liked the way they began to look at him, on about the tenth day of their being there, and he did not feel seventy-seven. He slid down out of the tree, walked across the clearing toward the largest woman, the one he had had his eye on, and took her hand, hugged her, felt her broad fat back, the backs of her legs, which were sweaty, and then her behind, while she giggled.

All that week, as the weather changed, they came drifting in, women from town, sometimes carrying lawn chairs, always wild-eyed and tentative when they saw the alligators and catfish, the people moving around naked in camp, brown as the earth itself—but then they would recognize someone, and would move out into the clearing with wonder, and a disbelief at having escaped. A breeze might be stirring, and dry colored hardwood leaves, ash and hickory, and oak and beech, orange and gold, would tumble down into the clearing, spill around their ankles, and the leaves made empty scraping sounds when the women walked through them, shuffling, looking up at the spinning fish.

At night they would sit around the fire and eat the dripping juiciness of the alligators, roasted—fat, from the tails, sweet, glistening on their hands, their faces, running down to their elbows. They smeared it on their backs, their breasts, to keep the mosquitoes away. Nights smelled of wood smoke. They could see the stars above their trees, above the shadows of their catches.

The women had all screamed and run into the woods, in different directions, the first time Buzbee leaped into the water after an alligator; but now they all gathered close and applauded and chanted an alligator-catching song they had made up that had few vowels, whenever he wrestled them. But that first time they thought he had lost his mind: he had rolled around and around in the thick gray-white slick mud, down by the bank, jabbing the young alligator with his pocketknife again and again, perforating it and muttering savage dog noises, until they could no longer tell which was which, except for the jets of blood that spurted out of the alligator's fat belly—but after he had killed the reptile, and rinsed off in the shallows, and come back across the oxbow, wading in knee-deep water, carrying it in his arms, a four-footer, his largest ever, he was smiling, gaptoothed, having lost two in the fight, but he was also erect, proud, and ready for love. It was the first time they had seen that.

The one he had hugged went into the hut after him.

The other women walked around the alligator carefully, and poked sticks at it, but also glanced toward the hut and listened, for the brief and final end of the small thrashings, the little pleasure, that was going on inside, the confirmation, and presently it came: Buzbee's goatish bleats, and the girl's, too, which made them look at one another with surprise, wonder, interest, and speculation.

"It's those berries he's eatin," said one, whose name was Onessimius. Oney.

"They tastes bad," said Tasha.

"They makes your pee turn black," said Oney.
They looked at her with caution.

Jesse didn't have the money for a car, or even for an old tractor.
He bought a used lawn-mower engine instead, for fifteen dollars.
He found some old plywood in a dry abandoned barn. He
scrounged some wheels, and stole a fan belt from a car rotting in a
field, with bright wildflowers growing out from under the hood and
mice in the back seat. He made a go-cart, and put a long plastic antenna with an orange flag, a banner, on the back of it that reached
high into the sky, so that any motorists coming would see it.

But there was never any traffic. He sputtered and coughed up the
hills, going one, two miles an hour: then coasting down, a slight
breeze in his face. He didn't wear his biking helmet, and the breeze
felt good.

It took him an hour to get to Hollingsworth's sometimes; he carried a sack lunch with him, apples and potato chips, and ate, happily,
as he drove.

He started out going over to Hollingsworth's in the midmorning,
and always trying to come back in the early afternoon, so that the
bikers would not see him: but it got more and more to where he
didn't care, and finally, he just came and went as he pleased, waving
happily when he saw them; but they never waved back. Sometimes
the one who had replaced him, the trailing one, would spit water
from his thermos bottle onto the top of Jesse's head as he rushed
past; but they were gone quickly, almost as fast as they had appeared,
and soon he was no longer thinking about them. They were gone.

Cottonwoods. Rabbits. Fields. It was still summer, it seemed it
would always be summer; the smell of hay was good, and dry. All
summer, they cut hay in the fields around him.

He was a slow movement of color going up the hills, with everything else in his world motionless; down in the fields, black Angus
grazed, and cattle egrets stood behind them and on their backs.
Crows sat in the dead limbs of trees, back in the woods, watching
him, watching the cows, waiting for fall.

He would reach Hollingsworth's, and the old man would be waiting, like a child wanting his father back. It was a ritual. Hollingsworth would wave tiredly, hiding in his heart the delight at seeing
another person.

Jesse would wave back as he drove up into the gravel drive. He would grunt and pull himself up out of the little go-cart, and go over to the Coke machine.

The long slide of the bottle down the chute; the rattle, and *clunk*. They'd sit on the porch, and Hollingsworth would begin to talk.

"I saw one of those explode in a man's hand," he said, pointing to the bottle Jesse was drinking. "Shot a sliver of glass as long as a knife up into his forearm, all the way. He didn't feel a thing: he just looked at it, and then walked around, pointing to it, showing everybody. . . . "

Hollingsworth remembered everything that had ever happened to him. He told Jesse everything.

Jesse would stir after the second or third story. He couldn't figure it out; he couldn't stand to be too close to Hollingsworth, to listen to him for more than twenty or thirty minutes—he hated it after that point—but always, he went back; every day.

It was as if he got full, almost to the point of vomiting; but then he got hungry again.

He sat on the porch and drank Cokes, and ate cans and cans of whatever Hollingsworth had on the shelf—yams, mushrooms, pickles, deviled ham—and he knew, as if it were an equation on a blackboard, that his life had gone to hell—he could see it in the size of his belly resting between his soft legs—but he didn't know what to do.

There was a thing that was not in him anymore, and he did not know where to go to find it.

Oney was twenty-two, and had had a bad husband. She still had the stitches in her forehead: he had thrown a chair at her, because she had called him a lard-ass, which he was. The stitches in the center of her head looked like a third eyebrow, with the eye missing, and she hadn't heard about the old days of yellow fever and what it could do to one person, or everyone.

That night, even though she slept in Buzbee's arms, she began to shiver wildly, though the night was still and warm. And then two days later, again, she shivered and shook all night, and then two days later, a third time: it was coming every forty-eight hours, which was how it had done when Buzbee and his father had had it.

Onessimius had been pale to begin with, and was turning, as if with the leaves, yellow, right in front of them: a little brighter yellow each day. All of the women began to eat the berries, slowly at first, and then wolfishly, watching Oney as they ate them.

They had built a little palmetto coop for their remaining chickens, which were laying regularly, and they turned them out, three small white magicians moving through the woods in search of bugs, seed, and berries, and the chickens split up and wandered in different directions, and Buzbee and all the women split up, too, and followed them single file, at a distance, waiting for the chickens to find more berries, but somehow two of the chickens got away from them, escaped, and when they came back to camp, with the one remaining white chicken, a large corn snake was in the rooster's cage and was swallowing him, with only his thrashing feet visible: the snake's mouth stretched hideously wide, eyes wide and unblinking, mouth stretched into a laugh, as if he was enjoying the meal. Buzbee killed the snake, but the rooster died shortly after being pulled back out.

Oney screamed and cried, and shook until she was spitting up more black blood, when they told her they were going to take her back into town, and she took Buzbee's pocketknife and pointed it between her breasts and swore she would kill herself if they tried to make her go back to Luscious—because he would kill her for having left, and in a way worse than spitting up black blood and even parts of her stomach—and so they let her stay, but worried, and fed her their dwindling berry supply, and watched the stars, the sunset, and hoped for a hard and cold winter and an early freeze, but the days stayed warm, though the leaves were changing on schedule, and always, they looked for berries, and began experimenting, too, with the things Buzbee and his father had tried so many years ago: cedar berries, mushrooms, hickory nuts, acorns. They smeared grease from the fish and alligators over every inch of their bodies, and kept a fire going again, at all times, But none of the women would go back to town. And none of them other than Oney had started spitting up blood or shivering yet. Ozzie, Buzbee's first woman, had missed her time.

And Buzbee sat up in the trees and looked down on them often, and stopped eating his berries, unbeknownst to them, so that there would be more. The alligators hung from the trees like dead insurgents, traitors to a way of life. They weren't seeing any more in the bayou, and he wasn't catching nearly as many fish. The fall was coming, and winter beyond that. The animals knew it first. Nothing could prevent its coming, or even slow its approach: nothing they could do would matter. Buzbee felt fairly certain that he had caught enough alligators.

Hollingsworth and Jesse made another approach a week later. Hollingsworth had the lariat, and was wearing cowboy boots and a hat. Jesse was licking a Fudgsicle.

Buzbee, in his tree, spotted them and jumped down.

The women grumbled, but they dropped what they were doing and fled, went deeper, to safety.

"Shit," said Hollingsworth when they got to the camp. "He saw us coming again."

"He runs away," said Jesse, nodding. They could see the muddy slide marks where Buzbee and the women had scrambled out on the other side. The dark wall of trees, a wall.

"I've got an idea," said Hollingsworth.

They knew where Buzbee and the women were getting their firewood: there was a tremendous logjam, with driftwood stacked all along the banks, not far from the camp.

Hollingsworth and Jesse went and got shovels, as well as old mattresses from the dump, and came back and dug pits: huge, deep holes, big enough to bury cars, big enough to hold a school bus.

"I saw it on a Tarzan show," said Hollingsworth. His heart was burning; both of the men were dripping with sweat. It was the softest, richest dirt in the world, good and loose and black and easy to move, but they were out of shape and it took them all day. They sang as they dug, to keep Buzbee and the women at bay, hemmed in, back in the trees.

Buzbee and the women sat up on their branches, swatting at mosquitoes, and listened, and wondered what was going on.

"Row, row, row, your boat!" Jesse shouted as he dug, his big belly wet, like a melon. Mopping his brow; his face streaked, with dirt and mud. He remembered the story about the pioneers who went crazy alone, and dug their own graves—standing at the edge, then, and doing it.

"Oh, say—can—you—see," Hollingsworth brayed, "by the dawn's—earl—lee—light?"

Back in the trees, the women looked at Buzbee for an explanation. They knew it was his son.

"He was born too early," he said weakly. "He has never been right."

"He misses you," said Oney. "That boy wants you to come home."

Buzbee scowled and looked down at his toes, hunkered on the branch, and held on fiercely, as if the tree had started to sway.

"That boy don't know *what* he wants," he said.

When Hollingsworth and Jesse had finished the pits, they spread long branches over them, then scattered leaves and twigs over the branches and left.

"We'll catch the whole tribe of them," Hollingsworth cackled.

Jesse nodded. He was faint, and didn't know if he could make it all the way back out or not. He wondered vaguely what Buzbee and the women would be having for supper.

The mosquitoes were vicious; the sun was going down. Owls were beginning to call.

"Come on," said Hollingsworth. "We've got to get out of here."

Jesse wanted to stay. But he felt Hollingsworth pull on his arm; he let himself be led away.

Back in the woods, up in the tree, Oney began to shiver, and closed her eyes, lost consciousness, and fell. Buzbee leaped down and gathered her up, held her tightly, and tried to warm her with his body.

"They gone," said a woman named Vesuvious. The singing had gone away when it got dark, as had the ominous sound of digging.

There was no moon, and it was hard, even though they were familiar with it, to find their way back to camp.

They built fires around Oney, and two days later she was better.

But they knew it would come again.

"Look at what that fool boy of yours has done," Tasha said the next day. She had gone to get more wood. A deer had fallen into one of the pits and was leaping about, uninjured, trying to get free.

Buzbee said his favorite curse word, a new one that Oney had told him, "Fuckarama," and they tried to rope the deer, but it was too wild: it would not let them get near.

"We could stone it," Tasha said, but not with much certainty; and they all knew they could not harm the deer, trapped as it was, so helpless.

They felt bad about it, and sat and tried to think of ways to get it out of the pit, but without shovels they were stumped.

They saw Oney's husband one horrible evening, moving through the woods, perilously close to their camp, moving through the gray trees at dusk, stalking their woods with a shotgun, as if squirrel-hunting.

They hid in their huts and watched, hoping he would not look down the hill and see their camp, not see the alligators hanging.

"Come on, baby," said Tasha, "find that pit." He was moving in that direction.

They watched, petrified. Oney was whimpering. His dark, slow shape moved cautiously about, but the light was going fast: that darkness of purple, all light being drawn away. He faded; he disappeared; it was dark. Then, into the night, they heard a yell, and a blast, and then the quietest silence they had even known.

And then, later: owls calling, in the night.

It was a simple matter burying him in the morning. They hadn't thought of letting the deer out that way; they had not thought of filling it in and making it not be there anymore.

"You will get better," they told Oney. She believed them. On the days in which she did not have the fever, she believed them. There was still, though, the memory of it.

It was escapable. Some people lived through it and survived. It didn't get everyone. They didn't all just lie down and die, those who got it.

She loved old Buzbee, on her good days. She laughed, and slept with him, rolled with him, and put into the back of her mind what had happened before, and what would be happening again.

Her teeth, when she was laughing, pressing against him, clutching him, shutting her eyes. She would fight to keep it in the back of her mind, and to keep it behind her.

Jesse rode out to Hollingsworth's in the go-cart. He took a back road, a different route. The air was cooler, it seemed that summer could be ending, after all, and he felt like just getting out and seeing the country again. It was a road he had always liked to ride on, with or without the pack, back when he had been racing, and he had forgotten how fresh it had been, how it had tasted, just to look at it. He drove through a tunnel of trees; a pasture, on the other side of the trees, a stretch of pastel green, a smear of green, with charcoal cattle standing in it, and white egrets at their sides, pressed an image into the sides of his slow-moving vision. It was almost cold down in the creek bottom, going through the shade, so slowly.

He smiled and gave a small whoop, and waved a fist in the air. The light on the other side of the trees, coming down onto the field, was the color of gold smoke.

He had a sack of groceries with him, behind the engine, and he reached back and got a sandwich and a canned drink. The go-cart rumbled along, carrying him; threatening to stop on the hill, but struggling on.

They went to check the traps, the pits, flushing Buzbee's troops back into the swamp, as ever.

"I'd hoped we could have caught them all," said Hollingsworth. His eyes were pale, mad, and he wanted to dig more holes.

"Look," he said. "They buried my mattress." He bent down on the fresh mound and began digging at it with his hands; but he gave up shortly, and looked around blankly, as if forgetting why he had been digging in the first place.

Buzbee and the women were getting angry at being chased so often, so regularly. They sat in the trees and waited. Some of the women said nothing, but hoped, to themselves, that Hollingsworth and Jesse would forget where some of the pits lay, and would stumble in.

Jesse and Hollingsworth sat on Hollingsworth's porch.

"You don't talk much," Hollingsworth said, as if noticing for the first time.

Jesse said nothing. It was getting near the twenty-minute mark. He had had two Cokes and a package of Twinkies. He was thinking about how it had been, when he had been in shape, and riding with the others, the pack: how his old iron bike had been a traitor some days, and his legs had laid down and died, and he had run out of wind—but how he had kept going, anyway, and how eventually—though only for a little while——it had gotten better.

The bikers rode past. They were moving so fast. Hills were nothing to them. They had light bikes, expensive ones, and the climbs were only excuses to use the great strength of their legs. The wind in their faces, and pressing back against their chests, was but a reason and a direction, for a feeling: it was something to rail against, and defeat, or be defeated by—but it was tangible. Compared to some things, the wind was actually tangible.

They shouted encouragement to one another as they jockeyed back and forth, sharing turns, breaking the wind for each other.

"I'm ready," Hollingsworth told Jesse on his next visit, a few days later.

He was jumping up and down like a child.

"I'm ready, I'm ready," Hollingsworth sang. "Ready for anything."

He had a new plan. All he had been doing was thinking: trying to figure out a way to get something back.

Jesse rode his bike to town, to get the supplies they would need: an extra lariat, and rope for trussing him up with; they figured he would be senile, and wild. Muzzles for the dogs. Jesse rode hard, for a fat man.

The wind was coming up. It was the first week in September. The hay was baled, stood in tall rolls, and the fields looked tame, civilized, smoothed—flattened.

They muzzled the dogs and put heavy leashes on their collars, and started out across the field. Owls were beginning to call again, it was the falling of dusk, and Jesse and Hollingsworth carried with them a kerosene lantern and some food and water.

When they had crossed the field—half running, half being dragged, by the big dogs' eagerness—and came to the edge of the woods, and started down into them, toward the swamp, they were halted by the mosquitoes, which rose up in a noisy dark cloud and fell upon them like soft fingers. The dogs turned back, whining in their muzzles, yelping, instinct warning them of the danger of these particular mosquitoes, and they kept backing away, back into the field, and would not go down into the swamp.

So Hollingsworth and Jesse camped back in the wind of the pasture, in the cool grass, and waited for daylight.

They could smell the smoke from Buzbee's camp, but could see nothing, the woods were so dark. There was a quarter-moon, and it came up so close to them, over the trees, that they could see the craters. Hollingsworth talked.

He talked about the space program. He asked Jesse if this wasn't better than riding his old bike. They shared a can of Vienna sausage. Hollingsworth talked all night. Chuck-will's-widows called, and bullbats thumped around in the grass, not far from their small fire:

flinging themselves into the grass and flopping around as if mourning, rising again, flying past, and then twisting and slamming hard and awkwardly down, without a cry, as if pulled there by a sudden force, hidden—as if their time was up. All around them, the bullbats flew like this, twisting and then diving into the ground, until it seemed to Jesse that without a doubt they were trying to send a message: Go back, go back.

And he imagined, as he tried not to listen to Hollingsworth babblings, that the bikers he had ridden with, the Frenchmen, were asleep, or making love to soft women, or eating ice-cream cones.

A light drizzle woke Hollingsworth and Jesse and the dogs in the morning, and they stood up and stretched, and then moved on the camp. Crickets were chirping quietly in the soft rain, and the field was steaming. There wasn't any more smoke from the fire. The dogs had been smelling Buzbee and his camp all night, and were nearly crazed: their chests swelled and strained like barrels of apples, like hearts of anger, and they jumped and twisted and tugged against their leashes, pulling Hollingsworth and Jesse behind them in a stumbling run through the wet grasses.

Froth came from their muzzles, their rubbery lips. Their eyes were wild. They were too hard to hold. They pulled free of their leashes, and raced, silently, like the fastest thing in the world, accelerating across the field and into the woods, straight for the camp, the straightest thing that ever was.

Jesse bought a bike with the reward money: a French bicycle, a racer, with tires that were thinner than a person's finger held sideways. It could fly. It was light blue, like an old man's eyes.

Hollingsworth had chained Buzbee to the porch: had padlocked the clasp around his ankle, with thirty feet of chain. It disgusted Jesse, but even more disgusted was he by his own part in the capture, and by the size of his stomach, his loss of muscularity.

He began to ride again, not with the pack but by himself.

He got fast again, as he had thought he could. He got faster than he had been before, faster than he had ever imagined, and bought a stopwatch and raced against himself, timing himself, riding up and down the same roads over and over again.

Sometimes, riding, he would look up and see Buzbee out on the porch, standing, with Hollingsworth sitting behind him, talking. Hollingsworth would wave, wildly.

One night, when Jesse got in from his ride, the wind had shifted out of the warm west and was from the north, and serious, and in it, after Jesse had bathed and gotten in bed, was the thing, not for the first time, but the most insistent that year, that made Jesse get back out of bed, where he was reading, and go outside and sit on the steps beneath his porch light. He tried to read.

Moths fell down off the porch light's bulb, brushed his shoulders, landed on the pages of his book, spun, and flew off, leaving traces of magic. And the wind began to stir harder. Stars were all above him, and they glittered and flashed in the wind. They seemed to be challenging him: daring him to see what was true.

Two miles away, up on the hill, back in the trees, the A.M.E. church was singing. He couldn't see their lights, but for the first time that year he could hear them singing, the way he could in the winter, when there were no leaves on the trees and when the air was colder, more brittle, and sounds carried. He could never hear the words, just the sad moaning that sometimes, finally, fell away into pleasure.

He stood up on the porch and walked out into the yard, the cool grass, and tried some sit-ups. When he was through, he lay back, sweating slightly, breathing harder, and he watched the stars, but they weren't as bright, it seemed, and he felt as if he had somehow failed them, had not done the thing expected or, rather, the thing demanded.

When he woke up in the morning, turned on his side in the yard, sleeping, lying out in the grass like an animal, the breeze was still blowing and the light of the day was gold, coming out of the pines on the east edge of his field.

He sat up, stiffly, and for a moment forgot who he was, what he did, where he was—it was the breeze moving across him, so much cooler suddenly—and then he remembered, it was so simple, that he was supposed to ride.

It was early November. There was a heaviness to all movements, to all sights. It was impossible to look at the sky, at the trees, at the cattle in the fields even, and not know that it was November. The clasp around Buzbee's ankle was cold; his legs were getting stronger from pulling the chain around with him. He stood out on the porch, and the air, when he breathed deeply, went all the way down into his chest: he felt good. He felt like wrestling an alligator.

He had knocked Hollingsworth to the ground, tried to get him to tell him where the key was. But Hollingsworth, giggling, with his arm twisted behind his back—the older man riding him, breathing hard but steadily, pushing his son's face into the floor—had told Buzbee that he had thrown the key away. And Buzbee, knowing his son, his poisoned loneliness, knew that it was so.

The chain was too big to break or smash.

Sometimes Buzbee cried, looking at it. He felt as if he could not breathe; it was as if he were being smothered. It was like a thing was about to come to a stop.

He watched the field all the time. Jesse raced by, out on the road, checking his watch, looking at it, holding it in one hand, pedaling hard; flying, it seemed.

Buzbee heard Hollingsworth moving behind him; coming out to gab. It was like being in a cell.

Buzbee could see the trees, the watery blur of them, on the other side of the field.

"Pop," said Hollingsworth, ready with a story.

Pop, my ass, thought Buzbee bitterly. He wanted to strangle his own son.

He had so wanted to make a getaway—to have an escape, clean and free.

He looked out at the field, remembering what it had been like with the women, and the alligators, and he thought how he would be breaking free again, shortly, for good.

This time, he knew, he would get completely away.

The blue line of trees, where he had been with the women, wavered and flowed, in watercolor blotches, and there was a dizziness high in his forehead. He closed his eyes and listened to his mad son babble, and he prepared, and made his plans.

When he opened his eyes, the road was empty in front of him. Jesse was gone—a streak, a flash—already gone.

It was as if he had never even been there.

Buzbee narrowed his eyes and gripped the porch railing, squinted at the trees, scowled, and plotted, and tried to figure another way out.

Ellen Akins

GEORGE BAILEY FISHING

(from *Southwest Review*)

Frederick's two main streets form an ellipse. They start at the high school, curve away from each other, bridge the St. Joe River, and come together again at the shopping mall. On the river bank under the north bridge George Bailey fishes. Some of the people of Frederick have come to think of that bridge as George Bailey's; but if anyone speaking to Bess Frederick refers to Bailey Bridge, Bess Frederick says that the bridge was Frederick's before it was Bailey's and will be Frederick's again. George Bailey, she says, is only clever enough to borrow a bridge and fishes under it because he feels at home with something going over his head. Since Bess is a Frederick and, unless another miracle like Elisabeth's occurs, the last, whoever is listening will let her talk.

Bess has a prominent position. Her house stands across the street from the courthouse and looks out over the St. Joe and George Bailey. Some people who are more on her side than George's say George Bailey fishes because he has nothing else to do. Some people are literal-minded and say he fishes for food, even though no one has ever seen him reel in anything more edible than a river weed, a beer can, a sprung tennis ball. Then there are those who can't help wondering whether George just lets his hook sink and every once in a while drags it across the riverbed for the fun of casting it out over the water again.

George wasn't always the source of such idle speculation. No one paid too much attention when he came home from college to think

130

things over and stayed. Though there's some question as to what it was he studied or whether he finished, it's generally assumed that he was a good student. But when he got home from school he said to the neighbors that his studies hadn't prepared him for any better life than this—he was clipping the shrubs when he said it, or idling the lawn mower or working up to inviting over the neighbor to admire his handiwork while the sprinkler played. And the neighbor went over, mostly for the satisfaction of going back home to his or her own children who were too young yet to be judged successes or failures.

From the first, the children didn't think of George Bailey as a failure. He showed them a game of hooking a balloon over the sprinkler and predicting where the nozzle would be pointed when the balloon finally shot off. A brave child would stand one step ahead of the spot he'd picked and stay there even when the strain on the balloon told him he'd miscalculated and would get wet. From the number of soaked children going home, you might guess that they liked being brave even better than being right.

George's parents weren't overjoyed with this arrangement, but weren't distraught either. Mr. Bailey stood on the porch, inches short of the sprinkler's reach and said resignedly, "I'm too old to have another child."

He and Mrs. Bailey resigned themselves to George and counted on their daughter Linda, who had gone off to college armed with two scholarships and an outstanding history of extracurricular participation. There was a balance to the Bailey family, people said, and a person could ask for more than that, but couldn't expect to get it.

Every step Linda took past average marked out a wider margin for George to inhibit unbothered. So, he made it his business to advertise his sister's advances. After telling the cashier at the grocery store or Mr. Doherty at the post office or Mrs. Clark at the TV repair shop that errands weren't as easy as they used to be for his retired parents, he would report Linda's grades and high scores in management training exercises. He was proud of the degree his sister was pursuing. He said that Linda might come home and manage Frederick out of its slump.

Since the Frederick Tool and Die Company had closed down twenty years earlier, the townspeople had come to a consensus that Frederick was a town with more past than future, a good place to raise children or retire. During the construction of the mall there had been a flurry of unnecessary busyness in town, along with talk of business to come; but soon enough it became clear that the new building would merely house the stores from the shopping center it had replaced, the only exceptions being a movie theater that showed *Mr. Deeds Goes to Town* and *Gone with the Wind* and *Dr. Zhivago*, and Hostler's, a department store that belonged to a chain and was run by people who came from Granger and Goshen and went to their own parties. Hostler's never really was a part of Frederick. Its crystal lamps and hush and refrigerated air made shopping there like a visit to another town.

Despite its size and strange glamour, the store wasn't doing well. People knew. So, when George said, "slump," nobody minded. If Frederick could extend its slump to Hostler's, it wasn't going to give in and flourish under Linda Bailey's management. The townspeople knew George didn't mean as much as he was saying.

He had no intention of seeing his sister come back to Frederick, where success was measured by how far away from Frederick a family spread. He made that clear, all teasing aside. That the career ahead of Linda demanded more than what Frederick had to offer was taken for granted until Linda suddenly came home.

For a few months, George had been sending her letters so long they required thirty-seven cents in postage. Right before Linda's return, the letters went out almost daily; and as he sent them, George told Mr. Doherty that school was out and Linda was about to come home for a breathing spell before submerging herself in business. Mr. Doherty told his daughter Katie, who told her mother. Mrs. Doherty told Mrs. Clark and Mrs. Clark told her son Tom who had been Linda's prom date. He told some of his and Linda's high school friends and it went on that way until word got all around.

When he wasn't mailing letters, George was down at the river, near the spot where he sits today. Sometimes he was actually in the river. Crabbed over with his wrists and ankles in the water, he was such an odd sight that a few people stopped on the bridge above long enough to see what he would do. He would lift a handful of stones which he'd push around with a finger, flicking them one by one off his palm. The one or two stones he had left he'd spin across the river's surface, three skimming splashes. Then he'd hunch down and start over. The procedure itself wasn't all that interesting, but

George's acute interest in it was enough to make some onlookers watch till two or three handfuls of stones had been dispatched.

George abandoned the river bank and went home for the weekend of Linda's arrival. There was a brief eruption of activity at the Bailey house. When George wasn't outside painting the screens or edging the grass along the sidewalk or weeding, he could be heard performing some task that entailed banging together pipes in the basement.

Saturday night, Mrs. Bailey drove away and came back with Linda. Through all of Sunday there was not a sound or sign of life from the Bailey house.

George emerged on Monday and started raking the thatched grass out of the yard. Linda sat on the steps and watched. George told the neighbor children who had come around the house that if they wanted to put the piling-up grass in bags, they could have it for stuffing pillows and mattresses and other clubhouse furniture. Until then, no one had heard of there being a clubhouse; and most people still didn't hear of it till pillowcases turned up missing in the houses where George Bailey had an influence.

Linda sat there all that morning; and during the week, she made a few outings. But because of George's touting of her, people thought she must have changed, and kept a tentative and respectful distance from her, even though she looked like the same old Linda, as nice as ever—if a bit remote.

Then she started working as a sales clerk in the domestics department at Hostler's. It was a sign that she could be approached. Her old friends, wondering why a girl so famous as a fine student with long-ranging plans would be selling sheets and towels, stopped by to say hello and renew their acquaintance. Linda was friendly and helpful, but didn't offer any explanation of her position.

Sometimes George would go to the mall and spend lunchtime with Linda. They became a familiar sight, sitting on the cement bench that ran around the fountain at the center of the mall, George talking and Linda eating a sandwich. When she went back to work, he stayed for a few minutes and chatted with whoever happened to be passing by. That was how a few people learned of Hostler's policy of starting management trainees in sales, where they could gain first-hand experience. But that didn't explain what Linda was doing at Hostler's in the first place—or in Frederick, for that matter.

The story filtered down from Sue Rafferty, who was one year behind Linda in school and home for the summer. She said Linda had talked to recruiters on campus and had interviewed in most of the major cities within a hundred-mile radius of Frederick. The Linda was too modest, Sue said; she was doing the right thing—getting into a position where what she did would be a boast, not what she told somebody in personnel. And everyone who'd known Linda remembered then that she was timid and had always achieved her reputation through hard work instead of pushiness, that she had never got easily or early into anything.

So her friends were shocked when Linda got laid off. She had been working for three months and George was confident of her approaching promotion. People around town had been receiving letters from Hostler's thanking them for their business and acknowledging their praise of Linda Bailey. The people who received the letters had never commended Linda Bailey in writing—not because they didn't think she was commendable, but because they didn't care one way or another about sending a letter to say a salesperson was good or bad. It seemed somebody—and George was the obvious candidate— was looking out for Linda Bailey. She should have been doing fine, but suddenly she was out of work.

At the time, George was going out with Sue. Nothing ever came of the alliance, except the story George told Sue on the night of Linda's dismissal. He claimed to have written Jim Manning, Hostler's store manager, a letter containing high praise for Linda, snatches of her sales philosophy, examples of mismanagement she'd observed and mentioned, and finally, the suggestion that she'd better serve the store in a position more instrumental than clerk. George said Linda said Manning said bad business was forcing him to cut back his staff. No one could argue that business was bad, George said, and no one could imagine it being any better in that veritable swamp of malfunctioning bureaucracy.

Anyone even remotely familiar with George Bailey's usual subtlety could see through his feigned unawareness that such a letter gave Hostler's grounds for firing his sister. It's speculated that he made up the letter to save Linda from the taint and shame that can attend dismissal. There's something modestly heroic in his taking the blame for his sister's layoff but pretending not to do so, even though it's possible that someone at Hostler's noticed a certain con-

sistency in Linda's letters of commendation, asked her for an explanation, and got none.

George also announced that he would not have anything from
Hostler's in his house. It's rumored that, until Linda started to work
there, George Bailey had not once set foot in the store and, after his
sister was hired, had only gone visiting, never shopping. Nonetheless, he began to return merchandise.

Bess Frederick's maid Beamer had been making frequent visits to
the customer service window at Hostler's. She was engaged in a battle Bess was waging to get a mail-order dress exchanged and delivered. Since Bess had to open the box to see the olive green mistake,
someone would have to pay postage to get the package returned—
and she was not about to be inconvenienced and made poorer in
order to correct someone else's error. She'd specified blue; they'd
sent army green. Hostler's had a policy strictly separating in-store
transactions from catalogue purchases. It was Beamer's job to force
the store to make an exception.

She was at the customer service window when George Bailey returned an electric blanket and a rug. She heard him tell the embat-
tled girl behind the glass that a timer ticked too loudly, a teapot
cooled too quickly, an avocado paper towel dispenser didn't match
the avocado paint on his kitchen walls.

By then, Beamer and the girl had struck up a friendship; and they
were chatting, the girl holding on to the edge of the window to sig-
nal that her business day was over, when George Bailey walked up
and put an iron on the sill and said it was too heavy. Beamer stepped
aside while her friend directed George to Mr. Seligman, the manager of customer service. George went into a room at the end of the
hall. A few minutes later, he came out, still carrying the iron.

Hostler's ran an advertisement in every evening's *Frederick Tribune*. This promise was boxed at the top of each ad: "We'll take it back
and refund in cash, no questions asked." On the day following
George's visit to Mr. Seligman's office, the *Tribune* printed a letter
from George Bailey on the editorial page, which was opposite the
women's page, which featured Hostler's ad. George's letter told the
story of Hostler's refusal to refund. It accused the store of false ad-
vertising and called upon the citizens of Frederick to protect themselves from such an underhanded practice and unethical business.

"In a town as small as ours," George wrote, "consumer affairs are family affairs."

Hostler's became busier than it had ever been. George had given the townspeople the perfect opportunity to test the store's attitude toward Frederick, whose attitude toward the store wasn't entirely sympathetic. Since people hadn't done much shopping there once the novelty of having a new department store had worn off, they had to make purchases before they could ask for refunds. A buying spree went on, the likes of which hadn't been seen since Christmas.

Only Beamer complained about standing in line at customer service. Mrs. Doherty and Mrs. Rafferty, who had adopted a quarrel of their daughters' and were still snubbing one another long after Sue and Katie had made up, found themselves in line together and started speaking and continued their conversation through three trips out to the household goods department and back to customer service. Beamer's boyfriend, who was used to having lunch in Bess's kitchen, stopped by to find out why Beamer hadn't come home. Mrs. Clark came looking for Mrs. Rafferty who had promised her a book. Tom came to find out why the repair shop was closed, and his mother gave him a juicer to hold. Mr. Seligman shut the window and taped up a sign that read, "Due to uncommon business, we do not have adequate funds on hand for cash refunds. Please come back tomorrow."

That broke the holiday spirit. Standing in line and holding their purchases, people read the sign in silence. Mrs. Clark tapped the juicer in Tom's arms and said, "I certainly will."

The next day Hostler's had to close its window earlier and on a longer line.

That evening, the *Tribune* printed a letter written by Bess Frederick. "George Bailey has perpetrated a lot of nonsense," the letter said, "and unless it stops, you will only succeed in running our biggest department store and business out of town and making Frederick that much poorer."

Not by any design most of Frederick congregated in front of the Bailey's. It started out simply, people strolling the street in pairs, but turned into an informal town meeting when the couples stopped in passing to exchange words. Everyone had read Bess's letter. Bess Frederick, they said, always had to make a controversy of an issue so simple that it had only one side. "Nonsense?" Mr. Clark said. "That juice-maker John got stuck with has a fancy price for nonsense." The next day was Saturday and free, so other men who were in predicaments similar to Clark's decided to go back to Hostler's with their wives.

There was not much to be said for Bess Frederick on Saturday when Hostler's didn't open its customer service window at all. People waited in line till noon, then filtered back through the store and were accompanied out by friends they intercepted in the aisles. When the store had emptied, Jim Manning closed and locked the metal grating that separated Hostler's from the mall concourse.

During the few days it had taken Frederick to test Hostler's, George Bailey had not been seen. He had not been dredging the riverbed. He had not been watering or mowing or raking or weeding. He had not been at Hostler's to watch Frederick's response to his alarm. It was almost as if George Bailey were waiting in seclusion for that moment when he would be proven right and appreciated for his civic vigilance.

Mrs. Clark hurried the moment by writing a letter to the *Tribune* saying that, contrary to Bess Frederick's assertions, "George Bailey has done the town a service and ought to be commended." It was the beginning of a campaign to get George Bailey commended. The townspeople wanted Mayor Rogers to put a period to the affair. They wanted him to do something that would reflect the festiveness of the first day at Hostler's, not the sour, unfinished air everybody was feeling. The mayor had often been accused of consulting Bess on matters of policy. Everybody knew where she stood this time; and if Rogers didn't do something, his credibility was as good as gone. He announced that he would present George Bailey with the key to Frederick.

Nobody minded that Frederick only had one key and that whoever got it had to give it back, or that it had already been handed out four times that year. It was only important that George Bailey's role in ridding the town of Hostler's be made a matter of record.

The ceremony took place on the courthouse steps on a Saturday morning. Linda Bailey was not there; Sue said she was interviewing in Goshen. Bess Frederick was not there, but anyone looking across the street could see her watching from an upstairs window of her house. The rest of the town was assembled.

For key occasions, Mayor Rogers had a standard speech that no one listened to but everyone knew by heart. It ended, "So, I am pleased to present this key to a man who will always be welcome in the town of Frederick." And it ended that way this time, even though the business about being welcome was meant for out-of-towners Frederick honored.

Then George said this: he didn't need a key to Frederick because he was inside and staying. And before the townspeople could guess what he was going to do, George pitched the key over their heads and into the St. Joe. It was so quiet, everyone could hear the splash.

Afterwards, there was a lot of talk. Some said George hadn't shown the proper respect for a symbol of the town's esteem. Some said the gesture was too flashy and didn't suit the occasion. But most of the people of Frederick agreed that what George had done was as right as what he had said, even though the town would have to come up with another key.

Bess Frederick said, "Of course George Bailey doesn't need a key. He'd be just the one to come in a window." People didn't mind her anymore. Things had settled down and George Bailey was setting up to fish. While he was situating himself on his river rock, Bess was standing on her screened-in porch, watching. For weeks after that, anyone on the bridge above George could glance up and see Bess Frederick looking down on him.

Finally, with Beamer in tow, she came out of her house and walked across the bridge. Beamer helped Bess pick her way down the bank, through the weeds, past the boys' abandoned tent and the rising stink of grass rotting. When she reached the rock above George's, Bess shook Beamer off and called out, loud enough for anyone on the bridge to hear, "You want that key after all, don't you, George Bailey?"

George didn't even look over his shoulder. He said, "I fished it out five times already. And every time, I threw the damned thing back—what do you think?"

For a minute, Bess stood above him, looking from neck to hem like a cylinder of blue metal. As she watched him start to reel in his line, her voice went ringing out. "If you were my son," she said, "I'd know exactly what to think." Beamer took ahold of her and led her back up the bank.

Since then, she's decided what she thinks, and takes advantage of every opportunity to say it. People let her talk. Frederick isn't so small, they say, that it can't contain George Bailey fishing and Bess Frederick saying what she thinks right across the river from each other with nothing but a bridge between them.

Barbara Kingsolver

ROSE-JOHNNY

(from *The Virginia Quarterly Review*)

Rose-Johnny wore a man's haircut and terrified little children, although I will never believe that was her intention. For her own part
she inspired in us only curiosity. It was our mothers who took this
fascination and wrung it, through daily admonitions, into the most
irresistible kind of horror. She was like the old wells, covered with
ancient rotting boards and overgrown with weeds, that waited behind the barns to swallow us down: our mothers warned us time and
again not to go near them and still were certain that we did.

My own mother was not one of those who had a great deal to say
about her, but Walnut Knobs was a small enough town that a person
did not need to be told things directly. When I had my first good
look at her, at close range, I was ten years old. I fully understood the
importance of the encounter.

What mattered to me at the time, though, was that it was something my sister had not done before me. She was five years older, and
as a consequence there was hardly an achievement in my life, nor
even an article of clothing, that had not first been Mary Etta's. But
because of the circumstances of my meeting Rose-Johnny I couldn't
tell a living soul about it, and so for nearly a year I carried the secret
torment of a great power that can't be used. My agitation was not
relieved but made worse when I told the story to myself, over and
over again.

She was not, as we always heard, half-man and half-woman, something akin to the pagan creatures whose naked torsos are inserted in
various shocking ways into parts of animal bodies. In fact, I was as-

tonished by her ordinariness. It is true that she wore Red Wing boots like my father. And also, there was something not quite womanly in her face, but maybe any woman's face would look the same with that haircut. I am sure that was what did it, even though her same head of hair, on a man, you wouldn't look at again: coal black, cut flat across the top of her round head so that when she looked down I could see a faint pale spot right on top where the scalp almost surfaced.

But the rest of her looked exactly like anybody's mother in a big flowered dress without a waistline and with two faded spots in front, where her bosom rubbed over the counter when she reached across to make change or wipe away the dust.

People say there is a reason for every important thing that happens. I was sent to the feed store, where I spoke to Rose-Johnny and passed a quarter from my hand into hers, because it was haying time. And because I was small for my age. I was not too small to help with tobacco setting in the spring; in fact I was better at it than Mary Etta who complained about the stains on her hands, but I was not yet big enough to throw a bale of hay onto the flatbed. It was the time of year when Daddy complained about not having boys. Mama said that at least he oughtn't to bother going into town for the chicken mash that day because Georgeann could do it on her way home from school.

Mama told me to ask Aunt Minnie to please ma'am give me a ride home. "Ask her nice to stop off at Lester Wall's store so you can run in with this quarter and get five pounds of laying mash."

I put the quarter in my pocket, keeping my eye out to make certain Mary Etta understood what I had been asked to do. Mary Etta had once told me that I was no better than the bugs that suck on potato vines, and that the family was going to starve to death because of my laziness. It was one of the summer days when we were on our knees in the garden picking off bugs and dropping them into cans of coal oil. She couldn't go into town with Aunt Minnie to look at dress patterns until we finished with the potato bugs. What she said, exactly, was that if I couldn't work any harder than that, then she had just as well throw *me* into a can of coal oil. Later she told me she hadn't meant it, but I intended to remember it nonetheless.

Aunt Minnie taught the first grade and had a 1951 Dodge. This is how she referred to her car whenever she spoke of it. It was the newest automobile belonging to anyone related to us, although some of the Wilcox cousins had once come down to visit from Knoxville in a Ford they were said to have bought the same year it was made. But I saw that car and did not find it nearly as impressive as Aunt Minnie's, which was white and immense and shone like glass. She paid a boy to polish it every other Saturday.

On the day she took me to Wall's, she waited in the car while I went inside with my fist tight around the quarter. I had never been in the store before, and although I had passed by it many times and knew what could be bought there, I had never imagined what a wonderful combination of warm, sweet smells of mash and animals and seed corn it would contain. The dust lay white and thin on everything like a bridal veil. Rose-Johnny was in the back with a water can, leaning over into one of the chick tubs. The steel rang with the sound of confined baby birds, and a light bulb shining up from inside the tub made her face glow white. Mr. Wall, Rose-Johnny's pa, was in the front of the store talking to two men about a horse. He didn't notice me as I crept up to the counter. It was Rose-Johnny who came forward to the cash register.

"And what for you, Missy?"

She is exactly like anybody's Mama, was all I could think, and I wanted to reach and touch her flowered dress. The two men were looking at me.

"My mama needs five pound of laying mash, and here's a quarter for it." I clicked the coin quickly onto the counter.

"Yes, Ma'am." She smiled at me, but her boots made heavy, tired sounds on the floor. She made her way slowly, like a duck in water, over the row of wooden bins that stood against the wall. She scooped the mash into a paper bag and weighed it, then shoved the scoop back into the bin. A little cloud of dust rose out of the mash up into the window. I watched her from the counter.

"Don't your mama know she's wasting good money on chicken mash? Any fool chicken will eat corn." I jumped when the man spoke. It was one of the two, and they were standing so close behind me I would have had to look right straight up to see their faces. Mr. Wall was gone.

"No, sir, they need mash," I said to the man's boots.

"What's that?" It was the taller man doing the talking.

"They need mash," I said louder. "To lay good sturdy eggs for selling. A little mash mixed in with the corn. Mama says it's got oyster shells in it."

"Is that a fact," he said. "Did you hear that, Rose-Johnny?" he called out. "This child says you put oyster shells in that mash. Is that right?"

When Rose-Johnny came back to the cash register, she was moon-eyed. She made quick motions with her hands and pushed the bag at me as if she didn't know how to talk.

"Do you catch them oysters yourself, Rose-Johnny? Up at Jackson Crick?" The man was laughing. The other man was quiet.

Rose-Johnny looked all around and up at the ceiling. She scratched at her short hair, fast and hard like a dog with ticks.

When the two men were gone, I stood on my toes and leaned over the counter as far as I could. "Do you catch the oysters yourself?"

She hooked her eyes right into mine. The way the bit goes into the mule's mouth and fits just so, one way and no other. Her eyes were the palest blue of any I had ever seen. Then she threw back her head and laughed so hard I could see the wide, flat bottoms of her back teeth, and I wasn't afraid of her.

When I left the store, the two men were still outside. Their boots scuffed on the front porch floor boards, and the shorter one spoke.

"Child, how much did you pay that woman for the chicken mash?"

"A quarter," I told him.

He put a quarter in my hand. "You take this here, and go home and tell your daddy something. Tell him not never to send his little girls to Wall's feed store. Tell him to send his boys if he has to, but not his little girls." His hat was off, and his hair lay back in wet orange strips. A clean line separated the white top of his forehead from the red-burned hide of his face. In this way, it was like my father's face.

"No, sir, I can't tell him, because all my daddy's got is girls."

"That's George Bowles' child, Bud," the tall man said. "He's just got the two girls."

"Then tell him to come for his self," Bud said. His eyes had the sun in them, and looked like a pair of new pennies.

Aunt Minnie didn't see the man give me the quarter because she was looking at herself in the side-view mirror of the Dodge. Aunt Minnie was older than Mama, but everyone mistook her for the younger because of the way she fixed herself up. And of course, Mama was married. Mama said if Aunt Minnie ever found a man she would act her age.

When I climbed in the car, she was pulling gray hairs out of her part. She said it was teaching school that caused them, but early gray ran in my mama's family.

She jumped when I slammed the car door. "All set?"

"Yes, ma'am," I said. She put her little purple hat back on her head and slowly pushed the long pin through it. I shuddered as she started up the car.

Aunt Minnie laughed. "Somebody walked over your grave."

"I don't have a grave," I said. "I'm not dead."

"No, you most certainly are not. That's just what they say, when a person shivers like that." She smiled. I liked Aunt Minnie most of the time. "I don't think they mean your real grave, with you in it," she said after a minute. "I think it means the place where your grave is going to be some day."

I thought about this for awhile. I tried to picture the place, but could not. Then I thought about the two men outside Wall's store. I asked Aunt Minnie why it was all right for boys to do some things that girls couldn't.

"Oh, there's all kinds of reasons," she said. "Like what kinds of things, do you mean?"

"Like going into Wall's feed store."

"Who told you that?"

"Somebody."

Aunt Minnie didn't say anything.

Then I said, "It's because of Rose-Johnny, isn't it?"

Aunt Minnie raised her chin just a tiny bit. She might have been checking her lipstick in the mirror, or she might have been saying yes.

"Why?" I asked.

"Why what?"

"Why because of Rose-Johnny?"

"I can't tell you that, Georgeann."

"Why can't you tell me?" I whined. "Tell me."

The car rumbled over a cattle grate. When we came to the crossing, Aunt Minnie stepped on the brake so hard we both flopped forward. She looked at me. "Georgeann, Rose-Johnny is a Lebanese.

That's all I'm going to tell you. You'll understand better when you're older."

When I got home, I put the laying mash in the hen house. The hens were already roosting high above my head, clucking softly into their feathers and shifting back and forth on their feet. I collected the eggs as I did every day, and took them into the house. I hadn't yet decided what to do about the quarter, and so I held onto it until dinner time.

Mary Etta was late coming down, and even though she had washed and changed she looked pale as a haunt from helping with the haying all day. She didn't speak and hardly ate.

"Here girls, both of you, eat up these potatoes," Mama said after awhile. "There's not but just a little bit left. Something to grow on."

"I don't need none then," Mary Etta said. "I've done growed all I'm going to grow."

"Don't talk back to your mama," Daddy said.

"I'm not talking back. It's the truth." Mary Etta looked at Mama. "Well, it is."

"Eat a little bite, Mary Etta. Just because you're in the same dresses for a year don't mean you're not going to grow no more."

"I'm as big as you are, Mama."

"All right then." Mama scraped the mashed potatoes onto my plate. "I expect now you'll be telling me you don't want to grow no more either," she said to me.

"No, ma'am, I won't," I said. But I was distressed, and looked sideways at the pink shirtwaist I had looked forward to inheriting along with the grown-up shape that would have to be worn inside it. Now it appeared that I was condemned to my present clothes and potato-shaped body; keeping these forever seemed to me far more likely than the possibility of having clothes that, like the Wilcox automobile, had never before been owned. I ate my potatoes quietly. Dinner was almost over when Daddy asked if I had remembered to get the laying mash.

"Yes, sir. I put it in the hen house." I hesitated. "And here's the quarter back. Mr. Wall gave me the mash for nothing."

"Why did he do that?" Mama asked.

Mary Etta was staring like the dead. Even her hair looked tired, slumped over the back of her chair like a long black shadow.

"I helped him out," I said. "Rose-Johnny wasn't there, she was sick, and Mr. Wall said if I would help him clean out the bins and dust the shelves and water the chicks, then it wouldn't cost me for the laying mash."

"And Aunt Minnie waited while you did all that?"

"She didn't mind," I said. "She had some magazines to look at."

It was the first important lie I had told in my life, and I was thrilled with its power. Every member of my family believed I had brought home the laying mash in exchange for honest work.

I was also astonished at how my story, once I had begun it, wouldn't finish. "He wants me to come back and help him again the next time we need something," I said.

"I don't reckon you let on like we couldn't pay for the mash?" Daddy asked, stern.

"No sir. I put the quarter right up there on the counter. But he said he needed the help. Rose-Johnny's real sick."

He looked at me like he knew. Like he had found the hole in the coop where the black snake was getting in. But he just said, "All right. You can go, if Aunt Minnie don't mind waiting for you."

"You don't have to say a thing to her about it," I said. "I can walk home the same as I do every day. Five pound of mash isn't nothing to carry."

"We'll see," Mama said.

That night I believed I would burst. For a long time after Mary Etta fell asleep I twisted in my blankets and told the story over to myself, both the true and false versions. I talked to my doll, Miss Regina. She was a big doll, a birthday present from my Grandma and Grandpa Bowles, with a tiny wire crown and lovely long blond curls.

"Rose-Johnny isn't really sick," I told Miss Regina. "She's a Lebanese."

I looked up the word in Aunt Minnie's Bible dictionary after school. I pretended to be looking up St. John the Baptist but then turned over in a hurry to the "L's" while she was washing her chalkboards. My heart thumped when I found it, but I read the passage quickly, several times over, and found it empty. It said the Lebanese were a seafaring people who built great ships from cedar trees. I couldn't believe that even when I was older I would be able, as Aunt

Minnie promised, to connect this with what I had seen of Rose-Johnny. Nevertheless, I resolved to understand. The following week I went back to the store, confident that my lie would continue to carry its own weight.

Rose-Johnny recognized me. "Five pounds of laying mash," she said, and this time I followed her to the feed bins. There were flecks of white dust in her hair.

"Is it true you come from over the sea?" I asked her quietly as she bent over with the scoop.

She laughed and rolled her eyes. "A lot of them says I come from the moon," she said, and I was afraid she was going to be struck dumb and animal-eyed as she was the time before. But when she finished weighing the bag, she just said, "I was born in Slate Holler, that's all. That's as far from here as I ever been or will be."

"Is that where you get the oysters from?" I asked, looking into the mash and trying to pick out which of the colored flecks they might be.

Rose-Johnny looked at me for a long time, and then suddenly laughed her big laugh. "Why, honey child, don't you know? Oysters comes from the sea."

She rang up twenty-five cents on the register, but I didn't look at her.

"That was all, wasn't it?"

I leaned over the counter and tried to put tears in my eyes, but they wouldn't come. "I can't pay," I said. "My daddy said to ask you if I could do some work for it. Clean up, or something."

"Your daddy said to ask me that? Well, bless your heart," she said. "Let me see if we can't find something for you to do. Bless your little heart, child, what's your name?"

"Georgeann," I told her.

"I'm Rose-Johnny," she said, and I did not say that I knew this, that like every other child I had known it since the first time I saw her in town, when I was five or six, and asked Mama if it was a man or a lady.

"Pleased to meet you," I said.

We kept it between the two of us: I came in every week to help with the pullets and the feed, and took home my mash. We did not tell Mr. Wall, although it seemed it would not have mattered one whit to him. Mr. Wall was in the store so seldom that he might not have known I was there. He kept to himself in the apartment at the back where he and Rose-Johnny lived.

It was she who ran the store, kept the accounts, and did the orders. She showed me how to feed and water the pullets and ducklings and pull out the sick ones. Later I learned how to weigh out packages of seed and to mix the different kinds of mash. There were lists nailed to the wall telling how much cracked corn and oats and grit to put in. I followed the recipes with enormous care, adding tiny amounts at a time to the bag on the hanging scales until the needle touched the right number. Although she was patient with me, I felt slow next to Rose-Johnny, who never had to look at the lists and used the scales only to check herself. It seemed to me she knew how to do more things than anyone I had ever known, woman or man.

She also knew the names of all the customers, although she rarely spoke to them. Sometimes such a change came over her when the men were there that it wasn't clear to me whether she was pretending or had really lost the capacity to speak. But afterward she would tell me their names and everything about them. Once she told me about Ed Charney Senior and Bud Mattox, the two men I had seen the first day I was in the store. According to Rose-Johnny, Ed had an old red mule he was in the habit of mistreating. "But even so," she said, "Ed's mule don't have it as bad as Bud's wife." I never knew how she acquired this knowledge.

When she said "Bud Mattox," I remembered his penny-colored eyes and connected him then with all the Mattox boys at school. It had never occurred to me that eyes could run in families, like early gray.

Occasionally a group of black-skinned children came to the store, always after hours. Rose-Johnny opened up for them. She called each child by name, and asked after their families and the health of their mother's laying hens.

The oldest one, whose name was Cleota, was shaped like Mary Etta. Her hair was straight and pointed, and smelled to me like citronella candles. The younger girls had plaits that curved out from their heads like so many handles. Several of them wore dresses made from the same bolt of cloth, but they were not sisters. Rose-Johnny filled a separate order for each child.

I watched but didn't speak. The skin on their heels and palms was

creased, and as light as my own. Once, after they had left, I asked
Rose-Johnny why they came into the store when it was closed.

"People's got their ways," she said, stoking up the wood stove for
the night. Then she told me all their names again, starting with
Cleota and working down. She looked me in the eye. "When you
see them in town, you speak. Do you hear? By name. I don't care
who is watching."

I was allowed to spend half an hour or more with Rose-Johnny
nearly every day after school, so long as I did not neglect my chores
at home. Sometimes on days that were rainy or cold Aunt Minnie
would pick me up, but I preferred to walk. By myself, without Mary
Etta to hurry me up.

As far as I know, my parents believed I was helping Mr. Wall because of Rose-Johnny's illness. They had no opportunity to learn
otherwise, though I worried that some day Aunt Minnie would
come inside the store to fetch me, instead of just honking, or that
Daddy would have to go to Wall's for something and see for himself
that Rose-Johnny was fit and well. Come springtime he would be
needing to buy tobacco seed.

It was soon after Christmas when I became consumed with a desire to confess. I felt the lies down inside me like cold, dirty potatoes
in a root cellar, beginning to sprout and crowd. At night I told Miss
Regina of my dishonesty and the things that were likely to happen
to me because of it. In so doing, there were several times I nearly
confessed by accident to Mary Etta.

"Who's going to wring your neck?" she wanted to know, coming
into the room one night when I thought she was downstairs washing the supper dishes.

"Nobody," I said, clutching Miss Regina to my pillow. I pretended
to be asleep. I could hear Mary Etta starting to brush her hair. Every
night before she went to bed she sat with her dress hiked up and her
head hung over between her knees, brushing her hair all the way
down to the floor. This improved the circulation to the hair, she told
me, and would prevent it turning. Mary Etta was already beginning
to get white hairs.

"Is it because Mama let you watch Daddy kill the cockerels? Did
it scare you to see them jump around like that with their necks
broke?"

"I'm not scared," I murmured, but I wanted so badly to tell the truth that I started to cry. I knew, for certain, that something bad was going to happen. I believe I also knew it would happen to my sister, instead of me.

"Nobody's going to hurt you," Mary Etta said. She smoothed my bangs and laid my pigtails down flat on top of the quilt. "Give me Miss Regina and let me put her up for you now, so you won't get her hair all messed up."

I let her have the doll. "I'm not scared about the cockerels, Mary Etta. I promise." With my finger, under the covers, I traced a cross over my heart.

When Rose-Johnny fell ill, I was sick with guilt. When I first saw Mr. Wall behind the counter instead of Rose-Johnny, so help me God, I prayed this would be the day Aunt Minnie would come inside to get me. Immediately after, I felt sure God would kill me for my wickedness. I pictured myself falling dead beside the oat bin. I begged Mr. Wall to let me see her.

"Go on back, littl'un. She told me you'd be coming in," he said.

I had never been in the apartment before. There was little in it beyond the necessary things and a few old photographs on the walls, all of the same woman. The rooms were cold and felt infused with sickness and an odor I incorrectly believed to be medicine. Because my father didn't drink, I had never before encountered the smell of whiskey.

Rose-Johnny was propped on the pillows in a lifeless flannel gown. Her face changed when she saw me, and I remembered the way her face was lit by the light bulb in the chick tub, the first time I saw her. With fresh guilt I threw myself on her bosom.

"I'm sorry. I could have paid for the mash. I didn't mean to make you sick." Through my sobs I heard accusing needly wheezing sounds in Rose-Johnny's chest. She breathed with a great pulling effort.

"Child, don't talk foolish."

As weeks passed and Rose-Johnny didn't improve, it became clear that my lie was prophetic. Without Rose-Johnny to run the store, Mr. Wall badly needed my help. He seemed mystified by his inventory and was rendered helpless by any unusual demand from a customer. It was March, the busiest time for the store. I had turned eleven one week before Mary Etta turned sixteen. These seven days out of each year, during which she was only four years older, I considered to be God's greatest gift to me.

The afternoon my father would come in to buy the vegetable garden and tobacco seed was an event I had rehearsed endlessly in my mind. When it finally did transpire, Mr. Wall's confusion gave such complete respectability to my long-standing lie that I didn't need to say a word myself in support of it. I waited on him with dignity, precisely weighing out his tobacco seed, and even recommended to him the white runner beans that Mr. Wall had accidentally overstocked, and which my father did not buy.

Later on that same afternoon, after the winter light had come slanting through the dusty windows and I was alone in the store cleaning up, Cleota and the other children came pecking at the glass. I let them in. When I had filled all the orders Cleota unwrapped their coins, knotted all together into a blue handkerchief. I counted, and counted again. It was not the right amount, not even half.

"That's what Miss Rose-Johnny ast us for it," Cleota said. "Same as always." The smaller children—Venise, Anita, Little-Roy, James—shuffled and elbowed each other like fighting cocks, paying no attention. Cleota gazed at me calmly, steadily. Her eyebrows were two perfect arches.

"I thank you very much," I said, and put the coins in their proper places in the cash drawer.

During that week I also discovered an epidemic of chick droop in the pullets. I had to pull Mr. Wall over by the hand to make him look. There were more sick ones than well.

"It's because it's so cold in the store," I told him. "They can't keep warm. Can't we make it warmer in here?"

Mr. Wall shrugged at the wood stove, helpless. He could never keep a fire going for long, the way Rose-Johnny could.

"We have to try. The one light bulb isn't enough," I said. The chicks were huddled around the bulb just the way the men would collect around the stove in the mornings to say howdy do to Mr. Wall and warm up their hands on the way to work. Except the chicks were more ruthless: they climbed and shoved, and the healthy ones pecked at the eyes and feet of the sick ones, making them bleed.

I had not noticed before what a very old man Mr. Wall was. As he stared down at the light, I saw that his eyes were covered with a film. "How do we fix them up?" he asked me.

"We can't. We've got to take the sick ones out so they won't all get it. Rose-Johnny puts them in that tub over there. We give them water and keep them warm, but it don't do any good. They've got to die."

He looked so sad, I stood and patted his old freckled hand.

I spent much more time than before at the store, but no longer enjoyed it particularly. Working in the shadow of Rose-Johnny's expertise, I had been a secret witness to a wondrous ritual of counting, weighing, and tending. Together we created little packages that sailed out like ships to all parts of the country, giving rise to gardens and barnyard life in places I had never even seen. I felt superior to my schoolmates, knowing that I had had a hand in the creation of their families' poultry flocks and their mother's kitchen gardens. By contrast, Mr. Wall's bewilderment was pathetic and only increased my guilt. But each day I was able to spend a little time in the back rooms with Rose-Johnny.

There were rumors about her illness, both before and after the fact. It did not occur to me that I might have been the source of some of the earlier rumors. But if I didn't think of this, it was because Walnut Knobs was overrun with tales of Rose-Johnny, and not because I didn't take notice of the stories. I did.

The tales that troubled me most were about Rose-Johnny's daddy. I had heard many adults say that he was responsible for her misfortune, which I presumed to mean her short hair. But it was said that he was a colored man, and this I knew to be untrue. Aunt Minnie, when I pressed her, would offer nothing more than that if it were up to her I wouldn't go near either one of them, advice which I ignored. I was coming to understand that I would not hear the truth about Rose-Johnny from Aunt Minnie or anyone else; I knew, in a manner that went beyond the meanings of words I could not understand, that she was no more masculine than my mother or aunt, and no more lesbian than Lebanese. Rose-Johnny was simply herself, and alone.

And yet she was such a capable woman that I couldn't believe she would be sick for very long. But as the warm weather came she grew sluggish and pale. Her slow, difficult breathing frightened me. I brought my schoolbooks and read to her from the foot of the bed.

Sometimes the rather ordinary adventures of the boy in my reader would make her laugh aloud until she choked. Other times she fell asleep while I read, but then would make me read those parts over again.

She worried about the store. Frequently she would ask about Mr. Wall, and the customers, and how he was managing. "He does all right," I always said. But eventually my eagerness to avoid the burden of further lies, along with the considerable force of my pride, led me to confess that I had to tell him nearly everything. "He forgets, something awful," I told her.

Rose-Johnny smiled. "He used to be as smart as anything, and taught me. Now I've done taught you, and you him again," She was lying back on the pillows with her eyes closed and her plump hands folded on her stomach.

"But he's a nice man," I said. I listened to her breathing. "He don't hurt you, does he? Your pa?"

Nothing moved except her eyelids. They opened and let the blue eyes out at me. I looked down and traced my finger over the triangles of the Flying Geese patch on the quilt. I whispered, "Does he make you cut off your hair?"

Rose-Johnny's eyes were so pale they were almost white, like ice with water running underneath. "He cuts it with a butcher knife. Sometimes he chases me all the way down to the river." She laughed a hissing laugh like a boy, and she had the same look the yearling calves get when they are cornered and jump the corral and run to the woods and won't be butchered. I understood then that Rose-Johnny, too, knew the power of a lie.

It was the youngest Mattox boy who started the fight at school on the Monday after Easter. He was older than me, and a boy, so nobody believed he would hit me, but when he started the name calling I called them right back, and he threw me down on the ground. The girls screamed and ran to get the teacher, but by the time she arrived I had a bloody nose and had bitten his arm wonderfully hard.

Miss Althea gave me her handkerchief for my nose and dragged Roy Mattox inside to see the principal. All the other children stood in a circle, looking at me.

"It isn't true, what he said," I told them. "And not about Rose-Johnny either. She isn't a pervert. I love her."

"Pervert," one of the boys said.

I marveled at the sight of my own blood soaking through the handkerchief. "I love her," I said.

I did not get to see Rose-Johnny that day. The door of Wall's store was locked. I could see Mr. Wall through the window, though, so I banged on the glass with the flats of my hands until he came. He had the strong medicine smell on his breath.

"Not today, littl'un." The skin under his eyes was dark blue.

"I need to see Rose-Johnny." I was irritated with Mr. Wall, and did not consider him important enough to prevent me from seeing her. But evidently he was.

"Not today," he said. "We're closed." He shut the door and locked it.

I shouted at him through the glass. "Tell her I hit a boy and bit his arm, that was calling her names. Tell her I fought with a boy, Mr. Wall."

The next day the door was open, but I didn't see him in the store. In the back, the apartment was dark except for the lamp by Rose-Johnny's bed. A small brown bottle and a glass stood just touching each other on the night table. Rose-Johnny looked asleep but made a snuffing sound when I climbed onto the bottom of the bed.

"Did your daddy tell you what I told him yesterday?"

She said nothing.

"Is your daddy sick?"

"My daddy's dead," she said suddenly, causing me to swallow a little gulp of air. She opened her eyes, then closed them again. "Pa's all right, honey, just stepped out, I imagine." She stopped to breathe between every few words. "I didn't mean to give you a fright. Pa's not my daddy. He's my mama's daddy."

I was confused. "And your real daddy's dead?"

She nodded. "Long time."

"And your mama, what about her? Is she dead too?"

"Mm-hmm," she said, in the same lazy sort of way Mama would say it when she wasn't really listening.

"That her?" I pointed to the picture over the bed. The woman's shoulders were bare except for a dark lace shawl. She was looking backwards towards you, over her shoulder.

Rose-Johnny looked at the picture, and said yes it was.

"She's pretty," I said.

"People used to say I looked just like her." Rose-Johnny laughed a wheezy laugh, and coughed.

"Why did she die?"

Rose-Johnny shook her head. "I can't tell you that."

"Can you when I'm older?" She didn't answer. "Well then, if Mr. Wall isn't your daddy, then the colored man is your daddy," I said, mostly to myself.

She looked at me. "Is that what they say?"

I shrugged.

"Does no harm to me. Every man is some color," she said.

"Oh," I said.

"My daddy was white. After he died my mama loved another man and he was brown."

"What happened then?"

"What happened then," she said. "Then, they had a sweet little baby Johnny." Her voice was more like singing than talking, and her eyes were so peacefully closed I was afraid they might not open again. Every time she breathed there was the sound of a hundred tiny birds chirping inside her chest.

"Where's he?"

"Mama's Rose and sweet little baby Johnny," she sang it like an old song. "Not nothing bad going to happen to them, not nobody going to take them." A silvery moth flew into the lamp and clicked against the inside of the lampshade. Rose-Johnny stretched out her hand toward the night table. "I want you to pour me some of that bottle."

I lifted the bottle carefully and poured a glass half full. "That your medicine?" I asked. No answer. I feared this would be another story without an end, without meaning. "Did somebody take your mama's babies?" I persisted.

"Took her man, is what they did, and hung him up from a tree." She sat up slowly on her elbows, and looked straight at me. "Do you know what lynched is?"

"Yes, ma'am," I said, although until that moment I had not been sure.

"People will tell you there's never been no lynchings north of where the rivers don't freeze over. But they done it. Do you know where Jackson Crick is, up there by Floyd's Mill?" I nodded. "They lynched him up there, and drowned her baby Johnny in Jackson Crick, and it was as froze as you're ever going to see it. They had to break a hole in the ice to do it." She would not stop looking right into me. "In that river. Poor little baby in that cold river. Poor Mama, what they did to Mama. And said they would do to me, when I got old enough."

She didn't drink the medicine I poured for her, but let it sit. I was afraid to hear any more, and afraid to leave. I watched the moth crawl up the outside of the lampshade.

And then, out of the clear blue, she sat up and said, "But they didn't do a thing to me!" The way she said it, she sounded more like she ought to be weighing out bags of mash, than sick in bed. "Do you want to know what Mama did?"

I didn't say.

"I'll tell you what she did. She took her scissors and cut my hair right off, every bit of it. She said, 'From now on, I want you to be Rose and Johnny both.' And then she went down to the same hole in the crick where they put baby Johnny in."

I sat with Rose-Johnny for a long time. I patted the lump in the covers where her knees were, and wiped my nose on my sleeve. "You'd better drink your medicine, Rose-Johnny," I said. "Drink up and get better now," I told her. "It's all over now."

It was the last time I saw Rose-Johnny. The next time I saw the store, more than a month later, it was locked and boarded up. Later on, the Londroski brothers took it over. Some people said she had died. Others thought she and Mr. Wall had gone to live somewhere up in the Blue Ridge, and opened a store there. This is the story I believed. In the years since, when passing through that part of the country, I have never failed to notice the Plymouth Rocks and Rhode Islands scratching in the yards, and the tomato vines tied up around the back doors.

I would like to stop here and say no more, but there are enough half-true stories in my past. This one will have to be heard to the end.

Whatever became of Rose-Johnny and her grandfather, I am certain that their going away had something to do with what happened on that same evening to Mary Etta. And I knew this to be my fault.

It was late when I got home. As I walked I turned Rose-Johnny's story over and over, like Grandpa Bowles's Indian penny with the head on both sides. You never could stop turning it over.

When I caught sight of Mama standing like somebody's ghost in the front doorway I thought she was going to thrash me, but she didn't. Instead she ran out into the yard and picked me up like she used to when I was a little girl, and carried me into the house.

"Where's Daddy?" I asked. It was supper time but there was no supper.

"Daddy's gone looking for you in the truck. He'll be back directly, when he don't find you."

"Why's he looking for me? What did I do?"

"Georgeann, some men tried to hurt Mary Etta. We don't know why they done it, but we was afraid they might try to hurt you."

"No, ma'am, nobody hurt me," I said quietly. "Did they kill her?" I asked.

"Oh Lordy no," Mama said, and hugged me. "She's all right. You can go upstairs and see her, but don't bother her if she don't want to be bothered."

Our room was dark, and Mary Etta was in bed crying. "Can I turn on the little light?" I asked. I wanted to see Mary Etta. I was afraid that some part of her might be missing.

"If you want to."

She was all there; arms, legs, hair. Her face was swollen, and there were marks on her neck.

"Don't stare at me," she said.

"I'm sorry." I looked around the room. Her dress was hanging over the chair. It was her best dress, the solid green linen with colored buttons and attached petticoat that had taken her all winter to make. It was red with dirt and torn nearly in half at the bodice.

"I'll fix your dress. Mary Etta. I can't sew as good as you, but I can mend," I said.

"Can't be mended," she said, but then tried to smile with her swollen mouth. "You can help me make another one."

"Who was it that done it?" I asked.

"I don't know." She rolled over and faced the wallpaper. "Some men. Three or four of them. Some of them might have been boys, I couldn't tell for sure. They had things over their faces."

"What kinds of things?"

"I don't know. Just bandanners and things," she spoke quietly to the wall. "You know how the Mattoxes have those funny-colored eyes? I think some of them might have been Mattoxes. Don't tell, Georgeann. Promise."

I remembered the feeling of Roy Mattox's muscle in my teeth. I did not promise.

"Did you hit them?"

"No. I screamed. Mr. Dorsey come along the road."

"What did they say, before you screamed?"

"Nothing. They just kept saying, 'Are you the Bowles girl, are you the Bowles girl?' And they said nasty things."

"It was me they was looking for," I said. And no matter what anyone said, I would not believe otherwise. I took to my bed and would not eat or speak to anyone. My convalescence was longer than Mary Etta's. It was during that time that I found my sister's sewing scissors and cut off all my hair and all of Miss Regina's. I said that my name was George-Etta, not Georgeann, and I called my doll Rose-Johnny.

For the most part, my family tolerated my distress. My mother retrimmed my hair as neatly as she could, but there was little that could be done. Every time I looked in the mirror I was startled and secretly pleased to see that I looked exactly like a little boy. Mama said that when I went back to school I would have to do the explaining for myself. Aunt Minnie said I was going through a stage and oughtn't to be pampered.

But there was only a month left of school, and my father let Mary Etta and me stay home to help set tobacco. By the end of the summer, my hair had grown out sufficiently so that no explanations were needed. Miss Regina's hair, of course, never grew back.

Jim Hall

GAS

(from *The Georgia Review*)

She'd thought it would be a gas to come home to Buck's Gap and put up a show. Visit her dad, shock the natives, maybe walk through a field, pick wildflowers—goofy rural stuff. Then get back to L.A. and tell Buck's Gap stories for the next six months. But here she was in her dad's kitchen baking dog biscuits.

Warhol, the family's ancient retriever, had lost his teeth. Now even Kibbles were too hard, wet food had some kind of ash or something that stirred up his liver problems, and the special vet food was too expensive. So she'd modified her chocolate-chip cookie recipe, dumping crumbs of ground round into the batter and then forming the nuggets into bone shapes. Almost immediately Warhol had become addicted to them, nosing her in the butt from the minute she got up around noon till four the next morning, prompting her to hand over another baked bone.

Her Clothing Art Show was supposed to go on at five-thirty that afternoon at Farmers Bank and Trust, but here she was at five o'-clock, peeking in the oven, trying to keep Warhol blissed out.

Her dad had been just as bad. The whole three days she'd been home, he'd been tagging along behind her soon as she was up, planting himself in the same room with her, carrying along whatever he was whittling at the moment. Droning on in that hillbilly voice about whatever batted through his mind. She loved him, sure, but sometimes he was too country to take seriously. Somewhere between Gomer Pyle and Li'l Abner.

She'd not walked through a single field since she'd come home, she was so busy baking bones and cleaning up her dad's little piles of shavings. At that moment he was sanding the edges and grooves of a chunk of walnut the size of a baseball and shaped into a perfect replica of a human brain.

"Kuru," he said, while Warhol swept his tail across the kitchen floor, flat on his stomach looking up at her. "Kuru's a disease that affects only the natives of New Guinea."

"Daddy-O," she said, turning the temperature off on the oven, "I got to get my things together for the show."

"It's a disease of laughter. They begin laughing and can't stop, can't eat, can't sleep or drink water or make love. I'd heard of hic-cupping to death, but this I hadn't heard of till I saw it on the TV. Damndest thing."

"It's wild all right," Tina Blue said. "Now I got to get my act in gear. You're coming, right?"

Her father pulled his penknife out of his pants pocket, opened it, dug out a small trail along the top of the brain.

"I hadn't got this medulla oblongata just right." He shook his head, frowned at the brain. "Course I'm coming, Tina Blue. Course."

"You'll freak," she said.

"I bet I will."

Tina Blue spent from five to five-fifteen stacking and spraying her black hair before studding the whole goopy mess with feathers and rhinestones. She put on a leopard leotard, then an aquamarine-and-fuchsia nun's robe on top. She carried a small leather shield that was actually a purse—she called it "the bicoastal-gladiator-bag." And she'd put on a few rubber rings and a necklace she'd made from the shells of dime-store turtles.

"That's a get-up," her father said as she came into the living room. She did a modeling spin, then a robot mechanical walk. The L.A. high-tech strut.

On their way down to the bank, her dad driving the Hudson he'd kept alive all these years, Tina Blue picked up her father's walnut brain from the seat and turned it this way and that.

"Dad, you're weirder than I am."

"Naw," he said.

"Why'd you want to do a brain?"

"I'm interested in them," he said. "That disease, kuru?"

"Yeah?"

"I wouldn't mind going that way, you know." He stopped in the middle of the street. No traffic light, no stop sign.

Tina Blue turned to check out the back window. A car had stopped behind them. The man waited a minute, then passed them slowly, smiling at her daddy and saying, "Howdy."

"But the only way the New Guineas get kuru is by eating human brains."

"Jesus, Daddy-O."

"I draw the line there. Not even to die laughing." He put the Hudson Wasp in gear and started off again.

"It's funny," she said. "In New York the audiences were frigid. I called them SoHo cool. They walk in, not saying a word about the show, and drink champagne—all of them dressed to the tenth power, very intellectually distant. Nobody wanting to crack a pose. It's like a high-school party when everybody was afraid to blow it. Out in L.A., man, they say whatever they think. Great things like, these are the kind of things a mass murderer has nightmares about. Or like how the only people who could actually wear clothes like mine would be the guys fighting for the Martian heavyweight wrestling championship. They get in there and try to outdo each other with smart remarks. I love it."

"When you get right down to it," he said, "I guess why I do it— carving so many brains—it's because of how Freddy Red turned out."

"Oh, God," Tina Blue groaned.

Freddy Red was her older brother. He'd been born with cretinism—some kind of thyroid disorder: wide flat saddle nose, tongue always hanging out, bloated belly, skin as coarse as a cedar plank, and thick hands and fingers. He was off in West Virginia living in a big hospital for people like him. Tina Blue had never visited him because, she told herself, she didn't want to stir him all up. She'd maybe said three words to him when she was little, just learning to talk, before they sent him off.

"It's given me an interest in brains," her father said.

She set the carving on the seat between them and looked out her window at the dogwoods blooming, the jonquils, the bright new shoots. In L.A. she'd forgotten about spring. Maybe in a way living in a place without a spring had given her creations more flare, sprouting all those impossible colors and textures and wild, capricious shapes and mixtures of traditions. Yeah, maybe she'd say something like that today at the bank, jazz up these hayseeds' vision of themselves. Because the corollary was that if you lived in a place like Buck's Gap that had a fantastic spring, then you let your own brain get drab; you put yourself in neutral, let nature do all your imagining for you. No, that might be too much of an overload for the audience of Buck's Gappers.

"I wished we hadn't moved around so much," her father said. He'd stopped again in the middle of Main Street, right in front of the Kiddie Korner Klothing Store, and the little traffic that there was—Buck's Gap rush hour—was flowing peacefully around them.

"I'm going to be late, Daddy-O," Tina Blue said.

"It was the only way I knew of making money. Fixing up a dump and selling it for double what I paid for it. It was a good income, but it wasn't any way to raise a family. I always thought it was why your momma run off. Never settled. Soon as we'd get the floorboards patched so you could walk through the house without falling through, we'd be out on the front porch, handing over the key to somebody."

"It was OK, Daddy-O. I liked it fine."

"I think how some people live their whole life in the same house—maybe even the same house where their daddy or momma was born. And I think of us, how we never let the dust settle but we were on to the next one."

"You been living in that one house now for five years—that's a long while," Tina Blue said.

"It's rented. That's somebody else's floor, their roof, their toilet. I'm renting their mirrors and sinks. I might as well be living at the bus depot."

Tina Blue raised the alligator-skin lid of her watch. Quarter till six—fifteen minutes after the show was supposed to begin. The clothes were hung already, back near the main vault, but still she should be there—at least to hear the corn-pone brains react.

"I'm glad we lived how we lived, Daddy-O. It gave me angst, a sense of outsiderness. Everybody feels that way in cities. It's existential. Not feeling at home in the universe. I got a head start on it and that's why I'm an artist. If we'd just lived in one house and had a safe, predictable, static life, I'd still be here in Buck's Gap probably, somebody's wife, living in the same house for the rest of my life. Going to see an art-to-wear show by some weird girl from L.A. and having no imagination myself, no unease. Nothing to overcome. You see what I'm saying, Daddy-O?"

He put the car in gear again, got underway, and said, "I wish I'd never sent Freddy Red off. I wished I had him near me now. I just got that old dog, not worth a damn."

"You got me, Daddy-O. What do you mean, you don't have anybody?"

Her daddy smiled and she thought for a minute he was going to stop again in the street, so she didn't give him a smile back. He slowed, looking over at her, but kept on going.

At the bank there was a crowd.

Tina Blue flowed in through the double glass doors as an old security guard bowed to her, seemed to consider clapping for a moment, then lowered his hands. The crowd opened for her, their murmuring dying out.

"Bravo!" someone called out.

"Speech!" a woman's voice chimed in.

The bank president was waiting for her back in the center of the exhibit. He stood next to an aluminum bathrobe that had Japanese Christmas lights for a belt. Next to where it was fixed to the wall was her winter collection of men's undershorts made from long red shag carpets with plastic fruit buried away inside the shag.

Her creations were strung up on the wall where usually a collection of old black-and-white photos were hung. They were the earliest photographs ever taken of Main Street and this or that wooden building or muddy street in Buck's Gap. Daddy-O's daddy had taken them back when photography was right up there with dynamiting at the quarry for dangerous jobs.

The president of the bank introduced her to Milton Mosley, the vice president. Tina Blue shook his hand, and Milton reminded her that he'd sat behind her in geometry almost twenty years back. She shook her head at him and smiled wanly. If her L.A. friends had heard that—wow, a guy from geometry class, how sweet.

The president cleared his throat and raised his arms to quiet the crowd.

"Would you like to say a few words, Tina Blue? I'm sure we'd all be edified by anything you might want to say to us."

When she hesitated briefly, someone called out from the crowd:

"Do you see your work as a paradigm for the way contemporary technological models have subverted the simplicity and practical beauty of American life?"

A man in overalls had worked his way to the front of the gathering. He handed her a program the bank had printed up, showing photos of her work, and asked her to sign it. "My daughter's got her sewing machine going a hundred miles an hour since she seen this brochure. Me and her momma are right happy about the things she's putting out. Nothing as good as this, but she's sure full of spit and fury."

As Tina Blue autographed the farmer's program, Milton Mosley said, watching her carefully, "There's a danger in creating something that hovers between the caprice and nobility of art and the utilitarian, don't you think?"

"Oh, I totally disagree," said the president of the bank. "Your terms of discussion are outmoded. Luck and accident are the main engines of the new quantum universe. Usefulness is no more than a stage in the life of any material. Leave your aftershave bottle open on the shelf overnight and you'll see how quickly what was once of use can still exist but have no use."

"I think what he means," said an old woman in a berry-covered hat, "is that a shovel that pretends to be a shovel but is only a counterfeit can be dangerous to those who are depending on its being a real shovel."

"It would seem to me," said Milton Mosley, "that art which announces itself as preposterous, which sniggers, has destroyed the tacit agreement between creator and audience. We don't need to be slapped awake by shag-carpet underwear, we need to be entranced by some new entertainment which is only a cockeyed and illuminating degree or two off what the past has prepared us for. Art which mocks and swaggers is not art at all, but public farting, don't you think?"

The bank president straightened his striped tie and said, "Look here, if we are to be true to a world in which radical mutants reach out to take some new frightening pathways into the evolutionary future, we must . . ."

Tina Blue backed away from the argument, watched the crowd heal up around her absence. She found her father near the front doors, talking to the security guard and showing him the walnut brain.

"Your father is a very weird man," the security guard said to her when she was beside them.

A feather had worked loose from her sticky hair and was dangling down across her forehead. She could feel the sweat running between her breasts, and the leotard was mashing her uncomfortably. She held her breath for a moment and listened to new voices speaking from the crowd. The argument had shifted and fresh opinions were being expressed. Tina Blue smiled uncertainly at her father.

"I'd like to go home," she said.

Her father said, "I never seen this bunch so worked up before. Have you, Billy?"

"Not since that Cherokee Indian with those dogs that could quote poetry."

"Oh, yeah—that," her father said. "That was hokum. I was disappointed to see everybody fall for that fellow."

"I was here and heard them dogs," Billy said to Tina Blue. "*Where ignorant armies clash by night*—I heard it coming from that spaniel's own throat."

"I liked to died laughing, myself," said her daddy.

"But it wasn't nothing to compare to your handiwork—not by a long way," Billy said to Tina Blue. "My goodness, this'll be the talk of Buck's Gap for years to come."

Milton Mosley came to call on her at seven the next night. He'd telephoned in the evening right after her show to apologize for his attack on her artwork. Her work had had such an effect on him, he said, such an intoxicating effect that he wasn't entirely responsible for the outburst. It was OK, Tina Blue said. She didn't take it personally. She was glad for any kind of reaction. But you seemed dizzy and upset when you left, Milton Mosley had said. And Tina Blue replied that yes, she'd been a bit dizzy, but it was from the change in altitude, nothing more.

So he came for her in his long black Ford Phaeton.

Tina Blue stood at a front window handing out bones to Warhol, staring at this man getting out of that other-worldly car. He wore a black shirt that had a single red slice of watermelon printed on a pocket, black pants, and red tennis shoes.

"What *is* this?" she said.

And her father, sitting at the dining room table concentrating on his medulla oblongata, asked, "He wearing that watermelon shirt?"

"Yes," Tina said.

"Oh, boy. Look out tonight."

"What?"

"Means he's going to ask you to marry him. Wears that every time. He's asked every woman south of the Ohio River and always wears that shirt."

Tina gave Warhol the last bone and slipped out the front door before he could begin begging for more.

"Hi," Milton said, standing on the sidewalk, looking too young and too nimble-eyed to be the vice president of a bank.

"You planning on asking me to marry you, you better just do it now," she said.

"OK," he answered. "I never met anyone like you. Ever. I don't think there is anyone like you, Tina Blue. I've asked many a woman to marry me, but I never asked anyone the likes of you. And I can't ever remember when I hoped a woman would say yes more than right now. I'm probably not what you had in mind for a husband, but there isn't a thing I wouldn't do to make you happy."

He paused only a moment. "And the fact is, I make a lot of money. I've got a lot put away, and I wouldn't mind letting you spend every penny of it if that was what you wanted. Plus, I kiss good. I been told I can make a chunk of marble groan, the way I do some things. And the woman I marry is the last woman I'd ever want."

After the wedding they spent two weeks in California, cleaning out her apartment and seeing all her friends. Milton charmed them all. He softened his hick accent just enough and asked lots of questions and nodded and made a lot of eye contact and stuck in a one-liner here and there, and her girlfriends would come up afterwards and say, "And he's rich, too?"

They drove up to the wine country and then to Sausalito, and he hadn't lied about making marble groan. When they returned to Buck's Gap in July, Tina Blue was warm and sleepy in a way she'd never been before.

They bought a big house out on Buck's Lake: five white columns across the front, a big terrace, sugar maples and Chinese elms. And her daddy moved into the servants' quarters out back.

"I want Freddy Red near me," he said to her one morning in August while she was changing a bobbin on her Singer. She'd been designing a cocktail dress made from the covers of *New Yorker* magazines that she'd enclosed in plastic pouches. But it hadn't been going right. It seemed ludicrous to her—absurd in a way that a three-headed baby might be absurd. Pointless and grotesque.

"I want him here in this big house where he'll be happy. Where we can be a happy family for once. I'm not happy. I never been happy. Never, ever. I sent my son off to live with idiots and morons and I regretted it every day of my life."

Tina Blue stared at her father, glanced back at the cover of one of those magazines. A dog walking through a snowstorm. She had no idea what *that* meant. Why was *that* a cover?

"You're happy, Milton's happy. Most every damn person in this town is happy, at least part of the time. But I'm not. Because my son's locked away."

"I'll ask Milton," Tina Blue said, still looking at that stupid dog walking through that snowstorm. The dog was a watercolor blue. Blue? What in the world was *that* about?

Freddy Red moved into the downstairs bedroom and took up a position in front of the little black-and-white TV. He listened to the news channel all day. He told Tina that he was following the desperate situation in the Middle East and it was very important to him not to be interrupted. "They need Eisenhower on this one," he said. "I'm doing the best I can, but a general is what's needed here." He waited for her reply, watching her with his blurry gray eyes, and when she said nothing he went away into the screen.

Her father seemed happy now. He was at work whittling a small intestine—a tangle of cedar, loops and whorls and corrugated surfaces. He sat out on the back porch within listening range of Freddy Red's TV and sliced and smoothed those guts, chuckling to himself as if he had been nibbling on human brains.

A few days after Freddy Red's arrival, Milton came into Tina Blue's workroom before he left for the bank. She was sitting at her Singer, feeding a hemline through the slot. She was almost finished with the *New Yorker* dress.

"I'm going to be late tonight," he told her. "There's a show at the bank this afternoon."

Tina Blue watched the gold thread stitching into the shiny orange fabric. She asked him what it was.

"Some gentleman from New York City who collects the bloody clothes from famous assassinations. He has Kennedy's shirt and two presidential candidates' undershirts. A lot of other things with blood on them, too, but I didn't pay that much attention."

"Why didn't you invite me to come?" Tina Blue said. She halted the sewing machine and swiveled to see how Milton would answer this.

"Bloodstains? You want to see a clothesline full of bloodstains?"

"Maybe."

"Well, come then. I just didn't think you'd care about such things."

When he'd gone, she sat still and was deeply, densely depressed. She spread the dress out and looked for the cover showing the dog in the snowstorm. Blue dog, white storm. Icy blue, pure white. It made her sadder still seeing that dog so hopeless, wandering like that without any idea of which way was home. It was lost, but still noble somehow. How had anyone been able to draw that? How had they known how to pour all those feelings into that one dog, that very ordinary snowstorm? Now *that* was art. *That* was the deep song of the soul.

Warhol shuffled into the room, even slower than usual, looking for her. He put his head in her lap and pressed heavily. This moment—with the TV babbling, the soft slur of her father's knife, his quiet laughter, and Warhol's heavy head—hurt her deep and true. But she had not cultivated the skill to hold and love such sorrow. She had learned to zing but she could not sing.

For several moments, her tears dripped onto the dog's nose. Then she drew the dress from the machine, undressed, and put it on. It was heavy and hot, and when she moved it made a noise like snow tires on summer pavement. But she kept it on, walking into Freddy Red's room and sitting in the lounge chair beside his. He glanced over at her, studied one or two of the covers, raised his eyebrows, and turned back to the TV.

"Freddy Red," she said. "There's a show at the bank today."

"Yeah?" He watched a Press-On Fingernail commercial, narrowing his eyes when the demonstration began.

"It's just a bunch of bloody clothes," she said, "but it might be good to get out. Show off my new dress. Want to go?"

"You going to wear that?" he said without looking away from the TV.

"I thought I would," she said. "I never wore anything I made before."

"I ain't going nowhere with you looking like some kind of crazy lady."

"Freddy Red!"

"You hadn't said beans to me all my life, then you want to take me out and show me off while you wear a dress like that. No way. No way in hell."

"If I wear blue jeans?"

"What else?"

"A work shirt?"

"What else?"

The news anchor came on, backed by a map of the Middle East. Then a film began playing of tanks rolling across the desert, and Freddy Red was gone again, gabbling quietly about Eisenhower.

When Tina returned to her sewing room, she found Warhol on the rag rug, mouth and eyes open. There was a drool of bloody foam that ran almost a foot from his mouth. She knelt beside him and ran her hand across his lumpy head, watching for any rise in his chest.

After a while she wrapped him in that ridiculous dress, took him in her arms, and carried him out onto the porch where her father was chuckling at a particularly humorous twist in his cedar intestines. Tina Blue walked down to the edge of the lake and laid Warhol in the tall grass. She returned to the house for a shovel.

It took her over an hour to dig what she considered a decent hole. By that time her father had noticed and joined her. He helped her lower the dog into the hole and squatted down beside her as she tucked the edges of that dress around the carcass.

"I guess that's the end of that," he said. And something between a sputter and a harsh laugh broke from him.

Tina Blue put her arm around his shoulder. Her eyes weren't working right. Some kind of static was blurring them. A hot bubble was growing in her throat.

She stood and hefted the shovel, running her hands up and down the smooth oak handle, feeling the narrowing and thickening of the wood. She found a good grip and took a spadeful of dark earth, lifted it, and let it fall into the hole.

Larry Brown

FACING THE MUSIC

(from *Mississippi Review*)

—FOR RICHARD HOWORTH

I cut my eyes sideways because I know what's coming. "You want
the light off, honey?" she says. Very quietly. I can see as well with it
as without it. It's an old movie I'm watching, Ray Milland in *The
Lost Weekend*. This character he's playing, this guy will do anything
to get a drink. He'd sell children, probably, to get a drink. That's the
kind of person Ray's playing.

Sometimes I have trouble resting at night, so I watch the movies
until I get sleepy. They show them—all-night movies—on these stations from Memphis and Tupelo. There are probably a lot of people
like me, unable to sleep, lying around watching them with me. I've
got remote control so I can turn it on or off and change channels.
She's stirring around the bedroom, doing things, doing something—I don't know what. She has to stay busy. Our children
moved away, and we don't have any pets. We used to have a dog, a
little brown one, but I accidentally killed it. Backed over its head
with the station wagon one morning. She used to feed it in the
kitchen, right after she came home from the hospital.

But I told her, no more. It hurts too much to lose one.

"It doesn't matter," I say, finally, which is not what I'm thinking.

"That's Ray Milland," she says. "Wasn't he young then." Wistful like.

So he was. I was too once. So was she. So was everybody.

But this movie is forty years old.

"You going to finish watching this?" she says. She sits on the bed right beside me. I'm propped up on the TV pillow. It's blue corduroy and I got it for Christmas last year. She said I was spending so much time in the bed, I might as well be comfortable. She also said it could be used for other things, too. I said what things? I don't know why I have to be so mean to her, like it's her fault. She asks me if I want some more ice. I'm drinking whiskey. She knows it helps me. I'm not so much of a bastard that I don't know she loves me.

Actually, it's worse than that. I don't mean anything against God by saying this, but sometimes I think she worships me.

"I'm okay," I say. Ray has his booze hanging out the window on a string—hiding it from these booze-thieves he's trying to get away from—and before long he'll have to face the music. Ray can never find a good place to hide his booze. He gets so drunk he can't remember where he hid it when he sobers up. Later on, he's going to try to write a novel, pecking the title and his name out with two fingers. But he's going to have a hard time. Ray is crazy about that booze, and doesn't even know how to type.

She may start rubbing on me. That's what I have to watch out for. That's what she does. She gets in bed with me when I'm watching a movie and she starts rubbing on me. I can't stand it. I especially can't stand for the light to be on when she does it. If the light's on when she does it, she winds up crying in the bathroom. That's the kind of husband I am.

But everything's okay, so far. She's not rubbing on me yet. I go ahead and mix myself another drink. I've got a whole bottle beside the bed. We had our Christmas party at the fire station the other night and everybody got a fifth. My wife didn't attend. She said every person in there would look at her. I told her they wouldn't, but I didn't argue much. I was on duty anyway and couldn't drink anything. All I could do was eat my steak and look around, go get another cup of coffee.

"I could do something for you," she says. She's teasing but she means it. I have to smile. One of those frozen ones. I feel like shooting both of us because she's fixed her hair up nice and she's got on a new nightgown.

"I could turn the lamp off," she says.

I have to be very careful. If I say the wrong thing, she'll take it the wrong way. She'll wind up crying in the bathroom if I say the wrong thing. I don't know what to say. Ray's just met this good-looking chick—Jane Wyman?—and I know he's going to steal a lady's purse later on; I don't want to miss it. I could do the things Ray Milland is doing in this movie and worse. Boy. Could I. But she's right over here beside my face wanting an answer. Now. She's smiling at me. She's licking her lips. I don't want to give in. Giving in leads to other things, other givings.

I have to say something. But I don't say anything.

She gets up and goes back over to her dressing table. She picks up her brush. I can hear her raking and tearing it through her hair. It sounds like she's ripping it out by the roots. I have to stay here and listen to it. I can understand why people jump off bridges.

"You want a drink?" I say. "I can mix you up a little bourbon and Coke."

"I've got something," she says, and she lifts her can to show me. Diet Coke. At least a six-pack a day. The refrigerator's crammed full of them. I can hardly get to my beer for them. I think they're only one calorie or something. She thinks she's fat and that's the reason I don't pay enough attention to her, but it isn't.

She's been hurt. I know she has. You can lie around the house all your life and think you're safe. But you're not.

Something from outside or inside can reach out and get you. You can get sick and have to go to the hospital. Some nut could walk into the station one night and kill us all in our beds. You can read about things like that in the paper any morning you want to. I try not to think about it. I just do my job and then come home and try to stay in the house with her. But sometimes I can't.

Last week, I was in this bar in town. I'd gone down there with some of these boys we're breaking in, rookies. Just young boys, nineteen or twenty. They'd passed probation and wanted to celebrate, so a few of us older guys went with them. We drank a few pitchers and listened to the band. It was a pretty good band. They did a lot of Willie and Waylon stuff. I'm thinking about all this while she's getting up and moving around the room, looking out the windows.

I don't go looking for things—I don't—but later on, well, there was this woman in there. Not a young woman. Younger than me. About forty. She was sitting by herself. I was in no hurry to go home. All the boys had gone, Bradshaw, too. I was the only one of the group left. So I said what the hell. I went up to the bar and bought two drinks and carried them over to her table. I sat down with them and I smiled at her. And she smiled back. In an hour we were over at her house.

I don't know why I did it. I'd never done anything like that before. She had some money. You could tell it from her house and things. I was a little drunk, but I know that's no excuse. She took me into her bedroom and she put a record on, some nice slow orchestra or something. I was lying on the bed the whole time, knowing my wife was at home waiting up on me. This woman stood up in the middle of the room and started turning. She had her arms over her head. She had white hair piled up high. When she took off her jacket, I could tell she had something nice underneath. She took off her shirt, and her breasts were like something you'd see in a movie, deep long things you might only glimpse in a swimming suit. Before I know it, she was on the bed with me putting one of them in my mouth.

"You sure you don't want a drink?" I say.

"I want you," she says, and I don't know what to say. She's not looking at me. She's looking out the window. Ray's coming out of the bathroom now with the lady's purse under his arm. But I know they're all going to be waiting for him, the whole club. I know what he's going to feel. Everybody's going to be looking at him.

When this woman got on top of me, the only thing I could think was: God.

"What are we going to do?" my wife says.

"Nothing," I say. But I don't know what I'm saying. I've got these big, soft nipples in my mouth, and I can't think of anything else. I'm trying to remember exactly how it was.

I thought I'd be different somehow, changed. I thought she'd know what I'd done just by looking at me. But she didn't. She didn't even notice.

I look at her and her shoulders are jerking under the little green gown. I'm always making her cry and I don't mean to. Here's the kind of bastard I am: my wife's crying because she wants me, and I'm lying here watching Ray Milland and drinking whiskey and thinking about putting another woman's breasts in my mouth. She was on top of me and they were hanging right over my face. It was so wonderful, but now it seems so awful I can hardly stand to think about it.

"I understand how you feel," she says, "but how do you think I feel?" She's not talking to me; she's talking to the window and Ray is staggering down the street in the hot sunshine, looking for a pawnshop so he can hock the typewriter he was going to use to write his novel.

A commercial comes on, a man selling dog food. I can't just sit here and not say anything. I have to say something. But, God, it hurts to.

"I know," I say. It's almost the same as saying nothing. It doesn't mean anything.

We've been married for twenty-three years.

"You don't know," she says. "You don't know the things that go through my mind."

I know what she's going to say. I know the things going through her mind. She's seeing me on top of her with her legs over my shoulders, her legs locked around my back. But she won't take her gown off any more. She'll just push it up. She never takes her gown off, doesn't want me to see. I know what will happen. I can't do anything about it. Before long she'll be over here rubbing on me, and if I don't start she'll stop and wind up crying in the bathroom.

"Why don't you have a drink?" I say. I wish she'd have a drink. Or go to sleep. Or just watch the movie with me. Why can't she just watch the movie with me?

"I should have just died," she says. "Then you could have gotten you somebody else." I guess maybe she means somebody like the friendly woman with her nice house and the nice nipples.

I don't know. I can't find a comfortable place for my neck.

"You shouldn't say that."

"Well, it's true. I'm not a whole woman any more. I'm just a burden on you."

"You're not."

"Well, you don't want me since the operation."

She's always saying that. She wants me to admit it. And I don't want to lie any more, I don't want to spare her feelings any more, I want her to know I've got feelings too, and it's hurt me almost as bad as it has her. But that's not what I say. I can't say that.

"I do want you," I say. I have to say it. She makes me say it.

"Then prove it," she says. She comes close to the bed and she leans over me. She's painted her brows with black stuff and her face is made up to where I can hardly believe it.

"You've got too much makeup on," I whisper.

She leaves. She's in the bathroom scrubbing. I can hear the water running. Ray's got the blind staggers. Everybody's hiding his whiskey from him and he can't get a drink. He's got it bad. He's on his way to the nut house.

Don't feel like a lone ranger, Ray.

The water stops running. She cuts the light off in there and then she steps out. I don't look around. I'm watching a hardware store commercial. Hammers and Skilsaws are on the wall. They always have this pretty girl with large breasts selling their hardware. The big special this week is garden hose. You can buy a hundred feet, she says, for less than four dollars.

The TV is just a dim gray spot between my socks. She's getting on the bed, setting one knee down and pulling up the hem of her gown. She can't wait. I'm thinking of it again, how the woman's breasts looked, how she looked in her shirt before she took it off, how I could tell she had something nice underneath and how wonderful it was to be drunk in that moment when I knew what she was going to do.

It's time now. She's touching me. Her hands are moving, sliding all over me. Everywhere. Ray is typing with two fingers somewhere, just the title and his name. I can hear the pecking of his keys. That old boy, he's trying to do what he knows he should. He has responsibilities to people who love him and need him; he can't let them down. But he's scared to death. He doesn't know where to start.

"You going to keep watching this?" she says, but dreamy-like, kissing on me, as if she doesn't care one way or the other. I don't say anything when I cut the TV off. I can't speak. I'm thinking of how it was on our honeymoon, in that little room at Hattiesburg, when she bent her arms behind her back and slumped her shoulders forward, how the cups loosened and fell as the straps slid off her arms.

I'm thinking that your first love is your best love, that you'll never find any better. The way she did it was like she was saying, here I am, I'm all yours, all of me, forever. Nothing's changed. She turns the light off, and we reach to find each other in the darkness like people who are blind.

Sunny Rogers

THE CRUMB

(from *The Quarterly*)

Haber Hill Culpepper was a simple man, and to fortify that simplicity of nature which he valued above all things and considered a judicious humility, he began this day, a disappointingly dank, dark, dreary, even—to carry out the consonantal theme—dismal day, which was also his fifty-seventh birthday, with a reading from the Scriptures, the beatitudes this birthday morning: Matthew 5:3–12. Haber Hill Culpepper was not, he was always careful to have understood, a religious man, but more a reverent one, and as he read verse twelve—"Rejoice, and be exceedingly glad for great is your reward in Heaven"—he knew he yet awaited divine disclosure with the same unmitigated certitude of its ultimate manifestation as he awaited the tinkling summons of his mother's sterling-silver tabletop bell, now heard, which announced she was awake, Haber, and ready for her "early breakfast" tray.

"In a minute, Mother!" Haber called, closed his worn and heavily annotated Bible, forced himself out of his cozy, quilt-spread antique four-poster bed and, with a girlish shiver he would have denied himself had there been anyone else in the room, pulled on his fawn-colored cashmere dressing gown. As fastidious as he was both simple and reverent, and over the now vehement convoking of the sterling-silver bell, Haber first brushed his teeth, carefully combed his thinning hair (the part, which was on the left side as had been his father's, was so clean and straight it appeared to have been cut into his scalp with a cutthroat razor), and then tucked into the breast pocket of his dressing gown a red silk handkerchief, his long and slender fingers fluttering and fussing until it flopped with that artless elegance he had always admired in his father and to which he had aspired even as a boy.

"Honestly, Mother!" Haber called with an exaggerated exasperation he hoped would speak volumes. It did not. The bell continued to convoke as Haber, tightening the silk-fringed sash of his dressing gown, hurried down the hall.

Haber Hill Culpepper had never lived in any other house than the severe and imposing Federal brick three-story whose hall he now hurried down, and neither had his mother, Amanda Lee Culpepper, called Mandy Lee in her youth but not now, who had been born in the exact same room from which she now so petulantly summoned Haber with the sterling-silver bell. (Mrs. Culpepper, soon herself to celebrate a birthday, her seventy-sixth, knew full well that Haber was hurrying to her, but she also knew he was prone to linger before the glass, and pocket handkerchief or no, she was ready for her pot of Fortnum & Mason's Earl Grey tea and her two slices of dry whole wheat toast that served to stave off famine until the housekeeper, Adele, arrived at nine-thirty.)

Of course there had been, many years ago, what Haber called his "New York adventure," but not for a single day had he considered the one-bedroom Central Park West apartment home, any more than he had considered himself, during the five years he had lived there, a New Yorker. Some of Haber's colleagues in the law firm where he was then employed (or "confederates," as Haber was unfortunately wont to call them) had, on occasion, risked the word "prissy" to describe the immaculately dressed and courtly Virginian suddenly come to earth among them, only to be scorned and hooted at by wives starved for the debonair airs and the endearing thoughtfulness Haber Hill Culpepper never failed to evince. Those manners and that air may have won every heart at which they were directed, but they also served to keep at bay other and, to Haber Hill Culpepper, far more threatening aspects of the female anatomy. Haber had had his few, and to him somewhat tedious, misadventures (immediately put out of mind and now totally forgotten), and although there was no denying that he courted and was invariably received with all the fervent kindnesses which were his just due (it was a rare evening, indeed, that Haber Hill Culpepper dined alone or at his own expense), there was also no denying that the kiss on both cheeks which he gave and received with such seeming spontaneity was, in fact, a consciously choreographed ballet of avoidance of even so much as the intimation of intimacy. It was all in good fun, and even if he didn't exactly sing for his supper, Haber Hill Culpepper earned his ladle of sorrel soup, his unctuous (Haber's word) sliver of smoked salmon, his properly aged and seasoned game hen, and all the claret (again Haber's word) he cared to drink by a studious focusing of all energy and attention on the source of such abundant bounty, his delighted and flattered and cosseted hostess, without the slightest chance that these attestations of admiration and affection would ever stray beyond drawing room, dining room, or kitchen.

But at last he had seen his museums, his Broadway shows, attended more than his fair share of openings and auctions; and Virginia did perpetually beckon. And then, unexpectedly (although admittedly providentially), his father had peacefully and painlessly passed away in his sleep, and Mother, who had no intention of rattling around in that big old house alone, had summoned, and Haber Hill Culpepper had brought his "New York adventure" happily to a close.

For the next ten years, to keep himself busy and "out of Mother's hair," Haber had taught what his mother called his "little courses" in estate law at the College of William and Mary until, tired of the twice-weekly commute to Williamsburg (or so he said), he gave it up and, between his gardening, his occasional tours of Europe, and his books, had quietly but nonetheless tenaciously begun his small quest for his perhaps negligible share of divine revelation. Certainly he had always had everything else that life purportedly had to offer, much of it served up on the proverbial silver platter, and even though the Bible did claim that it was easier for a camel to slip through the eye of a needle than for a rich man to ascend unto Heaven, Haber Hill Culpepper, proud descendant of governors and senators, recognized an expedient political statement when he heard one.

"Good Lord, Mother. Put that thing down," Haber said as he turned into his mother's room. "And turn on a light before I go crashing into something."

Haber Hill Culpepper's mother had been considered a great beauty in her youth and even now had the unblemished skin of a woman half her age and remarkable blue eyes still startling in their somewhat faded intensity. She was propped against several hand-embroidered, linen-encased, down-filled pillows, her snow-white hair pinned in a topknot on her head ("A concierge's knot," she called it, as if to emphasize that there was not now, nor had there ever been, a proud bone in her body), and like the obedient child she always became when she had got what she wanted, she placed the sterling silver bell on her bedside table and switched on a lamp.

"You could reply when I ring. Call out something," Mrs. Culpepper said.

"I did, and you know it," Haber said. "Don't go playing deaf, dumb, and blind with me, Mother."

"I believe we have cause for celebration today," Haber's mother said. "Happy birthday, son."

"Why, thank you, Mother," Haber said. "Another year older, but not, I'm afraid, any the wiser."

"I've invited Reverend Bogard to tea," Haber's mother said.

"Oh yes, the tree man," Haber said.

His usual reticence vanquished by several glasses of claret and two of port, Haber had recently broached the subject of his small quest for divine disclosure with the Right Reverend Clarence Bogard, only to be assured that there really was no need to go rooting around for God (and he had used the word "rooting," much to Haber's dismay), that God could be found even in the quiet contemplation of a tree. But then Haber had always known the Right Reverend Bogard was a banal man, whose weekly homilies, Haber had told his mother, were surely filched from Hallmark greeting cards.

"There is no need to be hard on Reverend Bogard," Haber's mother said. "He means well and we are not all as articulate as you are, dear."

"But rooting around for God, I ask you, Mother. I hardly think we are dealing solely with a lack of articulation here," Haber said.

"He was a rock when your father passed away," Haber's mother said.

"Oh, let's not begin the day with Clarence Bogard," Haber said. "Certainly not on an empty stomach, anyway."

Every time he entered the basement-level kitchen, Haber winced, and he winced now in the sudden, clinical glare of the tubes of fluorescent lighting (one of which annoyingly flickered) that the housekeeper, Adele, had declared she could not see even her hand in front of her face without and that gave the large and well-equipped kitchen, Haber thought, an institutional air untempered by the ruffled pink gingham curtains (again the housekeeper's doing) at the tall windows, two of which looked out on the boxwood-hedged garden at the back of the house, or the four ceramic doggy canisters the housekeeper had purchased at some yard sale. The dogs, a basset, a Yorkshire terrier, a poodle, and a spaniel, in their teeth held small placards that read SUGAR, FLOUR, SALT, and COFFEE and were eternally established in a begging position, their little paws held up into perpetuity as if for a pat on the head. But the kitchen was "Adele's domain," Haber's mother said, and it was therefore only proper that the housekeeper be allowed to do as she would within it. Easy for her to say, since she has never so much as cast her shadow across the door, Haber thought, and not for the first time. Mrs. Culpepper had, in fact, entered the kitchen at least once in her life, the night of her betrothal dinner, to thank the staff. "I'm so helpless I couldn't bake myself a loaf of bread were I starving to death," she would sometimes fret, as if decrying a style of life she had done absolutely nothing to alter, nor would Haber have wished her to alter it. Not for him a cookie-baking, cocoa-serving mother and the untidiness such an alliance implied, the miry sentimentality, the guilt. No, Haber was more than satisfied with the mother he had now and cherished the memory of the glamorous mother of his youth with her satin and velvet and taffeta ballgowns and her lovely triple-strand baroque-pearl necklace with the diamond-and-sapphire clasp. Not once had their somewhat ceremonial rapport been sullied by her personal attendance upon his intimate needs, not even when he was a small boy. Never had she bathed him, changed his soiled diaper, nor had she ever sat impatiently while he spat up whatever was being spooned into his mouth. There had always been other hands paid to attend to these things.

The two trays were on the worn and heavily scored butcher-block table, as Haber had known they would be, arranged by the housekeeper before she had left the night before. All Haber would have to do was brew the two small pots of tea, toast the four slices of whole wheat bread, and then, once he had delivered his mother her tray, he would be free to return to his bed, where he would read until the housekeeper arrived and had prepared what was known as the "proper breakfast," which was laid out under silver-domed servers on the Georgian sideboard in the dining room, a wild extravagance, Haber knew, since he was the only one to avail himself of the housekeeper's exuberant morning bounty, Mrs. Culpepper always taking her poached egg, her slice of cured ham, and her English muffin on yet another tray, this one prepared and delivered by the housekeeper, Adele.

While he waited for the water in the kettle to come to a boil, Haber read over the shopping list the housekeeper had made out the night before and allowed himself a smile when he came upon "birthday cake candles," the last item on the list but the only one that had been underlined. The dear old soul, bless her, never forgot, and knowing that seemed to more than compensate for the dreariness of the day. Oh, but it was a rather handsome existence, Haber thought, predictable in a soothing way, comfortable beyond even the meaning of the word, and not for a minute would he have changed a single thing about it, and neither, he was sure, would the divine disclosure he now sought do more than perhaps ripple the smooth surface of the calm and calming waters of his so carefully contrived, yes, even formal life. No, whenever it came and whatever form it would ultimately take, there would be no blinding light, no portentous shudder of the soul, no angel with whom he was yet destined to wrestle. "'Blessed are the pure in heart; for they shall see God' and quite rightly, too," Haber Hill Culpepper said aloud just as the kettle began its low and altogether pleasant whistle.

"I'm here, Miz Culpepper!" Adele, the housekeeper, bellowed from the bottom of the stairs, and Mrs. Culpepper, in her room, raised her eyes beseechingly to the ceiling and made a praying gesture with her hands, while Haber, in his, set aside his volume of Dickinson, flung off the quilt, and on the count of two silently mouthed, "Bacon's sizzling, folks!" in unison with the housekeeper's every-morning-at-nine-forty-five pronouncement. Now the housekeeper would pad back into the kitchen and Haber would shower and shave. On the dot of ten, Haber would descend the same stairs the housekeeper would at that very moment be ascending, bearing Mrs. Culpepper's second tray. The housekeeper would say, "You're looking mighty fine this morning, Mr. Haber," and Haber would say, "Same to you, Adele," with his usual distracted air, and another day at 415 Crawford Street would then be in full swing.

Adele Washington, now in her early sixties, had worked for the Culpepper family since she was a young girl. "In the olden days," as Adele would say when she reminisced, there had been a large staff: a cook; a washerwoman; a handyman, who also drove for Mr. and Mrs. Culpepper and tended the garden; and until he was sent to sleep-away school, a foreign-speaking nurse for Mr. Haber. But when Mr. Culpepper passed away, the handyman and the cook and the washerwoman had been let go and Adele had assumed entire responsibility for the house, and on this birthday morning, as on every other morning except Sunday morning (Sunday was the housekeeper's day off), she broke two brown eggs into her favorite blue-and-white mixing bowl and began to beat them with a fork just as the pipes next to the kitchen sink began to knock and rattle, which told her that Mr. Haber had turned on the shower.

Under the steamy shower, Haber, who liked to keep track of his daily rituals, reminded himself that, yes, he had read his passage of Scripture and, yes, his daily quota of poems (two). Now the morning paper awaited, brought in by the housekeeper and folded next to his place at the dining-room table, and after breakfast and the paper would come a Chekhov story and then his ten pages of Proust, and another seamless morning in the life of Haber Hill Culpepper would have passed.

Miss Emily Dickinson, Haber thought as he wrapped himself in a terry-cloth bath sheet, would always remain a bit of a mystery, but one of the poems he had read this morning did seem to strike close to home:

God gave a loaf to every Bird—
But just a Crumb—to Me—
I dare not eat it—tho' I starve—
My poignant luxury....

I wonder how the Rich—may feel—
An Indiaman—An Earl—
I deem that I—with but a Crumb—
Am Sovereign of them all.

Well, Haber thought, he might in fact be as rich as an earl but he was not greedy and would himself be more than satisfied with just a crumb if that proved to be his lot. And then he remembered that the Right Reverend Clarence Bogard was coming to tea, and he felt again, as he had often felt in the last few years, how isolated his life had become. There really was no one with whom he could discuss his small but nonetheless fervent quest for divine disclosure or, for that matter, even the books he read. How could you discourse about the delicious refinement, the subtle sensitivity of a Marcel Proust or the mystery of an Emily Dickinson with a man who talked of "rooting around for God"? But this was all so pointless, pointless and petty, Haber rebuked himself as he pulled the dove-gray cashmere crewneck sweater over the faded blue oxford-cloth button-down-collared shirt, and what possible difference would any of it make in the Grand Scheme of Things? *Rien n' a aucune importance.* And the disquieting possibility that he was in some way a fraudulent suppliant flickered through his mind. Did he seek, Haber wondered, the ennobling patina of great suffering born and transcended but without the necessity of wading through the brackish waters of anguish and pain? "Oh, but this is too much!" Haber said aloud as he pulled on his beige-and-gray Harris tweed jacket. A strong cup of coffee and a little of the housekeeper's morning bounty would set him right.

"Happy birthday, Mr. Haber," the housekeeper said as she mounted the stairs.

"Same to you, Adele," Haber said with that distracted air as he skirted by her.

"That boy of yours spends too much time with his nose buried in them books," the housekeeper said as she presented Mrs. Culpepper with her "proper breakfast" tray.

"Haber?" Mrs. Culpepper said. "Oh, but Haber is an intellectual like his father. Perhaps you had better make a fire in the library, Adele. I'm sure Mr. Haber will want to work in there and it is chilly this morning. Oh, and the Reverend Bogard will be joining us for tea."

"You want me to serve Mr. Haber's cake then?" the housekeeper said.

"Yes, I suppose so. Yes, that would be nice, I think, Adele," Mrs. Culpepper said, and while Mrs. Culpepper picked at the food on her tray and Haber spooned himself another helping of the housekeeper's buttery grits, the housekeeper made a fire in the library and laid a lap rug over the arm of Mr. Haber's favorite chair, started the water running for Mrs. Culpepper's bath, made Mr. Haber's bed, returned the fawn-colored cashmere dressing gown to Mr. Haber's closet, and then went to tidy Mr. Haber's bathroom. Mr. Haber needed fresh towels, the housekeeper noted, and his sheets would have to be changed tomorrow. Today she would change the sheets on Mrs. Culpepper's bed while Mrs. Culpepper soaked in her jasmine-scented bath, and because it was Mr. Haber's birthday, the silver ought to be polished, and if company was coming for tea, she would have to begin baking before three.

Lunch in the housekeeper Adele's "olden days" had been called dinner and had been the main meal of the day. Just as the grandfather clock in the black-and-white marble-tiled front hall had struck the hour of one, Mr. Culpepper had come in from his law office and Mrs. Culpepper, informally dressed in a silk shirtwaist and wearing her single strand of "day" pearls, had at last consented to descend the stairs. Often there had been guests (many of the guests were what Mrs. Culpepper called "prominent people" and what Mr. Culpepper designated "elected officials," whose pictures the housekeeper had often seen in the morning and evening papers), and almost always a brief respite after the big meal before Mr. Culpepper had been driven back to his office and Mrs. Culpepper had set out to shop or call on a friend. But now it was called "luncheon" and consisted of a bowl of hot soup if it was chilly, as it was today, and a sandwich if Mr. Haber wanted it—sliced chicken was his favorite. Mrs. Culpepper was usually satisfied with a wedge of hard cheese and an apple or a pear.

"Just soup today, Adele, and I'll take it in here," Haber said when the housekeeper came quietly into the library. Haber was seated in his favorite chair before the housekeeper's fire, the lap rug over his knees, a thick book in one hand, a pencil poised in the other.

"You saving up for a big slice of Adele's cake, ain't you, Mr. Haber?" the housekeeper said and, with a broad smile, rocked back on her heels.

"That I am, Adele, that I am," Haber said without looking up.

The bowl of hot soup, the fire, and the thimbleful of claret he always allowed himself at lunch had all served to make Haber drowsy, and when the housekeeper tiptoed in to remove the tray with its empty bowl, wine goblet, and balled-up linen napkin, Mr. Haber's head had dropped back and the thick book he had been reading had fallen to the floor. The housekeeper retrieved it and, careful not to lose Mr. Haber's place, laid it open-faced on the table next to his chair. The housekeeper knew that Mrs. Culpepper was probably resting her eyes, too, and after she had washed and dried Mr. Haber's bowl and cut-glass wine goblet, she would bake his birthday cake: a three-layered chocolate cake with dark chocolate icing that had been Mr. Haber's favorite since he was a little boy.

The Right Reverend Clarence Bogard was rummaging through the pockets of his black gabardine trench coat when Adele opened the front door. "I have a little something to mark the occasion," Reverend Bogard said in a stage whisper. "Or, at least, I hope I do. Ah yes, here it is," and he patted the breast pocket of his navy blue blazer with the bright brass buttons embossed with a cross. "A small tome for Mr. Haber," he said, and winked.

The housekeeper never knew quite what to make of the Right Reverend Clarence Bogard. For one thing, he liked to tell nasty jokes, and to the housekeeper's way of thinking, he was a little too particular about his appearance, certainly for a preacher, anyway. His salt-and-pepper hair was worn longer than she thought seemly for a representative of the Lord, and although she had long ago forgiven him the gold ring with the crest he wore on his left pinky, she could never bring herself to condone the slender gold bracelet that encircled his right wrist. And he wore a white turtleneck instead of a turned collar; and then there were those boots of his, black, and to the ankle, and so shiny you could see your face in the toes.

"Well, milady, lead me to the birthday boy," Reverend Bogard said, and to the housekeeper's indignation, he hummed a jazzy rendition of "Lead On, O King Eternal" as he followed her into the drawing room.

"Felicitations of the day, Haber old man," the Reverend Bogard said as he flung the housekeeper his coat. "Bearing in mind that quest of yours, I thought you might find this interesting," and he brought from the breast pocket of his navy blue blazer a small package wrapped in a balloon-patterned paper and tied with a silver ribbon.

"Thank you, Clarence," Haber said as he untied the silver ribbon. Inside the balloon paper was a $1.95 Penguin edition of *The Confes-*

sions of St. Augustine, a book that had always been in the Culpepper library and which Haber had already read.

"Never read it myself, and this fellow could well be a papist," Reverend Bogard said, "but from the title it sounded right up your alley."

"You want me to call Miz Culpepper?" the housekeeper said.

"Please," Haber said, and as the housekeeper was leaving the room she heard the Reverend Bogard say in that whisper of his that carried to the end of the street, "Before Amanda joins us, have you heard the one about..."

Haber watched with merry amusement as the Reverend Bogard "turned on the charm," as Haber's father would have said. He was recalling a recent sermon he had delivered on the efficacy of prayer and was sitting so far forward in his seat that Haber was certain one of his grand gesticulations would soon fling him onto the jewel-toned antique Sarouk carpet that Haber had purchased at an auction at Christie's in New York shortly before he had returned home.

"And I do honestly feel," Reverend Bogard said, "that whether one is, in fact, a believer or not—and I myself have certainly experienced my own Calvary of doubt, and I freely admit it—that whether one is a believer or not, prayer remains a potent power," and just then there was the crashing noise of things breaking and a muffled cry. Haber looked at his mother, who raised her eyebrows. "I'll go and have a look," he said.

When he came into the kitchen, the housekeeper was holding on to the worn and heavily scored butcher-block table as if for dear life and pain was deeply etched in her face. The teapot had shattered at her bare feet and her left foot appeared to have been burned.

"You've got no business walking around in this kitchen without your shoes on, Adele," Haber said crossly.

"But if I wore shoes when I cooked, the food just wouldn't taste the same, Mr. Haber," the housekeeper said, and before Haber could discreetly divert his gaze, a single tear rolled down her leathery cheek.

"Well, you've gone and burned your foot and you had better soak it in ice water," Haber said. But since it was obvious the housekeeper was in pain and probably hobbled into the bargain, Haber asked her where he could find something to put some water in and the housekeeper told him there was a plastic dishpan under the sink, and after he had flung a dishcloth over his arm like a waiter about to serve up a fine dish, Haber filled the pan with cold tap water and then two trays of ice cubes from the freezer.

"For goodness' sake, Adele, sit down," Haber said with a sharpness he hadn't really intended, but he was always at a loss when confronted with suffering and adopted a brisk air to cover that feeling of being emotionally all thumbs. "Here, stick your foot in," he said, and without pausing to think, he knelt before her.

"I'm fine, Mr. Haber," the housekeeper said. "You go on back with the folks."

"Be still," Haber said. "Has the burning subsided any?"

"I feels fine, Mr. Haber," the housekeeper said.

"Well, let's have a look, then," Haber said.

The housekeeper lifted her foot out of the pan of ice water and Haber, with but a second's hesitation, cupped it in the palm of his hand. The toenails were brittle, yellow as old parchment paper. There was a large bunion at the side of the big toe and corns on the second and third toes. The sole was a grayish white; the heel was cracked and webbed with deep lines. It had the coarse texture of an oyster shell and was so uncared for, almost deformed, that Haber had to get a grip on himself to keep from turning his face away or letting go.

"Not a pretty sight, eh, Mr. Haber? the housekeeper said as if she had read his very thoughts. "It's a poor old working woman's foot," she said, and Haber felt a prick of shame at his squeamishness.

"You're going to have a blister, I'm afraid," he said.

"Won't be the first," the housekeeper said with a quiet pride Haber did not miss.

"No, I suspect not," Haber said and, quiet suddenly, felt the absolute poverty, the utter selfishness of his own life. What marks of earnest work did his pale and soft and pampered body bear? Where was there so much as even an infinitesimal scratch to bear witness to a useful and purposefully lived life?

"Ah, washing the disciple's feet, are we?" Reverend Bogard said as he came into the kitchen, and whether it was out of spite or, in fact, an impulsive act of humility, Haber snatched the dishcloth from his arm and began drying the housekeeper's old and maimed foot.

"'If I wash thee not, thou hast no part with me' is, I believe, the message," Reverend Bogard said. "The other message I am pledged to deliver is that your mother is eager for her tea and wonders if the house is still standing."

"Mr. Haber, please," the housekeeper said, and she pulled her foot away and stood with such a sudden abruptness that she kicked the plastic dishpan of ice water and some of it splashed on Haber's trousers.

"Ah, dear Haber," Reverend Bogard said. "Not every act of contrition is received with open arms, I'm sorry to say."

"It was not act of contrition," Haber said in that tetchy voice he got when he was struggling to keep control of himself. "Commiseration, perhaps. Compassion, Clarence," he sputtered, and he turned on his heels and, with an oddly military bearing and crimson cheeks, marched out of the kitchen and, hurrying past the open door to the drawing room, sought a moment's refuge in the library.

The green damask curtains had been drawn, the lamps had been lit, and someone, Adele of course, had put more logs on the fire. With the curtains drawn and the lamps making pools of yellow light, the room had a semitransparent look as if it were but a thin membrane between Haber and the descending darkness outside, and he thought, It will be cold tonight, and I will not feel it, and for the first time in his life Haber Hill Culpepper allowed himself to acknowledge that he had never been cold without recourse to warmth, never been hungry without the immediate promise of nourishment, never had he burned himself, never so much as suffered a single callus, never, at least for as long as he could remember, had he even dirtied his hands. Dear God, no wonder it was easier for a camel to slip through the eye of a needle than for a rich man to ascend unto Heaven, he thought, and as if an aggressive act would make the room seem more substantial, and him within it, Haber took up the poker and struck at the logs. A flame danced nimbly, and when he struck again, a sequined shower of golden sparks went volleying up the chimney. Oh, but what a pathetically ineffectual man he was, ranting and raving, God help him, about compassion, of all things, and how utterly vain, vain and arrogant, was his foolish quest for divine disclosure. He struck again at the fire and another golden shower of sequined sparks flew up the chimney, and as he watched, as if in a trance, Haber wondered if perhaps he wasn't going about his quest in the wrong way. Instead of seeking God's approbation and approval, His esteem, which he now admitted was what he had sought, as he had, even as a child, sought these things from his father, why not send God, as if on these sequined sparks, some sign, some softly murmured prayer that he did indeed know that he was especially blessed and that he was grateful, grateful and glad, and never again would he take these manifold blessings for granted. And these whispered imprecations of atonement did seem to flare up into golden sparks and a modest peace did descend upon Haber Hill Culpepper, and he thought, as he put the poker away, he ought to thank God even for that, and so he did.

When, at last, Haber rejoined Mrs. Culpepper and the Reverend Bogard in the drawing room, Haber begged the Reverend Bogard for his pardon, and he received it, and soon the housekeeper came in bearing the eighteenth-century English sterling silver salver with another pot of tea and Haber's birthday cake ablaze with candles.

"Now that's what I call a cake," Reverend Bogard said, and rubbed his hands in avid anticipation.

"It's Mr. Haber's favorite," the housekeeper said.

"Just leave it, Adele, Mr. Haber can serve," Mrs. Culpepper said, and the housekeeper laid the sterling silver salver on the table next to Haber's chair. And as the housekeeper was turning to leave, Haber asked her to please wait a minute, and after a small struggle for the right words, he said, "Adele, Mother and I, I am sure, could never manage without you and I want you to know that."

"Thank you kindly, Mr. Haber," the housekeeper said, and she smiled, and as he watched the dear old soul hobble bravely out of the room, Haber Hill Culpepper thought that perhaps he had at last received his "but a Crumb," and if not a true epiphany, if some profound essence of divine disclosure were forever to elude him, he knew it to be enough, maybe even more than he deserved, and with a zestfulness that Haber Hill Culpepper had not allowed himself since he had been a small boy, he bent his head to the three-layered chocolate birthday cake and blew out the candles.

Pam Durban

BELONGING

(from *Indiana Review*)

I

One night, in a high wind that smelled of rain, a two-hundred-year-old water oak on the courthouse square in Timmons toppled over, its roots not as tough or deep as its age would have led you to hope, and for days, while the city workmen cut it up and hauled it off, people came by to stare at the wide paw of roots and to strip mistletoe from the crown. The tree fell in July, after almost fifty hot and rainless days, and its fall seemed to mark some boundary line between trouble and catastrophe. The peach crop was already ruined, and in the fields outside of town, half-grown corn and beans burned where they'd sprouted. Then the pines began to brown and shed their needles; the reservoirs shrank, and down at the Steakhouse, the Full Gospel Businessmen's Association cranked up the apocalypse machine. "Signs of the End Times!," the paper announced would be the topic of three prayer breakfast programs in one week. "Record Attendance," the paper reported when the week was done.

That summer the animals began to come out from where they live in good times. All over town, water moccasins and copperheads showed up in swimming pools; wasps drove their stingers into people's flesh, going for moisture, and everywhere it seemed, the lines between things dissolved in the heat. I have a picture from that summer, cut from the paper and saved all this time, because it reminds me of a kind of bond that flush times seldom make. The picture shows a deer, a *buck,* with a handsome rack of antlers drinking from a *saucepan* in somebody's backyard a block from the courthouse square. In the middle of the wrought-iron patio furniture, the whiskey barrels spilling over with impatiens, that buck drinks deep from the pan held out to him by a timid-looking woman wearing pearls and a round-collared blouse and flats. One morning, the paper reported, she came out and found the buck drinking out of her bird bath, and when she moved closer, it kept an eye on her and went right on drinking. That's how thirsty it was. The next morning it was back, and when she offered the saucepan filled to the brim with water, it came right up to her as naturally as if it knew her.

Of course, that was the summer I went back to Timmons. I couldn't wait for fall or winter or delicate, sweet spring. Oh, no. My marriage to Thomas had fallen apart; I had to act. Drought or no drought I was going home to where there was solid ground, not quicksand under my feet. So I headed for home in the middle of June. The divorce happened so suddenly. I won't burden you with all the gory details. Suffice it to say that when it was over I didn't feel whole anymore; I felt like a sheet of glass covered with hairline cracks. One tap in just the right spot, and who knows what? One month—March—we were deciding to get divorced and congratulating ourselves on how tender we'd managed to remain, even in this, to each other. By April, we'd hired lawyers; we spent all of May dragging our friends into court to testify to each other's failings and lacks in order that one of us would be judged more fit than the other to raise Christina, our daughter. We pulled out all the stops. I was amazed at my cunning and his, at what we knew about each other when, really, we'd stopped caring about discovering those things anymore. It seemed we'd discovered all over again depths and intensities that we'd first loved in each other. Only now we held them up, shook them in each other's faces. Look at your willful heart. See how you've failed me.

"Did you ever see Mrs. Holmes drink to excess?"

"Oh, yes, several times at parties."

"And what happened when she drank?"

"She would try and pick fights with Tom or anyone else who'd listen."

I sat there astonished, scrunched down in my seat, watching our lives go by as though they were a series of photographs taken on the sly by some greasy detective. *Pop!* Me holding a plastic cup full of beer, hair gone wild, shaking my butt alone on the dance floor at three A.M., eyes closed in private ecstasy. *Pop!* Thomas losing his temper, forcing Christina to wear a stiff new pair of shoes that made her trip and fall and bloody her nose. *Pop!* My leaving Christina asleep in her car seat while I ran into the grocery store for a jar of mayonnaise, finding her on the floor when I returned, screaming. *Pop!* I peeked at Thomas. He looked as sick as I felt, gnawing on his bottom lip as though he'd forgotten it. And it wasn't that I didn't recognize myself or him; the trouble was, I did, I recognized us both. We weren't unreal, just sadly magnified, our kinked, weak places blown all out of scale until our whole lives looked deformed.

When it was finally over, I went home and ran the tub full of the hottest water I could stand and sat there for hours. When the water cooled, I added more hot. I felt my pores open, felt the evil drain out, and as I soaked and purged myself, I looked out of the small, square window above the tub. This was Rochester, New York; there was a tall blue spruce beside the house, a bright blue sky beyond. The longer I looked, the stranger the place seemed, and the voices coming in from the street sounded harsh to me; they, and that place, all seemed part of the divorce and what I had become. I drained the tub and scrubbed it clean. I packed up our things, Christina's and mine—because I had won custody of her after all—and headed for home. To Timmons, South Carolina. Land of pines and sand and thick air and rich voices. You know the feeling. Home to recover a simpler sense of belonging.

At first, I thought it was going to be all right. There were signs. Timmons then was a faded little town on the fall line, the shore of the ancient eastern ocean that disappeared eons ago and left the place marked forever with the subtle drag of its ebb. Everything seemed to flow downhill there or pooled and lay dormant. I could rest there. Or so I thought, I was not in my right mind that summer, but whenever I walked downtown and saw the town huddled around the courthouse square and the inconsolable Confederate soldier keeping watch in the thick shade of water oaks, my heart lifted because I knew that no harm could come to me or to Christina there.

* * *

One day in July, when I'd been home for a month, I went down to my father's office to transfer the insurance on my car from New York to South Carolina. As I walked around the square moving slow through the heat like everyone else, I was pleased to recognize that I loved the heat; its thickness propped me up, and I didn't feel quite so capsized any longer. Papa had pull, and he'd helped me get a job at the Vaucluse County Tax Assessor's Office. Christina and I had rented a house over near the high school. I was young, starting over. Things were looking up.

I opened the door into Papa's office and the first thing I saw were the pictures. On the walls to either side of the door, like gates. On one wall, a portrait of Abraham Lincoln, the dark, sorrowful, aged Lincoln of the end of the Civil War. On the other, a painting in a gilt frame of a fireman carrying a golden-haired child clear of a burning building. Promotional pictures, compliments of Lincoln Life and The Fireman's Fund, companies his office represented. They'd been there all my life, but when I saw them that day, they seemed to jump out at me, illuminated, each line and color vivid and momentous as though they were messages or prophecies. At first, I couldn't speak. Then I put my hands up over my face and began to cry. It just flowed out of me as if those silly pictures had struck through a knot inside and this was what was behind that knot, waiting to be freed. Those silly pictures. Abe Lincoln, craggy and mournfully wise. The fire always burning, devouring the house, and the child, with its eyes as quiet as a newborn's, resting in the arms of the fireman who wore his high rubber boots and slicker like armor. Pictures from my childhood. "It's nothing," I said to Papa who had come to the counter and stood there, looking helpless, straightening the knot in his tie and frowning. "I guess I'm just a little emotional these days." How to explain to him the gratitude I felt. I could have dropped to my knees with thankfulness.

He nodded in a clipped way and went instantly grim which means his mouth clamped shut, his jaw hardened, his whole face looked belligerent. *Emotional,* of course, was a code word for what Thomas had done to me. Papa stared out the door with a challenging expression as if someone were coming up the steps who was responsible for my crying, and he intended to blast this person as soon as he dared to come through the door. I wiped my eyes with a paper napkin I'd found in my purse and I said, "It was me, too, Papa. It wasn't just Thomas."

He rapped his knuckles on the counter. "Who said anything about him?" he said.

I patted his hand, pulled my insurance policy out of my purse. "Don't worry, Papa," I wanted to say. "I am still the person who recognizes those pictures."

That night, it was late and hot and I couldn't sleep. The heat stuffed the room, the kind of heat that a fan spreads but can't dissipate. There is nothing to do in this kind of heat but to lie inside it, to lie very still, hardly breathing and not to get too worked up about anything, not even to think if you can help it. I was trying to do that, but every dog for miles around was barking. The schnauzer next door sounded like a squeeze toy that someone was stepping on again and again. Across the street, the German shepherd kept up the same hoarse, two-stroke carping, and the redbone hound in the pen one street over alternately howled and rasped out its misery while the clock moved from two to three and on into the deep darkness beyond. The longer I listened, the hotter it got and the darker my thoughts became. I tried to hold them up, but they kept sliding down, and soon I was thinking poison, poison and death, and the particulars of poison and death. I began to imagine the time of night when poison would be most potent. Four A.M., I thought, the pit of darkness; I imagined myself slipping along the fences from yard to yard, the fatal meatballs in my hands. I imagined the tone of voice I would use to cajole them to me, saw the meat wolfed down. I imagined the convulsions, then blessed silence.

At three-thirty, I got up weak, shaking from the depth and the darkness of these thoughts. There at home, in the place of safety, I felt the will to hurt, to *kill*. So I carried Christina, who was sleeping, and put her into the car and started driving out the by-pass, not knowing, really, where I was going or what I was looking for but looking for *something*, and knowing it. The Holiday Inn flashed by and the Datsun dealership with its Fourth of July sale banner still intact. Haloes of thick, pink air hung around the lights that lined the highway, and the sky looked as if it wasn't really night but day with a dark screen slid in front of it until it was time for the sun to rise.

As I drove, it began to dawn on me that I watched the rearview mirror almost constantly, waiting for the moment when the person following me finally switched on his headlights, announced himself. And then I became aware of a voice going round and round inside my head, ominous words set to a catchy melody, the song of my failings. *Snatched the child out of a sound sleep,* it sang. *Yanked her out of bed in the dead of night and put her in the car and drove around like a crazy woman and wouldn't tell anyone why she'd done it or where she'd gone.* It was Thomas's voice, of course, swearing and testifying, witnessing. *Capricious, it sang. Sullen, selfish, lazy. She flirts. She drinks. SHE AVOIDS HER RESPONSIBILITIES.* But it wasn't just his voice. Oh no. If it had been, I could have shut if off, maybe; it was *his* voice in *my* head, inside, deep, accompanied by big drums that carried for miles through the heavy air of night. How foolish of me to think I could escape this chorus, the one that goes: Unfit. *MO*– ther. Unfit. *MO*–ther. Unfit unfit unfit.

Meanwhile, I drove like the crazywoman of the courtroom scenarios, feeling stranger and stranger, as though I'd drifted into a place I did not know. I was south of Timmons by then, out where the by-pass curves around and joins the old highway that takes you to the coast. And just as the drums and the chorus were about to come around again, I saw the crown of a tree, a solid mass of darkness, dark against the dark sky, rising up at the end of a field as though it were growing wider as I drove towards it, and I knew that this was what I had been looking for. It was an oak, very old, with such an individual spread and shape, topping up over the cotton and the soybean fields at the edge of town like a dark boil rising and rounding into the sky, that for years, in the days when my father's family closed up the house in Timmons and moved down to Sullivan's Island for the summer, they had used it as a sign that they'd left town behind and were heading for the low country.

I'm not ashamed to tell you what I did next. When I saw that tree, I pulled over onto the shoulder and put my head down on the wheel and I cried until my whole face felt wet and soft. I didn't try to muffle it either, but Christina went right on sleeping in the back seat. Christina could sleep through anything and for this I'm grateful. And when I was finished, I wiped my eyes. I looked at Christina's sleeping face where all was quiet and untouched. No more weeping, I said to myself. And no self-pity. I am back where I belong, I thought. I am home. I am safe. I will not murder anyone's dog.

II

It didn't take much to change that. One day, I went over to Mother and Daddy's to pick up Christina after work. As I got out of the car it struck me how unchanged the house looked. From the outside, it looked the same as it had looked when I was growing up there, as it might have looked, judging from the photographs I've seen, when Daddy lived there as a child with his parents. Same slumped roofline and wide, sagging porches wrapped around three sides of the house. Same arbor in the side yard smothered in wisteria vine. If you wanted to, you could try, as I tried, to make the house into a kind of unmoving center. And that would work, as long as you stayed outside. But then you'd go inside and see that Mama had won her bid for central air, a new kitchen, a family room with an enormous brick fireplace at one end. You'd see all that, then step beyond those zones of light and fresh paint to find the dark pine floors, worn Oriental carpets and thin-skinned ancestors looking down from their heavy frames, and almost believe again if only you hadn't passed through the light.

Mother and Christina were back in the family room. Mother with her feet up, knitting, and Christina in her house under the card table. It was a white cloth house with a wooden spindle to hold up the peak of the roof and green shutters, a red door with a brass knocker, window boxes with red geraniums, all printed on the cloth so skillfully you'd think you could knock on the door and walk right inside. I bought it for her just after we moved back here. I set it up in my room beside my bed, but at first she would only sleep with me, pressed tight against me, holding my hand. Those nights I lay perfectly still, alert to every sound in the house, as if by keeping still that way, guarding her while she slept, I might heal her dreams and make her safe and ease trouble from her mind and heart as easily as the clouds I saw through the bedroom window glided across the sky.

When I came through the door, she stuck her head out from under the cloth and brushed her tangled light hair out of her eyes and said, very carefully, in the way she'd begun to speak since the divorce, "I'm sorry, Mother, but I have company. I can't go home right now."

"All right," I said. "You finish your visit and then we'll go." To indulge her that way, to give her room and time, to loosen a knot that I had tied around her life and mine during the divorce, gave me enormous pleasure, the kind of pleasure you'd feel if you shoved your hands into your pockets, tipped back on your heels until you were looking up into the whole sky and took deep breaths of a watery spring morning.

Mother sat in her recliner, tipped back halfway, knitting her way around one sleeve of a thick green sweater she was making for Christina, keeping an eye on the clock on the mantel. "Have a seat," she said. "Is it getting any cooler outside?"

"Not one degree," I said. "The bank clock said 101 when I came through town." I watched her hands; they are broad, flat, heavy hands, more suited to driving a team than knitting, and to see her hands working needles and yarn was like watching a miracle take place, one substance turned miraculously into another. Water into wine. Loaves and fishes. It has always been calming to me to watch Mother knit that way. It may have been one of my earliest memories. White yarn, then the feel of night and the yarn covering me and Mother's smell in the yarn. I remembered those things that summer. I counted on them.

"Well, shoot," she said. "I'm going to stop paying any attention to that idiotic weatherman. I think they pay him to be cheerful like that," she said, and she glanced up at the clock with her needles going.

"No doubt," I said. In that heat it was impossible to imagine a time when Christina would ever need a *sweater*, but Mother was knitting it now, and I loved her for it. I bent over and kissed the top of her head, and she leaned against me for a second. "What've you all been up to today?" I said.

She checked the clock again. Four minutes till five. "Oh, not much," she said. "We went down to the market after some of those pretty little butterbeans but it was slim pickings. This drought has just about done everybody in."

When the first note of five struck, she tucked her knitting down into a tapestry bag beside the chair, kicked the footrest down and stood. She smoothed down the front of her slacks. "Let's have our bourbon," she said, and before I could answer, she was at the counter. Glass, ice, silver jigger, Wild Turkey all appeared as if she'd drawn them down out of the air. One, two, she measured and poured the bourbon into a glass, like a scientist measuring something volatile into a beaker, then added a dash of water. "Join me?" she asked.

"Not just now, Mother, thanks," I said. "Not this evening."

"Suit yourself," she said and standing at the counter, she took a long pull at the drink. Then she wrapped a napkin around the base of the glass and came back to the recliner and sat down again with a groan.

She drank as if she'd been thirsty for years and this was the first oasis she'd come to. The glass was practically empty when she put it down on the table beside the recliner and picked up her knitting again, her face relaxed now. Watching her drink, it used to be that I could feel superior, horrified—she has always drunk with this barely controlled need, painful to see. My own thirst, I said to myself, was more dignified, controlled, but as I watched her that night, I saw myself too, in all those cheap courtroom pictures that Thomas's friends had sketched, and I realized that it was no good pretending that I didn't know what she was feeling. I did. I do. I know that thirst and the desire to quench it that grows more urgent with each glass, the feeling that the answer to the thirst lies at the bottom of the glass, until the thirst and the quenching of the thirst get all mixed up together.

In the middle of Mother's second bourbon, Christina crawled out of her house under the card table. She frowned and stood up with her fists on her hips. "They've gone now," she said.

Mother leaned way out toward Christina and her eyes got narrow and liquid-dark. "Did you have a good visit with your company, sugar?" she asked, and I thought of treacle, that odd English word from some storybook, the thick, sweet love that bourbon heated up for her, drizzled over Christina's head, over mine or Papa's. Christina was wary, I could tell by the way she stood, hands laced behind her back, twisting from side to side as she talked. "Yes," she said, "but they're very old. They ate up all my food."

Mother laughed. "Then you and your mother will just have to stay for supper won't you?" she said.

* * *

I meant to leave right after the meal, but as soon as I finished loading the dishes into the dishwasher and sat down in the rocker beside the fireplace, Christina crawled up into my lap and fell asleep like a stone sinking through water, the way a child can do, and then we were talking about Papa's retirement, which, I had learned, is not a subject I could walk out on. He'd been looking, Mother had said, for a last straw for two years now, some sign that he was getting too old to be traipsing around the countryside in the heat, selling houses to people who suspected that every word he spoke was a con, keeping up the insurance end of the business on top of that. Hell, he said that night, as he'd said on many other nights, he didn't even *care* about houses any more, so what was the point? There wasn't one, Mother and I agreed as we'd agreed before though neither of us could embellish that thought for him or give it more weight. He looked from Mama to me and back and when he saw we couldn't help him, he picked up the newspaper and snapped it open.

Christina was four years old then, heavy and solid in my lap, and I rocked her and rested my cheek on the damp crown of her head. I should have picked her up right then, said goodnight, gone home. But the only sounds in the room were the steady knocking of the clock, the creak of the chair, and the click of Mother's knitting needles building up the green yarn round and round. It felt good to sit there with those noises going round, weaving layer on layer. It felt safe. And then, Papa folded the newspaper and tossed it onto the hearth. He reached across the table that sat between their two recliners and poked Mama's arm. "Look here," he said. "I had a disturbing experience today. I was out in that new subdivision measuring a house and the heat just got to me." Mother's needles and my chair stopped at the same time. When he saw that he had our attention he ran his hand back through his hair and all over his face as if he were washing it. "Do you all remember that old tree that my family used to look for when we were going down to the beach?"

"Yes," I said. "I know the one you mean." I thought of the way it had looked, so wide and so dark against the sky, as if anything could find shelter there.

Mother looked at him with her knitting folded in her lap, her big hands resting on the wool, her eyes gone deep and brown and watchful. Drinking always makes her watchful as if some other sense had been activated in her and she were trying to divine with this sense the true meaning of what was being said. It was a warning, a flare, that look, but I missed it.

"Well, when the heat got to me, I thought I'd go sit in the shade of that tree for a little while and rest."

Yes, I said to myself, *yes, that would have been the thing to do*. Head for that tree.

He sat up straight with a beamish look on his face. He looked slyly at Mama and me and squeezed his folded hands between his knees. For a second, I was afraid he might giggle. I was not used to this brightness in him, the optimism he'd cultivated over the last few years, a defensive cheerfulness that hung on him like a cheap suit, a way of laughing that deflected angry words, angry looks. "Well, when I got there, son of a gun if it wasn't hotter in the shade than it was outside. It was so close I thought I was going to suffocate in there. I'm getting too old for all this," he said.

Mother didn't answer, but they looked at each other for a long time. "I think I'm going to go and retire some day real soon here," he said. "What do you say to that, old lady?" He looked from Mother to me and back, his eyes eager, waiting. I thought of my father and me and that tree. I thought of him running for cover, running for the tree, myself driving out the road that night. But at the edge of that shade, I lost him. I couldn't go in. Mine had worked and his didn't, and I wasn't about to give up that shelter.

Mother checked her chair, slowed it, and he kept his hand on her arm, resting there. "I've told you," she said, "*anytime* is fine with me." She gave him the same look she'd given me earlier, brown and sharp and wary, and drained her glass again and got up to make herself another one.

He shifted his attention to me; he held up his finger in the old tutorial style. "However," he said. "This kind of thing takes careful planning. It's not the sort of thing you just jump right into."

"No, Daddy, I know it isn't," I said.

But Mother was back by then, and he spoke to her. "This kind of thing is somewhat, ah, irrevocable," he said. "There are just a few things I have to take care of before I can let go."

"Such as?" Mother said, holding her head to one side and waiting, the way she used to wait when she helped with lessons.

"Such as?" he answered. "Such as?" and his eyes widened in mock astonishment. How could we not know? He ticked them off on his fingers impatiently for the benefit of the slow learners. "Such as getting the supplemental Medicare insurance in order; such as checking with the Social Security office and making sure the income would continue if something happened to me."

Mother looked at him tenderly as if he were a pitiful child who couldn't help his ignorance, and in that tenderness I saw, finally, the danger we were in. "You mean *when*, don't you?" she asked, as if she'd just said "How does meatloaf sound for dinner tonight?" and she picked up her knitting again. But my heart went cold and still, as cold as it had felt in the courtroom as I'd listened to the real story of my life, the one beneath the disguise of love and goodness I'd built so carefully, and what she'd said seemed to flash, a blue-white explosion high in the air, the thing that happens before the fire, before the noise and the wind. Papa's face reflected it, too. Shock, collapse, as if something carefully supported had fallen in. A few strands of hair lay plastered to Christina's cheek, stuck in the corners of her mouth. I pulled them free and smoothed hair behind her ears to steady myself because what Mother had said frightened me so much I wanted to hit her. To strike her and say *don't talk, don't talk*, the way Christina did when she flailed at me. But I knew I'd get about as far with Mother as Christina got with me, and meanwhile, Papa had faced into the flash.

He swallowed, forced a smile. "When *what*, Louise?" he said with such resignation and familiarity in his voice that for a moment I believe I saw what life was like for them day to day. The waiting, the anger, Mother trying to come to terms with something he wanted to refuse. He folded his hands, then opened them and stared down into his palms, and his whole face seemed to sag. Without unfolding his hands, he rubbed one palm with the other thumb.

"*When* something happens to you, not *if*," she said, holding the sweater by the shoulders, sizing it up.

"*Oh, Mother, really,*" I said, trying to keep my voice light, playful, only it came out like a joke told stupidly.

"Oh, Mother, what?" she said sharply. She raised her head; her mouth changed.

And then I stopped, I faltered. I couldn't answer. A few years earlier, I would have insisted, *You're not going to die.* I would have said, *You're going to live a long time yet. Your life will be good.* And it frightened me to think of how recently I would have insisted, argued. Hadn't I come home to find something like the faith it would take to say that again? And yet, I could not say it. Not even to Christina who breathed against me, moist and heavy and strong in my arms, and when I thought about that, I held her tighter till she grimaced in her sleep.

I tried to come up with another question, the right question this time, that would ease her toward the life-giving answer. *What's wrong with believing that you will live?* I would have asked once, only I didn't want to hear Mother's answer, the one she was ready to give, the one that made her back stiffen and her eyes dare anyone to ask. She had had two episodes, the doctor calls them, two incidents of breast cancer. Within a year she lost both breasts, and where they had been there were two long sutures, like lightning, healed white. That night, she had had two episodes of breast cancer, three bourbons, a year of chemotherapy and radiation, two years now of tests every three months, blood tests and bone scans and X-rays, and waiting to see what developed. And I thought of times in the room with her when she was changing clothes and I had seen those scars, and I knew why the question wouldn't come out right: it was the wrong question.

"Can't argue with that logic now, can you?" Papa's dismayed face addressed the air. The shine, the bluster of a few minutes before had drained out of him and left behind a kind of brittle puzzlement that crimped his mouth and hardened his eyes. Her illness had aged them both, I saw, the illness and the waiting. And I wondered if it might now have been the same face he'd turned to the shade that would not take him in, the shade he'd counted on that had smothered him. My father, who'd counted on so much.

"So," Mother said, and she shook herself. She looked calm again, as if she'd gotten free for the moment from something she was tangled in, and a little embarrassed. "Well, what are we going to do with all that time you'll have when you retire?" She didn't look up from her knitting, but she said it gently, almost playfully, she said it as if she knew what she'd said before. "I've always wanted to go on some of those cruises."

Seeing my chance, I jumped. "Now you're talking," I said. I wanted them to go someplace I could imagine them going, someplace I could be happy for them and imagine their contentment

again, not their weariness, not the corrosive facts of their lives. To
Disneyland, if that's what they wanted to do or the Caribbean, even
better. One long sun-drunk fiesta. I saw them tipped back in deck
chairs while a steward brought them tall, frosted drinks with exotic
names and little umbrellas stuck in the froth. At home, Papa would
return to the early pleasures of his life; he would putter in the yard,
study military history, carve duck decoys, raise pointer pups into
field trial champions. He would create with his life a dependable
symmetry and an old age which was the reward of a well-lived life
and the showing forth, the flowering of that life's meaning. "I'll bet
you're going to do a lot of hunting and fishing," I said.

He looked at me; he looked at Mama. "No," he said. "I'm going
to do some things that will surprise you both." He said it triumphantly, as if he'd smuggled diamonds past us. He sat back satisfied
and folded his arms across his chest and smiled to himself. Christina
sighed in her sleep and burrowed deeper into my blouse.

"Surprise us now," I said. Mother kept at her knitting, but you
could tell by the way she frowned at the needles that she was waiting
for him to speak.

"Well, now," he said quietly, "what would you say if I told you I
was going to learn to play the trumpet?" He said it as shyly as if it
were a dream nourished in silence, offered now, fragile and
exquisite.

Mother opened her mouth; she started to speak and though I
didn't, inside I said, *Let him go on. Let him finish in his own way for
once.* Then I felt very still, and I realized what I'd said. Finish, I'd
said. Let him finish. And that is the trouble, I think, with being
someplace and among people you know. You know what you see
there better than in other places. What you see and hear and how
you fit.

She closed her mouth and looked at him. Her eyes got soft. "Well,
wouldn't that be something?" she said. "Wouldn't it be something
to hear you play the trumpet?"

He swallowed and nodded and stared off at nothing in the same
way he'd nodded and stared when I'd burst into tears in his office:
like a soldier scanning the horizon for signs of the enemy.

I put my cheek down on the crown of Christina's head and
stroked the delicate line of her nose, and the feel of her head brought
back to me the way she had looked when I first saw her coming out

of my body, in the mirror that Thomas held between my legs in the delivery room while I pushed and blew and panted and her head crowned. What I saw then, through a haze of pain and astonishment, was the most perfect sight I have ever been blessed to see, her head stretching my body into a wide circle. Thomas saw it, too, I know he did, and somewhere back in some deep niche in our hearts, the belief rooted and grew that the sight of her head made the circle that could not be broken, that we were safe because of that perfection we had brought into the world, and that all we needed to do was to keep that dream, that vision close to our hearts, to live by it, and everything would be all right. And that summer, Thomas and I were divorced. We came to despise the sight of each other and the sound of each other's voices, and when it was over, he went back to Denver to live, the mile high city where the mountains still comfort him, no doubt, with the familiar and unchanging distances. His first child support check had come early, folded inside a blank sheet of typing paper and the night I got it, I sat with Christina and put my head down on her head and remembered her birth and felt strong again. That night with Mother and Daddy, no matter how tightly I pressed my check against Christina, the feeling wouldn't come back.

III

All that summer, Papa edged toward retiring like someone inching out and out toward the end of a high diving board. By the middle of August, and still no rain in anyone's future, he stood on the edge with his eyes closed, his toes already committed, ready to jump. And that's when Wallace Posey died.

Just like that is what people here call sudden death and that's what happened to Mr. Posey. They say it with palms turned up to try and show, I think, the suddenness, the mystery. It goes like this: hand closed tight, a fist, life. Then open, empty, gone. Just like that. Mr. Posey's wife, Thelma, was Papa's typist when he needed a clean, professional job done on a real estate appraisal or a report to the SC Board of Realtors, and that's how he met Wallace, and the two of them got to be friends. They went hunting a few times down in the Santee-Cooper and came back with nothing. Came back happy, though, and worn out. They went up to Clemson together to football games, decked out, Mother told me, in identical orange windbreakers with white tiger paws printed on the chests, like twins. Then one night, not long after he retired, Wallace was watching TV back in the family room with his granddaughter, and when a commercial came on he asked her to go get him something to drink. When she came back with the glass, he was slumped over in his chair and he was gone. Heart, of course. Stopped, between one beat and the next. "Run go get me a Coke before the show comes back on," is what people at the viewing repeated to each other as the last words Wallace Posey added to the long conversation that all of us are having on this earth.

When Papa heard about Wallace, he shouted. He was out in the yard with the floodlights on, working in the flowerbed outside the kitchen window, when Mama called him to come inside. *"What's this?"* he shouted, when she told him, and got red in the face, as though he'd come into his own house and caught somebody robbing him. "He *shouted* at me," she said. "Can you imagine?" I knew that I was supposed to say no, no I can't, it's impossible, but before I knew it, without thinking, I'd said *yes*. And I could, that was the amazing thing. I could imagine it. Imagine the evening when the temperature dropped a few degrees and all over town, people came out to water their lawns. Imagine Papa down on his knees in the dirt, the peaceful look that came over his face as he dug and pulled, the way I've felt sometimes, digging in the dirt, planting things, as if I'd left the world of air and measured time and had entered another world, the earth's world, where the smallest seed brings the most astonishing abundance, where the earthworm's turn back under the soil seems to carry with it a secret that takes me closer to the source of some life that I seem to be living, too. Then the shock, the news, your brain cold at the root, numb, refusing. The way I'd felt in court or when I'd learned about Mother's cancer. *No,* you shout. *Not to her. To him. To me.* What is there to do but shout when you hear those things, when the known world breaks up under your feet?

So Wallace died and Wallace was buried, big, kind-faced, slow-talking Wallace Posey, one morning when the sun sizzled in the sky. That evening, I went out for a drink with some people from work, and I didn't get back over to the house to pick up Christina until almost dark. Out in the side yard, Mama was refilling the humming-bird feeders, and a few of the tiny birds zoomed in and out of the light and hovered around her, chittering angrily. I almost yelled, "Look out," but I knew she would have shushed me, waved me away. She had developed a secret sympathy with the hummingbirds, their fierceness, their habits. But if you asked her about it, she would only wink and say, "They're some special birds," with a sly look in her eyes, nothing more. So I stood and watched, thinking how it must be getting close to time for their migration south. All summer they had hung around the feeder, the column of red sugar syrup, like do-mesticated jewels, their red throats pulsing, then had darted off to suck the flowers. But, toward September, they became industrious as ants, and fearless, stocking up for their long haul across the Gulf of Mexico, Mother said. Then they attacked each other, they dove at whoever came near the feeder. And Mother was out there among them, understanding their fierceness while they hovered and chit-tered around her—*robber, thief*.

"Just hold your horses," I heard her say, "I'm getting there as fast as I can."

"Howdy," I yelled.

Without turning, she said, "He hasn't moved since we got back. I told him he had no business carrying Wallace's coffin around out in that heat, but he still thinks he's thirty years old."

Let him alone, I wanted to say, but something in the set of her back stopped me. Not everybody has to live the way she had to live, not everybody has to expose the foolishness of things as if that fool-ishness, if it slipped by unnoticed, might destroy them. Not every-body has to measure their survival by how steadily they can look at the fire. But Mother did.

I hurried up the back steps and into the house. Daddy and Chris-tina were back in the den, him in the big recliner rocker, tipped back, watching Mama out the window, Christina on the floor pretending that the angel food cake pan was a record player and dropping old forty-fives on its spindle, singing to herself.

When I opened the door, she jumped up and ran to me and bur-ied her face in my skirt.

"What's all this?" I said, trying to pry her chin up so that I could look at her face. She pressed herself against my legs and wouldn't turn loose.

"It's me, I'm afraid," Papa said. He knocked his knuckles against the wooden arm of the chair. He looked pale and stern. A blue vein stood out near his temple, and the skin over the cut of his cheekbones looked thin. He wore his funeral suit, tie loosened, jacket thrown over the footstool of the recliner. His shoes were so new that only two light disks of scratches showed on the soles, and it occurred to me that he only wore those shoes to funerals, that those scratches were the marks left by the funerals of his friends. "I told her she couldn't go out and play in the yard, and she pitched one of her fits." Our eyes met in weary sympathy. Oh, yes, one of her fits.

"I'm sorry, Papa," I said. "Look at me, Christina," I said, but when she did I wished she hadn't. Her face was pinched, her eyes had a bald, rinsed, look. "Oh, baby," I said, stroking her hair. We were all, by then, too familiar with Christina's tantrums, those seizures of thwarted will and rage that twisted her face and stiffened her body and made her strike out at whoever came close. That summer there were times with her when I felt myself approaching an edge, when I'd almost convinced myself that she was not my child, the infant, who had looked at me with such quiet eyes, and if not my child, then someone I might hurt if she did not stop screaming. That summer, at night, with Christina screaming in her room where I'd sent her, I remembered how delicious it had been to imagine poisoning the dogs, ending the trouble, how easy it had seemed to turn on Thomas, to see him as a stranger and to hurt him, and it seemed to me that while I wasn't looking, things had become more real somehow, more dangerous, and I could no longer believe that cruelty was impossible, something that other people did. That summer, it seemed, I learned to discipline myself, to make myself recall that Christina in a rage was no monster: even then, she was my child. Growing more complex, past the point where I could guess her thoughts or know her completely, still my child. The night of Wallace Posey's funeral I stroked her back, her head, kept my voice low. "Just calm down," I said. "Why couldn't she go out?" I asked Papa.

"I couldn't chase her," he said. "I can hardly move. That man was just too heavy," he said angrily, holding up his hand, flexing it as if the weight of the coffin had stiffened it, as if the testimony of that weight still lay in his hand.

"Well, what did you expect?" I said. "Did you expect that he'd be lighter just because he was dead?" I said it because he frightened me talking that way, but as soon as I'd said it, I was sorry. He looked bewildered. Then his face pinched, as if a cold wind had blown onto it and his mouth clamped shut tight as a turtle's. I thought of Mother and her blunt ways, the things she feels obliged to say because of what's happened to her, as if her mission in life had become the stamping out of illusion. What is happening to me? I thought. I am not the person I was, that I always imagined myself to be.

Papa rallied. "It was his own fault," he said.

"What was?" I pried Christina loose from my skirt and pushed her hair back out of her face. She kept her eyes shut tight and slung her head from side to side. I tried to lift her, but she squeezed her arms tight against her sides so that I couldn't get my hands under her armpits. Closing me out, going deeper into her body, and pulling it shut around her. I felt the tightening of panic in my chest.

"Wallace should have known better," he said. "A man who's lived an active life can't just retire like that without something to do," he said.

Something to do. He folded his hands and looked at me, and I saw fear shining out of his face, a kind of tensed waiting, a straining to hear an answer, anything. In the past, I might have argued with him. I might have tried to convince him of the senselessness of fear. When I was a child, I spoke as a child. That day I looked at his face and I thought: he is talking about himself. He is thinking of Wallace's life as his own, ticking along next to his. Friends. Now this. And he is more in danger now for knowing Wallace's fate. Of course he was. Of course he wanted proof. Big Wallace Posey suddenly light as a husk, a wing, proof that his death was a fluke, a kink. And when there was not proof, no setting it aside or tossing it back, he needed someone to say *I know.* "Everybody needs something to do, Papa," I said. "You're right about that."

Relief loosened his face. "That's what I've always said. And when I find something to do, then I'll retire, and not before." He nodded emphatically, as if he'd just put the last elegant flourish on a winning argument.

Christina was close to the edge. I could tell by the tight feel of her shoulders under my hands. I used to feel helpless when she did that; I used to feel like weeping. No more. That night, I knew what to do. Surprise is the key. Action. I swept her up and kissed her loudly, then I set her down in front of the cake pan and the stack of records. "Play us a song, Christina," I said. She looked up at me with her mouth open, but it worked; she rummaged through the stack of records and picked one out. She dropped it onto the spindle of the cake pan and started to sing, a trickle of nonsense about the clouds in the sky and knickknacks on the shelves, whatnots and knickknacks and trifles until Papa dozed and I felt calm again.

IV

But he didn't retire. Not yet, he said. Not yet. And then it was early September and time for Mother's bone scan.

"Why me? Why not Papa?" I asked when she told me she wanted me with her this time, fear inside me like something with wings, beating against windows, trying to get out.

"He fusses like a mother hen," she said. "I don't want that."

"What do you want, then?"

"I want you to go."

There was no escaping that logic. And so, that morning, I woke up at dawn with my mouth dry, my heart pumping as if I'd been running, thinking about the hummingbirds, those tiny winged forms crossing the glittering water and Mother's sympathy with them, the way she hinted at a bond between her and those birds, an understanding. As I fixed our cereal and brushed Christina's hair and drove her to the babysitter's, my hands trembled. I couldn't stop thinking about the birds and the glittering water and Mother. Gaunt, tall, wide-boned Mother, not at all like a hummingbird. Surely, I thought, it is their beauty that she's drawn to, not their fragility, or the way they cross the glittering water.

Mother was dressed to the nines, classy, the way she can look, like an old-time movie star with her beauty parlor wave, her bright mouth and cheeks and nails, her high-heeled alligator shoes. That afternoon as she got into the car, she gave me her hand. "Am I glowing?" she asked.

I brought her hand up close to my face, pretended to study it. "Yep," I said, and we both laughed. This was her bone scan joke, her way of talking about the radioactive isotope they'd injected her with earlier in the day that had traveled through her bones and would show up in the scan. I had heard it before, but that day I saw that humor was the shape her courage had taken on, that her life had formed itself now around waiting and finding new shapes for courage when the old ones wore through. "Mama," I said. "You look great."

When the technician patted the table and said, "Hop on up here, honey," Mama did not hop. She had no truck with the cloying way medical people try to convince you that what you were going through wasn't life and death, it was fun. Instead, she climbed up onto the little footstool that stood beside the long stainless steel table and sat and swung her legs around and tucked her skirt down around her knees and lay back with a dignity that caught at my chest and throat. It seemed so necessary and so hard to do. She looked small on the large steel table. I walked to the edge of the table and took her hand. "You're doing fine, Mama," I said. "You're doing just fine." She nodded, her lips pressed tightly together.

"Please step back behind the monitor," the technician said, and she switched it on.

At home that night, late, I sat in my living room watching the shadows of leaves thrown by the streetlight dapple the curtains. The heat was so thick, I felt packed in it, but even the heat had a saving grace. At last, the dogs had been silenced. I imagined them pressed against the ground, begging for mercy, too smothered to bark. So, I listened to that quiet and tried to forget the trip to the hospital with Mother, and then there was a sound and Christina was at the door, waiting. I could tell by the way she stood that she hadn't slept yet; there was no drowse or slackness to her body. She stood there wakeful and tall; she'd gotten tall that summer, and with something of Mother about her bearing. "Come on over here, Christina," I said. I patted the cushion beside me on the sofa. "Come sit with me. It's all right." But when she'd been nestled in my lap for awhile, she was still awake and alert no matter how I stroked and smoothed her hair, no matter how low I made my voice. She wouldn't let go, relax, and so I said, "Sing a song, baby, would you do that?" I did it for her as well as for me, because her songs eased her, too; often, she would fall asleep in the middle of one of them. She nodded against me, fiddled with the top button on my nightgown, sighed.

We'd played this game often since we'd come back to Timmons. "Come over to my house and listen to some records," she'd say, watching me for signs of laughter or disbelief. "I'd love to," I'd say and crawl inside the house under the card table with her, sit down, take a cup of water, a plate of gravel—cookies—and Christina would select the first record and drop it onto the spindle of the angel food cake pan. Christina would start to sing, sitting up tall with her clear, narrow face turned up as if the song were falling on her like warm rain, her high, thin voice weaving it round and round.

I wrapped my arms around her, pulled her close, a sticky damp armful, smelling of soap. I needed her singing that night. At first it was just sing-song, la-la, here and there. Christina wandered, looking for the song, singing about the leaves on the curtains and her toys and Mama's funny nightgown. Then the song changed, her tone changed, or the way I listened changed, or it had been different all along and I'd just noticed it, but Christina wasn't wandering any longer; she was singing. A quiet song, almost whispered, as if she were telling a secret, about a tall lady with a blindfold on and big gray rocks and waiting in the sun. Solemn as a chant. Where had she gotten that song? I tried to make myself ask. What blindfolded lady? What rocks? What sun? But there was no sense in pretending that I didn't know. I did. I do.

One Sunday morning in the middle of the custody hearing, I took her to the courthouse because she wouldn't stop crying until I promised to take her to see the place where her father and I went every day. We stood on the sidewalk, I held her hand and pointed out the window in the gray granite wall, that looked into the courtroom where Thomas and I spent our days. Above that window, on a high pediment, a statue of blind justice stood, holding up her scales, and when Christina saw the statue, she covered her mouth with both her hands and buried her face in my skirt because, she said later, as I was putting her to bed that night, the lady looked as if she were falling, falling on Christina. No, baby, I said, holding her, no she wasn't falling. She didn't fall. And that was months ago, the months you always hope might be like years to a child in their power to heal, but it was not so, I heard it in her song.

I put my cheek down on the top of Christina's head as she sang. My child remembers trouble, I thought. It seemed as awesome a turning as her birth had been. She is not safe, I thought, any more than I am safe from what I am capable of, any more than Papa was safe from Wallace's death or Mama was safe that morning as the machine silently exposed every vulnerable inch of her bones. Not safe, not safe, I said to myself, rocking Christina, listening to her sing. I must love her differently now, I thought, with a different kind of alertness. I must take care to let her know that she is not alone, that trouble does not set her apart, it includes her.

Christina sang for a long time and when she was finished she twisted around in my arms until she could see my face. "Christina," I said, "that was very beautiful. I could listen to you sing all night."

So the bone scan was clear and Mother went on living. We are all still alive. I moved away at the end of that summer, and now Mama and Papa live in an apartment in a retirement home complex in Macon, Georgia, the city where my husband, David, and Christina and I live now. Papa is frail. He went down fast. First with a broken hip that mended wrong. Then with pneumonia, then hardening of the arteries. He has all sorts of problems, the abundance that comes to the old. He is frail, but still, his life goes forward in surprising ways. Now, he sits in his chair in the sun beside the window in the back room in their apartment most of the day, looking out onto the small yard where Mother has planted tomatoes, zinnias, marigolds, and one tall sunflower for him to watch. The sun comes through his hair as if it were a fine haze, spun from radiant filaments; it shines right into his skin. Sometimes he swears he sees worms on the tomato vines, he won't rest until someone goes out to check, and sure enough, nine times out of ten, there *will* be worms there, fat, horned, green ones. He likes to see them picked off the plants and squashed before he'll settle down again.

Much of the time, he doesn't speak or when he does, he shouts, and only Christina can get through to him and sometimes not even her. She is fifteen now, very tall and serious. She dresses in black and she's cut her hair so it stands up like a crest of porcupine quills. She stalks around and will not be consoled for things she cannot or will not name. But sometimes, without being asked, she'll up and take a checkerboard or a deck of cards over to Mama and Daddy's, and he'll be still for a couple of hours, as long as she stays with him. They play Slap-Jack and Go Fish, easy games. I see them there with her crest of strange hair bent close to his wispy white head, and my heart opens and opens until I'm afraid it's going to expand so far it'll knock itself out against the walls of my chest. One day when I thanked her for being patient with Daddy, she gave me that look like a glancing blow, the one that makes me want to curl up and die.

"God, *Mom*," she said, impatience curling the edges of her voice, "he's just Granddaddy." Scorn or no scorn, the way she said it made me remember something I'd promised myself not to forget it seemed like a hundred years before, and when we got out of the car at home, I kissed her, whether she liked it or not and said, "Thank you, love, anyway."

I am not as stalwart as Christina. All I want to do sometimes is run. You know that dream. Away from people's frailties that seem, if you let them be, so much your own, too, and everybody's. Run for the safe place. The haven outside of time and trouble. The first time Papa shouted at me, I had that dream again. The doctor told us that hardening of the arteries makes people like this—one minute lucid, the next, reliving some old hurt starring you as the tormentor—but the first time he shouted at me WAS I A DAMN FOOL? for trying to feed him custard from his lunch tray, I forgot all the doctor's reasoning. I threw the spoon down onto the tray and ran. Out of the room, down the hall, with no idea of where I was going so long as it was away. I pushed through a door and found myself in the empty auditorium where the church choirs sing for them at Christmas time and the Bingo games run hot and heavy on Friday nights. I climbed the stairs onto the stage and felt my way along the heavy red curtains until I came to the opening, and I pushed through and then the curtains felt so soft and heavy, I grabbed the edge of one of them and began to wrap myself in it. I turned and I turned until I'd wrapped myself tight as a mummy inside the cloth. I wrapped my head and everything until I could see only darkness, until I could barely breathe. But even there, I smelled alcohol and sickness in the curtains; I heard doctors and nurses being paged out in the halls. Back in the room Daddy dozed in the sun. I went over to his chair and said, "Hello, Papa," and when he looked up and saw me, he gave me the sweetest smile, and tears came into his eyes, as if he hadn't seen me in years. He gave me his hand, and I kissed it and put it back in his lap and moved the lunch tray out of sight.

If Papa is frail, Mama is tough, in just about equal measure. They have struck an amazing balance, as if when people have been married that long there's a kind of force, an impression or a dent they've made on life, that must be kept on being made, or they lose their place, and if one lays this force down, the other must pick it up. Whatever it is, Mama has two people's worth of energy. She gives everybody hell. Nurses. Doctors. Administrators. Social workers. The Christians who come to save their souls. Telephone solicitors peddling grave plots. Olan Mills Studios calling to sell them portraits of themselves for the grandchildren. Every day she rises, dresses, makes herself up, draws up her battle plan, then she wheels Papa down to breakfast in the sunny dining room. She doesn't eat breakfast, just tea and a sweet roll; she's too busy making lists, plans. Then she spends the rest of the day carrying them out: cornering doctors, bossing nurses, making appointments to see administrators about the abomination of a piano in the recreation room or the plumbing or the unpalatable food that upsets Daddy's stomach.

She calls David, my husband, at his law offices or at home and asks him to represent her in the *suits* (emphasis on the plural) she plans to bring against the world. He is very gentle with her, very kind, and for this, along with so much else, I love him. Sometimes it is enough to come into the room while he's on the phone with Mother and to rest in the sound of his voice as he talks to her, to listen and to feel doubt, fear, anger ebb away, carried on his calm voice. Sometimes, though, after he hangs up, he sags. I put my arms clear around him then and hold him close while he rests against me for awhile, the way I rest against the kindness in his voice as he talks to Mother.

And sometimes, when I've listened to one of her tirades and my head is so full of it that it feels as if it's going to explode, I cannot stand to look at her face. If I do, I think, I might turn to stone. She is all sinew now, all snap and bone and frozen face, someone I would like to make into a stranger, forget. But I cannot forget. I know, as surely as I knew that night what Christina was singing about, how all the waiting and the possibilities she faced, still faces, every day, have tightened and toughened her, until I think, sometimes, that she is one big scar. And thinking of the toughness, I think, too, of how fragile she must feel to be so ferociously tough, to try and order the world so that no harm can come in, and I know it is this fragility I must not forget else I will lose her and myself to the scars. Because it seems to me now that this fragility we share is both strength and peril, and that my life on earth is caught up in trying to remember love in the face of that fact.

Still, I know why the born-again Christians who work the halls at the retirement village, the joyful ones with their bright smiles and sure answers wait so hungrily for the Rapture. What a great day it would be, I think, as the last tide of evil and disgrace was about to be loosed, to be scooped off the earth and into Jesus's arms, to watch from the shelter of those arms while this cruel, evil, blighted earth is purged of sinners and decay, made ready for a new and unstained race to descend along with Jesus and to rule with Him for a thousand years of peace, a golden age of love. Who wouldn't shout hallelujah, fall down in a faint, need an otherworldly language, to profess such a faith?

Sometimes, I wake up in the middle of the night, and I cannot place myself in time or space or inside the confines of anyone's love. The room, the bed, David's back all seem strange, and I can't remember where I am connected or how or why. It is a long habit I cannot shake no matter how good my life has become; it's like another sense, a seventh or an eighth, a frightening perception of disconnection, isolation. It happens when Papa has had a bad day in his mind or I've been called to go over there and smooth down something Mama has roughed up. It happens for no reason at all. I go downstairs and make myself a glass of warm milk with a shot of brandy in it. I sit at the kitchen table and turn the glass between my hands and feel its warmth and try to put things back together because it seems then as if I can feel forces at work pulling things apart, blinding, silencing, isolating, and it seems that what I have to do is to remember. Remember what? I start with small things, work out. The table in front of me, for instance, the grain of the wood and the thousands of marks we've made on it. I run my fingers over those nicks and scratches and remember who made them and how. Then I move to the kitchen, my house, to David and Christina sleeping up in their rooms, Mama and Papa across town sleeping, mercifully sleeping, remembering along the way who they are and so, who I am. Sometimes, this is not enough and I cast a line way back. It catches here, there. Sometimes it catches on that summer I spent in Timmons and how I had come there, a kid with a kid, in search of some far-fetched sense of belonging, a safe place. I have to laugh then when I think of that dream and to love the innocence of the person I was then with the tenderness I feel when I think of Christina and her songs. And sometimes when I think of that summer, I remember the buck that came out of the woods in search of water. It drifts up out of the shelter of the trees, through the shimmering heat, drawn by its thirst to a dangerous place and there, in that dry summer, though it is not safe, never safe, it takes water from a human hand. I sit here and remember until I feel myself surrounded again, to the ends of this earth surrounded, by my own kind.

Nanci Kincaid

LIKE THE OLD
WOLF IN ALL THOSE
WOLF STORIES

(from *St. Andrews Review*)

We saw Annie weaving her way through the woods down to our house. She came about suppertime every night to use our telephone. Mother had taught her how. Annie had memorized the number because it was the only one she ever called. It irritated Walter to have his supper interrupted. "Tell that girl she's got to find another phone. She can't be coming down here every night," he said.

Walter was my mother's new husband, not my real daddy. Mother got up from the table. "It's not every night," she said.

But it was practically every night. Melvina sent her down to our house to call the Blue Bird Café. Annie always dialed the number carefully, waited for an answer and then said, "Mama said tell Alfonso Williams come home." That was it. Almost every night.

"Why Melvina wants that man home for supper is beyond me," Walter grumbled with his mouth full.

"I like Alfonso," Roy said.

"Not that Alfonso, dummy. The daddy," I said. "And you better not like him. You better be scared of him."

"I'm not," said Roy.

"Thank y'all, Mrs. Sheppard," Annie hollered on her way out of the kitchen. The back porch door slammed and barefooted Annie started through the woods back home. She just lived next door. There was a little patch of woods between our house and Melvina's, but we could see her house well enough. And we could hear pretty good, too.

I don't think I ever saw Alfonso up close. The daddy. It seemed like he was always at the Blue Bird down in French Town. French Town wasn't too far from where we lived. It was close enough so Alfonso would walk home when Melvina called him. The Blue Bird was kind of the main thing around there—right at the red light, right at the main part of French Town.

French Town was sort of like Melvina's house in a larger way— how you wanted to go in it, but felt nervous about it and plain un-welcome. How you'd pass the Blue Bird Cafe and think to yourself you wish you could get out and walk right up into the yard and somebody would wave at you or come over and slap you on the back glad to see you showed up there. Like they'd say to you, "Hey there, Little Lucy," real friendly and all. And they'd say, "Does your Mama know you're up here at the Blue Bird today? Up here in French Town? You just come on in and drink you a cold drink. We're gon buy you a cold drink ourselves and then you got to run on home. But we're sure glad you dropped by here, little Lucy. Real glad."

Like you'd go inside and there would be Alfonso, just as neat as a pin with an ironed white shirt on and this nice look on his face and all, and he'd say, "This here little girl, she my neighbor, Lucy here. Me and her Daddy is the best of friends. I'm gon look out for this little one, her being my neighbor girl and all." And he would smile and be a complete gentleman and drink nothing but orange Nehi drinks. And you'd be thinking to yourself how completely wrong you are about things you don't know. But, somehow you know it won't ever happen like that.

Walter would drive us through French Town on our way different places. Mother, too. It was the shortest way, right through French Town. Right past the Blue Bird. I loved to go by there. Me and Roy always thought we saw Alfonso—he was the one leaned up against the wall out front smoking cigarettes, or the one with a stocking on his head sitting on a car fender talking to some ladies, or the one taking a pee over by the side edge of the Blue Bird with his back to the street and his legs spread far apart so his pants don't get wet. We always thought we saw him. We liked it when our car got stopped at the red light on the corner by the Blue Bird. It gave us longer to look things over and pick out which one was Alfonso.

The Blue Bird Cafe didn't look like that much by itself. A small grey cinder-block square with a messy painted sign outside above the door that said BLUE BIRD CAFE and had a funny-looking blue bird that looked more like a blue chicken hand-painted on it. And no windows. Not a single window. Walter said that was because those people wouldn't do anything but break them out first thing, just bust them things right out. He said you'd have to sell a heck of a lot of booze to keep a place like the Blue Bird in windows. All I thought was that it must be some kind of hot inside there, some kind of sweatbox. Every place in Tallahassee needed windows, open doors, electric fans, that's what I thought. There was a beat-up old wooden door that led inside, into pitch darkness. And there was some music. Walter said the only good thing you could say about that kind of music down at the Blue Bird was that it was loud enough. And it usually was.

Some colored folks were always gathered up around the yard at the Blue Bird, talking and laughing and whispering. Once in a while fighting and yelling. When we ever saw fighting going on we knew for sure that that one must be Alfonso. There'd be commotion going on in the Blue Bird's yard and Walter would drive right by in a calm, regular way like he never even noticed, and me and Roy would be halfway hanging out the window trying to watch. We had a real curiosity about the Blue Bird and French Town. Like why they called it French Town. Seems like it didn't have anything to do with France. We never were clear on it.

We never were clear on anything that had to do with colored people. At least I wasn't. Seemed like they were all keeping some kind of secrets or something. Like they knew something they weren't telling. And I wanted to know it so bad it liked to kill me sometimes. The secret. It wasn't just old Alfonso, and the Blue Bird and all. It was Melvina too, and her kids, and her crazy little fall-down house next door. Walter said one good hard wind would blow that little house clean across town, and he wished it would. But not me. I liked that house close by, because it was my best chance to find things out, colored people things, and I watched that house like a hawk. There was always a lot of screaming and yelling up at Melvina's. There were all those kids, Melvina, and sometimes Alfonso, all staying in that little two-room house. And there was hollering all the time, and dogs barking.

When Alfonso got good and drunk Melvina would lock him out of the house and then he would get so mad he would turn mean. It was always at night. Some nights we could halfway see Alfonso stumbling around on the porch and we could more than halfway hear all the screaming and crying.

"I'm gon kill you, woman," Alfonso would roar. "I got me a knife and I'm gon cut you up. I'm gon slice your ugly face, you no-count woman." And inside the children would wail like a chorus of terrified crickets.

Melvina tried to hush the children so she could hear where Alfonso was and what he was doing. Sometimes he tried to crawl in a window, but Melvina would bang him on the head with a stick or a shoe or a rock. And then the biggest boys would grab something to hit him with. "You ain't gon hurt Mama. You a ole drunk dog. You a dog!"

Some of Melvina's real dogs would take offense at this and start yelping and baying and yapping at Alfonso's heels. Once Alfonso sat outside cussing his head off and throwing rocks up at the house. Sometimes he'd yell for Melvina to come outside so he could show her something. "I got something you sure do want to see. Come on out here. I ain't gon do nothing to ya." Melvina would just sit inside very still. And I could picture all her little children huddled up around her, listening. "Mama, you ain't gon go out yonder, are you? Mama don't mess with him."

Sometimes old Alfonso would get tired and pass out in the yard someplace. Melvina would just leave him out there all night and in the morning he'd be laying there like a dirty dog with his tongue hanging. Melvina's dogs would be lying right beside Alfonso like a pack of old wolves worn out from a night of trying to kill sheep and little baby lambs. It seemed like that. Alfonso was just like the old wolf in all those wolf stories.

Once on a rainy night Alfonso was drunk and talking about what he was going to do with a razor. Melvina locked him out and for a while he circled the house like a vulture, his arms waving wildly in the darkness. We could see his silhouette when he passed in front of the window or got under the porch light. The rain hitting the tin roof of the house was loud enough to make Alfonso's yelling useless. And from time to time his legs would give way to his swaying body and he would slip down in the mud. He would disappear from sight for a while, then in a little bit here he would go again. He had to be getting tired when a bolt of lightning cut through the night like a jagged saw blade, and thunder followed—loud thunder—that shook the ground under old Alfonso's feet. He disappeared then, and for just a minute it crossed my mind that maybe he had got struck down by the lightning, and dropped dead in the yard someplace. That maybe God had had enough of Alfonso's doings and just went on and called his number right then and there with one fiery stroke of lightning. But no. Twice more we saw him, both times making a run for the porch and standing out there pounding on the door.

Later on Melvina told us that when he seemed to disappear all it was was him crawling up underneath the porch, and that her yard dogs had gathered up around him under there, licking him and scratching him. She said everytime he would roll over one of the dogs would yap and move out of the way and Alfonso would splat back down in the mud like a half-dead fish. He wanted her to give him a quilt, but Melvina wouldn't do it. She said she never saw no kinda pig-in-the-mud that slept with a quilt. Then old Alfonso said tomorrow he was gon get the wood ax and chop off Melvina's head. He said she was a dead woman tomorrow for sure.

But she wasn't. She was down at our house just like always. The only difference was she was about a half hour late since she wouldn't let the children outside until Alfonso was gone. She said he didn't wake up good till way after daybreak and that the children watched out the window while he crawled out from under the porch, dried mud on his face and clothes like grey paste. Said his hair was caked with mud, too, and he looked like an old, old grey ghost. He looked like a spook or a haunt and the children had watched him wander up the road with the muddy dogs trailing behind him, their fur matted in little tufts and points. She said they watched as wide-eyed and quiet as children who had just seen the devil hisself rise up from hell.

Me and Roy watched this stuff too, as much as we could, before Mother would come and try to shame us for it, try to make us find something better to do as she put it. Shoo us off and then stand at the window herself and watch. Mother and Walter had got used to the uproar next door. Some nights Mother sat up in the kitchen listening and worrying about it. She listened to all those little boys screaming while Alfonso banged on the door and tore things up. Walter usually went on to bed. He said he was not gon let the likes of Melvina and them keep him up half the night. He had a day's work to do tomorrow. "That's just the way niggers are," he told Mother. "No use in sitting up there worrying about it. They ain't happy unless they're into a fight. It's their way," he said, "you might as well come on to bed." But Mother wouldn't.

Walter tried to tell Mother that old Alfonso was mostly talk, that he was like one of them dogs whose bark is a lot worse than his bite, but that was just because he never did see the looks of Melvina after Alfonso beat her. He never saw her half tore to pieces like Mother and us did—and I didn't guess he ever would since Melvina would not allow it, a white man like Walter in her personal business. She said she could tolerate a lot of things, but not that.

So Mother knew better than Walter about the actual fighting itself, cause whenever old Alfonso actually got ahold of Melvina and beat her up bad, then she'd come down to our house the next morning as soon as Alfonso and Walter both were gone off. And when we saw her coming me and Roy would holler for Mother who would meet her at the door. And then me and Roy would freeze solid like a couple of useless nothings, like we were paralyzed, like we were just a couple of sticks of furniture in the room. We'd get as still as two dead children, couldn't do nothing with us but bury us. And Melvina would go along with it, us not being real, the way she walked past us—all bloody and beat up—and would not look at us same as if we were invisible. Her just crying and crying. And goodness knows Mother got to crying right with her, and then she'd send us out to play or off to school and if we could we would get somewhere close by and be real quiet and listen to Mother and Melvina. Sometimes outside under the kitchen window.

Mother would say, "Melvina, next time he comes around up there I'm calling the sheriff and I mean it."

But Melvina would practically swoon. "No, Mrs. Sheppard. Don't you never do that. Don't you never call the sheriff. Alfonso'll kill me for sure," she'd wail. Mother would get some ice for Melvina's eye and a warm rag to wipe off the dried blood, and she would pour Mercurochrome into her cuts which would make Melvina holler and start up crying again.

"If I had a gun I'd shoot Alfonso Williams myself," Mother said. "I would, Melvina. He is no good. I swear you'd be better off dead than living with a man like that."

"Alfonso don't hardly give me no money."

"He ought to be shot, Melvina." Mother would speak like someone spitting. "I mean it!"

"He stay drunk," Melvina said.

They would drink some coffee and Mother would say, "Do you love him, Melvina? Are you that crazy?"

And Melvina would shake her head and say, "It ain't his fault."

This all happened a hundred times and Mother always ended up promising not to call the sheriff—not ever. And Melvina always went home cleaned up and cried out. And then me and Roy got back to normal.

After a while Walter laid down the law about Annie using our phone. He said Mother ought never to have got that started showing her how to use the phone and all. He said no way in hell was Melvina gon keep on calling Alfonso home from the Blue Bird. "She ought to hope he just stays there and drinks hisself to death. Melvina is as much a fool as he is."

"We don't understand," Mother would say.

"The hell we don't."

"We can't understand," Mother said.

"Understand what?" Walter said. "Tell me that. Understand what?"

One late night old Alfonso got going again. Only worse this time. I woke up, not because of the racket at Melvina's, but because Mother woke up Walter over it and he was so mad it woke me.

"I've got a mind to get my gun," Walter said. "I'm sure as hell calling the sheriff this time." And he did, without Mother even trying to stop him.

Up at Melvina's Alfonso was locked out of the house. He sat out in the yard lighting matches and talking crazy. He lit a match and set it to an old dog's tail, but it didn't take and the old dog just lay there. "I'm gon burn up this old dog," Alfonso hollered. "Then I'm gon set a match to you. I'm gon catch that house on fire." The children shrieked just to hear him say it. Melvina got up and planted herself at the window. We could see her.

Alfonso lit a second match and this time he set it to the fur on 'the old dog's back. That old dog set out a blood chilling yelp that raised the hair on my neck. He yelped and jumped and started rolling in the dirt like a dog that had got into a bed of red ants. Alfonso laughed.

"He be setting them dogs on fire," Skippy hollered at Melvina. "Oh Lord, he gon burn us up!" And inside the house was the most screaming and crying you ever heard, and Melvina could not get them to hush.

"Y'all don't open that door, then I'm gon burn the house down," Alfonso yelled. "You a woman that's gon burn in hell," he laughed.

"Mama!" the boys screamed. "Mama!" Annie was hollering so loud we could hear her plain down at our house.

Alfonso lit a match and started toward the house. That wood house would burn like a stack of kindling—Melvina knew that. She stood at the window and watched Alfonso out there playing with fire.

Down at our house Mother turned on every light. She lit it up like a Christmas tree. She wanted Alfonso to know we were up and watching him. But it didn't seem like he noticed. Walter was walking around out in the yard with his flashlight, ole one-eyed George beside him. If Alfonso noticed Walter, he didn't pay him any mind, either.

I sat in the kitchen and Mother didn't even try to make me go back to bed. It wasn't too long until we saw the sheriff's car go by and we knew exactly when he pulled in at Melvina's because the yelling and crying stopped. There was dead silence up there. The red light on the sheriff's car flashed like a big heartbeat in the sky.

Walter went on up to Melvina's as soon as the sheriff got there. He said that Melvina wouldn't open the door. The sheriff said he'd have to knock it down if she didn't. Walter said the children sat still and quiet, the little ones still crying some.

Melvina told the sheriff she didn't know where Alfonso was. She said they were not having any kind of trouble and there was no need for the sheriff to bother hisself with them. She said she could look after herself and her kids.

The sheriff and the man with him found old Alfonso up under the porch, mostly because of the dogs. Walter shined his flashlight under there for them. "Boy, if you don't come on out of there by yourself I got a dog can convince you," the sheriff said.

Melvina stepped into the doorway, her big shoulders almost reaching from side to side and heaving up and down with each breath she took. She was quiet.

Alfonso came on out and the sheriff and his man led him to the car, his hands cuffed behind him. Alfonso drug his feet as he walked as if they were tied to something heavy at the end of a rope. His head hung forward and his eyes stared down at the dirt. In the night with the red light flashing Alfonso looked old and small. Not like something to be afraid of.

And as soon as the sheriff's car drove off then Walter came on home and made me go to bed, but I could not sleep a wink for thinking about it. Alfonso gone. And Melvina—her just standing there in the doorway like that, and Walter said she did not act one bit grateful. He said he guessed she would like it better if he had just let old Alfonso go on and burn the house to the ground—and all them with it. "Guess she'd appreciate that better," he said. He said Melvina stood right there and told the sheriff a bold-faced lie like only a nigger can. And I couldn't get away from thinking about it.

Melvina was quiet about things afterwards. Mother too. Melvina came to our house the next day as usual. She didn't seem any different to me. She seemed the same. Any secret Melvina's got is safe forever. I see that plain. Nothing gon make the colored people secrets come loose from Melvina. It bothers me. Why does Melvina make me so mad—and Mother, too?

Walter said being rid of old Alfonso felt like when you finally run off some old dog been getting into your trash can night after night, making a mess you got to clean up over and over again. He was satisfied with it—old Alfonso gone. But I kept on wondering what the sheriff did with Alfonso after he got him. Did he hang him? Walter said he hoped they taught him a lesson he'd remember. Mother said she guessed they put him in jail for a while. Melvina said when old Alfonso came back we better all watch out.

METROPOLITAN

(from *Grand Street*)

Mr. Hebert parked his green Impala in the lot beside the railroad tracks. I watched as he stepped from the car and locked the door. He smoothed back his hair with both hands like a swimmer surfacing and glided across the street toward the Metropolitan. He moved slowly, in a limp black suit, yellowed shirt and dark wool tie even in the hot Louisiana summer. His long face was criss-crossed with tiny red veins and his skin hung loose, almost billowing from the cheekbones. He turned his head cautiously from side to side as he walked, as if he expected at any minute to be confronted. But no one stopped him. I saw him nod to an old man as they passed on the sidewalk, then quickly look away toward the display window where the pink neon sign flashed "Metropolitan" above dust-covered aspirin bottles, after-shave lotions and two heart-shaped boxes of white, rock-hard nougats and stale caramels. By the time the bell over the front door jingled, I was busy spraying Windex on the beveled glass of the perfume counter.

"Good morning, Neva," he said. Mr. Hebert's voice was dry and cool.

I moved my dust cloth back and forth across the glass as I smiled and told him good morning. Mr. Hebert and I had exchanged few words since he'd hired me; in fact, he rarely spoke to anyone except Skelly. He was in the store a few hours each morning and again before closing. The rest of the day he worked as a land surveyor. Val-Jean told me he wasn't interested in pharmaceuticals—that only a provision in his father's will kept him from selling the store. He'd closed down the soda fountain rather than keep it clean enough to be relicensed; the polished oak counter had been rebuilt to house cosmetics. Perfume bottles and a few pieces of bright, cheap jewelry were scattered on the glass shelves of the pie case.

This morning Mr. Hebert did not walk past me as usual, but stood quietly at the counter. His eyelids were wrinkled and thick, and he blinked a little as he looked at the perfume displays.

"Neva," he said finally. "What have you done with my Wind Song?"

His question so startled me that I could feel my face growing hot.

"Over there, sir," I said, pointing to a cluster of crown-shaped bottles I'd arranged in a pyramid on the top shelf.

He looked at me severely and then looked at the bottles.

"Elegant," he said, and walked away.

I was temporary. I'd been working at the Metropolitan Drug Store for three weeks that summer. Val-Jean got me the job.

"We need a little high-school girl to work part-time," she told my mother. "Somebody to help out over the summer so I can take some time off now and then."

She and my mother were talking on our back porch about tomato plants. She brought my mother a seedling in a plastic pot tied with an orange ribbon.

"Welcome to the neighborhood," I heard her call. "Sure hope you like termayters."

We'd moved to Beauville only a few days earlier. I was fourteen and high school was still a year away, but I was pleased that Val-Jean thought I was older. She lived with her husband in the house behind us. I'd seen her barbecuing hamburgers in their backyard, but I'd never spoken to her. In the evenings when I helped my father clear the tangle of undergrowth from the shrubbery, I saw Val-Jean walking back and forth on the deck of her house in tight white shorts and a halter top. When she leaned over the grill, the vertebrae bulged along her spine. She looked twenty-seven or -eight, but her skin was already leathery from sun, and above the waistband of her shorts a small ruffle of brown skin hung like the fluting on a pie crust. Her eyes were so brown they seemed pupilless and I had never seen hair as coarse and dark.

"The color of a crow's wing," my father said once when he stood to light a cigarette and caught me watching her.

It was past one, and Val-Jean was taking another of her long lunch breaks. All week she'd been taking off for two to three hours in the middle of the day. I got nervous if Mr. Hebert wandered into the store while she was gone, but he never asked where she was or even seemed to notice she was missing.

As I Windexed the glass, I heard him talking to Skelly at the back of the store. Skelly had a television set in the room where he filled prescriptions; he had a hot plate and a recliner. Green and amber bottles lined the shelves of his small chamber, and someone long ago had sewn print curtains for the two doors—one leading to the store proper, the other opening onto the supply room. Skelly's room was a gathering place for his friends and the salesmen from the drug companies. In the afternoons, they watched their stories on TV and drank the thick chicory coffee Skelly brewed. The only bathroom in the store was a cubicle at one side of the supply room, and when Skelly's friends were visiting I didn't go back there. The men snickered when they heard the toilet flush; when I came back through the door, they grinned. Skelly never interfered with them. He counted pills into bottles with his head bent and a thin smile on his face.

That afternoon I heard the shrill voices of cartoon characters from Skelly's TV as I wiped the caked lipstick from the samples on the Yardley display. I'd read that the model whose face sulked on the cardboard backdrop was friends with the Rolling Stones and didn't mind being six feet tall. I'd grown two inches taller that summer, and as I looked at my big hands fumbling among the lipsticks, I hated the knuckles, the wide, flat nails too broad for polish, the small brown freckles that had appeared at the base of my thumb the previous weekend. The lipsticks were pale beige, pink, apricot—colors iridescent as shell, almost glowing inside their clear cases. I put down my dust cloth and slipped the palest of the samples from the display.

"We had five hatch this morning," Skelly said as I leaned toward the mirror, and Mr. Hebert answered, "Five. Well, well. Five is a good number."

They were talking about Mr. Hebert's quail. Val-Jean said to me once that Mr. Hebert was interested in only two things, and the other one was his quail. I thought about this as I watched my lips turn pale and slick. The main thing Mr. Hebert was interested in was his surveying business, I supposed, but I was skeptical that the quail had competition. Mr. Hebert's visits to the Metropolitan seemed motivated only by the nervous desire to see if they were hatching. The eggs incubated in the heat of the supply room. Boxes of laxatives, shampoos and toothpastes had been pushed aside to make room for the wire and plywood frame that held the nests, and the effect was that of a shrine. Low-watt bulbs circled the frame and shone dully through the old bedspread that covered it. The smell in the room was overwhelming—a heavy, wild-animal odor mixed with a wave of hot dust and the thin, sweet smell of the merchandise. I complained, but Skelly and Val-Jean said they couldn't smell anything.

They both warned me not to breathe a word about the birds to anyone—not even to my parents. I promised, though it seemed silly to think of so much secrecy over a few wobbly downies and the small white eggs there seemed to be more of every time I peeked into the supply room. Sometimes, when I was waiting on customers out front, I heard the downies chip-chipping in the back room. I was always surprised that no one ever asked where the noise was coming from.

As I stepped back from the mirror, I thought that any other drugstore would be an oasis: cool, immaculate, the air drenched with the medicinal balm of healing. The clammy air that hung in the Metropolitan that afternoon left condensation on the display windows and smelled of wildlife and mildew. I opened my eyes until they were wide and startled looking, and pushed my tongue behind my bottom lip to create a pout that almost matched that of the Yardley girl. I tried to imagine how I might look to someone seeing me for the first time—how Mick Jagger might see me if he walked into the Metropolitan at that instant.

The bell over the front door gave a sharp, excited little ring as Val-Jean, returning from lunch, pushed open the door with one hand square on the glass. The faint, greasy print of her palm was the first thing I saw when I looked up from the mirror. She gave her chewing gum an emphatic pop and walked past me with her head bent as if looking at me would have been too much trouble. She put her purse into a drawer behind the counter and began poking in her hair with a comb.

a   "Bring me that Bubbling Burgundy sample, why dontcha?" she
said, keeping her back to me. She pointed with her comb to a lavish
new display in which all the lipsticks were named after wine.

I picked out the tube of violent magenta high-frost. "But it's so
dark, Val-Jean," I said.

She sniffed. "You think I'd look better wearing one of those
shades like you've got on?" She pointed to the London Lights display. "One of those colors that makes you look like you've rubbed
Clorox on your lips?"

"It's the style," I said.

"So what? I've got strong coloring," she said. "I can handle rich
shades."

I handed her the lipstick. When she turned to take it from me, I
saw the dark swelling beginning to settle beneath her left eye.

"Who hit you?" I said in wonder, reaching out to touch her face.
I'd never seen a black eye in person.

She pushed my hand away. "I wish you could have seen how you
looked when I walked in just now," she said. "Everybody walking
past on the sidewalk probably saw you, too. You looked like you
thought you were Miss America. You were so funny looking, I
thought I'd die."

By two-thirty I was bored with polishing the glass. It was a terrible day. We had only two customers all afternoon. Val-Jean had been
grumbling to herself behind the counter since her return, refusing
to speak to me or wait on customers, refusing to do anything. Skelly
and Mr. Hebert were still cloistered in the back room.

"Gotta be careful when they're this young," I heard Skelly say
when I went to the back to ring up a sale, and Mr. Hebert answered,
"Yessir. That's a true fact."

I gave up trying to look busy. Mr. Hebert came from the back
room only once since he entered it that morning, and that was to
call for Val-Jean.

"Would you come here please, Val-Jean?"

She didn't budge. She looked out the window and picked at her
fingernails. After a while, Mr. Hebert turned and went back into the
room.

In the days when Mr. Hebert's father owned the store, the Metropolitan had been a hang-out. The soda fountain churned out
frappes and sundaes to the beat of a Wurlitzer jukebox. The old

Wurlitzer was still wedged in place between a rack of greeting cards and the front door, and it was this I leaned against as I looked through the display windows at Lee Avenue. The pink neon sign blinked "natiloporteM" like an advertisement for some narcotic with which we hoped to lure customers.

I hated Beauville. After a month, I already knew what kind of place this was. Most of the boys my age who passed by the store looked like they worked on cars every spare minute. And some of the girls were even worse. They wore neat pastel blouses, cuffed shorts and white sandals, their hair rolled into flips or tied back in ponytails, their faces at once benevolent and cunning. I knew they would all be relentless.

"Why dontcha turn on that jukebox?" Val-Jean said from behind the counter. "So we won't have to sit here and listen to each other breathe."

She'd shown me how to operate the jukebox without money by turning a switch at the back of the machine. Another switch controlled the volume. When customers played their selections, Skelly sometimes came from the back room to turn down the volume if he didn't like the song.

I was tired of humoring Val-Jean. "Any requests?" I made my voice sound as flat and unfriendly as hers.

"Don't play anything stupid," she said. "I don't care what you play as long as it isn't rock and roll."

I punched the buttons for Sinatra. My mother listened to Sinatra at home.

When I was seventeen, it was a very good year.

"Shit," Val-Jean said. "What does he know?"

"He didn't write the song," I said. "He's just singing it."

I didn't know why I was defending Frank Sinatra.

Val-Jean came to the end of the counter so that we stood only a few feet apart. Her left eye was a deep blue crescent now and her right eye was puffy, as if she'd been crying or rubbing it. I was sure she'd been walloped and wondered vaguely if her husband—a lanky, soft-spoken meter reader for the gas company—was capable of catching her off guard with a smart right hook. I decided no.

"That song stinks," she said. "I don't care who wrote it. Frank Sinatra put his name on the label. That means he's responsible for what it says. If he's going to sing something, then he damned well better be ready to defend what it says."

"Okay," I said. I was really tired of Val-Jean now. "Let's call him up. Let's make him defend himself. 'Mr. Sinatra,' we can say, 'just what do you mean by saying that you had a good time when you were seventeen?'"

Val-Jean slowly shook her head. "Sometimes, Neva, you are so dumb," she said. She picked up a bottle of Toujours Moi from the counter and sprayed cologne along her wrists. "Let me tell you something. When I was seventeen I was working time-and-a-half out at the paper mill just to keep my head out of the mud. My husband—not Sam, but my first husband Spider Loftin—you know Queen Loftin who comes in here sometimes? Her son. She's my mother-in-law. My ex-mother-in-law, thank God. I don't know who I was happier to get rid of, Queen or Spider. When we were married, Spider was working offshore, so he was home for two weeks and gone for three—though to tell the truth, him being home wasn't much different from him being gone, because he was drunk all the time he was home."

"I didn't know you'd been married before," I said.

"Ha," Val-Jean smirked. "There's a lot you don't know about me. You'll never know how much you don't know about me. I could tell you stories. But that's not what I'm saying. What I'm saying is that Frank Sinatra has no idea about what being seventeen is all about. Or twenty-one, either—all that malarky about city girls with perfumed hair. He has no idea. And you know why?"

"No," I said.

"Las Vegas," she said. "He sings all those songs like every place in the world is Las Vegas."

I thought for a minute. The song always reminded me of my mother's stories of her girlhood during World War Two—the excitement of USO dances, bare legs painted to look like seamed stockings, handsome soldiers fox-trotting with girls in Augusta, Georgia, one week and shipped out to a Japanese island the next.

I shrugged. "My mother's life was sort of like that," I said.

"Oh, come on," Val-Jean said.

"It's true," I said. "She's told me all about it."

"And you're probably dumb enough to believe it," she said, folding her arms across her chest in a satisfied way.

I looked out the window, where the sun made a rail glint like the blade of a knife on the railroad tracks. The deserted avenue seemed to be wavering in the exhaust of all the cars that weren't there.

Sinatra's song ended. The jukebox stopped whirring. I looked hard at Val-Jean. For the first time, I noticed that the mass of black curls perched on top of her smooth hair was secured with hairpins.

"Is that a rat?" I said.

Val-Jean put her hand self-consciously to her head. "Oh," she said. "Sure it is. It's those birth-control pills. Don't you ever take them," she wagged her finger at me. "I started up a few years ago and now I'm addicted. And my hair's falling out on top."

"Why don't you want to have a baby?" I asked.

"I can't," Val-Jean leaned closer. She put her hand over her heart. "I've got palpitations. Sometimes they get so bad, I think I'm dying. Remember last week? That morning I was late coming in? My heart was knocking around so, I had to call the police to give me CPR."

Her eyes sparkled. For a moment, I thought she would say something more. She looked at me the way my best friend Gayle used to look when she detailed her dates with GIs. I was searching for the right question to ask that would make Val-Jean tell me what she knew. But at the same moment, we both became aware that Mr. Hebert was creeping down the hair-care aisle.

"Val-Jean," he said softly. "Skelly and I need some help in the back room. Would you mind?"

Val-Jean stared at him. She seemed to have lost all self-consciousness about her shiner.

"No, sir," she said in a loud voice. "It would be a pleasure."

She glanced at me triumphantly, then headed towards the back with Mr. Hebert following.

We'd turned the volume on the Wurlitzer down low for Frank Sinatra, and I kept it down as I ran through all the Rolling Stones selections on the jukebox. There weren't many: "Satisfaction," "You Can't Always Get What You Want," "Honky Tonk Women." Cato Pruitt, the arcade man who came to change the records, knew our clientele and kept the machine stocked with all the new George Jones, Tammy Wynette and Merle Haggard singles. Cato had shown me how the plays were tallied on the machine, so I played the Stones songs over and over to drive up their score.

I was standing at the window watching the 3:35 K.C.S. run through town, singing *Baby better come back maybe next week 'cause it seems I'm on a losin' streak* and swaying my hips and shoulders in a way I'd seen Jackie De Shannon do on television the night before, when Mr. Hebert said softly at my shoulder, "Neva, could we talk with you for a minute in the back?"

Val-Jean and Skelly were leaning against the prescription counter and when I came into the room they both smiled as if they hadn't seen me in months. Mr. Hebert indicated that I should sit in Skelly's green leatherette recliner. He sat on a high stool on the other side of the room, next to the TV. He asked me if I'd like a cup of coffee, but I told him I didn't drink coffee.

"Good girl," he said.

"Wish I'd never started up," Val-Jean said. "If I don't have my two cups in the morning, I'm not good for anything all day."

"I knew a man once," Skelly said. "Drank coffee in the morning to wake up and drank coffee before he went to bed at night so he could sleep." He smiled his thin smile and wiped a hand over his bald head.

There was a silence. Mr. Hebert cleared his throat. Skelly and Val-Jean looked down at their feet.

"Neva," Mr. Hebert said. "Remember when we hired you, we said we needed somebody here so Val-Jean could take some time off now and then?"

I nodded.

He looked at me for a few seconds as if to make sure I'd really understood him. "Well," he continued, "she's been doing a little work for me in my surveying business this week."

"Errands and things," Val-Jean said.

"Exactly," Mr. Hebert said, looking at her. "And so she's been taking time off during the day when she'd normally be working here."

I nodded. "Okay," I said.

He placed the tips of his fingers together and studied them. Both forefingers were deep brown with nicotine.

"Well," he said. "It's not exactly working out. Val-Jean ran into a little trouble this morning, and it looks like she may not be able to continue doing the work for me."

"Nothing serious," Val-Jean said.

"Of course not." Mr. Hebert glanced at me. "It's just that—well, it's complicated, to tell the truth. Val-Jean's lived in Beauville all her life, she has a lot of friends in town. People who might tend to misjudge her intentions."

"I see," I said, though I didn't.

"I've been doing some surveying work out at Drew Pike's place," Mr. Hebert said. "Been working with him out there for about a year now. And times have gotten a little difficult for old Drew, so he's not been able to meet my bills."

"Gee, that's really tough," I said. Mr. Hebert clearly expected my sympathy, but I barely knew these people. I didn't know what else to say.

Mr. Hebert frowned. "Yes, it is tough. Tough for all of us. I have my own bills to pay, too, you know. Got a fine staff over at the surveying business, and they got their own responsibilities. Clifton Frazar over there, his wife just had a new six-pound baby girl last week."

"Ginny Frazar?" Val-Jean wrinkled her nose. "I didn't know that. Lord, I thought that baby wasn't due until September."

Mr. Hebert ignored her. "The thing is, Drew can't pay me in money, so we've worked ourselves out an exchange. You know I'm a quail man," he said. "And Drew's a quail man, too. So we've decided to operate on a kind of bartering system."

"You mean he'll give you quail in exchange for the work you're doing?" I said.

"Sort of," he said. "Yes, sort of like that. Only not the birds themselves, but the eggs. And Val-Jean's been collecting them for me this week."

"So after he gives you the eggs, you bring them back here and put them in the incubator?" I asked her.

Val-Jean nodded. "Yeah, only Drew's pretty busy with his cattle all day, so he said I could just go get the eggs myself from the pens."

"Oh," I said. Val-Jean's shiner was almost purple, and puffed so her eye was scarcely open. I looked from her to Skelly then back to Mr. Hebert. None of them would meet my eyes. "I'm not sure what the problem is," I said.

Mr. Hebert cleared his throat delicately. "Mrs. Pike saw Val-Jean out there this morning, and thought she was perhaps paying a visit of a romantic nature to Mr. Pike."

I laughed because I didn't know what to say. I looked at Val-Jean, hoping she would laugh too, but she didn't. I'd seen the Pikes together a few times in the store. He was a bent, rawboned man at least as old as Mr. Hebert; he chewed tobacco and spit the juice in a Dixie cup he carried with him. And she was monstrous—easily three hundred pounds—with long black hair and a squint.

"So she's the one who belted you?" I asked Val-Jean.

"Sure wasn't the mama hen," Val-Jean said and popped her gum.

"Ora was just upset," Mr. Hebert said. "I've known her for years and have always thought she was one of the most charitable ladies in the world. But now she's on the rampage against Val-Jean, so it's not exactly good for Val-Jean to be doing business for me out there."

There was a brief, embarrassed silence and then Skelly shifted slightly and said, "We were thinking that maybe you'd be able to do the collecting for us, Neva."

"Yeah," Val-Jean said. "Nobody would ever think their husband was after you."

Mr. Hebert nodded. "The birds are nesting now, Neva, so it would only be for another week or two at the most."

"I don't know," I said. "It sounds kind of scary. Besides, I can't drive."

"That's okay," Val-Jean said. "I can drive you out there. All you've got to do is get the eggs."

Fennel Road was unpaved, rutted and covered in fine white dust that flew up from the wheels of Mr. Hebert's Impala as Val-Jean slowly guided the big car towards the Pikes'. For one who seemed so reckless about life, Val-Jean drove like an old woman. The red needle of the speedometer hovered at twenty, and she drove with both hands firmly on the wheel. When I tried to talk with her, she told me to shut up.

"I can't concentrate with you yapping at me," she said. "Wait until I park this thing before you start talking."

So I looked at the landscape creeping along beside the car. The long grass grew like spears punched into the dirt at the side of the road. Insects floated lazily over the green tips that wavered a little in our wake. Here and there, the fields were broken by a farm, usually a trailer turned parallel to the road, some outbuildings, a silver silo brilliant in late sunlight, a small herd of cows watching calmly as we passed and two or three chickens scattering back from the road. The insects popped softly against the windshield. On the steps of one of the farmhouses, a young woman in a ruffled pink dress turned to see what disturbed the thick air. She lifted her hand to us, then turned and sat down.

The entrance to the Pike farm was at the end of the road, which I saw just a few hundred yards ahead of the trail where Val-Jean made a sharp left turn. She steered the car to a clump of pine trees and parked in a small clearing that couldn't be seen from the road. She wiped her hands on her skirt.

"I hate driving this old thing," she said. "I'm not used to power steering. The car feels like it's flying all over the road."

"Val-Jean," I said. "What are we doing in the woods?"

"Listen," she said. "If that old bitch had been after you this morning, you wouldn't be asking such a stupid question. I know what I'm doing. The Pikes ought to be sitting down to supper right about now."

She got out of the car. "Come on," she said. "I'll walk down to the pens with you."

From the back seat she took a small cardboard box with the lid tied down with string—the same kind of box she brought from Grummacher's Bakery once in a while.

We walked through the woods in silence. Val-Jean never hesitated as we wove between the trees and scuttled through the undergrowth. She'd taken her stockings off when we first got into the car and replaced her high heels with a pair of dirty white sneakers she produced from beneath the front seat. I had on Earth Shoes—heavy brown-leather sandals that rocked me gently backward with each step. My toes were black by the time we reached the edge of the woods and the soles of my feet felt gritty.

"You should've worn better shoes," Val-Jean pointed out.

I pushed a sweaty strand of hair from my forehead and glared at her. "I had no idea I'd be tromping through the woods after work." I felt perspiration soaking through my thin cotton blouse and running in rivulets between my skin and the denim fabric of my skirt. Somehow, I'd imagined all this would be different—that the birds, being delicate, would be kept someplace cool and sterile. My face felt as if it had been smeared with Crisco, my eyes smarted, and as I slapped at the mosquitoes buzzing around my head I turned on Val-Jean. "Where are we? This is a terrible place."

Val-Jean shrugged. "You'll get used to it," she said, looking across the strip of meadow that skirted the woods.

I could see the pens huddled there, between the woods and the fenced pasture—a squat, gray assortment of boards and wire fencing with a square of white dirt before it, surrounded by chicken wire to make a sort of cage. On the horizon I saw Drew Pike's farm and in the nearer distance his cows were scattered like pieces of a black-and-white jigsaw puzzle against the green pasture.

"This morning," Val-Jean said, "Ora Pike came swooping down out of nowhere while I was standing right here. She must've been waiting for me."

The heat created an odd, humming noise inside my head. "Why didn't you just tell her you'd come for the eggs?" I said. "Why'd you let her think what she was thinking?"

"Miss Cosmopolitan," Val-Jean said. "If you had half a brain, you wouldn't have to ask those kinds of questions."

She ran her shoe along the trunk of a fallen pine. The tree was rotten and the bark flaked off in chunks that turned powdery when they hit the ground.

"I want to tell you something," she said. "And don't you ever tell a soul I said it. The only reason I ever do things like this is for what I can get out of it. And this isn't half the worst thing I've ever done. People, you know, they think they're using you. But you've just got to turn around and be sure you get more out of them than they're getting out of you."

"Wait a minute," I said. "Is Mr. Hebert paying you to come out here and get these eggs?"

"I'm not doing it for laughs," Val-Jean said.

"He didn't say anything to me about money."

She smiled and kicked at the tree.

"I don't think that's fair," I said.

"So what?" she said. "Listen, you're just a kid. You don't know anybody here in town and nobody knows you. You think anybody would pay attention to anything you had to say?"

"About what?" I said.

"About these stupid birds," Val-Jean said. She shook the bakery box gently. I heard things rolling around inside.

"Listen to me," she said. "This is what I want you to do. You go into the pen, and Pike's got the nests all marked so he can keep track of what's what. You go for the number two, the number seven, the number fifteen and the number twenty-two nests. They're the nests

I was supposed to clean out this morning. You take the eggs out from under the brooders and replace them with the eggs that are in this box."

A heaviness was starting to creep across my chest. I felt a pricking sensation along the back of my neck.

"What's the difference?" I said.

Val-Jean untied the box. "These eggs are from Mr. Hebert's quail. Domestic bobwhites. Drew Pike's brought in a strain from Mexico called Elegant Quail that Mr. Hebert's taken a liking to and wants to start raising."

"Elegant Quail?"

"Right," she said. "Now all you have to do is switch the eggs and then beat it back over here as fast as you can. Somebody's going to be coming after those cows pretty soon and one black eye a day is enough."

She pushed the box into my hands. It bulged slightly at the bottom and was heavier than I'd imagined.

"You're crazy," I said.

Val-Jean pressed her lips together in annoyance, an expression I'd seen countless times when she was waiting on customers who were slow to make up their minds. She dug her fingernails into my shoulder and shook me twice, hard, just as the undergrowth crackled and a broad expanse of daisy-print fabric began to streak toward us from between the trees. For one frozen moment, I saw Ora Pike's red face and her mouth open in a round, astonished shape like a baby's. Val-Jean commanded me to run like hell.

I ran. Ora Pike thundered behind us as we tore between the trees. The breath ripped from her throat in great muffled gasps as her feet slapped against the path. I clutched the bakery box to my chest, pumping along behind Val-Jean. The muscles in her rump moved like machinery under the thin summer fabric of her skirt. She ran so fast that the pins slipped from her hairpiece and the rat flopped wildly from one side of her head. Following her lead, I leapt over roots, fallen branches and puddles. Ora Pike's breath seemed to be against my neck and as she ran she cursed and called us names. As the woods sped by on either side of me, I found myself concentrating on her words; my running became mechanical, pure motion.

She shouted, "I been waiting for you all day, I knew I'd catch you," just as I leaped over the roots of a fallen tree and almost lost my balance. Then I heard Ora Pike hit the path with a grunt and when I slowed to look back, she was spraddled in the pine needles, clutching her ankle. Our eyes locked for an instant and she screamed, "If I'd brought my gun, you'd be two dead bitches."

Val-Jean kept the Impala at forty-five all the way to the highway. She gripped the wheel so tightly her knuckles were white. My lungs ached and my throat felt caked with dust. After running so hard, I felt weightless, capable at any second of flying out the window. I crushed the bakery box to my chest.

She parked the car in the alley behind the Metropolitan. Mr. Hebert opened the back door and motioned us inside, but Val-Jean sat down on the steps and began to take off her filthy sneakers. She made him wait while she tied the two shoes together and put on her glossy white pumps.

"We didn't get them," she said, handing him the car keys.

His skin was purple; each tiny vein seemed to have a life of its own as it throbbed in his old face.

"What happened?" he said thickly.

Val-Jean pulled the last few hairpins out of her rat and stuffed it into her purse. She slung her shoes over her shoulder.

"Remind me to tell you about it sometime," she said.

Skelly now stood beside Mr. Hebert in the doorway, looking from Val-Jean to me with a nervous little smile.

"What's happened?" he said. "Neva?"

I was afraid to say anything. I was sure the moment I started to speak, Val-Jean would tell them I'd backed out.

"Come on now," Mr. Hebert rasped. "I got money tied up in this."

I was frightened by his look and by the hard, flat way he was speaking. I figured that a confession would be better than Val-Jean's accusation.

"I didn't understand," I burst out. But Val-Jean's hand clamped down hard on my shoulder.

"Ora was onto us," Val-Jean said. "When she comes in here on Monday raising hell, I'll send her back to talk to you fellers."

Her laughter sounded high and thin. Skelly looked at Mr. Hebert and then away. Neither of them said anything.

I suddenly remembered the bakery box and offered it to Mr. Hebert. He immediately opened it and then his face went blank.

"Broken," he said. "Every last one of them."

He handed the box to Skelly. And when Val-Jean and I started off down the alley, the two men still stood in the doorway, looking at the eggs.

Val-Jean's scalp gleamed faintly through her coarse black hair as we walked home down streets still stifling at twilight. People fanned themselves on porch swings and called out to Val-Jean as we passed, but she barely spoke to them and walked so fast I couldn't keep up. Finally, I stopped and rummaged in my purse.

"Here's a scarf," I said, handing her a square of Indian cotton swirled with mauve paisley.

She shook it out and tied it over her hair. "It's good thing Sam's out playing softball," she said. "He'd have a fit if he saw me come walking in the house dressed like this."

"What are you going to tell him about your shiner?" I asked.

She shrugged. "I don't know. I'll think of something. There's plenty of ways to hurt yourself around that store." She looked at me coolly. "Don't waste so much time worrying about these things. They happen all the time. Nobody's going to blame you."

"She saw us," I said, my voice sounding tight and small. "She looked right at me."

Val-Jean waved her hand at me, irritated. "You chickened out. She won't forget that. And I don't care—I've been paid for my trouble. I told Mr. Hebert we couldn't count on you anyways. I'm no fool. Ora Pike is his little red wagon."

We walked the last block in silence. At the corner she turned and faced me. The shiner didn't look so bad now; it was still purple but seemed less swollen. I thought maybe I was just getting used to it.

Val-Jean smiled. I saw myself reflected in her dark, pupilless eyes—two images, left and right, but each distinct: one locked in, the other born opposed to it and seeming to float outward. Val-Jean was moving away.

"Grow up," she called over her shoulder. "You hear what I'm saying? I'll see you Monday."

I lingered. I looked down the street at my house half hidden behind the overgrown shrubs. On the porch sat my mother, filing her nails into perfect ovals. My father was mowing the lawn. In his T-shirt and baggy army shorts, he trudged back and forth behind the big Yazoo. His white legs looked thin and birdlike in black socks and black oxfords that were almost obscured by the stream of grass and leaves the mower spewed out. When he looked up and saw me standing there, he waved, then turned the machine at a crazy angle to do the edging.

BIOGRAPHICAL NOTES

Ellen Akins, a Chicagoan, has published work in the *Southwest, Southern* and *Georgia* reviews. Her first novel, *Home Movie*, is forthcoming from Simon & Schuster.

Rick Bass is a Southerner by birth (Fort Worth) and by raising (Houston). He went to college in Utah, lived in Mississippi for eight years, and is now a resident of Montana. The recipient of a 1987 General Electric Younger Writer Award, he has published his stories in several magazines, including *The Paris Review, The Quarterly, The Southern Review,* and *Shenandoah*. A collection, *The Watch,* will be published in early 1989 (W. W. Norton & Co.).

Richard Bausch, who teaches writing at George Mason University, is the author of three novels—*Real Presence, Take Me Back,* and *The Last Good Time*—and one collection of stories—*Spirits, and Other Stories*. He has received fiction fellowships from the National Endowment for the Arts and the Guggenheim Foundation. He lives with his wife, Karen, and their four children in Fairfax, Virginia.

Larry Brown was born in Oxford, Mississippi, in 1951. He served in the Marine Corps from 1970 to 1972, and joined the Oxford Fire Department in 1973. He and his wife, Mary Annie, have a small country store at Tula. *Facing the Music,* his first collection of short stories, is newly published (Algonquin Books of Chapel Hill).

Pam Durban grew up in South Carolina and was educated at the universities of North Carolina (Greensboro) and Iowa. She has published short stories in many magazines including *TriQuarterly* and the *Georgia, Ohio,* and *New Virginia* reviews. She published her first collection of stories, *All Set About With Fever Trees,* in 1985 (David B. Godine, Publishers, Inc.) and received a Whiting Writer's Award in 1987. She teaches at

Georgia State University in Atlanta, where she lives with her husband, Frank Hunter, and their son, Wylie.

John Rolfe Gardiner grew up in Fairfax County, Virginia. He attended the Sidwell Friends School and Amherst College. He is the author of the novels, *Great Dream from Heaven* and *Unknown Soldiers*, and the story collection, *Going On Like This*. His new novel, *In the Heart of the Whole World*, will be published this fall by Alfred A. Knopf, Inc. He lives now in the village of Unison in Loudoun County, Virginia, with his wife Joan and daughter Nicola.

Jim Hall has published four volumes of poetry, the most recent of which is *False Statements* (1986, Carnegie-Mellon University Press). His short stories have appeared in many literary journals, and his novel, *Under Cover of Daylight* (1987, W. W. Norton & Co.), was a Literary Guild alternate selection, a Mystery Guild Main Selection and will soon be a movie. A new novel, *Islamorda*, is also forthcoming. Mr. Hall lives in Key Largo, Florida, and is a professor of English at Florida International University.

Charlotte Holmes was born in Georgia, raised in Louisiana, and now lives in Pennsylvania, where she teaches in the writing program at Penn State. Her short stories have appeared in *The New Yorker, The Southern Review, Grand Street*, and *Carolina Quarterly*.

Nanci Kincaid, currently enrolled in the MFA Creative Writing Program at the University of Alabama at Tuscaloosa, was born in Tallahassee, Florida. Her work has been published in *Owen Wister Review, St. Andrews Review, The Rectangle*, and *The Gyre* and received a fiction award at the Southern Literary Festival in Oxford, Mississippi. She is married and the mother of two daughters.

Barbara Kingsolver grew up in rural Kentucky and lives now in Tucson, Arizona, with her husband and daughter. She is a fiction writer, poet, and journalist whose work has appeared in a variety of magazines and anthologies. Her first novel, *The Bean Trees*, was published this spring (Harper & Row).

Trudy Lewis was born in Oklahoma, raised in Nebraska, and educated in the South. She holds degrees from the University of Tulsa, Vanderbilt University, and the University of North Carolina at Greensboro. She is now teaching in a private high school in Newark, New Jersey.

Jill McCorkle, a native of Lumberton, North Carolina, graduated from the University of North Carolina at Chapel Hill and received her M.A. from Hollins College. She is the author of three novels—*The Cheer Leader, July 7th*, and *Tending to Virginia* (Algonquin Books of Chapel Hill).

She lives with her husband in Boston and teaches writing at Tufts University.

Mark Richard was born in Lake Charles, Louisiana, and grew up in Franklin, Virginia. A graduate of Washington and Lee University, he has recently turned from newspaper work to fiction writing. His short stories have appeared in *Shenandoah, The Quarterly, Equator,* and *Esquire;* and a first collection, tentatively entitled *The Ice at the Bottom of the World,* will be published this fall (Alfred A. Knopf, Inc.).

Sunny Rogers was born and raised in Portsmouth, Virginia. She has lived and studied in Europe and the Middle East and now resides in New York City and Rhinebeck, New York. "The Crumb" is her first published short story.

Annette Sanford lives in Ganado, Texas, with her husband. Her fiction has appeared in a number of literary magazines and in *Best American Short Stories, 1979.* She has twice been a recipient of fellowships from the National Endowment for the Arts.

Eve Shelnutt was born in Spartanburg, South Carolina. In 1972, she received an MFA from the University of North Carolina (Greensboro) and, since then, has published three collections of stories—*The Love Child, The Formal Voice,* and *The Musician* (Black Sparrow Press); two collections of poetry—*Air and Salt* and *Recital in a Private Home* (Carnegie-Mellon University Press); and a book about teaching writing to children—*The Magic Pencil* (Peachtree Publishers). She teaches in the MFA Program at the University of Pittsburgh.

Shannon Ravenel, the editor, was born and raised in the Carolinas—Charlotte, Camden, and Charleston. After graduating from Hollins College, she went to work in publishing. For the last eleven years, she has served as Series Editor of *The Best American Short Stories* series and, for the last six, as Senior Editor of Algonquin Books of Chapel Hill. She lives in St. Louis with her husband, Dale Purves, and their two daughters.

STORIES FROM PREVIOUS VOLUMES

SUGAR, THE EUNUCHS, AND BIG G. B., by Lewis Nordan (*The Southern Review*)
THE PURE IN HEART, by Peggy Payne (*The Crescent Review*)
WHERE PELHAM FELL, by Bob Shacochis (*Esquire*)
LIFE ON THE MOON, by Lee Smith (*Redbook*)

HEART, by Marly Swick (*Playgirl*)
LADY OF SPAIN, by Robert Taylor, Jr. (*The Hudson Review*)
ACROSS FROM THE MOTOHEADS, by Luke Whisnant (*Grand Street*)